"The Story People have lived here for ages," the boy says. They moved in when the books moved in."

"Where are they now?" The girl looks frightened.

"They're out in the bookstore gathering stories."

# THE STORY PEOPLE

*a novel*

## HEATHER KAUFMAN

CONCORDIA PUBLISHING HOUSE · SAINT LOUIS

*To Andrew, with love*

**The girl is lost.** *She is in the middle of a row of book-shelves that she is too short to see over and now she is beginning to feel the first twinges of panic. She realizes too late the wisdom of staying with an adult when you are told to stay. But she is a brave girl, and she does not cry.*

*The girl sees a door and thinks this is the way out, but when she opens it, she sees it's just a cluttered old closet. Now she thinks she will cry. In fact, she has just decided to do so when she sees a sliver of light against the far wall. There is another door, only this one doesn't look much like a door. She would never have seen it if it weren't cracked open. It is not much wider than she is, and she is barely five and not that big at all. She has never seen a door this narrow. It doesn't seem like a way out. It seems like a way in. Still, she is a brave girl, and she decides to explore.*

*The girl opens the strange door. There is no doorknob, so she must push. Now she sees a narrow passageway and, far ahead, another glimmer of light. The girl moves forward slowly. She thinks of Lucy and the wardrobe in the book her grandmother is reading to her and wonders if this, perhaps, is how Lucy felt when she reached out her hand to find a tree branch instead of a coat.*

*The girl reaches the light when she hears the noise—a soft, clearing-the-throat noise.*

*This is when the girl realizes that she is not alone.*

# CHAPTER ONE

## HE DIDN'T FEEL MUCH OF ANYTHING AFTER ALL

B en didn't typically wish to be shorter, but he wished it now—not anything drastic, a few inches less would suffice, just enough so he could fold himself behind the billowing standing banner, which advertised Palermo's Books. Instead he found himself fumbling clumsily, with limbs poking out from behind the banner, giving away his position to the ever-approaching Mrs. Matilda Gardner. He knew he looked ridiculous, but the thought, rather than making him move, just made him embarrassed, which in turn made him more zealous to hide himself.

He'd left the relative safety of his shop in order to bring in the banner before the growing storm blew it away, and just now he caught sight of Mrs. Gardner's hunched form scurrying across Main Street toward his store. Her oblong shape and tendency to walk with her chest shoved forward gave her the figure of a penguin perched for flight—made all the more ridiculous by the impossibility of takeoff. Her distinctive form never failed to spark a flutter of panic in Ben. Inevitably any conversation he held with Mrs. Gardner turned to the fact that he, a grown man of twenty-nine, was unmarried and, good heavens, didn't he think that was unfortunate, and what on God's green earth did he intend to *do* about it? Now, as he bobbed and weaved in time with the banner's erratic movements and became steadily soaked by the rain, he wished he'd stayed inside.

A quick peek informed Ben that Mrs. Gardner had nearly made it to his shop. Her face, pink and shiny from exertion, swiveled back and forth as if scouting for any number of disasters, and her bustling form looked like she was trying to outdo the raindrops, which were managing to soak her gray, curled updo despite her best efforts to shield it with her purse. Just as she reached the awning of Palermo's Books, another woman tugged at her arm, causing her to spin with a squeal. Ben watched Mrs. Gardner's face light up in anticipation of juicy gossip as the two settled into a comfortable conversation. He sighed in relief, for he knew she wouldn't be inside for at least another half hour. Taking advantage of this momentary distraction, Ben ducked around the banner, slid behind Mrs. Gardner, and leaped up the front steps, cringing as the bell above the doorway chimed his presence. He headed back to his swivel chair behind the counter and scanned the first floor of his store. No one was directly in sight. Quickly he tugged on his T-shirt, pulling it up and swiping at his face to remove the last of the rain.

The bookstore was three stories tall with the flight of stairs in the middle. The first floor was the coziest, with the front desk immediately to the left of the entrance and a quiet reading alcove in the back of the store. The used books, children's, romance, and classics were all on the first floor; nature, poetry, and nonfiction were on the second; and hobbies, travel, cooking, and clearance were on the third.

Ben plopped down on his chair and glanced at the doomed banner through the front window. "It's not worth it, JC." Petting the small mutt, who looked like a mix between a Chihuahua and a miniature poodle, he took a swig from his now-cold cup of coffee. "We'll just have to chance the banner." JC groaned in an agony of joy and tilted his head into Ben's palm as Ben continued to scratch behind the ears. "JC? Jesus Christ?" people often asked, looking at him askance as if he'd committed blasphemy. "No," he'd clarify, "Julius Caesar."

The drizzle had begun midmorning, with a lull around noon, but as the afternoon progressed, the mass of black clouds condensed and let loose its rain with renewed vigor. Awnings up and down Main Street now shielded fidgeting people who were pawing at their umbrellas in nervous anticipation. Ben crossed his ankles with a grunt, picking up a splayed paperback from the counter as he let his eyes roam from the banner to the window, watching as the raindrops smeared across the glass.

It was mid-July, and the rain was a welcome change for many in New Holden, Indiana, who'd spent the last few weeks gazing at the sky and clicking their tongues in dissatisfaction. No rain for the local farmers' crops meant no roadside stands with tempting fresh corn on the cob come late summer. With the downpour came renewed visions of bright yellow corn dripping with butter and sprinkled with salt. Family outings were already being planned to celebrate the coming bounty.

For Ben, rain had a more mercenary implication. Poor weather meant visitors would be forced away from the outdoor offerings of New Holden—horseback riding; canoeing, fishing, and picnicking by the Wabash; visits to the local historic mill and picturesque covered bridge. It would all be out of the question, and instead, a stream of wet and disgruntled people would trickle in to take refuge in the shops. Wet days, so often toxic to other businesses, proved invaluable here in New Holden's historic district. This was one of the early lessons Ben had learned about his new home.

Three years before, Louis Palermo had passed away and bequeathed Palermo's Books to his only nephew. Ben had grown up visiting the store, and it held an enduring nostalgic place in his memory. Summer wasn't complete until the Palermos packed up the old cherry-red Suburban and made the long drive to visit Uncle Louie. Ben's memories of his uncle were so tightly connected to those of the store that it was hard to separate the two. He'd spent countless hours roaming the store and "helping" his uncle behind the front desk. Evenings were cozy and revolved around family and food, his father and Uncle Louie swapping childhood stories, their big laughs prompting laughter from Ben, even if he didn't always follow their inside jokes.

Those happy summers came to an end, however, when, on a drive home from a Christmas party, his parents were hit head on by a too-tired semitruck driver. Ben was just fourteen. He had gone to live with his grandma on his mother's side, and the trips to visit Uncle Louie had ended. But the bookstore took up permanent residence in Ben's mind, a symbol of happier, less complicated times.

When Ben received the news that the bookstore was his, he'd been an eager twenty-six-year-old MBA graduate who'd spent the past year working as financial manager for a college friend's start-up software company in Chicago. The news came unexpectedly, and he'd waffled on what to do, finally deciding to go for a year. He'd felt panic in leaving friends and his job for something so uncertain, but he'd maintained sanity by telling himself he'd only be gone for a year. He'd go, assess the business, sell, and then return home. His friend had agreed to hold Ben's job until he returned, but then the one year turned to two and then to three, and the job was no longer on the table, and the connections with Chicago slowly unraveled.

Ben hadn't expected to stay, didn't intend to stay, and

yet somehow he stayed. His uncle's life, he'd found, was one of quiet elegance, and he'd enjoyed steeping himself once again in the simple charm of small-town life. Ben had looked around at the business and realized there was more than loss or profit—there was legacy, and it was hard to put an estimate on that. The people, too, had been so pleased to have Ben there, so grateful to have Louie's family running their beloved bookstore, that before he knew it, he'd blown by his time frame. But Chicago was still there, representative of the future, while New Holden confronted him daily with the past and all the loss it contained. He'd found it increasingly difficult to shoulder his uncle's life, however briefly. Ben prayed daily for the strength and clarity to live out this part of his life well and to not be consumed by the emotional baggage it inevitably brought.

Uncle Louie's bookstore gave insight into a life thoughtfully lived, and Ben had enjoyed coming to understand what his uncle had built. But Ben was young and had given up a promising job to set up shop in the middle of nowhere. This beautiful community sucked you in, and no one heard from you again. The small town had a way of turning you into camouflage so that the lines between you and it became increasingly blurred. At first this was charming—and then it was suffocating. The three stories of Palermo's Books, so tantalizingly quaint at the beginning, now felt oppressive. Some mornings, Ben sat at the front desk and simply focused on breathing. In, out, in, out. *It will be okay.* A customer would move on a floor above, and Ben would listen to the creaking and imagine that the books, along with the walls, were slowly settling, adjusting themselves, moving downward, inward, until their combined weight crushed him. And then he wouldn't be able to breathe. No matter how hard he focused, he'd be smothered beneath a heap of C. S. Lewis, George R. R. Martin, and Dr. Seuss.

The quietness of this present life meant that the loudness of his past had freedom to crowd and clutter his thoughts. He was a young man on a quaint island left with reminders of all he had lost. How had he reached this point? Was it possible to simply "end up"? Ben had a growing suspicion that life was not as intentional as he'd once believed, that it was entirely possible to wake up one morning filled with confusion and displacement. Yet here he was, year three, and the people of New Holden were gradually beginning to associate the store with him rather than with Louie, and he had slowly progressed from "Louie's nephew" to "Ben." He loved his customers. In fact, that was what kept him sane most days, the jingle above the door a Pavlovian signal for loneliness to subside, for look—here was another person! Ben was not, after all, the last living soul on earth, about to be crushed by literature and memories.

With a start, Ben realized he'd been staring at the same page for five minutes without reading a word. Grunting, he rose to his feet, snapped the book closed, and crossed the room to slide the volume back onto the bookcase. When he wasn't consumed with the business side of Palermo's, the books themselves served as effective distractions, but not today, it would seem. On his way back to his chair, the bell chimed another presence. Ben smiled as he caught sight of the well-known customer. Professor Jenson harrumphed noisily in the doorway and struggled to close his umbrella while keeping the door propped open with one foot. Finally succeeding, the Professor shook his umbrella of the last few raindrops and let the door swing shut behind him with a dull thunk, but not before Mrs. Gardner's cackle sounded from outside, indicating that she was still carrying on a monologue with her friend.

"The weather in this town never ceases to disappoint me." Professor Jenson ran an arthritic hand through his white hair and cleared his throat of the last of its phlegm, his full mustache quivering as if attempting a mad escape. The Professor was one of Ben's more interesting customers and New Holden's more eccentric residents. He'd gone back to school at the age of fifty-five and earned his PhD in botany; he was now committing his latter days to studying fungi. The Professor ambled up to the front desk and covered JC's head with one large hand. JC peeked through the thick fingers and wiggled with the joy of being noticed. "Why on earth does this bookstore have three floors?" He spoke through the mustache hairs lying lankly in front of his lips. "Combined with the steps out front, the entire experience is exhausting. The least you could do is put in an elevator."

"An elevator, unfortunately, requires two things: space and money. So . . ."

"Well, at least your nature section is only one flight up."

"I categorize my books by popularity. The topics that are least popular are on the third floor."

"Ah, then the fungi books should be on the first floor! Today I am on the hunt for more information on the *appendiculatus*. Tell me, what can be nobler, what can be more worthwhile than that? Nature in all its various and rare forms doesn't deserve to be shoved out of sight, and it would save me a climb up these obnoxious stairs."

Ben knew the Professor was perfectly in earnest; he took his fungi seriously. The Professor had just begun pulling himself up the steps, a hand on each banister, when the bell let loose another announcement: Mrs. Gardner had indeed decided to grace Palermo's with her presence.

Mrs. Gardner's chest entered first, shoved completely off center from the rest of her stout form. The remainder followed in a slow sway as she shouted out a cheery "Hallooww!" Ben put on a practiced smile and went to her with open arms. Complete and utter involvement was the only way to minimize an encounter with Mrs. Gardner. At the mere hint that you wished to be elsewhere, she would sink her conversational fangs in deeper. An overabundance of cheer and charm was the surest way to get Mrs. Gardner moving along.

"Ben, dear, I've just had a most interesting conversation with Mrs. Dean. Her son, Jeremy, called yesterday from the camp he's volunteering at, Camp Something-or-Other—I can't remember the name. Oh, wait. It's Camp Arcadia. That's it! Do you remember Jeremy? Big boy with blond hair, blue eyes? Anyway, he's working at that one camp up there in Minnesota I think, or maybe it's Montana. No. It's Michigan. Anyway. He called his mother yesterday saying he's found this girl there who actually lives just a few hours from here, and he's bringing her for a visit when he comes home. Name's Anna, or Hannah, I can't seem to remember which at the moment."

As Mrs. Gardner attempted to recall whether Jeremy had discovered an Anna or Hannah, Ben braced himself for what he was sure would follow. *Any moment now she'll wonder why I don't bring home an Anna or Hannah.*

"Ah, well, no matter." Mrs. Gardner shook her head resignedly and shifted her eyes to Ben, narrowing them with a hint of agitation. "Was that Professor Jenson I saw coming in here a moment ago?" She leaned to the right and glared suspiciously at the stairs, which no longer contained the Professor's huffing and puffing form.

Ben blinked, surprised that the threat had passed and he was unscathed. "Yes ma'am."

Mrs. Gardner swatted at the drops of rain in her hair. Ben watched as her nose flared and her lips began twitching, and he knew he was about to hear a speech on the subject of her next-door neighbor. "I suppose he went straight upstairs to soak himself in that idiotic nonsense of *fungi*. Why doesn't he call them by their proper name, anyway? They're just plain old mushrooms." She sidled over to Ben, disdainfully sidestepping JC. "I heard from Mary, who, as I'm sure you know, used to housekeep for Professor Jenson before he became so hard of hearing. Everyone says she quit her position because he was constantly shouting at her, and it wasn't discovered until later that it was because he was beginning to go deaf. Now, by that time, he had gotten another girl, and poor Mary was quite distraught because she did so love working for him, it was only because she can't stand anyone raising their voices and—oh dear, where was I?"

"Mary said— "

"Oh my, yes! Well . . ." She paused for effect, lowering her tone to a whisper. "Mary said that he doesn't even *like* mushrooms. You know, on pizzas or salads. He absolutely cannot stand them."

"I think that's perfectly normal," Ben mused. "The man likes to study mushrooms, not eat them."

Mrs. Gardner drew her lips into a severe line. Nodding her head in the fashion of a sage about to impart all her earthly knowledge, she murmured, "Well, he's bound to go crazy from all that nonsense. Just you wait and see."

"The Professor seems to think that romance novels are nonsense." Ben grinned and winked at her.

"Aha, but I have most of the world on my side. My novels are on the first floor of your fine store and are read by millions, whereas whatever books he reads are, I'm sure, read by only a select few, too snobby and self-involved to know a good story if it up and slapped them in the face!" The crispness of her tone, the arched eyebrow, and the heavy breathing that accompanied this speech implied an impassioned state of mind laced with self-righteous fervor, not an uncommon combination in Mrs. Gardner. "And speaking of matrimony, when am I going to receive the happy news that there's a Mrs. Palermo on the horizon?"

Ah yes, there it was at last. If the topic didn't come up

naturally, then, never fear, Mrs. Gardner would superimpose her agenda on even the most unlikely of conversations. Ben cleared his throat. "Well, I can't give you an exact time frame." He placed an arm around her shoulders and began walking her toward the romance section. "But when I have news to share in the romance department, you can expect to be the first to receive it, ma'am." Ben leaned in conspiratorially and gave her a large, dimpled grin.

Mrs. Gardner's blush raced all the way to her hairline. "Just see that you don't keep me waiting, young man." She paused in the aisle and tilted her head. "Oh, and you might want to bring that banner in before it gets blown away." Turning, she scuttled away to dig through the many shelves of star-crossed gazes, mournful sighs, and brawny heroes.

A boom of thunder let loose as the storm rolled up its sleeves and got down to real business. As Ben ran outside to rescue the banner, he saw five more people making a mad dash for his bookstore. Ah yes, the magic of a stormy day was once again at work.

◇◆◇

When Ben inherited Palermo's, he'd also inherited the ground-level apartment at the back of the building. With two small bedrooms, a living room, a kitchen, and a bath, it was more than enough to meet his needs. He'd thought about moving many times. Perhaps if he did, he'd feel less like he was house-sitting and more like his own person, but he could never quite do it. It was just too convenient to be located in the same building as the shop, not to mention financially smart as well, and so he'd stayed. It was a bit creepy at first. Uncle Louie's bedside drawers were still full of crumbled tissues and prescription medications. His fridge housed sprouting vegetables and a smell that could only be curdled milk. His armchair sagged in odd places, cultivated as it had been over the years for a very specific rear end. The overall effect was that the house was rejecting him, fundamentally denying Louie's absence. A yard sale had helped matters a bit. The armchair had gone to a photography studio to serve as a prop, the bedroom furniture had gone to a college student in need of cheap furnishings, and the remaining bric-a-brac had been happily scattered throughout the community. Still the house seemed unwilling to accept him. The new overstuffed chair he'd purchased looked out of place and uncomfortable in its surroundings. The new bed, as well, seemed mockingly new, an upstart individual among the remains of Louie's life.

Admittedly there was a certain predictable comfort to Ben's life. His routine was set for him; all he need do was follow it through until the well-worn end of each day. The business side of actually running the store kept him busy, occupied, and challenged. He felt ungrateful for not settling into himself more fully. Instead, he increasingly entertained thoughts of selling Palermo's—the ultimate betrayal of uncle and community. He'd gone so far, in fact, as to begin researching commercial real estate agents, finally remembering that Professor Jenson had a cousin in the business. He had yet to make the phone call, but the number was there, speared to a corkboard in the kitchen, daring him to action.

The rain that had been so ferocious earlier had died down after dinner, much to JC's apparent delight, for now he could legitimately pester Ben for a walk. Clipping a leash onto JC's collar, Ben let himself out by the back door and circled around his store to reach Main Street. He paused at the corner of Fifth and Main, trying to decide his destination for the evening, finally settling on the familiar path to Fischer Park. New Holden's Main Street was paved with chipped and jagged bricks. It was a street ill-suited for vehicles, which only added to its charm, but it was inconvenient for residents, who complained about the potholes and unevenness, all the while knowing nothing would be done because it would ruin the "aura."

Turning left, Ben crossed Fifth Street and headed west toward the park. As he walked, his gait settled into its normal pace, and JC happily trotted along, his tiny nose sniffing the air and every once in a while snuffling a discarded candy wrapper or cigarette butt with intense interest. The crickets were out, their steady chirp punctured by JC's claws as they ticked across the brick like an impatient woman's fingernails.

Most of the buildings in New Holden's historic district were devoted to businesses, but there were glimpses of cozy homes down side streets. Each home nestled in its spot, huddled in the evening with lights winking outward. Visitors often drove through these neighborhoods, especially during the Christmas season, with noses pressed to glass, heat from their mouths fogging the view as hushed exchanges filled the car. "Would you look at *that* one!" "Oooh, I can see inside!" New Holden homes elicited nostalgia for other people's childhoods, the kinds of childhoods filled with a Thomas Kinkade glow—or so motoring passersby imagined.

The night felt close and muggy after the rain, and the mosquitoes were beginning to casually latch on and off anyone with exposed skin. Ben quickened his pace, walking past Charlotte's consignment boutique, Carley's Café, Rhonda's florist shop, and a few doors down, Peter Peters's antique shop and Gene Mendleson's barbershop. Running a hand through his thick curls, Ben made a mental note to visit the barber within the week. Mendleson's shop was next door to Peters's shop, and the two men had been close friends for more than twenty years. From all accounts Louis Palermo had been the third musketeer to their two. In fact, they had taken his death so hard that Ben had yet to see them enter the bookshop. He knew firsthand how place was an intensifier of memory. Some memories left their mark more deeply on certain places, their grooves so fixed there was no separating the two.

As Ben neared the entrance of the park, he could just make out the tip of his church's steeple peeking above the tree line on the far end. St. John's Lutheran Church and the familiar rhythms of church membership had been and continued to be a lifeline for Ben. More specifically, Pastor Dale Andrews had been an unexpected friend when Ben had needed one most. Not much older than Ben himself, Dale brought a passion and vitality to his congregation that Ben admired. A week didn't go by that Dale didn't make a well-anticipated trip to Palermo's to root through the shelves in the Religion section, to ask after the latest Bible commentary, or as was most common, to just lean against the front counter and talk, a momentary distraction. Ben had gladly offered the store as a location for Dale's Thursday night men's study, which had grown in size to more than a dozen regular participants.

Ben had always felt slightly skittish around pastors, perhaps because he'd always had a hard time seeing them as people just like him, until Dale upset his expectations. Here was a like-minded soul with an expansive mind who saw beauty and potential in his neighbors and who, oddly enough, saw Ben not just as a congregant but as a person, a friend.

Now, as Ben left Main Street behind and entered the park's tree-lined path, JC picked up his pace, pausing only to make authoritative dashes at suspicious-looking sticks or to shout a word of caution to passing squirrels. Ben headed for the fountain at the center of the park, passing an older couple and a few kids on bikes making their way home to their respective bedtime routines. The fountain was still this evening except for the rainwater steadily dripping from the stone surface. After wiping at the wet concrete in a futile attempt to dry it, Ben finally took a seat at one of the five benches surrounding the fountain and slapped his knee in invitation. JC accepted and leaped onto the cold bench next to him, shivering a bit and nestling against Ben's thigh just as the streetlamps began flicking on.

Ben hunched forward and stared down at a puddle harboring three dead worms. He shifted the toe of his left foot so that it dipped into the puddle. With a flick, he splashed a good portion of the water onto the surrounding pavement. He continued in this way, dip, flick, dip, flick, for several minutes as if it were suddenly of the utmost importance that he empty the greedy puddle of its water and equally distribute the moisture elsewhere. He felt the dampness seep through the seat of his pants, rapidly turning his flesh numb. Normally he would have gotten up so as not to get soaked, but this evening he found himself burrowing in deeper, egging on the wet, daring it to make him move. Dip, flick, dip, flick.

Contrariness had slowly built up in him over the past year, and he hadn't stopped to analyze it yet. If he were pressed to give an explanation though, he supposed he would begin by saying he felt claustrophobic. But he could already hear the counterargument. "That's ridiculous, Ben. You can't feel claustrophobic when you've been conveniently handed a full and satisfactory life and you have the freedom and resources to build upon it." Okay, he'd admit. Okay, fair enough.

He supposed, then, that what he was feeling was loneliness. "That's equally laughable, Ben. You can't possibly feel alone when you're surrounded by people who care about you. Everyone knows that." True, true, he'd concede. Never mind, then, he must have been mistaken.

Under the glow of a nearby lamp, Ben watched a stranded worm under an adjacent bench struggle to peel itself off the pavement. Two birds alighted on the fountain in front of him and stared at the exhilarating bounty of worms in varying stages of distress. They hopped an elaborate dance of ecstasy with each other before descending and partaking.

"You're quite right," he'd acknowledge. He didn't feel much of anything after all.

**The boy is sitting on the floor with a book, a flashlight, and a bag of Sour Patches.** *He is enjoying the pleasure that comes from being intentionally alone. The light is illuminating the page, creating a bright island of words. His right hand is growing stickier and stickier as he steadily consumes the bag of candy. He must use his left hand to turn the pages, otherwise he will get gunk on them. Each page turn is filled with small calculations. Lick the sweetness from his fingers, transfer the flashlight from left to right, turn the page, transfer the flashlight back, and continue. He is utterly absorbed in this process when he hears the soft intake of a panicked breath.*

*This is when the boy realizes that he is not alone.*

# CHAPTER TWO

## "HEAVEN HELP THE GIRLS OF NEW HOLDEN"

The next morning, at the corner of Sixth and Main, three women sat talking in Carley's Café. Their friendship spanned decades, reaching back to grade school at St. John's and extending to the present and their work with various women's ministries. The three women were fixtures at St. John's, in New Holden, and in one another's lives. With the years had come a familiarity that allowed the women to sink happily into their well-worn roles. There was no doubt that Mrs. Gardner was presiding over the meeting; she was the flurry of words around which the other two orbited. "My friend Sheri called yesterday and, as usual, spent most of the time talking about her granddaughter who is bound to be famous someday, but she did have one piece of interesting news. You'll never guess." Mrs. Gardner paused and waited eagerly to be prodded for more information.

Mrs. Baumgartner sat across the table, sipping at her coffee and eyeing the pastries at the counter even though she had a bagel in front of her and was steadily consuming it. There was nothing Anita Baumgartner loved more than a fresh-baked pastry. Food of any kind, really, was one of God's best gifts to humankind. Her round features gave her an owlish look, which intensified as she pried her wide eyes from the pastries to turn them to her friend. "No, dear. What?"

Mrs. Gardner seemed dissatisfied with the lackluster inquiry and so compensated by replying with extra gusto. "Benji is engaged!"

Mrs. Emma Frank raised her eyebrows and left them suspended in the middle of her forehead like two squiggly question marks. "Really? Now, that *is* surprising. He's the youngest grandchild, correct? The effeminate one?" Mrs. Frank was a tall, thin woman with hair that was pulled back into a severe bun, a suitably serious style for a suitably serious woman. Her voice was even and measured, as if each word were sifted and deliberated over before delivery. "It's hard enough that the poor young man looks like an adolescent girl, but to be saddled with such a name?"

"I know, it makes me think of that one song—B-E-N-J-I, Benji was his name-o!" Mrs. Baumgartner belted out this last phrase in an uncomfortably loud tone, making the other two women quick to shush her.

"Honestly, Anita, no need for a concert. And no, you're thinking of 'Bingo,'" Mrs. Frank hissed.

"Although Benji is, indeed, a famous dog. Made into movies and everything," Mrs. Gardner placated. "Anyway, I thought it was surprising news."

"Yes indeed," Mrs. Frank agreed. "Makes you realize there is someone for everyone, as they say."

"Yes . . ." Mrs. Gardner's voice trailed off as she quickly looked away from the table. "I certainly found my 'someone' in Robert. It just hasn't been the same since he died . . ."

"Oh gracious, here we go again." Mrs. Frank drew her thin lips into a line, her expression one of forbearance at having to hear an oft-told story again.

"Oh, don't be cruel, Emma!" Mrs. Baumgartner waved a plump hand at her friend, her thin, reedy voice trilling above the noise in the café. "We all know the story, dear."

She patted Mrs. Gardner on the hand affectionately, her bagel suspended in the other hand.

"But really . . . it really was my fault! If I had only paid better attention to his symptoms and taken notice when he complained—"

"Nonsense." Mrs. Frank's nose twitched. "You know you couldn't have done anything differently. And it was fifteen years ago, Matilda. *Do* be reasonable."

Mrs. Baumgartner frowned viciously and then crooned once more to her friend. "I'm sure it must be hard to be all alone in that great big house of yours."

"Oh, you have no idea, no idea." Mrs. Gardner sighed and calmed herself with a sip of tea. "It's one of my biggest sorrows that we were never blessed with children, but at least Robert and I had each other for nearly thirty years. Thirty years is something, you know."

"Of course it is," Mrs. Baumgartner agreed vigorously, coughing up crumbs as she did so, finally putting down the bagel to swig her coffee in an effort to clear her throat.

"To a lot of people, it's a headache," Mrs. Frank snorted.

"Oh, you're just a sourpuss!" Mrs. Baumgartner's jowls quivered indignantly, causing her to choke on another crumb.

Being friends for such a long time had its certain advantages, one being an absolute lack of pretense, which allowed Mrs. Gardner to interject a wholehearted "You're always so negative, Emma!" at this juncture in the conversation, which allowed Mrs. Frank to reply with a "Well, someone has to balance your unnerving cheerfulness" without so much as a hiccup in the friendship. Mrs. Baumgartner, ever the liaison, sided with everyone in an effort to maintain peace. Barbs were given and received and forgotten just as rapidly.

"I think it's so very wrong for a person to be alone in the world," Mrs. Gardner sighed, staring into her mug as if into a wishing well. "True love. There's nothing like it. You know," she went on meditatively, "it really is a shame that Benjamin Palermo doesn't find himself a nice girl and settle down. How can he truly be a part of our community if he doesn't have a wife by his side?"

"I agree," Mrs. Baumgartner nodded, willing and ready to talk about anything with anybody. "He's such a fine-looking young man too."

"He's not so young anymore," Mrs. Gardner said. "He's twenty-nine, and in my opinion—"

"In your opinion, every man would find his soul mate at eighteen. Honestly, Matilda, you're such a sappy romantic!"

"Oh, pooh," Mrs. Gardner sniffed. "I was going to say that in my opinion, twenty-nine is much too old to be remaining a bachelor."

"Twenty-nine is still young, and look at Professor Jenson. He's reaching eighty, and *he's* still a bachelor," Mrs. Frank reasoned.

"In *my* opinion, Professor Jenson is insane," Mrs. Gardner snorted.

"Professor Jenson is a very wise, very sane man. If there were more people like him in the world, there would be less in the world to complain about."

"Why, Emma, I do believe you are showing a hint of sentimentality!" Mrs. Baumgartner giggled, the action causing the extra flesh in her neck to shake merrily.

"Nonsense." Mrs. Frank uttered her favorite word once again, looking mortified that anyone could possibly connect her to such a concept as sentimentality.

"Nonsense is right," Mrs. Gardner agreed. "How can anyone be a very wise, very sane person when all they talk about is mushrooms?"

"I see your point there." Mrs. Baumgartner bit her lip as she thought. "I guess he is a bit eccentric."

"Again, I say, nonsense," Mrs. Frank said calmly as she

methodically dunked her tea bag. "He is a genius on plant life and specializes in fungi. Just think, the both of you, if there were no Professor Jensons in the world, we would have no idea which mushrooms are poisonous and which are edible."

Mrs. Baumgartner's eyes grew wide and she clutched at her coffee mug convulsively. "Oh gracious! Thank God for Professor Jenson!"

Mrs. Gardner sighed. "Can we please find something to talk about *besides* the Professor? How did we ever get on that topic anyway?"

"How does one get on any topic?" Mrs. Frank turned philosophical. "Life is full of rabbit trails."

"Rabbit tails? I've never heard that expression before! Aren't they supposed to be good luck?"

"I said trails, not tails, and it's rabbit *feet* that bring good luck. Honestly, Anita, you *can* be infuriating." Mrs. Frank suddenly sagged a bit and placed a hand on her forehead. "Oh goodness, my blood pressure!"

"You and your soaring blood pressure!" Mrs. Gardner was clearly fed up with her friend. "If you would control your temper, you wouldn't have a problem with your blood pressure. Now, as I was saying, twenty-nine is such an awfully old age."

"If twenty-nine is old, then we might as well call the mortician," Mrs. Frank moaned.

"And I really think it a shame. You know what, girls?" Mrs. Gardner freshened as an idea came to her. "I think it's about time that our dear Mr. Palermo found some happiness in this life."

"How do you know he's unhappy?" Mrs. Baumgartner was concerned.

"Well, it's really rather obvious, Anita. Don't you see how he talks to his dog all the time? Just as if it were a real person! And he hasn't any family to speak of, not with poor Louie gone, and his parents—so tragic!" She paused and clicked her tongue sadly. "Why, the poor thing is simply desolate!" Mrs. Gardner was warming up to her topic. "What he really needs is a loving wife to look after him, a woman to stand by him through the trials and tribulations of life, someone to cook and keep house for him."

"He is going to be hard-pressed to find someone like that nowadays," Mrs. Frank commented. "Housekeeping and child-rearing are deemed unsuitable for the modern girl. Ha! *The modern girl.*" Mrs. Frank stressed the words to show just how she felt about such a person. "We wouldn't want Ben to get stuck with one of *those.*"

"Now, that is the first bit of sense you've spoken yet!" Mrs. Gardner chirped cheerfully. "Of course Ben's wife will have to be cut of better stuff, and *we* will be the ones to bring her to him!"

"Like matchmaking!" Mrs. Baumgartner was aglow, her wide eyes growing even wider with anticipation. "Oh, how *fun!*"

"I think this whole idea is ridiculous," Mrs. Frank emitted. "Ben is a grown man and can handle his own affairs."

"But if we allow him to do that, you just *know* what he'll do," Mrs. Gardner persisted. "He'll sit in that bookshop of his, piled under a mountain of books, and he won't come out for the world."

"Perhaps he's safer there," Mrs. Frank observed drily.

"But just think how wonderful it would be to see him happily married with young ones toddling about his shop and his wife humming from the rear of the store. Oh, how darling it all will be!"

"You speak as if you already have someone in mind, Matilda."

"Oh, do you? Do you, Matilda?" Mrs. Baumgartner said eagerly.

"Now now, I haven't given it much consideration yet."

"As usual."

"Now, Emma, don't be so sour. I think I'll go home and start compiling a list."

Mrs. Frank raised her eyes upward. "Heaven help us, a *list*?"

"Naturally." Mrs. Gardner rose from her seat, placing a few bills on the table to tip the server. "Since tomorrow is quilt-tying day, let's plan to meet up afterward; by then I'll have all sorts of possibilities."

Mrs. Baumgartner and Mrs. Frank rose as well, the former squealing as if she couldn't contain her joy. "You think up the most fun things, Matilda!"

Mrs. Frank wore a pained expression. "I know you'll thoroughly interrogate all the unfortunate women you place on your wretched list." She sighed and shook her head as all three left the café, her mood emanating from her and forming a palpable cloud of dismay. Looking upward as she stepped out onto the street, Mrs. Frank murmured, "Heaven help the girls of New Holden."

**The girl looks past the light to see a Room.** *Well, it's more of an extended closet than a Room. It doesn't have any windows, and the girl can now see that the light is coming from a flashlight, its beam muted by a blanket. The girl is not sure what she is seeing. Two chairs are in the Room, one on each side, the blanket draped over them, and in the middle is the light, bouncing slowly. As her eyes adjust, she sees a bended knee sticking out, and she gasps.*

*The girl watches as a head slowly emerges from the blanket. A boy with wild black hair is staring straight at her. In the semidarkness, his eyes look black, and they are directed right at her. The flashlight, too, is now beaming at her. She blinks and feels more lost than ever in its light.*

*The girl decides to speak quickly, otherwise she is afraid she will cry.* "Hi," *she says. She is a brave girl. This boy will help her.* "I'm lost. Where are we?"

# CHAPTER THREE

## MAYBE THIS NEW SENSE OF LIGHT
## WAS CATCHING

Rosemary picked up a weathered volume in the used book section of the bookstore and opened it carefully: a biography on Lucas Cranach the Elder. She was a sucker for biographies. Eagerly she began to pore over it, employing her Four-Check Method: (1) read the back cover, (2) read the table of contents, (3) skim any preface or foreword, and (4) begin the first chapter. Only then could she decide if it was a book worth buying. Time passed and suddenly she realized someone was watching her. A bit self-conscious, she slowly raised her head to stare into the eyes of the cashier. The front desk was directly across the room, giving him a front-row seat to observe her. He was looking at her with a half-amused gaze that made her feel uncomfortable. Shifting her weight, she positioned her body so he couldn't get a clear view of her face. A minute passed and Rosemary found that she was reading the same line over and over. Sighing inwardly, she glanced up again. He was still staring at her as if committing her to memory for future reference. *I can't believe this guy!* She ducked her head and let one more minute pass before attempting another glance. She was glad to see him finally looking away.

She'd come to New Holden for a month to take care of her grandmother, who was recovering from a hip replacement. It was her chance to reconnect not only with Oma but also with the town she'd grown up visiting. This bookstore, in particular, held many fond memories. "Get any book you like, dear," Oma would say as they entered the store. And off Rosemary would go in search of a book to take home. It'd been years since she'd been here. She hadn't realized how nostalgic this old place would make her feel—and here was this annoying man, ruining it for her.

Rosemary took advantage of the man's turned face to study him. He seemed balanced between unusually handsome and unusual, his odd features arresting enough to draw a second look but not quite conventional enough to be convincingly attractive. His hair was a deep black, thick, and in terrible need of a cut. The nose was wide with flared nostrils, which gave him a perpetually hungry look, and his eyes were kind of desperate looking, but not necessarily in an unpleasant way. Just at that moment, his eyes flicked in her direction. Rosemary was so absorbed in observation that his sudden attention shocked her into action. She jerked her gaze away and lurched awkwardly into the aisle. In an attempt at recovery, she cleared her throat, flipped a few pages, and then turned back around and casually looked at him again to prove that he was just a fellow person and she was in no way bothered or influenced by his presence.

He was grinning, a bit too broadly. His teeth and dimples were showing now, giving her further study material. Rosemary turned a deep shade of pink and hid her face within the depths of the book. She hated that she blushed so easily.

"Excuse me." He was speaking to her now. Gone was the hope of being a casual wallflower.

"Yes?" Rosemary tried to plaster on her best "Who? Me?" expression and hoped she looked convincingly unperturbed by his presence.

"Can I help you in any way?"

Rosemary realized with relief that there was still a book in her hand—blessed book, mother of all distractions. "Yes, actually, how much is this book? I don't see a price."

He came over and took the book from her, glancing down to see what she had been reading. "So, you're an art history buff." He pursed his lips; in approval or critique, she couldn't tell which. "Or perhaps you're more interested in him for his connection to key figures of the Protestant Reformation."

Rosemary did not feel sociable and she couldn't tell if he was being genuine or genuinely being a snob. "Um, sure, something like that. How much is the book?"

Forming his face into a philosophical expression, he handed the book back. "Twenty dollars."

Rosemary opened the book again and gave it a last perusal, aware that the man was still standing by her side. She could practically feel his breath on her neck. Although she could also now smell his cologne, and that part was kind of pleasant.

"So, what brings you to New Holden?" The man was peering down at her, apparently oblivious to the social norms of personal space. "I don't remember seeing you around here before."

Rosemary groaned. She should have known better than to engage him. He seemed overeager, and engagement of any sort was usually interpreted as reciprocal interest by overeager guys. "I actually grew up visiting this place, so I'm quite familiar with the town." She'd meant this to shut him down, but it seemingly only intrigued him more.

"Really? And here I was getting ready to give you the scoop on all the local attractions."

"No need." Rosemary shelved the book. Her Four-Check Method had been sufficiently disrupted, but she wasn't ready to be done with the bookstore. She hadn't even been able to explore the other floors as she'd planned. She'd need to revisit this another day. "Thanks anyway though. This really is a beautiful shop. I'm glad to see it's still here." She started toward the door.

"Yes, this place is a beauty. I'm fortunate to be a part of it." He was *still* talking. "So you must be here on summer break?"

"I'm just here for a month. Helping my grandmother." Rosemary cared too much about politeness; that was her problem.

"You looking to attend college locally? There are some wonderful schools in the area."

"Attend . . . no, I actually finished graduate school over a year ago."

"Oh, wow! I'm sorry . . . I shouldn't have assumed . . . I mean . . ."

Rosemary was done with the conversation. With the countenance of a seasoned soldier, she marched from the store, leaving the befuddled cashier staring after her.

◇◆◇

"There was this guy at the bookstore. He completely threw me off. I didn't get a chance to look around. I'm going to have to go back, hopefully when he isn't there," Rosemary vented.

"What did this person possibly do to get you worked up like this?" Oma looked at her granddaughter with concern on her face.

"I don't know! He—well, for starters, he thought I was a high school kid!" Rosemary paced and waved her hands in front of her. "I'm twenty-five years old, and I would hope by now that I look like a mature adult." True, she was a twenty-five-year-old college graduate, and on top of that, one who had been forced to move back in with her mom while she looked for a full-time job that paid enough for rent. She'd graduated with her MFA in studio art over a year ago and since then had been busy with freelance work. Currently, she had a contract with a publishing company, providing illustrations for their new K–6 curriculum. Still, not a day went by without that pesky "What now?" question looming in her mind. She didn't need assumptions of youth. She felt young enough as it was, given her current situation.

"Honey, someday you'll appreciate looking younger than your years, just trust me," Oma laughed. "By the way, was he married or single?"

"Single, unless he lost his ring—" Rosemary stopped short, choking on her words, her face turning bright red. She looked at Oma, who was laughing quietly. "What are you insinuating? You know it's perfectly natural to observe whether someone is wearing a wedding ring or not. People do it all the time. You know, you just naturally glance at people's left hand to see whether there's a ring or not. Plain curiosity."

"I don't do that." Oma displayed an innocent face to her granddaughter, which only flustered Rosemary more. "Why are you so upset over this?"

"I am not upset!" Rosemary paused and caught Oma's eye. "Well, okay. I am. But the only reason is that he was playing with me. He was so sure of himself, like he's used to having women fawn over him or something. Like he expected me to just swoon at his feet right there. Seriously! But the odd thing was that he wasn't really that attractive."

"Oh?"

"I mean, he was, but he wasn't."

"I'm not sure I follow."

"Oh, never mind," Rosemary sighed. She couldn't stand cocky men, and the possibility that she would see this one again was very high. There was one thing Rosemary knew about this small town—you couldn't hide from anyone.

◇◆◇◆

Rosemary wasn't quite sure what a pomegranate looked like. She frowned at the tattered grocery list in her hand. The fruit's sticky, sour kernels were a common sight in Oma's house. The cracks in her crooked fingers held dark stains where the juice had settled over the years. But Rosemary wasn't sure what the actual fruit that housed the kernels looked like. Grocery shopping for someone else was a lot harder than she'd expected. Other people's preferences and habits were hard to get right when confronted with an unfamiliar store and aisles upon aisles of choices.

She was slowly wheeling past the oranges when she caught sight of the guy from the bookstore standing at the deli. His tall form was hard to miss, as was the abundance of black curls. Rosemary's heart paused and then raced. *Silly* . . . she wasn't even attracted to him. She was just nervous. That was all. Because he so obviously had been flirting with her the other day—which, come to think of it, was kind of pedophilic of him, since he'd also assumed she was a recent high school graduate. Thus arming herself with fresh indignation, Rosemary continued past the fruit, forcing herself to go slowly. Why should she rush out of the produce section? His presence meant nothing and did not bother her in the slightest. *If* he recognized her, surely he wouldn't strike up another conversation; their first one had ended so awkwardly. Oh dear, he was waving. And walking in her direction.

"Hi! We met the other day."

*Play it cool, Rosemary.* "Oh yes, at the bookstore. Hi."

"I want to apologize. I feel bad. Like maybe I upset you. I don't know why I go around saying such awkward things. I should know better than to guess people's ages, right? I mean, who does that? I'm sorry if we got off on the wrong foot."

He was clutching a package of salami and looking completely earnest. Rosemary was unsettled. It would have been a lot easier and simpler if he'd been as awkward as the other day; then she could have simply solidified her dislike. But here he was, challenging her first impression. "Oh no. I mean, I get that all the time. You don't need to apologize."

"I'm Ben, by the way." He stuck out a hand.

"Rosemary." She shook it and noticed that it was a pleasant handshake. Strong, big hand, firm grasp. *Yes, very pleasant as handshakes go.*

"I hope I haven't scared you away from the store. We're having a discount day on Saturday. Maybe you'll stop by?"

"Sure, I've wanted to check out the store ever since I've been back here. It's such a great place."

"Then consider this a personal invitation to stop by on Saturday. Your grandmother is welcome too."

He might be trying a bit too hard to impress her, or possibly to redeem himself, what with the apology, invitation, and now the thoughtful inquiry after her grandmother. But Rosemary didn't care; it was working. "Thanks, but she's not quite up to moving around much. I'm actually doing her grocery shopping now. It's hard on her, not to be able to do the things she normally does. But I'm glad I can be here to help her for a while."

"I'm sure she appreciates it." Ben looked like he wanted to say more, but they were blocking a good portion of the fruit aisle and throughout the conversation had been systematically sidestepping to allow shoppers access to the surrounding produce. There was an awkward pause, during which Rosemary shuffled to the left for a young mother with twins and apologized to an elderly gentleman whom she bumped into.

"Well ..." Ben cleared his throat. "I should probably let you get back to it. But I'll look forward to seeing you Saturday."

"Yes, Saturday, great. That sounds delightful. So nice to meet you." Rosemary watched him walk away. *That sounds delightful? Really? That sounds* delightful? *Who says* delightful *anymore?* Why on earth did that word pop into her brain and out of her mouth? Had she said anything else equally ridiculous? Rosemary started running through the conversation, word for word. No, nothing too horrible. Had she been awkward in any other way? She began cataloging her physical movements during the conversation but finally stopped herself. No, this was silly. She'd drive herself crazy obsessing over every little thing. She'd see Ben on Saturday and then she could correct any weird impressions she might have made today.

Rosemary looked down. Pomegranates $2.17/lb. Funny, they looked like Christmas ornaments—hard, red, bulbous Christmas ornaments. She'd been walking circles around them for ages. Rosemary gratefully filled a bag and tried to pretend that her heart rate was normal.

Palermo's Books was crowded on Saturday. When Ben had extended a "personal invitation," she hadn't been sure if that had meant she should seek him out or not, so she decided to play it safe and just mingle with the crowd. Never a good idea to come across as too interested. Because she wasn't. Interested, that is.

She had everything planned to the last detail. Mingle, explore the store, and if their paths happened to cross, a politely happy "Oh, hello again!" What she hadn't planned on was Ben standing right at the front entrance, personally greeting each customer at the door.

"Rosemary, I'm so glad you came." Ben's face jumped into action at the sight of her. His eyebrows shot up, his grin got bigger—which meant his dimples showed through. Was it her imagination, or was his greeting to her more pronounced than to the others? And then there was the handshake again, just as wonderful as she'd remembered.

"Oh, hello again. So good to see you again. Wouldn't miss this sale for the world!" *Smooth, that was smooth. Great.*

"Come, follow me." Ben touched her arm as he left his post and led the way to the back of the store.

Rosemary had to jog to keep up with his long strides. "Where are you taking me?"

He just smiled. As they neared the back of the store, Ben struck up a conversation. "So, your grandmother . . . anyone I know?"

"Carol Berg."

"Carol, yes. She's a member of my church, although we don't really know each other that well."

He was a member of St. John's? So his overly knowl-edgeable small talk from the other day had perhaps been genuine after all. *Calm down, Rosemary. There's no such thing as the perfect guy. He's probably engaged or secretly horrible in some way.* Not that she cared one way or the other. "Then she probably knows you too. She hasn't been able to get to church for a while now. I'll be taking her tomorrow though."

"I'll be seeing you twice in one weekend? Nice."

*Oh my goodness.* Rosemary didn't know how to re-spond to such an obvious flirtation, so she just smiled and laughed and then stopped abruptly because it sounded squeaky and annoying, which it often did when she got nervous.

"Here we are." Rosemary watched as Ben folded his big limbs so that he could squeeze through the makeshift bookshelves that were set up for the discount day. "Now where is it . . ." He clicked his tongue and ran his fingers lightly over the bindings. "Aha! I knew it was here some-where." He pulled out the huge volume she had been pe-rusing the other day. Ben came triumphantly over to her with the tome displayed in outstretched hands like an offering. "All you ever dreamed of knowing about Lucas Cranach, knowledge without end. Amen." He plunked it down in her hands. "Half off."

Rosemary squealed. She couldn't help herself. And Ben laughed right out loud, enjoying her enjoyment. Rosemary hugged the book and looked up at him. "I am so glad you spotted this. Thank you so much."

"Oh, it's nothing. I love books as well. Good thing, right?" He shrugged in the direction of the shelves as if the books had ears and the potential for hurt feelings, should he not do their relationship with him justice. They shared a laugh, and Rosemary let herself be curious.

"What kinds of books do you like?"

They were headed back toward the front of the store by this time. "I read a bit of everything. I've always been that way, dipping into every topic I can find. How about you?"

"I love biographies. I'm a firm believer that everyone, famous or not, is telling a story with their lives. There's something powerful about sharing in another's story, don't you think?" She didn't wait for an answer and instead con-tinued to talk nonstop, simply raising her voice to be heard when the crowd thickened. Rosemary momentarily forgot her embarrassment, forgot to be self-appraising, for she was on her favorite topics—books, stories, people—and had found a listening ear. By the time they reached the front of the store, their discussion had meandered from historic religious figures to sci-fi to memoir, finally culmi-nating in the discovery of their mutual dislike of sparkling vampires.

"Why don't you come back next Wednesday, say, around three, and I can give you a tour of the place? Might be nice for you to rediscover the store, and maybe we could talk more books."

Rosemary couldn't stop grinning. So what if he continued to flirt with her and make quirky, odd remarks? Rosemary was suddenly tired of her natural suspicion. Maybe he was just a genuine guy. And didn't she owe it to herself to try to get to know a genuine guy? And this bookstore—she hadn't realized how much she'd missed it until now.

She was lighting up the store, literally lighting it up, with the sun catching her honey hair just right and glinting at him like an insider wink. But more than that, her enthusiasm, her passion, her insistence on seeing the potential in everything energized him. She glanced at his shelves, peered into his dusty life, and saw meaning. The books that seemed so weighty yesterday sprang to life beneath her gaze, every corner of the store responding to her presence. What was it that she had said? Something about sharing in other people's stories? That was golden! He wished he had the same level of confidence she exhibited, the same passion and drive. Oh, for the ability to see possibilities instead of limitations! She said she'd grown up visiting this town. He wished their paths had crossed before this. She said she'd be here for a month, and Ben wondered how the town would suit her, if perhaps she could gaze into its streets and corners and see the possibility she'd drawn from his shop that day. Maybe this new sense of light was catching.

**The boy pokes his head out from underneath the blanket.** He sees a girl standing in the doorway, one hand flat against the wall, the other pressed to her face, where she is sucking on her fingers. The boy is surprised. He's never been found before. She is just a little kid, years younger than himself. Her hair is light and frizzy and glows oddly in the beam of his flashlight.

The boy doesn't know what to say. He watches the girl take her fingers out of her mouth and rub them on her shirt as if to dry them. She looks like she is about to cry, but instead she says, "Hi," her voice sounding as if she's found the monster under her bed. "I'm lost. Where are we?"

# Chapter Four

## "OH DEAR, OH DEAR, OH DEAR!"

It was a blinding Sunday morning; the sun spread buttery rays across the rooftops and streets of New Holden, not yet hot enough to drive people indoors. The service at St. John's was just letting out. The small stone building was one of the oldest in the town and had a quiet charm about it, albeit not-so-quiet acoustics. Ben walked out into the sun and squinted. He could still hear the choir singing the Doxology, their voices blending and resonating throughout the little church. A stream of people were leaving behind him, eager to shake the pastor's hand. Ben turned back toward the gaping double wooden doors, looking for Rosemary and her grandmother in the exiting crowd. He hadn't seen them during the service. Then again, he usually sat near the front, and he guessed that they would have been sitting near the back. He was still looking when a shrill voice wavered over the crowd.

"Ben! Oh Ben! Wait up for me!" Mrs. Gardner was side-stepping people this way and that, her tattered Bible tucked dutifully beneath one arm and her bright pink handbag dangling from the other as she maneuvered through the obstacle course of God-fearing people. Her high heels furiously clicked and clacked across the concrete as if in competition with the choir.

"Mrs. Gardner, what's the rush?"

"I just wanted to be sure to catch you before you left." Mrs. Gardner was panting and clutching at her hat, which had begun to slide off her head. "You must come with me this afternoon. I have an invitation from my niece, Dora Henley, to come to lunch right after church. You remember Dora, don't you?"

"Ah, we met . . . once or twice . . ."

"She attends Saturday evening service, so you probably don't know her from church, but she's highly involved in the community. Surely you know her from her stray cat initiative with the local animal shelter?"

"I really . . . I don't . . . I'm not involved with—"

"You must come with me to her house. I am sure you must be famished, and I insist that you join us for lunch. A Sunday lunch shouldn't be eaten all alone. It wasn't meant to be. So, you see, you really must join Dora and me and make it a snug three."

Mrs. Gardner had latched on to his arm and was steadily dragging him down the sidewalk. "She only lives down the street so you can easily walk back to get your car after we've had our lunch. You don't have any other plans this afternoon, do you?"

"No, I don't, but—"

"Excellent! I'm sure you and Dora will hit it off wonderfully. She really is a sensational cook."

Ben broke her string of words with a question. "Won't she mind you bringing someone to lunch on the spur of the moment?"

"Fiddlesticks!" Mrs. Gardner was adamant. "She will be delighted!"

Ben shot one last desperate look over his shoulder. No Rosemary. Perhaps her grandmother hadn't felt up to attending church that morning after all. "All right, you've talked me into it." Ben patted Mrs. Gardner's arm. "Just wait a moment while I put my Bible in my truck."

Leaving Mrs. Gardner dancing impatiently on the side-walk, Ben hurried over to his blue pickup in the parking lot. Quickly he unlocked the doors and was about to place his Bible inside when he caught sight of a golden head bobbing among the vehicles. *Rosemary.* He set his Bible on the dashboard, locked the doors, and dashed in her direction, slowing before she saw him so as not to appear *too* eager. "Hi there. I was beginning to think I'd missed you."

Rosemary turned and flashed her wide smile at him. Her green eyes latched on to his face and stayed there. He instantly felt warmer. She was one of those rare people who exuded joy. It was a palpable presence. To be near her was to be instantly ushered into its warm glow. "Good to see you, Ben. I think you know my Oma." Rosemary turned to the older lady at her side. "Oma, this is Ben, that guy I was telling you about from the bookstore."

*That guy I was telling you about from the bookstore—* Ben was quite happy with this title, for it implied that he'd been previously discussed and all that was now needed was a modifier: "that" guy. Anxiety quickly followed on the heels of this happiness, however, as he found himself analyzing the intonation. Had it been more along the lines of "*that*" guy as in "Save me now, Oma, it's *that* guy"?

Oma, however, was giving him a seemingly genuine smile and leaning over her walker to grab his hand. "Yes, I don't believe we've formally met, though I knew your uncle, of course. It's so nice to meet you and to finally be back at church. Pastor Andrews has been wonderful. He's visited me every week since the surgery. But there's nothing like being in the house of the Lord, is there?"

"Definitely, ma'am. I'm glad to see you back in the pew. It looks like you're doing well."

"Much better, thank you. It has been such a blessing to have Rosemary visit. She's been taking good care of me. She just cheers up my whole house!"

Ben was looking at her grandmother, but he was acutely aware of Rosemary's eyes still on him. That was another thing he liked about her. Her attention, once on you, stayed there. It made you feel special and important, to be the center of such attention and focus. Ben turned to meet her eyes and noticed that she was a bit flushed even though the day wasn't that warm yet. "Yes, I can see that. She could cheer any place up, I'm sure."

"Ben! Where are you, dear?" Mrs. Gardner's voice sounded across the parking lot. Ben started and turned around. He'd forgotten that someone was waiting for him. Mrs. Gardner had left the sidewalk and was winding her way through the parking lot. "Dora is expecting us any minute."

"I'm so sorry." Ben turned back to Rosemary. "I promised to be somewhere for lunch, but I'll see you Wednesday?"

"No worries; we don't mean to keep you."

Ben's disappointment was sharp as he turned and jogged in Mrs. Gardner's direction.

◇◆◇◆

Rosemary slowly guided the car out of the parking lot. She was silent, but Oma had a lot to say on the subject of "that guy from the bookstore." "I didn't realize you were talking about Ben, Rosemary. And I don't know what you meant when you said he isn't handsome. He has that dark, suave, Italian look about him. A family trait. And he is definitely single."

Rosemary finally piped up. "Yes, but he apparently has a lunch date with someone named Dora."

"Yes, Matilda Gardner's niece."

"So she's young, then? Like around my age?"

"You sound jealous!"

"Really I'm not; I hardly know Ben."

"I suppose so, but what is this about meeting him this Wednesday, hmmm? You didn't tell me about that."

Rosemary sighed and gripped the steering wheel tightly. "He's going to show me around the shop a bit. That's all, honestly. You can come too, if you're so curious." Inwardly she cringed and silently begged her grandmother not to take her up on the offer.

"That sounds nice, but I don't think I'll quite be up for it. All those stairs . . . thank you anyway, dear." Silence reigned in the car for the rest of the short drive home. As Rosemary pulled the car into the driveway, Oma sighed. "Did you just see how he gave me a little bow as he left? Such a gentleman."

◇◆◇◆

"Aunt Matilda, who is this?" Miss Dora Henley did not look as "delighted" as promised. She stood silhouetted in her doorway, peering down at her aunt with a hint of accusation cloaked in a smile. Ben thought she looked a bit like a scarecrow, and not the heartwarming Wizard of Oz kind. She stepped aside to admit her guests. None of the lights were flicked on, so it took a moment for Ben's eyes to adjust from the brightness outside to the dimness of Dora's front hallway. As they adjusted, mounds of papers, magazines, laundry, and odds and ends greeted him. He felt slightly embarrassed. He shouldn't have dropped by unannounced. She didn't look ready for visitors.

"You remember Benjamin Palermo, dear, don't you?" At Dora's blank look, Mrs. Gardner prompted, "He's the fellow who runs Palermo's Books downtown."

"Oh, I go by that place all the time." Mrs. Gardner beamed at her niece's words. Dora continued. "But I've never been inside. Frankly, I don't remember the last time I read a book. Probably when I had to for school. I think part of the problem is time; I just never seem to have the time, what with my work for PAWS and all. These days my 'bookstore' is the magazine rack in the grocery store checkout line." Dora laughed as if she'd told a great joke.

Mrs. Gardner laughed nervously and cleared her throat. Ben tried not to take the offhanded comment personally, but it was hard not to when his profession had been so easily dismissed.

As she showed her guests into her dining room, Dora continued, "I like to read things that are fresh and relevant to me today, things that are happening here and now. Books take too long."

Ben smiled and waited until the women were seated before he took his chair. The dining room was no less cluttered, with a flowerpot full of receipts serving as a centerpiece and cats lazily draped across chair seats as if they were part and parcel of the decor. "Well, we do have magazines and newspapers for sale at Palermo's." Ben hoped his tone was pleasant enough and didn't sound quite as forced as it felt. "I hope to see you drop in sometime."

Dora sniffed, her sharp nose twitching spasmodically. "That's okay; I get mine from someplace else."

"Well, folks!" Mrs. Gardner clapped her hands with a desperate air. "How about we start on lunch!"

"I only set the table for two, Aunt Matilda." Dora rose and deliberately crossed the room to the china cabinet. China—Ben noted with astonishment the fine china on the table, placed like glistening spots of cleanliness among the rubble. *Why bother with china when she hasn't bothered with anything else?* Ben squelched the ungracious thought. *Don't judge a book by its cover, Ben,* he counseled himself. Dora was rummaging around in the cabinet. "You will have to wait a moment for your food while I set the table for a third person." She glanced at Ben and pursed her lips.

"Don't worry about that, dear. I'll get the third setting ready while you bring out lunch."

Dora consented, and Ben rose to his feet. "Do you need help with anything, Miss Henley?" He didn't dare call her by her first name. Somehow he sensed that wouldn't go over well with his hostess.

There came a cool "No. Thank you. I can manage." And then she was gone.

"I'm so sorry if Dora offended you." Mrs. Gardner carefully balanced a china plate, bowl, cup, and saucer in her hands as she approached the crowded table. "She can come across rather stiff sometimes, but underneath her prickly exterior shines a heart of gold!" Quickly she set out the china, plopped down some silverware, and scurried into the next room to find another cloth napkin.

Ben sat in his chair and fiddled with a spoon. His head was filled with thoughts of Rosemary. *She must be an incredible person to give up a month to help her grandmother.* He wondered what she did for a living, where she was from. He found himself growing nervous at the prospect of seeing her again. Just one sight of her made him crave her approval in a vague and unsettling way. Each time he saw her, she became more and more impressive, and Ben was beginning to feel unequal to the task of interesting or impressing her.

A clash from the kitchen drew his attention away from his spoon and his ruminations. He didn't know what to make of this whole situation. The predominant feeling was one of awkwardness: awkwardness over intruding upon Miss Henley uninvited; awkwardness over witnessing how breathlessly eager Mrs. Gardner was that they get along; awkwardness over sitting here, playing with a solid silver spoon next to a lightly snoring cat using an unidentifiable piece of laundry as a pillow. Mrs. Gardner had been so adamant that he come . . . Ben paused and chuckled to himself. If he didn't know any better, he would suspect Mrs. Gardner of trying to hook him up with her niece!

Dora and Mrs. Gardner came back in at the same time, the one carrying a steaming pot of what turned out to be chicken and rice soup and the other a carefully embroidered cloth napkin. After a quick table prayer, which Mrs. Gardner insisted that Ben lead, the meal was underway.

Poor Mrs. Gardner tried her best to find some similarities between the two young people at the table. "Dora hand-embroidered these napkins, Ben. Isn't that right, Dora?" Dora was sipping at a spoonful of broth, so she only nodded yes. "So many girls these days don't know how to embroider." Mrs. Gardner paused sadly over her buttered roll. "It really is a shame. Your mother embroidered, didn't she Ben?"

Ben looked up, surprised. "Ah, actually, I don't remember. She was more of an outdoorsy person. She loved hiking and camping."

"Well, Dora likes to camp, don't you dear?"

"Aunt Matilda," Dora explained patiently, "you know I don't like camping."

"Oh yes, that's right." Mrs. Gardner laughed softly and dabbed at the corner of her mouth with her napkin. "How silly of me to forget." She frowned and bit her lip, gazing at the two young people in apparent displeasure. Both were busily eating and not saying a word. Ben reached out for a second roll just as Mrs. Gardner eagerly commented, "These rolls are delicious, aren't they?"

Ben nodded appreciatively. "They are quite good. Did you make them, Miss Henley?"

"Yes, I did."

"You did an excellent job."

"Thank you."

Mrs. Gardner beamed at this brief exchange. "So many girls these days don't know how to make bread—a simple thing like bread! Now, Dora here started baking her own bread at the tender age of eight."

"Actually, I was eighteen."

"Well, eight or eighteen, it doesn't make any difference,

you're a wonderful cook now and that's all that matters," Mrs. Gardiner snapped and threw down her napkin. Quickly she regained her composure and nudged Ben, leaning in conspiratorially. "It's good practice for whenever she becomes a wife and mother, isn't it?"

Ben cleared his throat. "Ah, yes, I suppose."

Dora looked completely fed up with her aunt. "I'll bring in the dessert now."

Dessert consisted of an apple tart topped with a dollop of vanilla ice cream. Mrs. Gardner was practically wringing her hands by this time, throwing out topics like conversational lifelines. "Um . . . Ben has a dog who keeps him company at the store."

"You keep your dog in the store with you?" Dora seemed incredulous. "Isn't that a little thoughtless?"

Ben frowned. "How would it be thoughtless?"

"Well, what if some of your customers are allergic to dogs or just don't like to have a dog yapping and prancing about them while they do their shopping?"

Ben dropped his fork with a clatter. "Excuse me, Miss Henley, but Julius Caesar does not yap or prance around the store. He is a very well-behaved dog. I wouldn't keep him in the store if he weren't."

Dora's hard face cracked and she began to snort and gasp. At first Ben thought she was having a seizure, and he jumped from his chair in alarm, but then he realized Dora was simply laughing. He abruptly sat back down.

Between snorts and gasps, Dora managed to say, "Y-your dog's name is-is *Julius Caesar*?"

Ben cleared his throat, his body rigid. "Yes, JC for short. You find that funny?"

"W-what a silly name for a *d-dog!*"

Mrs. Gardner had been watching the conversation, her anxious eyes darting back and forth as if at a testy tennis match, but now she gasped loudly at her niece's rudeness and, at the look on Ben's face, quickly stepped in. It was a well-known fact that Mrs. Gardner wasn't exactly fond of JC, but it was equally known that she was incredibly fond of his owner and by extension was protective of anything he loved. "You're wrong about JC, Dora. He's a wonderful, adorable dog. Please don't make fun of him. I'm sure that if you saw him you would just fall in—"

"I am not much for dogs." Dora had quickly gained her composure and was now wiping the tears that were running down her red cheeks. "They're so . . . smelly and . . . unnecessarily large. Now cats, on the other hand—"

"I don't really care for cats," Ben interrupted her. His normal mannerly self had flown out the window at Dora's snorting and gasping. *A woman who laughs like that*, he thought, *ought to be gagged and tied.* "In fact, I find cats to be the smellier of the two. And as far as largeness goes, I've seen many cats who are larger than JC, such as that fellow over there." Ben gestured toward a large gray mass that had somehow managed to haul itself to the top of the china cabinet. "Although I've never heard of 'largeness' being any animal's fault or an inherently bad trait. But what do I know?"

Dora narrowed her eyes at him. "Aunt Matilda, why did you bring this rude man to my house?"

Mrs. Gardner had been sitting with her mouth agape in an expression of horror-struck fascination for the past few seconds, but now she seemed to unglue her tongue. "I'm sorry you two didn't get along. Well, um, uh, we better get going, Ben."

Ben rose to his feet and placed the hand-embroidered napkin on the table. "I'm so sorry for dropping in on you unexpected and uninvited, Miss Henley. The meal was delicious. I am very glad that you can embroider and make bread. And I shouldn't worry if I were you; camping, books, and dogs aren't everything in the world. You have been getting along well enough without them, and I'm sure you will continue to survive for many more years without them. I better get going now and get out of your hair. I'm sorry to have been a nuisance." Ben turned to Mrs. Gardner. "You're right, she is a sensational cook." He nodded at Dora and then let himself out, leaving her to gasp and splutter as her face turned a tint of purple.

Mrs. Gardner grabbed her purse, flustered about a bit until she finally found her Bible, gave one last look at her purple niece, and hurriedly followed Ben out of the house, mumbling the entire time, "Oh dear, oh dear, oh dear!"

**The girl enters the Room.** *She watches as the boy climbs out from under the blanket. He is a tall boy, and his eyes still frighten her, but she has decided that he is not a scary boy.*

*"Where are we?" the boy repeats her question. "We're in the Room," he says matter-of-factly.*

*The girl frowns. She has never heard of this Room.*

*"The Story People live here," the boy explains.*

*Now the girl is frightened. Apparently they are in someone's home. Perhaps these people will be mad if they come back and find strange children in their house. "Shouldn't we leave, then?" she asks, and now, finally, she begins to cry. "B-b-before they come back?"*

# CHAPTER FIVE

## EXITING UNDER A KALEIDOSCOPE OF EMOTION

Monday morning found Ben kneeling in his sale room, boxing up books to donate, still railing at himself. He had been rude and inconsiderate at Dora's house, and quite frankly, he was shocked at the little speech he had given before he left. True, she had deserved it. True, she had been an awful hostess. True, she really didn't know how to make an apple tart. But these were no reasons for him to go against character and snap at her the way he had. Not a small part of his irritation was the fact that his encounter with Dora had cost him potential time with Rosemary. If it hadn't been for Mrs. Gardner's invitation, he'd have asked Rosemary, and her grandmother of course, out to lunch. Instead he'd been stuck in an awkward situation and he'd made the worst of it.

Ben paused and leaned back on his heels. He needed to slow down, or the books would arrive at the church worse for the wear. The annual church bazaar was fast approaching, the funds collected going toward a youth mission trip, and Ben had promised Dale a box of books for the event. With a groan, Ben took the books back out of the box and started over, more carefully this time.

The drive to the church took no more than five minutes. The day was especially fine with low humidity and clear, crisp sunshine, so Ben opened his windows and let the breeze sweep away his irritation over the previous day. He'd also promised Dale that he'd help set up the fellowship hall for the event. "I'll have a shortage of muscle tomorrow, Ben, so any help you can give with the tables would be much appreciated," Dale had mentioned before church yesterday. Ben didn't mind; in fact, he was looking forward to spending time with Dale and the chance to help out at church.

There was a decided uptick in his mood as Ben pulled into the church parking lot. The cars of fellow volunteers were sprinkled throughout the lot. As Ben jumped out of his truck and headed to the bed to unload the books, he heard the loud bang of the church's side door. Looking up, he watched as Rosemary left the church and headed toward the open trunk of a car. Ben watched her hike a box onto her hip and head back into the building. Only then did he realize that he was hiding behind his truck, deliberately positioning himself so as not to be seen. What was wrong with him? He'd been so eager to see her the other day, but now his nerves were getting the better of him. *Pull it together, Palermo*, he told himself. She was only the most elegant, composed, thoughtful person he'd met in a long while. Or at least she appeared to be. What did he really know about her? Name: Rosemary. Age: post–graduate school—she'd made that abundantly clear! Pastimes: ministering to her grandmother in a time of need. Occupation: bringer of joy and light. Summary: Scripture was correct in encouraging a hospitable outlook on life, for there are indeed angels among us! To top it all off, there was something about her that felt decidedly familiar. Ironically, the more he basked in this feeling of familiarity, the more nervous he felt. It was becoming increasingly clear that this was no passing attraction but rather one he was beginning to feel compelled to do something about.

Ben cleared his throat, rolled his shoulders, and popped

his neck, mentally preparing himself. He hadn't expected to put on his game face today, that best-foot-forward self intended to woo and persuade. He looked at his clothes: sneakers, ripped jeans, and a gray T-shirt. *Great.* Hoisting his load of books, Ben emerged from behind the pickup and headed toward the door recently vacated by Rosemary.

St. John's was built without fuss or fanfare, a simple L shape with the foyer and sanctuary in the main building and the offices, classrooms, and fellowship hall jutting off the side. Ben entered the side door and made his way down the corridor, following the sound of amplified voices coming from the fellowship hall. The preparations were well under way. A couple of teenage boys were wrestling battered round tables from a side closet while a handful of ladies taped a banner to the wall. One corner of the room held a pile of items, which were being methodically sorted by Rena, the church secretary. Conspicuously absent, however, was Rosemary.

"Hey, Ben, over here!" Dale waved him over to a table. "Set those down right here; thanks." Ben gratefully eased the box onto the table and shook his friend's hand. Dale was a short, thin man. His small frame and the way his ears stuck out from his head gave a deceiving impression that was shattered once he opened his mouth. Dale's big voice filled a room, and his presence filled the pulpit each Sunday as he enthusiastically preached God's Word. It was nearly impossible to feel unloved in Dale's presence. To be near him was to be reminded that everything would, after all, be well.

"What treasures have you brought us?" Dale began unpacking Ben's box, but Ben, usually so eager to showcase his books, found himself merely mumbling something in reply. *Where is she? Has she already dropped off her box with Rena? But if she did, then I would have seen her leave.*

"I appreciate your helping out this way," Dale continued. "I suppose Nick is watching the shop?"

"Hmm? Yes, Nick. Yes." Ben acknowledged the existence of his sole employee and craned his neck to look past the ladies with the banner.

"If you're looking for more tables, they're right this way." Dale began walking toward a second closet. "Logan and Levi have the round tables under control, so if you could help with the long ones, that'd be great."

Ben was finding it difficult to concentrate. *Did she see me and duck out on purpose? No, she can't be avoiding me, right? She didn't give me that vibe the other day.*

"Hey, Ben. You okay?"

Ben looked up to see that Dale was already halfway across the room and had needed to shout this last phrase. "I'm sorry. My head is just not in the game today." Ben gritted his teeth and shook his head in apology. "Let's get this show on the road."

Physical labor was always a good distraction. Yet as Ben lifted tables, moved chairs, and carted mounds of sale items to various locations, he found himself surreptitiously eyeing the hallway and any persons coming and going, which, as a result, made him painfully aware of how he looked and moved. He was careful not to show too much exertion, just in case Rosemary happened to walk by. He wouldn't want her thinking a few tables and chairs were too much for him to handle.

◇◆◇◆

"For the longest time the twins kept calling my belly 'ball.' They're at that age, you know, where the concept of a baby is just not real yet."

"That's cute." Rosemary smiled and leaned more to her left so she could see out the kitchen door, into the fellowship hall, and across the room to the closet where Ben was lifting a table in the air like it was a feather. Ben. He was everywhere! She couldn't move two steps in this town without a Ben sighting. Rosemary watched the way Ben shifted to get a better grip on the table, his bronzed features looking suitably rugged against his tattered attire. She didn't mind this view. Not in the least.

"Dale and I bought them baby dolls of their own to 'practice' with. We help them hold the dolls, comb their hair, and change them. But the other day I came across Laura coloring on her doll's face, and Anna's doll is now somehow mysteriously missing a leg, so I'm thinking maybe we did more harm than good with this whole baby doll idea!"

Rosemary laughed out loud. She'd met Sarah Andrews a week ago and was already enchanted. "And when are you due again?"

"Two weeks." Sarah sighed. "This is way longer than I made it with the twins. I thought I couldn't be any more uncomfortable than I was with them, but I was wrong."

"You look so great. I'm happy for you both." Rosemary realized she'd scooted behind the island in the kitchen, out of alignment with the door. The idea of Ben seeing her made her heart pound. After learning he'd spent time with *Dora* yesterday, he'd become larger than life in her mind, occupying way too much mental space. Somehow, the idea of him spending time with someone other than her had made her jumpy and had solidified what she'd previously denied: she was attracted to him. *Oh my goodness, yes.* And seeing him today—casual, natural, unguarded, and completely unaware of her—had only added fuel to this conviction. Not only that, but the way he'd interacted with Oma had impressed her. The gregariousness she'd originally found suspicious had morphed into a charming and genuine trait. His whole personality now seemed open and inviting.

Her eyes were drawn to him from across the room, and even as she longed to see and talk to him, she also felt too self-conscious to make the first move. In the back of her mind, the question of Dora wiggled around, as unasked questions tend to do. She knew if she saw him, her insatiable desire to know about Dora would rise to the surface, and there really wasn't a subtle way to ask about it. She knew she needed to just let it go. It could, after all, have been a completely casual lunch date. It had seemed like Mrs. Gardner would be in attendance, so really, how romantic could it have been? Maybe Dora was an older niece. It was possible, right? Rosemary had seen Mrs. Gardner sitting next to a couple of other women at church; maybe one of them was Dora. Yes, maybe Dora wasn't the young, attractive, single woman Rosemary had been imagining. Perhaps she was an older woman—married, even!

"And you're sure you don't mind?" Sarah was talking again, looking up from the list she'd been referencing.

"Two dozen cookies. Nope, I don't mind at all. How does chocolate peanut butter sound?"

"Yum, that sounds perfect, thank you! If you could have the cookies here by Friday that'd be great."

Rosemary had brought over several boxes and bags full of old items from Oma's home for the church sale. It hadn't been easy to convince Oma to go through her crowded basement, but in the end, the good cause of the youth mission trip had won her over. Still, she'd strictly overseen Rosemary's cleaning. If Rosemary had been left alone, the church would have received ten times the amount she'd ended up bringing.

"Well, I think I'm finished in here for now," Sarah said. "I just need to bother a few more people for baked goodies and then we'll be all set." She capped the pen she'd been using to compose her list and headed toward the door. "You coming?" She paused, one hand on the doorframe, the other on her rounded stomach.

"Oh, um, yes. I will in just a minute. You go on without me."

"Okay." Sarah shrugged, most likely wondering why Rosemary would linger by herself in her grandmother's church's kitchen. "Thanks again."

Rosemary scuttled to the left, in line with the door once more, and watched Sarah cross the room to her husband, who was helping Ben unpack several boxes. How would she leave without Ben seeing her? She was going to see him the day after tomorrow anyway, so why avoid seeing him now? But still she lingered, waiting until Ben crossed the room to the closet once more. Only then did she emerge, holding an empty box like a shield and keeping to the side of the room, exiting under a kaleidoscope of emotion.

**The boy watches the girl cry and feels bad for scaring her.** He's never had to comfort someone before. "Don't worry," he consoles. "They're out in the bookstore all day, gathering stories. They won't come back until late tonight."

This seems to calm the girl. She has, thankfully, stopped crying. The boy feels embarrassed for sharing the secret of the Story People with the girl. What if she laughs at him? But instead she is moving forward and sitting down, crossing her two skinny legs and clasping her small hands in her lap.

"Tell me more about the people," she says.

And so he does.

# CHAPTER SIX

## "CHOP IT ALL OFF"

Today was the day. It made Ben want to lie down, elevate his feet, get the blood rushing back to his head. Rosemary would be coming to see the store—to see *him*—and there was no avoiding the question dancing in his mind. Ben had been practicing all morning. "Would you like to grab a coffee sometime?" "Do you like coffee?" "There's this coffee shop in town. Want to try it?" "Coffee—yes?"

It had been a while since he'd been interested in anyone. He certainly hadn't met anyone since moving to New Holden. The store was such a consuming distraction that he'd put relationships on hold. And honestly, a guy could go only so many years without meeting anyone before he just kind of stopped looking.

The bell above the door jingled, pulling Ben from his state of nervous anticipation. Mrs. Baumgartner scuttled in, wearing a sage-green jumper and leather sandals. She spotted Ben and hurried over to him. Ben rose and nodded his head to her. "It's wonderful to see you again, Mrs. Baumgartner. If I can be of any assistance, just let me know."

"Thank you, Ben." Mrs. Baumgartner patted JC on the head. She smelled of strawberries—she always did—and not for the first time did Ben imagine her as a character in Candyland: Berry Baumgartner of the Strawberry Caves.

Her sweet scent and sweet manners could win anyone over.

Turning large, innocent blue eyes on him, Mrs. Baumgartner moved a bit closer to Ben. "I've brought my granddaughter with me." Ben looked behind her but saw no one. Mrs. Baumgartner saw his puzzled expression and turned as well. "Oh my. She must not have seen which store I went into. Excuse me, Ben." She scuttled back outside, leaving a waft of berry in her wake.

Ben was putting on his mental kid hat, thinking up questions to ask about the granddaughter's reading interests and running through a list of his best sellers. Nancy Drew was a classic, and he always had some of those in stock . . . unless the girl was too young for chapter books. What picture books might he recommend? Amelia Bedelia? The bell above the door jingled again and all thoughts of spunky girl detectives and annoyingly literal maids flew out of his head, for in walked the most colorful woman Ben had ever seen. She wore leopard-print leggings and a lime-green, inappropriately low-cut top. Her hoop earrings were so large that Ben was afraid they'd snag on objects as she passed by, and her shoes made her at least six inches taller than she really was, which in turn made her sound like she was clomping around on stilts. Her face, although quite attractive, was heavily done up in makeup, and her bright red lips smacked as she chewed a wad of gum.

Ben didn't know where to look. His gaze flitted here and there, like a bird looking for a safe landing. He finally settled on staring fixedly at the girl's forehead. He thought he'd heard once that this was something people did when they were nervous. But no, that was for public speaking, so now he just felt ridiculous.

"So sorry, Grandma, but I was looking at the clothes shop next door. Ooh, they have the cutest tops!" she squealed.

"There was this glitzy one that had a neckline like this." She drew a long, manicured finger across her chest in a painful progression that included dips where Ben hadn't realized there could be dips. He found himself groaning inwardly as he sat down and looked away. Who would have suspected that Berry Baumgartner would be grandmother to Tutti Frutti?

"That's fine, dear, but I want to introduce you to Ben. Ben, this is my granddaughter Natalie, who has come to visit me for a week."

Ben inwardly groaned again and stood. "I hope you will enjoy your stay in New Holden, Natalie."

"Ooh, I'm sure I will." Natalie took him in from head to toe. He had taken extra pains to look nice for Rosemary, but now, beneath Natalie's gaze, he wished he hadn't done so.

Mrs. Baumgartner didn't seem to take notice of Ben's discomfort. "I promised Natalie you'd show her the shop. She wants to get a feel for New Holden and its people, and I could think of no better beginning than right here." Seeing Ben's hesitant look, she added, "You don't mind, do you, Ben?"

Ben heard off-key humming coming from the classics section that was unmistakably his employee, Nick, entertaining himself while shelving books. A lightbulb went off. "I'm actually, um, kind of busy right now." Ben grabbed at some random papers on the desk and shuffled them importantly. "I could have Nick do the tour." Hearing his name, Nick popped his head up over the shelves and turned in the direction of the front door like a submarine periscope homing in on potential danger.

"Couldn't *you* do it, dear?" Mrs. Baumgartner's eyebrows knit together. "You know the place so well, and I promised Natalie you'd be the one to show her around."

What could he say? "No, I don't want to take your granddaughter on a simple tour"? "No, I don't like how your granddaughter looks or how she's looking at me"? Rosemary wasn't coming for another half hour, so he couldn't use that excuse; and Nick had quite unhelpfully ducked back down, safely submerged once more in Shakespeare, Milton, and Dickens, so he answered, "Ah . . . sure. Let me just ask Nick to fill in at the desk for me for a few minutes."

"Wonderful!" Natalie crooned as she swung herself around the desk and latched on to his arm.

Ben was too surprised to move for a moment, but finally he was able to get himself and Natalie out from behind the desk. Carefully he extricated himself from the girl and smoothed his dark green polo shirt. "Nick!"

Up popped the head again. "Oh, hey there," Nick said innocently, as if this were the first time he'd noticed there were other people present. Ben glared, his gaze saying in no uncertain terms, "Thanks for nothing, Buster."

"Front desk, please?" Ben indicated Natalie, who had somehow ended up back on his arm. As Nick fully surfaced and settled himself behind the desk with a half-amused, half-guilty grin, Ben turned to Natalie. "Yes. Well. What would you like to see?"

"Ooo, anything and everything," the girl murmured as she sidled closer to him and gazed up into his face. She couldn't be more than eighteen or nineteen—although he'd been known to mistake ages before. He thought of Rosemary with a pang of longing. Why on earth would Mrs. Baumgartner do something like this to him? And where was she, anyway? Wasn't she coming along on this expedition? But no, Mrs. Baumgartner was nowhere to be seen. Sighing, Ben removed his arm once again from Natalie's grip and began.

The tour should have taken no more than ten minutes, but in the end it took forty. The extra time was spent trying to squeeze out from under Natalie's clutches and listening to her drone on about herself and her long line of boyfriends. He found out in the course of their forty-minute tour that she actually didn't like to read all that much and when she did read, it was the latest celebrity gossip columns. She had never heard of Tennyson or Wordsworth and asked if they were kinds of drinks. As far as the classics went, she had heard of Charles Dickens and wasn't he the fellow who wrote *War and Peace*? When she found out that no, Leo Tolstoy wrote *War and Peace*, she only mumbled that she knew it was some sort of classic and that most people didn't even know *that* much and didn't he know what she meant? Oh yes, Ben knew what she meant.

He mentioned several times that he must get back to the desk, but somehow they would manage only to descend to the next floor, and then she would start in on something else. By the time they reached the first floor again, Ben was absolutely desperate. He was feeling nauseated from Natalie's perfume, which, she had explained, was called The Passion Fruit, and his arm was beginning to ache from her constant clutching and grasping at it. He wished he could somehow accidentally lose her in one of the aisles, but she was staying much too close to his side for that. Perhaps he could feign an emergency. How did one actually feign an emergency? Cardiac arrest seemed too dramatic, bathroom too juvenile, and everything else too easily dismissed by the relentless girl at his side. In the end he settled for repeated mumblings of "Oh, we better hurry. Wouldn't want to keep your grandmother waiting. My, it must be getting late."

The only clock in Palermo's Books was on the first floor, and Ben was not wearing a watch, so it wasn't until he had reached the first floor that he finally realized it was ten minutes past three. Dismayed that he might have caused Rosemary to wait and even more dismayed that she would catch him with the bright and colorful Natalie on his arm, Ben hurried to the desk.

Rosemary stood in the doorway. Her hair was loosely tied at the neck. Soft curls floated about her face, slightly frizzed, no doubt, from the recent humidity, and the light behind the door made the flyaways shine like a halo. She was wearing shorts that showed off just the right amount of a shapely pair of calves, a loose purple top, and jeweled sandals. In essence, she was the very picture of beauty without pretense. He looked into her clear face and saw it light up when she caught sight of him. That was a promising sign. Maybe this coffee question would go over well, after all. But then he watched her face cloud over, and a laugh at his elbow told him why.

Natalie had latched on once more to his arm and was hanging on him closely. She caught sight of Ben gazing at Rosemary and tugged on his sleeve, asking loudly, "Who is that, Benny?"

Rosemary smiled and came to meet them. "I'm sorry, Rosemary," Ben said as he detached Natalie's hand. "I lost track of the time."

"Hmmm, I'm sure you did." Rosemary glanced at the girl next to him. "No need to worry, I was late anyway, just got in a second ago, but since you're busy, I'll just come back another time." She started to leave.

"Oh no, no." Ben hurried toward her eagerly but was snagged by Natalie after only two steps. "I'm not busy now."

"It sure looks like it." Rosemary smiled indulgently at him, and it was then that he saw she was carrying books.

"You brought some books."

Rosemary looked down at them as if seeing them for the first time. "Oh yes, well . . . just a few things I was going to show you, but we'll save it for some other time."

"Oh no, really, Natalie is just—"

"Benny, please come help me find Grandma. I'm sure she would like to hear about our tour."

"Your tour?" Rosemary looked at him with such a pained expression that he wanted to weep.

"No, please, let me explain."

"What is there to explain?" Rosemary was at the door now, one foot in, one foot out, her voice tight and controlled. "We had arranged for a tour and a chat, but you're too busy today. There is nothing to explain. Good-bye, *Benny*." Her voice cracked on the last word as she quickly turned and left. Ben could detect a wisp of her perfume, modest cucumber.

Ben lunged for the door, intent on finding Rosemary and convincing her to listen, but again he was jerked back by Natalie's grip. He turned on Natalie with gritted teeth. "Excuse me, but will you *please* let go of my arm?" He had tried to remain calm, he had tried to keep his voice down to a whisper, but in the end he fairly shouted the last few words, attracting the attention of several customers who were milling about.

Instead of giving him the injured look mixed with rage that Dora had reserved for him, Natalie simply dropped his arm and huffed, "Well, I'm not the one who suggested this stupid tour. I don't even like books."

"Oh boy, you can be sure I had nothing to do with arranging this!" Ben wanted to say more but remembered his outburst at Dora's home and held his tongue.

"Hello, gang!" Mrs. Baumgartner scurried over from the back of the store. Two stark glares greeted her. "Um, well . . ." Mrs. Baumgartner cleared her throat and fiddled with her purse. Finally she grabbed Natalie by the arm and began to drag her toward the door. "Natalie, dear, you can tell me all about it outside. Thank you, Ben, for complying so . . . um . . . graciously."

Ben looked anything but gracious as he watched them leave the store. Marching over to his desk, he strove with all his might not to throw something. Nick looked up from the computer, where he'd probably been playing solitaire. "That tour was more than a few minutes, Ben."

Ben growled. Nick gave him an apologetic face and pointed his chin toward the door. "You look like you could use a walk. I'll hold down the fort for a while. Take a breather; you need it."

"Thanks." Ben strode out the front door. He didn't want to even think of what he had missed with Rosemary or what he had just been forced to go through with Natalie. And he'd been all geared up to ask her out too. Would Rosemary believe his sincerity if he asked her now? He was too much of a pushover, that's what his problem was. He was too nice. He needed to stand up and say no every once in a while. If he had, he wouldn't be in this situation. What was with all of these young ladies being thrown at him anyway? It was like the whole town was conspiring against him. "Lord," he fumed, "what is the deal here?" He felt a twinge of guilt, for lately his prayers had all begun similarly. "Sorry, I just feel so frustrated right now."

He stopped in front of the barbershop and plopped down on a bench, leaning to rest his forehead on his fist. His heartbeat slowed its frantic pace, and Ben's mind began to clear. "I just need direction, God," he started over. "I feel beaten at every turn." His mind quieted and the face of his friend Dale came to mind. Dale had been coming to visit him in the shop for years. Perhaps it was time for Ben to pay his friend a call on his home turf.

"Need a cut, Ben?"

It was embarrassing how easily Ben spooked. Up came his head, down came his fist to thwack his thigh, and out came a yelp.

Gene Mendleson's bald head gleamed in the afternoon sun. "Sorry, didn't mean to scare you. Saw you out here and just assumed." Gene's owlish eyes transitioned from apologetic to mischievous. "And seeing the state of your head, I also assumed . . . so you need a cut?"

"Well, yes—but no, that's not why I'm here. I mean, I didn't come here specifically, I just needed to . . . I don't know." Ben sighed. *Oh, why not?* "Sure, Gene. Chop it all off."

**"The Story People have lived here for ages,"** the boy says. "This is an old building, and they've lived here since the building was built. They moved in when the books moved in. That is how they live, by eating the stories. I come here to read while they're away."

"They don't sound very nice." The girl looks like she is still afraid.

"Nice?" The boy thinks for a moment. "They're not mean or nice; they just are."

The girl considers this for a moment. "What do they look like?" the girl asks. She is sucking on a curl and her eyes are huge.

"They can look like anything you want them to," the boy says. "What do you want them to look like?"

# CHAPTER SEVEN

## HER BLUSH GAVE AWAY HER PLEASURE

Rosemary breathed in the familiar smell of vinegar and cookies. Home, family, safety. Somehow, Oma's house always smelled sour and sweet at the same time. It was a smell well ingrained since her childhood. No sooner would she cross the threshold than Oma would be after her with a vengeance, plying her with food. "Have just one more, dear. You sure you don't want some pickles too?" Now, as Rosemary huffed through the front door and passed through the kitchen on the way to the spare bedroom, Oma's voice called out, reining her in.

"What's your hurry, dear? You just missed Pastor Andrews. I asked him to stay, but he had other shut-ins to visit. Will you take a coffee with me instead? Oh, and I've just started some sausage, and I was thinking of frying up an onion to go with it. How does that sound?"

"No, Oma, I don't want an onion and sausage."

"Nonsense. Are you going to make an old woman eat alone? No, you are not. Come sit down and eat."

Rosemary didn't think she could keep herself together. Seeing Ben taking someone else on their tour had hurt more than she'd thought possible. What had he been thinking? He knew they had a meeting. It was as if he'd intentionally staged the moment to humiliate her. She'd gotten her hopes up too high. All the good impressions she'd been forming of him over the last week began to wobble beneath the weight of her hurt and something else. Anger. Yes, anger, over the fact that she'd been played. Taking one woman out to lunch one day, parading another woman in front of her the next. What a man! And to think that she had almost become one of many in his lineup! It was too much. How could she have let herself be deceived in such a way? He had lulled her with his talk of literature, had given her the sedatives of Lewis and Shakespeare, and she had taken them oh so readily. How humiliating. And to think, to just think, that she had planned on showing him her book. Oh, the wretchedness of it all!

"You really do look like you need some food." Oma placed a gentle hand on her shoulder. "Are you sure you don't want anything?"

Rosemary turned her face away and squeezed her eyes shut. She was hurting way more than she should be. She needed to take her mind off of everything Ben-related. "You know what? That onion and sausage is sounding better by the minute. You definitely know how to convince people to eat." She turned and hugged Oma, burying her face in the top of Oma's head. "If you start the food, I'll come join you in a minute."

"Yes, wonderful!" This was all the incentive Oma needed. Her cane sounded soft thuds as she made her way to the stove. Rosemary ducked into the hallway and dashed for her room, the copies of her book still clutched in her hand.

For Rosemary there could be no greater invitation into her life than through the window of her book. *Spectrum* was about a little girl who lives in black and white until one day she picks up a book and enters a full-color world of imagination. As the girl makes subsequent trips back and forth between her world and the world of the story, her world gradually begins to exhibit color. The first trip back brings blues yawning across the sky. The second trip back brings greens jumping across the fields. The third trip adds a dash of buttery yellow into her world. The more the little girl reads, the more color is added until her real world is just as colorful and bright as the world she imagines in her story. *Spectrum* was a lifetime in the making. Even as a little girl herself, Rosemary spent hours sketching, escaping the mounting tension between her parents by pouring herself into imagined worlds of her own creation. She'd hidden her art from her parents for years. It was something that was hers, only hers, free from the incessant shouting and unavailable as ammunition in the ongoing war between mother and father. And then it was just Rosemary and her mother, and the house grew quiet and safe, and Rosemary had slowly emerged, art in hand.

In high school, she'd turned to charcoal and pastels as her preferred media and continued to work diligently on the same concept that had gripped her as a child. Some of her more vivid spreads in *Spectrum* were imagined and sketched years ago. The book finally took shape in graduate school where, under the direction of several beloved art professors, she finished *Spectrum* for her final project. That it would go on to be published and receive such accolades as "Whimsical fun," "Haunting illustrations with a story that encourages creativity and wonder," and "Perfectly captures the inquisitive mind of a child" was beyond Rosemary's dreams. Having finished *Spectrum* and been astonished at its impact, Rosemary wondered if another book was in her future, if perhaps this was the direction she should take with her life.

Bringing *Spectrum* to share with Ben had been an invitation to know her more fully, an invitation that felt humiliating and ill-placed at the moment. Now Rosemary closed her door and set the books on the sagging bed, where they spread out with sad, upturned faces. The spare room housed Oma's wedding furniture: a rickety full bed with the original mattress, a dresser and mirror, and an armoire. There was nowhere else to sit but on the bed, so Rosemary joined the books, the springs screaming out in protest. She missed her room at her mother's house, mainly because it housed her old rolltop desk and she'd always been comforted, sitting at that desk. It was a world unto its own with cubby after messy cubby stuffed with half-used pieces of charcoal and chalk pastels, erasers, and scraps of paper. She missed the order her mind settled into while surrounded by all that mess.

The smell of frying onion reminded Rosemary that Oma was waiting for her in the kitchen. After slipping her shoes off and retying her hair, Rosemary ventured out.

With the grip of her cane in one hand and a long-handled fork in the other, Oma prodded some sausages and onion around in an old skillet. The food was well lathered in butter and was hissing and popping happily in its marinade. Rosemary opened a cabinet and set some plates on the countertop. "That smells delicious. Then again, anything with butter is delicious."

Oma gave her a sideways frown that intimated that some sort of barb had been lovingly given and only halfway understood. "*Anything* I make is delicious."

"This is true." Rosemary leaned a hip against the counter. "Anything I can do to help?"

"You can start a pot of coffee."

By "coffee," Oma meant espresso. A day didn't go by that Oma didn't consume several pots of "coffee." Rosemary opened the stove-top espresso maker and began scooping grounds.

"Weren't you supposed to still be out? Didn't you have a date with Ben?"

Rosemary suppressed a cringe. "No, not a date. He was just going to show me around the bookstore, but he ended up being too busy, so . . ."

"That's funny. It's not like Ben to not keep a promise."

"Well. How well do you really know him, Oma?"

"Not well," she admitted. "But I knew his Uncle Louie very well, and from how he talked about Ben, you would have thought the boy invented sunshine." She laughed at her own joke.

"Uncle Louie is the guy with the big black mustache, right? The one who owns the store? Where is he anyway?"

"Oh dear." Oma briefly ceased her onion shoving and looked at Rosemary. "He passed away over three years ago."

"Oh! I honestly didn't know. That's so sad. I remember I was always a bit scared of him, growing up. He had such a big voice and was so huge."

"Not that big, really. You were just a scrawny little child." Oma smirked, probably pleased at having successfully lobbed a barb back.

Rosemary wrinkled her nose and stuck her tongue out. "Uh-huh. That's sad though. He's a big part of my memory of that place. What did he pass away from?"

"Heart attack. Too much soppressata, if you ask me."

Rosemary looked from the sizzling butter to her perfectly earnest Oma and raised an eyebrow but said nothing.

"He left that place to Ben, you know. He thought the world of him."

Rosemary nearly choked on the water she'd been sipping. "Wait, he *owns* the store?"

"Yes, what did you think?"

"I don't know. I guess I just assumed he worked there as an employee, certainly not as the owner."

"It couldn't have been easy coming out here to a small town, but Ben did it. He has a fancy degree and everything—the NBA, I think."

"MBA." Rosemary corrected Oma automatically, her eyes wide, her face fixed in surprise mode.

"Yes, that's it. From what I hear, he left a cushy job. I don't remember what he did—something with keeping the books for a friend's company out of Chicago—but we were all pleasantly surprised when he came here and kept the place running. There were so many rumors that he'd simply sell. I'm sure he has as many memories of the place as you do, which is perhaps why he didn't sell. Anyway, he's done a good job in keeping the store going." Oma took a plate from Rosemary and slopped some food onto it.

Rosemary's mind was a whirlwind. Just when she was ready to throw in the towel, the man took on more nuance. "So he's Ben Palermo and he owns the store."

"Yes, dear." Oma was putting the plates on the table one at a time and sprinkling salt over the steaming heaps of food. She carefully backed into a chair and waited for Rosemary to take her seat before folding her hands and leading them in prayer. "Come, Lord Jesus, be our guest, and let Thy gifts to us be blessed. Amen."

"Amen," Rosemary echoed, again on automatic.

"What's on your mind, dear? Why are you so surprised?" Oma questioned her.

"I'm not. Surprised, that is. Just curious." Ben Palermo. The name wasn't exactly familiar, but now Ben himself did seem a bit familiar. "So, did he come here as a kid or something?"

"Yes, he spent most summers here. You might have been in Vacation Bible School with him a few summers."

Rosemary shook her head no. "I never went to VBS at St. John's. Only at home."

"Oh, that's right. Anyway, he spent summers with Louie until that tragedy with his parents."

"Tragedy?" Rosemary popped a forkful of food into her mouth, realized it was too hot for consumption, and opened her mouth, breathing shallowly to let the food cool before chewing. "Whaa agedy?" she managed around the food.

"It's really very sad." Oma shoveled a bite in and swallowed; apparently she'd burned off her nerve endings long ago. "Both parents died in a car crash when he was barely in high school. Poor boy. Lost so much so young. He went to live with a grandmother up in Kenosha, I think, and that's when his trips to New Holden ended. I remember Louie being so upset. He would have taken Ben himself, but I guess the grandmother was the guardian or something. I really don't know. Just that he never made it back to this town. Until three years ago, that is, when he inherited Palermo's."

Rosemary had finally swallowed and was pouring them both small cups of espresso. "That's so sad. He must have felt passionately about the bookstore to uproot his life like that."

"Must have," Oma agreed. She set her fork down and stretched out a hand to Rosemary. "I just had a brilliant thought. Why don't you bring your book over to Palermo's? They sell children's books, you know. I'm sure he'd be interested in selling your book."

"Oma, I don't know . . ."

"Why on earth not? Do you want to make money? Then people should know there is a book to buy! How else will you sell copies? How else will you get paid? And it's such a beautiful book, a masterpiece!"

Rosemary fought the urge to cry. "Thank you, and yes, your thinking is logical. I just don't know. My book is a big part of me, and I don't know if I really like Ben all that much, and it just feels awkward."

"Like him? I thought you liked him quite a bit!" Upon receiving Rosemary's glare, she continued, "All's I'm saying is . . . oh, what's that saying? Don't judge a cover by its book."

Rosemary masked a smile. "I believe it's the other way around."

"Yes, whichever way, the point is, sometimes things worth reading are worth reading twice. There's more there than a skim or initial impression, if you know what I'm saying."

Actually, Rosemary did, and the thought gave her pause. She leaned across the table and gave Oma a peck on the cheek. "Thank you. I needed to hear that. You are wise beyond your years, young lady."

"Oh, get out of here." Oma swatted at her, but her blush gave away her pleasure.

**Together the girl and the boy give shape to the Story People.** *First off, they are huge, colossally huge, with long, long arms that they snake through the shelves in search of food. They are huge, but they can easily hide and not be seen during the day, so perhaps they are also thin. Yes, thin as a sheet of paper so they can hide behind the shelves and no one will know. They sneak around by day and return to this hidden Room at night, their bellies full from eating all the stories they can get their sticky fingers on.*

*The more the girl and the boy give form to these people, the more the girl forgets she is lost, forgets she is scared. They are sharing the Sour Patches now, their fingers wet and sticky, the flashlight passing between them like a slippery silver fish, its beam nodding enthusiastically into the corners.*

# Chapter Eight

## THE PURPOSEFUL SILENCE HURT THE MOST

Out of habit, Ben reached up to run a hand through his hair, but he stopped short in surprise when he found decidedly less hair there than expected. He'd regretted the drastic haircut almost immediately, but he would never let on to Gene. No sense in making someone else feel guilty for his own rash decisions. Lesson learned: never make personal grooming decisions while in the throes of relational turmoil.

A week had passed, and Ben had yet to see Rosemary again. His time spent volunteering at the church sale had proved fruitless. Well, actually, the sale itself was a huge success and more than met the desired monetary goal; however, Ben's secondary motive of reconnecting with Rosemary had gone woefully unfulfilled. One good result from the sale—aside from the funding for the youth mission trip, of course—was that it had given him an idea. He'd snagged a copy of the church directory and had looked up Carol Berg's address: 307 Washington Avenue. *Ha!* If he couldn't run into Rosemary naturally, then maybe he could corner her at home. But no, that seemed incredibly stalker-like. He should probably just leave her alone, but he couldn't get that last look on her face out of his head—brow furrowed, lips pressed in a line, her eyes surprised and sad. Ben groaned at the memory and sat in his armchair. Digging into the side of the chair, he yanked open the footrest, letting it spring outward with a dull thunk. He leaned back and listened as the grandfather clock ticked off the time and the refrigerator hummed like an accompanist. JC lay curled up in his lap, snoring steadily. The evening hours stretched before him. He needed a distraction, and he needed it fast. He was just reaching for the TV remote when the phone rang.

Startled, Ben jumped from his seat, causing JC to tumble from his lap. The little dog yelped, righted himself with an indignant shake, and jumped onto Ben's vacant seat, giving him a withering glare. "Sorry, boy." Ben raced into the kitchen to catch the phone before the fourth ring. "Hello?"

"Hello, Ben, this is Emma Frank."

"Hi, Mrs. Frank."

"Listen, I hope I'm not disturbing you."

"Oh, not at all." Ben looked over to JC, who was by now perfectly content in the warm chair. "Did you need something, Mrs. Frank?"

"Actually, yes. You see, I was going to come in tomorrow to pick up that book I ordered."

Ben frowned and thought. "Ah yes, the one on vegetable life."

"That's right, but I will be out of town tomorrow, ah, um . . . visiting . . . my cousin . . . yes, my cousin."

"That's okay; you can pick it up anytime. I'll hold it for you."

"Well, you see, my cousin's niece, Elaine, will be at my house tomorrow. Same cousin I'm visiting. So I'll be there and Elaine will be here. That's not strange at all. It's just that she's eager to see my book."

"She's eager to see a book on vegetable life?"

"Um . . . yes. Anyway, I was hoping, that is, if it wouldn't be too much trouble for you . . ."

"You want me to run the book over to your house." Ben smiled grimly. Another young lady was being thrown his way.

"That's right! I don't live horribly far from the bookstore, and I thought you could drop by after your store closes."

"Mrs. Frank, couldn't your niece just come to the store and pick up the book herself?"

"Oh, you see that's where the trouble lies. Poor Elaine is so delicate and the weather is forecasted to be extremely hot. She's prone to migraines, poor thing, and I really cannot have her out in the heat for more than a few minutes."

"Ah, I see." Yes, Ben saw perfectly well. He paused for a moment before replying. He could hardly be snagged this time. All he had to do was drop the book off at her house. He didn't even need to go inside. "Okay, Mrs. Frank, I'll drop off the book after the store closes. Could you give me your address?"

"Certainly, it's 305 Washington Avenue."

Had she said 305 Washington Avenue? As in next door to 307 Washington Avenue? Ben's heart rate picked up pace, and he realized he was breathing rather heavily into the receiver.

"Ben, are you okay?"

"Yes, sorry . . . 305 Washington Avenue. All right, got it . . . night, Mrs. Frank."

"Good night, Ben, and thank you."

Ben hung up the phone and stared at it. Could this be a sign? Did God work that way? It couldn't be coincidence, could it? Surely this meant he was supposed to go over to Carol Berg's house and . . . do what? Apologize. The answer came to him softly. Yes, apologize for seemingly brushing Rosemary off when that had been the furthest thing from his intention. It was settled; he'd make the move tomorrow.

◇◆◇◆

At a quarter to five the next day, Ben left Nick to close up the shop and headed off on his errand. He had decided to walk since Washington Avenue was so close, and he figured he could use the exercise. After much thought and second-guessing, Ben had settled on flowers as his gesture of apology. Who knew? Maybe his apology could segue into something more.

As Ben descended the front steps, he caught sight of the florist's shop. He could see Rhonda through the glass storefront, which wrapped around the side and gave him a full view of the shop. Ben watched Rhonda preparing to close shop as he crossed Fifth Street and came to a stop in front of the window. He rounded the corner and went inside.

"Hi, Ben." Rhonda glanced up at him with a smile. "I'll be with you in just a second." While Rhonda carted some flowers into the back, Ben wandered over to the refrigerated case where there were beautiful bouquets behind glass.

"Now, can I help you with anything?" Rhonda approached him with a gleam in her eyes.

"Yes, I'm looking for a small bouquet of flowers."

"We-e-e-ll," Rhonda crooned, "I don't think you've ever bought a bouquet of flowers before. What kind of occasion is this for?"

At the sound of her syrupy voice, Ben looked up abruptly. "Rhonda, I don't like it when you look at me that way. Don't go getting any ideas into your head. This bouquet is simply for a friend to tell her I'm sorry."

"Oh dear, you had an argument. I'm sorry, but here's a piece of advice: Don and I have been married for fifteen years, and fighting is just a part of marriage. The important thing is that you're able to make up afterward. So don't let a little argument ruin your relationship."

Ben knew he was turning red. "We're not in a relationship. This is just to say sorry for some bad impressions I made."

Rhonda bit her lip thoughtfully and gazed steadily at him. "Okay, whatever you say. I suggest you get her yellow roses. They're not only the symbol of friendship but also apology. Quite fitting, don't you think?"

"That sounds good; I'll take those." Ben got out his wallet as Rhonda opened the glass door of the case and took out a delicate bouquet.

"If you want, you can write her a little note on this card." Rhonda handed him a heart-shaped card.

"Umm, do you have any different cards?"

Rhonda frowned a bit but took him to the front desk where she showed him an assortment of options. As Ben looked through the cards, she rang up the purchase, keeping an eye on her customer to see which one he chose.

Ben chose the simplest card he could find. It was white with a faint floral pattern around the edges and looked almost like a business card. Now, what to write? Ben picked up the pen and held it poised. He glanced up and found Rhonda staring at his hand. She started guiltily and moved to the rack of tissue paper next to the counter. "Would you like it wrapped in yellow paper?"

"Sure." Ben turned back to the card and started to write. *They say first impressions are often right*— He looked up and caught Rhonda wrapping the flowers slowly while trying to read upside down. He cleared his throat, and she jerked her gaze to the flowers and began studying them as if she'd never seen a flower before. Ben continued writing: *but I feel bad for the other day. Please stop by Palermo's anytime and we'll take that tour. —Ben*

"That's a sweet note!" Rhonda exclaimed, handing Ben the flowers. Ben scowled and handed her the money.

As he left the shop, Ben turned down Fifth Street with a hopeful heart and a spring in his step. Making his way toward Washington Avenue, he carried the flowers in one hand and a thick hardcover book entitled *The Functions, Life Cycles, and Growth of Green Leafy Vegetables* in the other.

It was the first week of August and the air hung humid and hot over the little town of New Holden. As Ben reached Washington, he gazed down it and marveled at its beauty. The oldest houses in town were on this street, along with the most ancient trees. Their leafy branches and towering trunks nearly blocked out the sky, and Ben noticed at least a ten-degree difference in their shade. He hummed a tune as he walked down the old brick sidewalk with the moss growing up between the mortar and bricks. He passed several houses looking for number 307, eager to see Rosemary's face when he handed her the flowers. He came upon number 305 first and paused to look at the two-story brick-faced beauty. Ivy climbed all up the front, giving it an air of tasteful decay. An old iron fence surrounded the front yard. Just as he continued on toward 307, someone shouted his name.

"Hello, you must be Ben! I've been expecting you!" A young woman stood from where she'd been lounging on lawn furniture under a tree and began picking her way to him through an obstacle course of lawn ornaments.

Ben hovered by the gate, wondering if he could just toss the book inside and make a mad dash toward 307 and safety.

"I'm Elaine, but you probably guessed that by now." The young woman laughed as she reached the gate and propped it open for Ben, its rusty hinges squealing in complaint, mimicking the protest in Ben's mind. Elaine stood looking up at him expectantly. Her hair hung lank and heavy on either side of her face. The part at the top of her head was wide and raw beneath the sun, as if her long hair were slowly peeling off of her head. Her eyes, likewise, appeared to be dripping from her face, large and like a basset hound's; they seemed barely able to stay open. The overall effect was of a person melting before Ben's eyes. Ben seriously considered denying who he was, but then there was the incriminating book in his hands.

"Don't just stand there; come on in!" Elaine grabbed his wrist and led him into Mrs. Frank's front yard. Turning, her eyes shifted from Ben to the bouquet in his hands. "Oh, how lovely. You brought me flowers. How thoughtful of you!"

"Uh . . . um . . . ah . . . no . . . you see . . ."

Elaine gently took them from his hands as if she were handling a newborn baby. "You really didn't have to, Ben. I mean, we don't even know each other."

"I didn't. Those aren't for—"

"But Aunt did say you were sweet."

"There's been a mistake."

"And now I see she was right." Elaine held the flowers in one hand and with the other playfully swatted at Ben's forearm before burying her nose in the flowers and inhaling theatrically.

Elaine, he could tell, was definitely the soppy type, and Ben was too flustered to know what to do. He looked from Elaine to the flowers and back again, his mind a whirlwind of panic. Before he knew what he was doing, he'd reached out and grabbed the bouquet back, never mind how it would appear and never mind if it offended her. The action caused the card to flutter to the ground.

Elaine looked at him in surprise as she bent to retrieve the card. "Are you okay?" She glanced at the card and then turned it to face Ben. "What on earth is this supposed to mean?" She looked at him quizzically, her large, mournful eyes looking more and more doggish. "You certainly don't have anything to apologize for." She swatted at his arm again with a laugh. "In fact, quite the opposite." Her tone grew flirtatious.

It was just at that moment that Ben noticed the porch next door. He froze; Rosemary was sitting in a wicker chair. She practically had a front-row seat to the little drama being played out in Mrs. Frank's yard. She had a spiral notebook in her hand and looked as if she had been busy writing or perhaps sketching, but now she was staring straight at them, her face puckered into a frown. Ben knew she couldn't have heard what they were saying, but she definitely had seen what they were doing. When she caught him looking at her, she stood crisply to her feet and went inside. Ben fairly ground his teeth in frustration. He looked back at Elaine and a thousand suspicions arose in his mind.

"Let me ask you a question. Do you happen to suffer from migraines?"

Elaine looked taken aback. "Why, no—"

"Aha! Just as I thought. And do you happen to be the least bit interested in the functions, life cycles, and growth of green leafy vegetables?" It was at this juncture that he shoved the book into Elaine's arms. As he turned to leave, Elaine stared at him as if he were out of his mind, her mouth hanging open and her basset eyes fairly popping from her head. Ben reached the gate and fumbled with the latch, but it refused to open without patience, which Ben had none of at the moment. Muttering under his breath, Ben placed a foot onto the lowest rung and prepared to swing himself over.

"But the flowers!"

Ben didn't respond. Once on the other side of the fence, he strode away without a backward glance.

Reaching the intersection of Washington and Fifth, he paused, breathing rapidly, both from distress and from the quick pace. He had to explain himself. Circling around, he approached 307 from the opposite direction. Elaine was nowhere to be seen. Taking the front steps two at a time, Ben knocked on the front door and then knocked again when no one answered. The bouquet was still clenched in his hands, the flowers worse for the wear. Ben shifted the bouquet from hand to hand as he listened to the raised voices coming from inside, but no one came to the door. If only he hadn't tried to multitask with the flowers and the book. Who knew multitasking could be so disastrous? If only he'd called Rosemary first so she knew he was coming. If only he'd told Mrs. Frank that no, he couldn't deliver her book, and she needed to come pick it up herself. His mind was ablaze with the many "if onlys" that now relentlessly presented themselves as such attractive alternatives. Instead he was left with a horrifying conclusion to an originally promising day. *Why, why, why did this have to happen?*

Ben knocked once more, calling out, "Rosemary, can you please open up? It's Ben. Please let me explain." He wasn't sure if she could hear what he was saying or not, but there was no way she could miss his persistent knocking. The voices on the other side of the door died down and then silence, just silence. Ben stared hard at the door, willing it to open. He knew knocking again would be pointless. Sadly he knelt and placed the flowers on the doormat where she would be sure to see them. He no longer had the note, which was most likely now in Mrs. Frank's trash can, and he had nothing with which to write another. The lonely bouquet with the now-twisted and ripped tissue paper would have to be enough. Ben was shaken to the core as he slowly descended the steps. She was inside, and she knew that he knew that she was inside. And yet, she did not open the door. The purposeful silence hurt the most.

**The Story People have become larger than life.** *To the girl, they are a wonderful world that she can help mold and shape. She has breathed new life into the story that has grown stale to the boy. Together they weave something fresh and new.*

*The secrecy of the Room coupled with the creepiness of the old building has created the ideal atmosphere for pretending: pretending that the bookshelves stretching throughout the store are currently being raided by long-armed, semi-scary people; pretending that this small Room is the home of these people and that the two of them are the clever ones who have discovered it. They share in endless pretending until they both forget that there are people who might be looking for them, people who might be worried, that they are not alone but connected and accountable and probably at this moment being sorely missed.*

# CHAPTER NINE

## ALL DISSENT EVAPORATED
## AT THE PROSPECT OF LOSING BEN

Rain struck Mrs. Frank's windows in intermittent spurts. The sunny morning had turned into an indecisive afternoon with the sky spitting bouts of rain, holding back and raising hopes, and then spitting more rain. Mrs. Gardner sighed, and Mrs. Baumgartner adjusted the ball of yarn in her ample lap. The three friends had a weekly knit-along to make shawls for the Ladies' Aid prayer ministry. This particular session was being held at Mrs. Frank's home, which meant they were nestled in her enclosed patio and had a front-row view of the gray afternoon. "This weather is certainly dreary. I don't recall ever getting this much rain so late in the season," Mrs. Gardner said, breaking the silence.

Mrs. Baumgartner agreed wholeheartedly. "I really dislike rainy days," she complained. "They make me feel depressed."

"Well, I, for one, enjoy a bit of rain," Mrs. Frank commented, her long, thin fingers maneuvering her knitting needles with record speed.

"That is only because you like being depressed, Emma."

"Oh come, Anita!"

"Now you two," Mrs. Gardner warned. "Please let's not start yet another argument."

Mrs. Baumgartner submitted herself to this admonition and settled once more into the overstuffed chair, her fingers moving nimbly all the while. "It is just too bad that our matchmaking efforts were all for nothing."

"I didn't like the idea in the first place," Mrs. Frank muttered.

Mrs. Gardner turned to Mrs. Baumgartner and spoke gently to her. "Now Anita, you did choose rather an ill-suited girl for Ben. I mean, Natalie really isn't Ben's type. She's just too . . . too . . ."

"Too what, Matilda? Remember, she is my granddaughter." Anita Baumgartner rarely showed any signs of anger or bad temper, but when it came to blood relations, she was a tigress, and Mrs. Gardner knew this.

"I mean no disrespect, Anita, you know that, and I certainly don't want to offend you. All I meant was that Natalie was just a bit too . . . worldly for Ben."

Mrs. Baumgartner was just about to be offended when Mrs. Frank butted in. "Matilda, that may be so, but Dora certainly wasn't a better fit. She's too much of a pickle for Ben."

"What?"

"You know what I mean. Ben needs a woman who is all warmth and softness. Dora is cold and prickly."

"Why, I never—"

"Ben needs someone who is sweet, not sour."

Mrs. Gardner finally found her tongue. "Why, look who is talking! You can be an old sourpuss yourself, Emma."

"I know it," Mrs. Frank replied softly, uncharacteristically admitting a fault of hers. "But we are not trying to marry Ben off to me, thank the Lord."

"And what about Elaine?" Mrs. Gardner questioned.

"Well, unfortunately, Ben did not get a chance to talk to Elaine. She told me that he acted extremely odd when he came to visit her."

"Even though they didn't get a chance to talk, I know they wouldn't have hit it off," Mrs. Gardner said firmly.

"How can you be so sure?" Mrs. Frank frowned. "I intend to give it another try."

"Elaine is too serious and soppy for Ben."

"What?"

"Oh, you know how it would have gone." Mrs. Gardner warmed to her topic. "Elaine would have invited him in and then would have proceeded to talk the entire visit of pestilence and famine. She would have offered him some cake and when he took a slice, she'd say, 'Eat it all up. There are starving children on the other side of the world to whom such a cake would be a feast.' Once she had instilled guilt firmly into her visitor, she would begin to get teary-eyed and talk of all the orphans in the world. By the time the poor man left, he would believe that nothing in the world is good and that no man is to be trusted."

"Utter nonsense. Every word of it!" Mrs. Frank snorted. "Elaine is a sensible girl with a sensitive heart."

"I guess I won't dispute that point."

"What is that supposed to mean?"

"Ladies!" Mrs. Baumgartner suddenly began to laugh. "Ladies, calm down! I believe I have found the problem." This arrested the others' attention immediately. "I have been sitting here thinking while you two have been gabbing, and I have come to realize that the three girls we have tried on Ben are really nothing like the girl we want for him."

The other two considered this. "I believe you are right, Anita," Mrs. Frank finally said.

"I wonder why on earth we did such a thing," Mrs. Gardner pondered.

"I know." Mrs. Baumgartner looked mischievously at her two friends. "Each one of us wanted Ben in the family, so we took a relative and tried to make it work."

The other two stared at her, and then all three began to laugh. "You know, you are absolutely right!" Mrs. Gardner said when she had found her breath. "I wasn't really thinking of Ben, I was thinking of how wonderful it would be to have him for a nephew!"

"We've been so selfish!" Mrs. Frank agreed. "Anita, for once you are entirely correct."

Good-natured Mrs. Baumgartner took this as a huge compliment and beamed. Peace settled upon the room, and for a while, the only sound was the pattering of the rain and the clicking of knitting needles.

Eventually Mrs. Gardner broke the silence with a question. "Well, what are we to do about it?"

"I say we give the whole thing up."

"Oh, but Emma, we can't!" Mrs. Gardner exclaimed. "Not when we have invested so much in it already."

"That is true," Mrs. Baumgartner agreed. "We have come awfully far to go back now."

Mrs. Frank snorted. "We haven't made any progress, so quitting will do us no harm, and besides, Ben must be suspicious by this time. He is probably suspecting that a fourth girl will be thrown at him and will be on his guard."

"That is true," Mrs. Baumgartner relented. "Poor boy, he must feel as if he is being hounded."

Mrs. Gardner dismissed all these comments and continued to knit furiously. "We have to press forward. This is for his own good, after all."

"Well, it may not really matter in a little while." Mrs. Baumgartner sighed, her statement giving the other two pause.

"What do you mean by that, Anita? Do you know something we don't?"

"Oh no, nothing really. I shouldn't even mention it."

The other two dropped their knitting, leaned forward, and dug in. "You absolutely must. Come on now, what is it?" Mrs. Gardner was not someone you said no to, so Mrs. Baumgartner complied with another sigh.

"It's just that while Ben was giving Natalie the tour of his store the other day, I ran across something . . . suspicious. I had to make myself scarce, so I ducked into a back room, only it wasn't a back room, it was Ben's house, and—"

"Wait a moment, just wait a moment." Mrs. Frank raised a hand for silence, paused, and then said in a level tone, "You *broke and entered*, Anita? Really? You broke and entered Ben's home?"

While Mrs. Frank sat agog with horror, Mrs. Gardner was eyeing her demure friend with a new level of appreciation.

"Well, I didn't know it was his home!" Mrs. Baumgartner looked wildly between her two friends. "Honestly, I thought it was the bathroom—and who doesn't keep the door to his home locked, for goodness' sake?"

"Please tell me that you instantly left as soon as you realized your mistake." This came from Mrs. Frank. Mrs. Gardner was still silently marveling at the deviousness of her friend.

"I mean, yes, I did leave . . . eventually."

"Oh, dear Lord."

"I was just so embarrassed that I didn't want anyone to see me leave. I figured I'd wait until I heard Ben and Natalie leave the first floor and then I'd duck back out."

"I don't even know you anymore, Anita Baumgartner. Am I the only sane person in this room?" Mrs. Frank was holding her head as if in physical pain.

"So in the meantime, I just sort of sat in his living room. I mean, his recliner was right there. I wasn't going to go snooping or anything. I'm not that horrible, after all!"

Mrs. Gardner was smiling from ear to ear, leaning forward in intense pleasure, living vicariously through her friend. "Go on, go on. What did you see? What did you find?"

"I was just sitting there, as still as possible. I wasn't going to touch anything. I was barely even looking around, I promise."

"Yes, Anita, because you not moving a muscle completely compensates for *breaking and entering* Ben's home."

"Anyway . . ." Mrs. Baumgartner was flushed and her hands were fluttering by her face. "Like I said, I was just sitting there, waiting the appropriate amount of time before leaving, when I just saw on the side table a bunch of brochures and newspapers with items circled."

"Isn't breaking and entering a felony? Does knowing about this after the fact constitute being an accessory to the crime? Oh, dear God, forgive me!"

"So I sort of just leaned over and looked at what he'd circled. I didn't touch anything; I just looked."

Mrs. Gardner was blocking out Mrs. Frank's moans, single-minded in her focus. "Was it help wanted ads?"

"No, it was real estate agencies! The brochures, too, were all for real estate agencies."

Mrs. Gardner sat back in disappointment. "He's probably just looking to move to his own place. Does he need the space for the store, perhaps? I wonder why he's moving."

"Oh, I don't know. Maybe because people are *breaking and entering* into his current home," Mrs. Frank snapped.

"That's just it though. They were all agencies that specialized in commercial real estate."

"How closely were you looking at these papers, Anita?"

"Commercial as in *buying* a piece of business property?" Mrs. Gardner's brows furrowed.

"But think about it: why would Ben be buying another piece of commercial property? Isn't it more likely that he's selling a piece of commercial property?" Mrs. Baumgartner's eyes were pleading. "Oh, I don't know. I'm probably reading too much into this. I shouldn't have mentioned anything. I'm sorry, this is ridiculous and completely irrelevant to our earlier discussion."

"Completely irrelevant? How could you think that this is completely irrelevant?" The light had come on and the alarm set off in Mrs. Gardner's head. "Oh my goodness! Ben is selling Palermo's!"

"What?" This piece of information finally cut through Mrs. Frank's disgust and paranoia. "But he can't sell it! Louie built that place up himself. It's an institution in this town. He can't just sell it."

"That's what I thought." Mrs. Baumgartner's face exhibited relief as her friends confirmed her suspicions. "There can be no other plausible explanation. He must be selling the place."

"I wish you had brought this up earlier, Anita." Mrs. Gardner was standing at this point, her knitting scattered on the floor as she began to pace and gnaw her lower lip. "This changes everything. Everything!"

"I don't exactly follow . . ."

"We can't exactly set him up if he isn't *here*, now can we? Without Palermo's, there's nothing to keep him in New Holden. We'll lose our beloved bookshop and Ben all in one blow! This absolutely cannot happen."

"But what better way to keep him in New Holden than to find him a wife?" Mrs. Baumgartner timidly suggested.

Mrs. Gardner dismissed this statement with the wave of a hand. "I'm not suggesting that we drop the endeavor, simply that we shift focus. Let's ensure that Ben doesn't sell Palermo's and then we can find him a wife."

The room grew solemnly silent as the three women considered this strategy. Mrs. Frank finally broke the air of contemplation. "Yes, I do think this is the wisest move. The question, then, is how? How are we to ensure he doesn't sell?"

When the stakes were high, Mrs. Gardner's mind worked at top speed. "He must be planning on showing the store to a real estate agent, who, I believe, will help list the property. What if we make sure that no agent will want to come near the place? What if Palermo's is falling apart and . . . and even *haunted*?"

"Haunted?"

"Yes, haven't you seen that ghost busting show, or whatever it's called? Old buildings are always supposed to be haunted, right? I know it sounds crazy and maybe even wrong, but what choice do we have?"

Silence descended once more. The ladies knew they were treading on shaky ground. But in their state of desperation, no plan was too dark or too devious when it came to preserving something they loved. All dissent evaporated at the prospect of losing Ben.

**The girl and the boy lose track of time until their chatter is abruptly interrupted by a voice.** *The voice is faint, almost like a memory rather than something real, but still it is enough to make the girl and the boy sit as still as they can and listen. Have the Story People heard them? Have they been found out? What will happen to them now?*

*The girl is young enough to still believe in being snatched away by imagined creatures, and even though the boy is old enough to know better, he is still young enough to forget this fact.*

*The voice comes again. A searching voice. A frightened voice.*

*"Rosie!"*

# CHAPTER TEN

## HE RECOGNIZED HER AS BEAUTIFUL

Rosemary tucked her feet between two couch cushions and opened her laptop. Her toes, as usual, were freezing, even though it was the dead of summer, but she was too lazy at the moment to get up and find a pair of socks. Oma was sleeping in her recliner, her slippered feet propped up, an afghan half-on, half-off, the television flickering in the background. Rosemary reached for her mug of tea on the side table and methodically dunked her tea bag as she stared at the colorful spinning ball on her screen, waiting for her email to refresh. It was a comforting gesture, this soft dunking, and the anticipated warmth of the tea was enough to make her momentarily forget that her feet were cold.

Only a week remained of her visit with Oma. The sadness of the thought was overshadowed by a sharp sense of relief. She would finally be free of Ben. Seeing him march right up to another woman with a bouquet of beautiful flowers had surprisingly not hurt. Instead, she'd felt numb. This numbness had spread to outright anger as she'd opened the front door later that evening to find what appeared to be the same bouquet on her doorstep. There had been a heated discussion about that bouquet.

"Perhaps he intended to give you the flowers all along," Oma had advocated.

"I really don't think so." Rosemary had held the flowers out from her as far as possible as if they reeked of betrayal. "You should have seen it, Oma. He was very obviously giving the flowers to the other woman. There's no doubt. He saw me watching him too, and I'm sure he could see I was upset. What I don't understand is why give me the same bouquet? Is he trying to make some sort of weird point? Did he take them away from that poor woman to give to me? I just don't understand."

"Then ask him," Oma persisted as Rosemary dumped the flowers in the trash.

But Rosemary would do no such thing. It was becoming increasingly obvious to her that Ben had simply been leading her on. Was he handsome and interesting and alluring? Yes, but also not worth her time and definitely not worth the emotional turmoil. She'd miss Oma, but leaving New Holden meant no more awkward encounters with Ben, no more confusing signals, no more semi-flirtations. It had been flattering, yes, to be noticed, to feel attractive to someone, but how could she trust him if he was also simultaneously throwing himself at every other woman in town? Even going so far as to give women the same bouquet—or perhaps regifting the bouquet. It was all a confusing mess. Oma might think she knew Ben through reputation, but just because Louie had been a nice guy didn't make his nephew one too. And sure, it spoke well that Ben had taken over his uncle's store, but then again, maybe he was just opportunistic. It was upsetting, too, that he'd seemed to be such a genuine Christian guy. His actions just weren't meshing with what she'd expect from a man of faith.

Rosemary had never had much luck with guys, so why should this one be any different? In college, one of her guy friends had told her she was intimidating. Apparently he had several friends who would have asked her out ages ago but were too afraid to ask. Rosemary had never quite understood how this was her fault. Still, just because dates were not forthcoming, that didn't mean they wouldn't have been welcome. It hurt that no one had really sought after her or liked her enough to make an effort and take a risk. People typically described her as focused and driven, which helped when it came to her studies and her final project but perhaps not so much outside of class. Her driven personality and focus probably derived from having to be self-sufficient for most of her childhood. With parents too absorbed in managing their failing marriage and surviving their divorce to parent her, she'd learned that the best way to help them was simply by taking care of herself. She could be one less thing they had to worry about. Head down, eyes forward, don't rock the boat. When her father had finally left and it was just Rosemary and her mother, she'd felt like she'd failed them somehow. Would they have been happy if they hadn't had her? Was her father upset with her and that's why he'd left? All these questions had flooded her mind as a young girl, but she'd been afraid to ask them, so she returned to what she knew: head down, eyes forward, don't rock the boat.

Perhaps openness was something she needed to work on. Still, rather than alter her personality just to score dates in college, Rosemary preferred to find someone who would see her for who she was and love her because of and in spite of it. Which is why Ben's attention had felt so nice. Pretty much the only quality time they'd had was during the discount day, and his enthusiasm had felt genuine then. But you never could tell with some people. Oma's analogy about books from the other day extended only so far. At some point you had to put a bad book down and pick up something else.

With a start, Rosemary realized that she'd been violently dunking her tea bag for much longer than the recommended brew time. A sip told her that yes, the tea had turned bitter and the water was now tepid at best. The reality of her cold feet now hit her full force. She balanced the laptop on the armrest and shuffled down the hallway to root through a dresser drawer. Coming back moments later, sporting a pair of bright orange fluffy socks, she heard the ding of incoming email. Eagerly she snuggled back on the couch and began sorting through her inbox to see if there was anything she needed to respond to.

There was a message from the publishing company reminding her of the upcoming deadline for her illustrations. She dashed off a reply, affirming the deadline, and then turned her attention to a message from Liam Johnson. In just a few weeks, she, Liam, and a couple of other friends were headed to an SCBWI conference. The Society of Children's Book Writers and Illustrators Midwest Regional Conference was in Chicago this year, and she couldn't wait. The four had been friends since their undergraduate years and had kept in contact even after going in different directions after graduation—some, like Rosemary, for graduate school, others for jobs. This trip would be a great reunion. Rosemary scanned the email from Liam, sensing that this would be an exuberant message, dripping with details of their forthcoming itinerary. Sure enough, the message started out with a loud "What's up, Clooney?!" Clooney, Liam's nickname for her, was something to do with Rosemary Clooney, although Rosemary looked absolutely nothing like the classic American singer and actress. She couldn't even carry a tune. Rosemary grinned and shook her head, rolling her eyes though no one was there to see them roll. Liam was full of plans, attaching the conference schedule with his preferred sessions highlighted. He'd also included links to Navy Pier, Giordano's stuffed deep-dish pizza, and the Willis Tower Skydeck. For all of his loud and carefree manner, Liam was a planner, and Rosemary had been happy to leave this trip in his capable hands.

Rosemary leaned back and breathed a prayer of thanks for good friends and highly anticipated trips. One of her professors had introduced her to SCBWI and she'd continued her dues upon graduation, making it to a national convention just last year. This regional convention with a few close friends promised to be a welcome distraction from the pointless Ben drama. It was also a pleasant pit stop before confronting the uncomfortable fact that she still had no solid future plans. Staying with Oma for a month had given her purpose, and she'd enjoyed working on the curriculum illustrations, but that job was now coming to a close along with her stay at Oma's, and she wasn't exactly looking forward to the time when she'd pull back into her mother's driveway and confront, once again, the big "What now?" question. This conference would give her a productive focus. Rosemary dashed off an enthusiastic reply, pausing to wonder why Liam hadn't copied the others in his initial message. She forwarded it to Clare and Becca and included the line, "Look what Liam just sent! Say goodbye to a relaxing weekend!" Rosemary closed her laptop, shifted it onto the couch, and adjusted the blanket around Oma, bending to kiss her cheek and breathe in her musky perfume, missing her already.

Professor Jenson peered through the thick venetian blinds and out onto his front porch. The summer heat had taken a toll on his potted begonias flanking the front entryway. He dropped the blinds and opened his front door tentatively, casting a wary eye next door. Professor Jenson strategically timed his trips outdoors so as to avoid his neighbor, Mrs. Matilda Gardner. The woman was relentless with her cheerfulness and intrusive personal questions. Professor Jenson had one goal in life: to be left alone.

He preferred to engage people on his own terms and was tirelessly impatient with those who had no respect for personal boundaries and instead planted themselves in other people's business, invited or not. Live and let live—a tired saying, but true nonetheless.

Having assured himself that Mrs. Gardner was nowhere to be seen, Professor Jenson snatched up his watering can and made his way to the kitchen to fill it at the sink. He knew his aversion to his next-door neighbor was mutual. Mrs. Gardner insisted on prying into his life every chance she got, but he could tell she thought him ridiculous. Professor Jenson wasn't really a professor—had never, in fact, led any sort of classroom and, indeed, found the mere thought of forming and molding young minds to be alarming and futile. However, he'd earned the Professor nickname thanks to his chosen course of study, a nickname he didn't mind except when Mrs. Gardner uttered it. It wasn't quite an endearing term when she said it.

Professor Jenson emerged onto the front porch and had just begun watering when a loud "Yooo-hooo!" resounded from his side yard. Dropping the watering can, Professor Jenson let out a yelp and clung to the doorjamb for support. Mrs. Gardner was walking across his yard, waving a gardening trowel in one hand as if her loud cattle call hadn't been enough to draw attention.

"Good heavens! Where on earth did you come from? Do you just lie in wait for me to come outside?"

"Don't be ridiculous," Mrs. Gardner snipped. "I'm hardly skulking about in the side yard staking out your front door." She wiped at her sweaty forehead with a thick forearm, leaving a streak of dirt behind. Professor Jenson smiled in mischievous delight at the sight. "Can't a neighbor say hello to another neighbor without being hideously accused?"

"You just surprised me." Professor Jenson watched as she ascended his front steps. Her oblong shape never failed to remind him of a *Coprinus comatus*. Today she sported a fuzzy sequined blouse, which intensified the image. It wasn't an altogether unpleasant comparison.

"I was just in the middle of mulching my hosta bed when I heard your front door open and it reminded me that I've been meaning to come over here and ask you something."

*Oh, good grief.* Her chatter was already beginning to make his head hurt. Professor Jenson placed one hand on the porch rail and extended the other to the fallen watering can, already beginning the process of tuning his neighbor out. He'd long practiced the introvert's art of well-placed nods and affirmative grunts. It was much simpler than conversing. "Uh-huh."

"I was just wondering if you still have that cousin. Well, not if you still *have* him. Sorry, that came out wrong. I'm not asking whether he's deceased." Here she paused and inserted a nervous laugh and then abruptly stopped and clutched at her floppy sun hat. "He's not, is he? Dead, I mean?"

Professor Jenson sighed. "I have many cousins, Matilda. Many cousins. I assume you have a particular one in mind?"

"Donald, I think? The one in real estate?"

"Arnold."

"Yes, yes, Arnold. Alive and doing well, I hope?"

"Yes, he's still with us."

"Oh good, good, that's very good. And still in real estate?"

"Yes, though he should be retiring soon."

"I see, I see. So he's still practicing, then? Now, I mean? Currently?"

"Matilda, why the sudden interest in Arnold? You do know that he's married with five grandchildren, right?"

Mrs. Gardner blushed a deep red and quickly averted her eyes as if too embarrassed to look him in the face. "Oh goodness, no! I'm not looking for a romantic connection. What an idea!"

Professor Jenson grunted and turned to his begonias. *Dratted plants.* He should have left them to wither in agony.

"Anyway, I really was just wondering if you still had a cousin in the real estate business."

"Uh-huh." Most of the water had spilled when he'd dropped the can, but there was still enough to give the plants a sufficient soaking. There was a strained silence, during which he finished with the watering, wiped his hands on his pant legs, and turned to go back inside. Only then did he realize that Mrs. Gardner was still standing on his porch, her stout figure swaying slightly as if she were a plant in a strong breeze. Professor Jenson groaned. "Was that all you wanted, Matilda? To confirm the existence of cousin Arnold?"

"I . . . um . . . I was just wondering if you perhaps could give me his phone number?"

"You looking to sell or buy a piece of property?" Professor Jenson felt a spark of interest and instantly chastised himself. *Live and let live.*

"Well, not exactly. I'm just curious about any potential clients of his."

"Clients?" Professor Jenson shook his head. No business of his. "I probably have an extra business card of his lying around somewhere." He turned to enter his home. The sooner he gave her what she wanted, the sooner she'd be on her way. Never mind why on earth she wanted it. He headed for the hall table where he kept the phone book and other odds and ends.

"Thank you for checking."

Her voice was right by his side. Professor Jenson jumped for a second time and clutched at the table for support. He turned in horror. She was in his house. In his peaceful, quiet, usually Matilda-free house. "Go wait outside!"

"Don't be ridiculous." Mrs. Gardner slapped his arm playfully.

Professor Jenson turned and fumbled with the drawer, shuffling the contents frantically. Where on earth was the card? Home was the ultimate sanctuary. Outside, one was fair game. But inside, well, inside was safety—until now. "I can't find it," he mumbled, racking his brain for where else it could be. Finally, a happy thought came to him. "It's funny you should ask for it, though, because I recently gave his number to Ben Palermo. You might try asking him. I can't find it anywhere. Ben can help you." He said this while ushering her to the door. Thank God he could pass the buck this time. It was always a happy surprise when one was able to legitimately foist one's problems onto someone else.

"Ben?" Mrs. Gardner dug in her heels and gripped his arm with surprising ferocity. "You gave his number to Ben?"

"Yes, go find Ben and—" Professor Jenson's words were cut short by a soulful sob, and he watched in shock as Mrs. Gardner flung herself onto a nearby hall bench.

"Oh oh oh! It's true! In my heart of hearts, I'd been hoping that Anita had simply imagined this whole horrible thing, but it's *true*!" Mrs. Gardner's floppy sun hat had been dislodged by her graceless descent onto the bench and was now dangling unhappily around her neck by its chin strap. She was still clutching the gardening trowel, and the swipe of dirt across her face, so amusing earlier, now looked like a pathetic spectator to the unfolding emotional breakdown.

Professor Jenson was completely at a loss. What did one *do* for a woman who was hyperventilating in one's front hallway?

"And now we'll lose not only Ben but also everything Louie worked so hard to build. They'll probably tear down the building and put in a McDonald's. Oh, I can't stand it!"

She was weeping—actually weeping—in his front

hallway. For all his brusqueness, Professor Jenson couldn't stand seeing anyone cry. He placed an uncertain hand on her shoulder. He'd seen people do this sort of thing before in order to extend comfort to a grieving person. Somehow it was deemed reassuring to have someone's hand on one's shoulder. Perhaps he should do something with it rather than just have it lie there like an inanimate object. Professor Jenson commenced patting her shoulder. Did she look any less hysterical? He wasn't sure. Matilda Gardner always looked a bit hysterical.

"Oh, thank you." Mrs. Gardner placed a plump hand over his own and squeezed. Professor Jenson froze. Now what? Hesitantly he sat down next to her on the bench, his hand still clutched in her own and resting on her trembling shoulder. Her hand was soft with a thin layer of calluses at the base of her fingers and fingertips, most likely from gardening and endless hand wringing. Her grip was desperate, like she needed to draw strength from his presence. Professor Jenson grunted and shifted, casually dislodging his hand and letting it trail back to his lap. There was an uncomfortable warmth spreading through his chest—not exactly pleasant—almost like a minor heart attack. It made him uneasy to be physically affected by the sniffling woman at his side.

"You must think I'm crazy." Mrs. Gardner let out a shaky laugh.

"Oh no, no." *Yes, yes*, Professor Jenson thought as he shook his head.

"I owe you an explanation."

"No. Not necessary." Professor Jenson finally thought of something to do and reached into his pocket for a handkerchief. Maybe he could encourage her to calm down enough to leave.

"Oh, thank you." Mrs. Gardner snatched at the proffered handkerchief with both hands and brought it to her face with a sigh. "You see, Anita Baumgartner suggested to Emma Frank and me that Ben might be thinking of selling Palermo's Books."

This got Professor Jenson's attention. "Selling Palermo's? That place has been a part of our community for a long time. Why would he do such a thing?"

"Exactly!" Mrs. Gardner's eyes widened and she motioned with both hands to Professor Jenson as if showcasing him as a case in point. "I half disbelieved Anita and thought I'd do some investigating before we take any preventive steps." She paused in her explanation to give him a sideways glare. "Although how this is news to you, I have no idea. Didn't you wonder why he'd want Arnold's number? Why would you keep that to yourself?"

"Well, I . . . I don't ask nosy questions," Professor Jenson blustered. "None of my business what people do or do not intend to do."

Mrs. Gardner sighed. "Yes, but you didn't even *wonder*?" At Professor Jenson's crusty stare, she rolled her eyes and continued. "Oh well, the important thing now is that I know. I am aware, and so I can take action."

Now Professor Jenson really began to feel uneasy. How did this happen? How did he end up sitting side by side with Matilda Gardner in his own front hallway in witness to one of her confounded schemes? "I don't know about this, Matilda. This sounds like interfering to me. It's not your place or anyone else's place to butt into someone's business."

Mrs. Gardner whipped around and grabbed at his hand again, causing him to jerk back and blush. Why the sudden fascination with his hand? He wished he'd never placed it on her shoulder. Apparently now his hand was hers to do with as she wished. "Stop and think, Mark."

His first name. He couldn't remember her ever calling him by his first name. He sat up and obediently listened.

"Stop and imagine for a moment that Ben sells the bookstore to some greedy developer. That's a historic building right in downtown. It's part of the heart of this community. Imagine having no more bookstore, no place to buy your . . . *fungi* books. Imagine, instead, some retail store or fast food chain. Imagine greasy cheeseburgers. Imagine gaudy storefronts. Imagine, Mark!"

Professor Jenson was imagining. Mrs. Gardner had finally struck a chord. The only thing he loved as much as fungi was books on fungi, and if the beloved local bookstore closed, then he might be forced to go to the dreaded Internet. He shivered. "Surely the building is protected. It's not as if they can go about knocking down historic old buildings."

"Oh, who knows how these things work?" Mrs. Gardner's eyes were wide as she slowly shook her head. Her voice was infused with mystery as if discussing cosmic concerns rather than the finer points of commercial real estate. "At the worst, they tear down the building to make way for some impersonal store. At the best, the building stays and is repurposed as a . . . a . . . *yoga* studio, or one of those Web cafés or whatever they're called. You know, the places where people go to look at who knows what on that Internet. Neither option is appealing."

"Perhaps Ben will change his mind?" Professor Jenson threw out feebly.

"Do you really want to take that chance?" Mrs. Gardner spoke the words slowly, her hands still clasping his with steadily increasing pressure, her eyes latching on to him, challenging him. "I know you love that bookstore. Perhaps even more than I do. Isn't that where your Thursday night Bible study is held? What will happen to your men's group should the bookstore fold?"

"I suppose Pastor Andrews would just move it to the church," Professor Jenson conjectured, his face fallen, tone dejected.

"But it wouldn't be the same, now would it?" Mrs. Gardner persisted. "If there was even the slightest chance that you could do something, *anything*, to keep Ben and Palermo's here, tell me you wouldn't do it."

"Well, when you put it that way . . ."

"I know I can be a busybody. I know I can butt in uninvited and unwanted." Mrs. Gardner had released his hand to dab at her eyes. Professor Jenson took advantage of this release by stuffing both his hands in his pockets, safe and out of reach. "But it's only because I care so much." Her tone had shifted. A level of artifice had dropped, and for the first time Professor Jenson sensed that Matilda Gardner was trying to be vulnerable. He had no idea how to handle this new development. "And this," Mrs. Gardner continued, "this is different. This is for the well-being of our community." At this point she rose from the bench just as gracelessly as she'd fallen onto it, stumbling a bit and throwing out an arm for balance. "Some things are too precious, too valuable to leave alone. Some things are worth butting in for."

Professor Jenson stared at her in amazement. She was making sense, and it frightened him. Before he quite knew what he was doing, he was wobbling to his feet and opening his big mouth. "Tell me what I can do."

Mrs. Gardner smiled up at him. Her sequined top caught the sunbeams streaming through his front window and blinked the light into his face. He squinted beneath the brilliance of the light and her smile. For the first time he recognized her as beautiful.

**The boy looks at the girl and realizes with surprise that he will miss her.** *It has been nice to share his secret place with someone else.*

"I have to go," the girl says. She looks sad and maybe a little relieved.

"Will you be back?" the boy asks.

"Yes, but maybe not for a while."

"Well, when you do come back, you can come here, to the Room. I'll leave you a message to find."

The girl's eyes grow wide and she gives a little jump of excitement. "A message, yes! And then I can leave you a message back!"

The boy smiles. It's nice to have someone be excited about his Room, to understand how special it is, to join him in seeing its possibilities.

They will leave messages, and in this way, the Story People will continue—a secret they share and keep alive.

# Chapter Eleven

## DID HE LIKE THE IDEA
## OF STAYING ANY BETTER?

Ben sat on the first-floor stairs and watched the last of the light stream through the front windows and spill across the weathered wooden floorboards. This time of day was always beautiful, but especially when observed from this vantage point—quietly and in the presence of thousands of books. Ben's chest ached at what he'd just done. He looked at the business card in his hand, finally shoving it back into his pocket. He'd finally broken down and called Arnold Jenson, the first step in a very long, confusing, and emotionally draining process. Arnold walked him through what to expect and gave him a list of all the information he'd need to gather. Because of the historical nature of the property, Arnold had recommended that they have the property appraised before listing it. Ben looked at the pad of paper next to him on the step. It was filled with his chicken scratch handwriting. He'd circled and starred the most important pieces of information, the biggest one being August 30, the date by which he needed to get all his records together and prepare for the appraisal. He looked up from the paper to the store. He felt like he'd been tasked with grooming a child for sale, the sense of betrayal ran that deeply.

Ben looked at the curved front desk, which sectioned off an entire corner of the first floor. This was where he had the most memories of his uncle, in that corner amid all his important-looking papers and receipts, swiveling backward and forward in his cracked and dirty office chair, calling out to customers, leaning against the counter, inviting a very happy little nephew to come join him behind the counter, making him feel like a king. Ben would play for hours behind the front desk, realizing now that he must have been somewhat of a nuisance, always underfoot, but his uncle had never let on. Instead, he let his only nephew dip into the candy jar he left on the counter and play with the cash register. It was Ben's chief delight to press the button that released the cash drawer, reveling in the soft click and then the whoosh and loud ding followed by a thump as the drawer leaped obediently outward and then caught itself. Then there was the pleasure of shoving it back in and starting over: click, whoosh, ding, thump.

His uncle had a deep-throated chuckle, exactly as one would expect from a big man with a big mustache and a big smile. Everything about his uncle matched. As a boy, Ben imagined that his uncle was the smartest man in the world. Ben had been too young to realize that there were more books in the store than any one person could read in a lifetime, but in his mind, his uncle had read them all and therefore he must know everything there was to know. His uncle added to this perception by quoting books endlessly to him, gifting him with books over the years that he'd handpicked for Ben, grooming his nephew to be a dedicated reader just like he was. Uncle Louie always had a dog-eared paperback splayed on the front desk, waiting for a pair of big hands with thick fingers to pick it up again. He had a funny way with reading. Certain books were tied to certain places. Instead of taking a book from place to place until he finished it, Uncle Louie would simply pick up whatever book was nearest and continue reading. The front desk, the living room recliner, the kitchen table, the nightstand—they all housed books that stayed there, waiting for him to enter the room and pick them up. He read books like he ate, a bite at a time, just whenever he felt peckish and whatever was at hand.

When Ben lost his parents, he also lost his uncle. It was as simple as that. Uncle Louie had come to the funeral, had brought Ben a book, had held him and cried deeply into Ben's hair, and then he was gone. Ben was fourteen and living with his maternal grandmother. Trips to New Holden stopped as Ben entered high school. But the gifts of books continued faithfully; every birthday and Christmas, the books came with a Palermo's Books bookmark on the inside. And Ben read them, faithfully, and missed his uncle and missed his parents and tried to keep looking forward to keep from looking back.

He'd considered a trip back in college, but somehow it'd never happened. There were tests to study for, friends to make, and soon enough his grandmother's funeral to plan. In graduate school, he was busier than ever, and then the demands of his friend's start-up were all consuming for a while. Ben thought back on those years with regret, not fully understanding why he'd stayed away. It was a pattern in Ben's life—this habit of pushing himself forward. It was easier to cope with loss, he supposed, if you didn't focus too much on what exactly had been lost. Because when you lose someone, you don't just lose that person. You lose all the possibilities that came with that person. Better to focus on the possible, on the next step, than to dwell on the vastness of what had been lost. But living in New Holden had taught him that it was hard to keep looking forward because he was literally living in the past. Everywhere he looked there were reminders, and it was both sweet and bitter. During trips here with his parents, they'd camp out in Louie's home, the three of them in the living room, his dad on the couch and him and his mother on an air mattress on the floor. And now it was Ben's living room, and he found himself each evening sitting in his new recliner and stubbornly looking past the spot on the floor where they used to put the air mattress. Ben didn't know how to move forward while stuck in the past. He loved the bookstore and he couldn't bear the bookstore; he needed it and didn't want to need it all at the same time. Best to continue on this new course, he thought, to finally move forward by letting Palermo's go. His year stint, turned to three, needed to come to a close, but at least no one could say of him that he hadn't tried.

Ben rose from his hunched position on the stairs and headed toward the back. He'd avoided reminiscing all throughout high school and college, but now it was seemingly all he did. Rosemary and all the confusing feelings she'd elicited had felt like a refreshing giant leap forward. For the first time he'd captured that sense of looking to the next thing. But that had all come crashing down on her grandmother's front porch. He understood that she must be incredibly frustrated with him right now. She'd caught him in numerous confusing situations. But still, to pointedly refuse to answer the door just seemed petty and childish. In essence, she was refusing to hear him out, refusing to consider that perhaps her impressions weren't gospel truth. And what had she made of those flowers on her doormat? Ben had yet to hear a word from her and was regretting leaving the bouquet—was regretting a lot of things. Ben realized he was clenching his jaw again. He'd relived that front porch experience over and over: the humiliation he'd felt when he'd heard the voices inside, the sting of knowing he was being actively ignored. Maybe he'd misjudged her. Maybe Rosemary was too self-assured for her own good, too confident in her own opinions. If so, that spoke of a closed-mindedness that he wanted nothing to do with.

Entering the living room, he shut the door behind him and locked it. He'd developed a bad habit of leaving the connecting door unlocked, so he'd been trying to be better about consistently locking up, especially at night. It was just that leaving it unlocked made popping back and forth between home and store that much easier. JC trotted over to greet him, and Ben picked him up and tucked him under an arm. "Hey, buddy. Let's get some grub." As Ben filled the dog's bowl and began dinner preparations, he tried to quiet and redirect his mind away from anger, away from sadness. As he so often did in the privacy of his own home, Ben prayed out loud. It helped fill the silence and helped him focus on God as a friend, as someone close by. "Lord, I really need wisdom right now. I don't know what I'm supposed to do here. Some days it just hurts too much to be here. Should I keep living here or move forward with something else?" He paused. JC's loud crunching filled the kitchen, and the living room clock could be heard ticking away. Ben finished making dinner: French toast and sausages. Thank goodness for breakfast food.

As Ben scrounged around for the maple syrup, he couldn't seem to shake the unease. He didn't like being mad at Rosemary. Seeing her with her grandmother reminded him of his own grandma, now passed. He should have appreciated her more for taking him in and caring for him during a formative time in his life. He should have comforted her in her grief at losing her daughter. He should have cared for her the way Rosemary so obviously cared for her grandmother.

Ben wanted to see Rosemary again but didn't know what to say anymore. He didn't know what was going on in her head and so he couldn't figure out how to approach her, what to do or say, especially now that she so clearly had resorted to the silent treatment. Ben located the syrup and poured a large amount over the French toast, causing the pats of butter to swim appealingly. He sat down at the small table and patted his lap for JC to join him. The small dog circled quietly in Ben's lap in preparation for lying down. Once settled, he let out a half squeal, half yawn as Ben bowed his head over the food and gave thanks before digging in.

Looming over the tension with Rosemary was the anxiety over selling Palermo's. August 30. He wasn't looking forward to someone appraising Palermo's, poking around and talking about assets and liabilities, looking at this beloved place and seeing only cents and dollars. No, he didn't like that at all.

The question was, did he like the idea of staying any better?

**The girl misses the boy and she misses the Room.** She tells herself not to worry, that the next time she visits, there will be a message waiting for her. The thought of this message makes her happy every time she's tempted to feel sad. She thinks of the boy and the Room and the message often, and she wonders if maybe she imagined it all. So it is with both hope and doubt that she goes in search of the Room the next summer.

The girl learns that it is much harder to find a mysterious place when one is actually looking for it. Much easier to simply stumble across it. The girl knows it is on the third floor. She is looking for a door behind a door. There is only one door on the third floor, and she opens it slowly. There is no guiding light this time, just a small, dark closet with a bare bulb sticking in the ceiling. She finds the light switch, and the bulb winks to life. The girl feels silly creeping about in the closet, but she has to know, she has to see if it is still there. So she places both hands against the back wall and runs them back and forth until she finds a crack, and then she pushes. Nothing happens, so she pushes again, harder this time. Something happens. The crack widens, the door opens, and she is staring down a narrow hallway.

The girl's heart is in her throat. She half expects to see a flashlight ahead, a curly head beneath a blanket, a goofy smile. But no, as she enters the Room once more, there is no boy to greet her. The light from the closet snakes in and illuminates all but the corners of the small Room, and by its light she sees the chair and on the chair a piece of paper, folded carefully—waiting.

# Chapter Twelve

## LIKE THE QUICK SMART
## AFTER RIPPING OFF A BANDAGE

Stephanie Berg welcomed her daughter home with a pan of brownies. "Honestly, you're worse than Oma!" Rosemary chided as she hugged her mom.

"Where do you think I get it from? How is your Oma?"

"Feisty as ever." Rosemary pinched off a corner of a brownie and popped it into her mouth.

"I know she appreciated your help. I'm going to head over there myself next month, check up on her. Do you need help unpacking?"

"No thanks, I'll be fine." Rosemary gave her mom a peck on the cheek before ducking back into the hallway and trekking back to the car for the last of her bags.

Her mom was a beautiful forty-two, her hair just beginning to show hints of silver, her laugh lines jumping out in welcome, her figure curved and youthful. She'd had Rosemary at just seventeen, marrying her father at nineteen. "We were two kids raising a kid," she often told her daughter, causing Rosemary to wonder if her arrival on the scene had artificially thrown her parents together, forcing two people who were not right for each other to simply end up with each other.

Rosemary had gradually pieced together the details of her parents' marriage as she matured. Her parents' young age coupled with her father's addictions and instability had made for a rocky start to their family. It wasn't until years later that Rosemary learned just how much her mother had shielded her from, the ugliness she made sure stayed behind closed doors. She'd been too busy parenting her husband to parent her daughter, something she continued to try to make up for, cramming years' worth of missed memories into carefully crafted family moments now that it was just the two of them, possibly trying to distract Rosemary from the fact that her father had left her behind without a backward glance. The overparenting was excessive at times, but it made Rosemary love her all the more. Her mother, she'd come to realize, was one of the strongest women she knew.

Rosemary scooped up the last of her bags and entered her childhood bedroom, tired from the drive to their cozy Indianapolis ranch home and dreading the task of unpacking only to have to pack again for the trip to Chicago. She couldn't waste any time though. Her friends were picking her up in just three days.

Rosemary dumped her purse on her bed and looked around the expansive room. She had the run of the finished basement, half of which had been converted to her bedroom while she was in high school. The obsessions of her younger self were apparent. Her sketches and artwork were tacked to the walls, their edges fluttering as she passed, her bags in tow. One wall was lined with bookcases, which held an assortment of tomes, double-stacked and often arranged horizontally so as to maximize space. Pictures from numerous youth mission trips hung in a collage over her bed, and several concert posters for Michael W. Smith hung on the opposite wall. But it was her rolltop desk that arrested her attention. Rosemary sank into the squeaky office chair and ran her hands over the grooved surface of the desk. She swiveled around and looked at the mess of suitcases and duffel bags she'd deposited at the bottom of the stairs. It had been hard to leave Oma, even though she was doing much better and would at least be able to move around without a walker and take care of herself. Rosemary had promised a return trip before Thanksgiving. She hoped that by then, time and space would have made things less awkward with Ben, so if they happened to cross paths again, she'd feel less like sprinting in the opposite direction. The problem remained that she never got the full reunion with the bookstore that she'd been craving. Unfortunately, she didn't see an easy way to get it now, not with Ben owning the store and her passion to avoid him.

Just as she was getting ready to pull herself out of her seat, her cell phone buzzed. Rosemary grabbed it and nestled it between her cheek and shoulder. "Hey, Clare, what's up?"

"I got the job!" Clare's bright voice filled Rosemary's ear.

"Congratulations! That's so awesome! I knew you would."

"Yeah, I start in two weeks, can you believe it?"

"I'm excited for you." Rosemary pulled herself to her feet, grabbed a bag, and dumped its contents out. Best way to unpack was to just dump everything out and then sort from there. "So now you'll be a big-shot copywriter, convince all us lowly consumers to buy a bunch of stuff we don't need, right?"

"Something like that," Clare chuckled.

Rosemary continued to dump out the contents of her suitcases as she listened to Clare talk about the particulars of the job. Pretty soon a massive pile of clothes, toiletries, food, and other odds and ends had formed in front of her bookcases. Rosemary sat cross-legged and began to sort.

"Hey, so how is your grandma?" Clare switched topics abruptly.

"Oh, she's doing fine."

"And your time there? Was it weird being there so long?"

Rosemary paused to consider her reply, her gaze drifting to the books in front of her. There were old, cloth-covered, and beautifully illustrated editions of *Anne of Green Gables*, *Little Women*, and *Black Beauty* that she'd gotten from Palermo's Books when she was a girl. "It wasn't really weird being there so long. It was just weird seeing all the places I used to visit as a kid." She ran her fingers along the spines in front of her. Oma had always given her suggestions for books to purchase but left the decision up to her. Whatever book Rosemary chose was the one they'd read together during her visit. As soon as Rosemary would step through the front door, Oma would squeeze her tight and say, "We need to go get us a book, pumpkin. Something without horses this time, okay?"

"I went to this beautiful old bookstore I used to visit all the time as a child."

"Ha, that's too perfect. I can totally see you in a bookstore, camping out, refusing to leave."

"Yeah, well, it was neat to see it, but there was this guy . . ."

"Oooh, a *guy*, please do tell."

Rosemary grinned and settled back against the bookcase. She loved talking like this with Clare. "Okay, so get this. There's this cute guy running the bookstore, and he acts like he's interested in me. He goes so far as to single me out. Just overall sending me *that* vibe. But then I realize he's kind of a small-town version of a ladies' man, nothing too dangerous, just some good old-fashioned catch-and-release going on."

"What in the world?"

"Yeah, he's got three different girls going at any one time, apparently." Rosemary relished Clare's squeal and dug into her story with enthusiasm, embellishing a little here and there. "The sad part is, he was so cute and I kind of liked him for a little while. He reminded me of . . ." Rosemary stopped short, choking on her next words. He reminded her of BJ.

"Of what? He reminded you of what?"

"Huh? Oh, nothing. It was just so weird walking into the bookstore again, like a time warp."

"Well, I guess even New Holden has its share of players."

Rosemary laughed, but her heart wasn't into it anymore. BJ—she wondered if she still had his letters. "Hey, I have a lot of unpacking and repacking to do."

"Yeah, for sure, I'll let you go. See you in a few days."

Rosemary ended the call and stared again at the Palermo's books on her shelves. Now that the thought of BJ had entered her mind, it wouldn't go away. It wasn't until she'd talked through the whole event with Clare that Rosemary realized why Ben had seemed so familiar. It had to be a weird coincidence. A dark-haired guy in her bookstore . . . no wonder she'd thought of BJ. Surely she still had the letters. Rosemary got to her feet and checked her closet, feeling around on the top shelves for anything that might be housing letters. She pulled a few boxes down, but they contained old sheet music and dried-up gel pens. She yanked open the larger bottom drawers of her desk but found only old stationery, a fountain pen set that had gone woefully unused, and a mountain of sketches. There was only one other storage area in the room—beneath the bed. Getting down on her hands and knees, Rosemary began dragging out all the contents from under the bed, not caring that instead of unpacking, she was, in fact, making her room even more unmanageably messy. An old shoe box looked promising, and as Rosemary lifted the lid, she smiled in relieved pleasure. There they were, bundled together with a hair band. Goodness, she hadn't looked at these things in years, though the memory of them never failed to fill her with a poignant longing. The letters were out of order, the first one she opened being one of the last ones she'd received. "Rosie, I wish I could see you again. The Story People have been chattering nonstop about you. I hear them at night, and they tell each other stories about us." Rosemary smiled and thumbed the page fondly. She reached for another. "Rosie, I almost got caught by Uncle Louie today."

Rosemary stopped and read the line again, her heart suddenly racing so hard it felt as if her veins were pulsing through her skin. "Uncle Louie," she read out loud. She'd just assumed that everyone called him Uncle Louie, like an affectionate nickname, but now she wondered. Her eyes jumped to the signature line: BJ, as in short for *Benjamin*?

"Oh my goodness!" Rosemary lurched to her feet and began pacing, waving the letter in front of her like a flag. "No, it can't be!" She made herself take deep, calming breaths. She picked up the shoe box and sat on her bed, her body trembling with adrenaline. She took the letters out and spread them on the bed one by one, placing them in the order received. Quickly she began reading the letters, looking for clues as to BJ's true identity. It had to be just a coincidence.

But it wasn't. The more she read, the more Rosemary picked up and pieced together. "Rosie, my uncle still doesn't know where I sneak off to in the afternoon." "Rosie, I was hoping this visit that I'd find you here again. My parents wonder why I'm so eager to visit my uncle all the time." "Rosie, it's hard to hear above my dad's snoring, but I think the Story People are whispering to each other tonight." The repeated references to *Uncle* Louie, the implications that BJ was sleeping in the same building and visiting with his parents, and then the fact that his name was BJ and possibly a nickname for Benjamin . . . Rosemary sat and stared at the letters before finally collecting them in her hands. She held them silently, letting the revelation sweep over her, and with the revelation, the attraction. She'd been holding on to it by a thread, dismissing and distrusting it, but in the light of this discovery, she was helpless to avoid it. Could Ben really be her BJ? She closed her eyes and tried to picture BJ as she'd last seen him. She'd been nine? He must have been thirteen. Curly black hair and goofy dimpled smile—how could she have missed it before?

With surprise, Rosemary realized she was crying. She caught the tip of her sleeve between thumb and fingers and swiped at her eyes. She hadn't thought of BJ in years and yet the tears reminded her of how pivotal he'd been in her young life: his letters a predictable bedrock, the shared secret a source of comfort and inspiration. When she couldn't show her art to her parents, she showed it to BJ. He'd been a safe place for her. It'd hurt when he'd gone silent, abruptly and with no explanation. She'd visited the Room for years after his abrupt silence, each time leaving a letter even though the last one was still there, each time letting herself feel a tug of hope until finally the pain of the silence had kept her away.

Rosemary realized now the tragic reason behind the silence and began crying even harder. He'd been there to help her through the deepest crisis of her childhood, but she hadn't been able to return the favor. He'd felt alone and she hadn't been able to tell him that he wasn't. She dug through the letters, searching for one in particular. "Rosie, I'm sorry to hear about your parents' divorce. Does it make you feel alone? You should never feel alone. I broke our agreement and spoke to the Story People. It seemed like they should know about this. They told me to tell you that they're here for you and that they've never known a girl who is as brave as you are."

Rosemary cried and cried, muffling the sound in her pillow to keep her mother from coming down and investigating. *Ben!* How she wished she had put two and two together when they'd met this summer, and how she regretted laughing about him only moments ago with Clare. How alone he must have been in the years following the last letter. Did he still remember? Had he kept her letters as she'd kept his? Was their Room still there, or had the Story People finally gone silent, written over, as childhood dreams tend to be, by time and distance?

Professor Jenson had been trying to catch Mrs. Gardner all day. He'd hoped to see her outdoors, but after several hours of loitering by his front windows, he gave up. He'd even made an additional—and pointless—trip to the mailbox just so he could peer searchingly into her yard. He knew there wouldn't be any mail to retrieve—he'd already fetched it this morning—but he just had to talk to Mrs. Gardner. *Confounded woman!* When he wasn't looking for her, she intruded into his life at every turn, and now that he actually needed to talk to her, she was nowhere to be found. Perhaps she was on vacation? Perhaps she was running errands? Perhaps she was avoiding him?

He was not so self-unaware that he couldn't appreciate the irony of how the tables had turned. He imagined her locked in her home, anxiously waiting for him to stop stalking her yard, and he chuckled. If only that were the case, then she could finally appreciate his daily dilemma. He'd considered knocking on her front door but quickly dismissed this option. Better to shout this news over the fence than to risk being dragged into her home, sat down, fed, talked at. No, much better to deliver the news and then run for the safety of home. He would wait.

Four o'clock rolled around, and Professor Jenson began thinking of dinner. As he puttered about in the kitchen, his impatience turned to anxiety. He must relieve himself of this news before the day ended. He had, after all, been tasked with only two items: provide the fungus and deliver the date.

"Can you handle this, Mark?" Ever since this whole fiasco started, Mrs. Gardner had called him by his first name, as if trying to emphasize how utterly seriously she was taking it all and how crucial to the operation she thought he was.

"Yes, as long as you don't throw anything else my way. I want to be as tangential as possible." Two tasks, and both completely behind the scenes and as unconnected as possible to the shenanigans brewing in Mrs. Gardner's mind: provide the fungus and deliver the date.

Professor Jenson was so absorbed with repeating his two tasks to himself that the ring of the phone spooked him. "Hello?"

A pause, then, "Mark, you sound out of breath. Everything okay?"

"Matilda!"

"I just wanted to check in with you and see if you'd heard anything from Arnold."

"I . . . I . . ." Professor Jenson's words were failing him. The phone! Why hadn't he thought of ringing her? Did he even know her phone number? "Yes, I talked with him this morning."

"And you waited until this late hour to tell me?" Mrs. Gardner's tone was incredulous. He could just envision her clutching the phone in both hands, wagging her head at him even though he wasn't there to see it. "Sorry, sorry, I'm just anxious and perhaps a little guilt-ridden."

Professor Jenson's ears perked up at this. He sensed an opportunity to steer this ship in a different, brighter, and more honest direction. "Now Matilda, if you're having second thoughts, I think we really should consider—"

"It's not second thoughts," Mrs. Gardner interrupted. "Oh, I don't know, I just don't like deceiving anyone."

"Exactly!" Professor Jenson's heart began to beat wildly with hope. "In light of this, perhaps we should—"

"I don't *like* deception, I really don't, but what's that they say? The ends justify the means," Mrs. Gardner cut in.

"Uh, I think that is correct, but I think that's always meant as a negative thing. As in, the ends don't really justify the means."

"Are you sure about that? I thought the maxim was meant as an encouragement to do whatever it takes for the right outcome."

"No, I'm almost certain it's meant as a warning. It's, uh, what people in the wrong tell themselves to make themselves feel better about what they're about to do."

"What! Are you trying to say I'm a bad person, Mark Jenson?"

"No no, not at all!" Professor Jenson blustered. Really, he'd thought it was bad enough with a hyperventilating Matilda in his hallway the other day, but this telephone debate on ethics was worse, so much worse.

"Don't you take the moral high ground with me, Professor."

There it was. He was back to the nickname. "I'm not taking high ground or low ground. No ground is being taken, Matilda!"

There was silence and then a prolonged sigh. "Even if the ends don't justify the means, at least there is grace," Mrs. Gardner finally said.

"Yes, well, the apostle Paul did say not to sin in order for grace to abound." He bit his lip as soon as the words left his mouth.

Surprisingly, Mrs. Gardner just chuckled. "You really are a good man, aren't you?"

Professor Jenson felt the heat rise in his cheeks. If he didn't know better, he'd describe her tone as tender.

"Well, enough of this. What did Arnold say? I hope Ben didn't follow through with his plans!"

"Well, that's just it—he did." Professor Jenson cringed, preparing for a loud utterance of disapproval. "Ben made an appointment with an appraiser, who, I understand, will assess the property to decide what it's worth and how to list it."

Mrs. Gardner interrupted him, and Professor Jenson was surprised at the levelness of her tone: no hysterics, just a cool, calm, and collected voice purring into his ear. "The date, Mark. What is the date?"

The use of his first name again filled Professor Jenson with a confusing level of satisfaction. "August 30. Two o'clock."

"Thank you, Mark. You've been most helpful. Please have the specimen ready a couple of days beforehand. I'll be by to pick it up."

"Yes, of course." There was a soft click and Professor Jenson was left staring at his handset and marveling that the first of his two tasks was over in a moment. And even though she hadn't taken his half-proffered advice, in the end, it hadn't been so bad. Like the quick smart after ripping off a bandage.

**The boy hopes the girl found his note.** *It would be so disappointing to enter their Room and find his note still there. He is not disappointed. He finds a folded piece of paper lying on the floor next to the chair, as if it'd started on the seat of the chair and by some mysterious force had ended up on the floor.* Perhaps the Story People knocked it off, *the boy speculates and grins.*

The boy unfolds the paper eagerly. Inside the girl has sketched a long, thin man with a huge nose and disproportionately large mouth. He is reaching for a book with one hand while shoving another into his cavernous mouth. A bubble above the head says "YUM!" There is no other message, just the large, uneven letters of her name.

The boy laughs out loud at the picture and begins planning a reply.

# CHAPTER THIRTEEN

## SHE SAW THE TRUTH IN THEIR EYES

The hotel was decent as hotels go, with comfortable beds and ample space. Still, the four friends were reluctant to call it a night. Their spirits were running high after the first day at the conference, and they'd gathered in the girls' room for late-night snacks.

"Oh man, I've missed this." Clare leaned forward and snagged a bag of chips from Becca. "Can we just stay here and avoid going back to real life?"

Becca snatched the bag back, her short figure stretching as far as it could without tumbling off her perch on the side of the bed. "I don't know what you're complaining about. You have a cushy job waiting for you." Her tone was laced with frustration as she settled back against a pillow; her frizzy brown hair spiked out like spokes, her head the hub.

"I know," Clare sighed, licking her cheddar-encrusted fingers. "I'm just half-terrified that a week in, they'll realize they've made a horrible mistake and kick me to the curb." Her lanky, five-foot-eight frame was draped across the bed, her blond hair pulled into a messy bun.

"Oh, stop worrying. You excel at everything you do!" There was a not-so-subtle hint of hostility behind Becca's words of encouragement, and Rosemary grimaced as she observed the two, hoping there would be no ugly confrontations. Clare and Becca had both graduated from the same English program, but Becca had returned home to a retail job and had no patience for Clare's imagined woes. Liam, who'd been sitting uncharacteristically silent next to Rosemary, jumped in and smoothed over the tension.

"Well, I don't know what either of you have to complain about. I'm just happy to be in the company of adults!" Liam, passionate, buoyant, and oftentimes ridiculous, was entering his second year as an elementary school teacher. Clare and Becca smiled and laughed, and Rosemary nudged Liam's knee with her own, silently showing her gratitude. Liam bumped her shoulder with his and gave her a grin. "How about you, Clooney? As the only real artist and storyteller among us, what are your thoughts about the conference so far?"

"Oh, I don't know about that." Rosemary sighed and snuggled deeper into her spot on the bed. "I don't know. Today was great, but I have mixed emotions. On one hand, it's inspiring to hear other authors and illustrators, but it's also a little frustrating. I guess I feel like I've peaked," Rosemary confessed. "*Spectrum* was a lifelong passion of mine, and I just can't imagine getting up enough energy and enthusiasm for anything else. Does that make any sense?"

"Definitely, but just give yourself time." Liam patted her knee. "It's only been . . . what? A year since your book was released? You'll find something else that you're passionate about, don't worry. You're too crazy talented to lie dormant for long." Clare and Becca exchanged pointed looks.

"Thanks. I'm kind of hoping I'll find inspiration here. It'd be nice to have another project." Rosemary didn't mention that part of the reason behind her fractured enjoyment of the conference was a mental preoccupation with Ben. She'd gone from shock over the revelation of his identity to grief over their lost connection and had finally settled on a cocktail of confusion and frustration. It was weird putting a grown-up face to BJ. He'd existed for so long as a part of her childhood that she didn't know how to mesh her memories with the current reality. BJ had been imaginative, loyal, kind, and sweet. Ben, she wasn't so sure of. It made her angry to imagine BJ giving a woman flowers one day and linked arm in arm with another woman the next. BJ jumping from date to date like a honeybee among flowers. She felt sad for BJ, as if Ben had somehow let his younger self down. Maybe the years after his parents' deaths had changed him, altered his personality. She longed to know for sure but shrank every time she thought of confronting him. "Hey, remember me? I'm Rosie. You know, from sixteen years ago. See? Look at all these letters from you I saved. You were kind of a big deal in my childhood. So . . . coffee?" One word: awkward.

"Earth to Rosemary." Becca was waving a hand in front of her, her dark eyes probing Rosemary's for any sign of life.

"Sorry." Rosemary shook her head. "What were you saying?"

"We were just talking about our plans for tomorrow. There are two morning sessions, break for lunch, then one afternoon session. That should give us enough time in the late afternoon and evening to go do something. I'm thinking Navy Pier?"

"Sure, sounds good to me, although I may have to be late in joining you for any evening plans. My deadline on this current project is tomorrow, so I'll need some time to wrap things up, but I can easily catch up with you all."

"We don't mind waiting," Liam commented quickly.

"Yes we do," Becca butted in. "I'm not going to sit around a hotel waiting on you, Rosemary. Just text us when you're ready to join us and we'll let you know where we are."

Rosemary smiled. "Deal. So what sessions are you all doing in the morning?"

"I think we were all interested in going to the one on book proposals." Clare gestured to the other two. All three had manuscripts at various levels of completion.

"Isn't that the same time as the one on storytelling through picture books?" Rosemary pulled out her schedule. "I really want to go to that one, so how about I just meet up with you three afterward?"

"Oh no, I'll go with you," Liam jumped in. "It's no fun to go to a session by yourself."

"You sure?" Rosemary frowned. "You seemed excited about the proposal session."

"Yeah, I'm not worried. I'd rather you not have to go by yourself. You don't mind me keeping you company, right?"

Rosemary couldn't help but notice how Clare and Becca cleared their throats and looked at each other out of the corners of their eyes. Becca spoke up, "Well then, you all have fun, but we'll be learning how to put together a rock-solid proposal while you two schmucks do whatever."

"Rosemary doesn't need to learn about proposals, not with a book already published!" Liam said. "I'll just bask in her glow, thank you very much."

"Knock it off, Liam!" Rosemary laughed. Becca and Clare just rolled their eyes.

◇◆◇◆

Rosemary yawned into her hand and hoped no one saw her and mistook it for boredom. There were fifteen minutes until the session started, and she was waiting for Liam to show up. They'd stayed up late until the girls had finally booted Liam into the next room so they could all get some rest. Becca and Clare fell asleep almost immediately, but Rosemary, who had opted for an air mattress on the floor, couldn't get comfortable, and not just because she was pretty sure there was a hole in the mattress. She sprawled and shifted, but it wasn't the slowly deflating mattress that was keeping her awake as much as it was her mind. As hard as she tried, Rosemary could not shake thoughts of BJ and Ben. She'd come to separate the two in her mind, like a Dr. Jekyll and Mr. Hyde scenario. Whenever she closed her eyes, she came face-to-face with BJ, and then she'd toss and turn, wondering what had happened to him in the silent years that had followed their friendship. Then, just as suddenly, she'd be confronted with Ben's face, smiling at her in a mischievous, knowing way, causing butterflies to leap in her stomach. And then she'd imagine him in someone else's arms, and then someone else and someone else, until she couldn't see his face anymore. Then she'd be back to BJ and she'd long to reach out and comfort him and find him again. It was all very unsettling and confusing. As one hour rolled into the next, she tried to still her mind with prayer, but she was too distracted even for that, finally resorting to a deep moan into her pillow. "Lord, please help me." With BJ. With Ben. With the more immediate need of sleep. Rosemary had been grateful when the alarm had finally gone off.

"Hey, I got you a coffee." Liam approached her breathlessly, sliding a fragrant, steaming cup into her hand and taking the seat next to her.

"Thanks! I really need some." Rosemary took a sip. "Is this caramel?"

"Yup, found a Starbucks kiosk on the first floor. Much better than the hotel coffee. Caramel Macchiato is still your favorite, right?"

"Yes, thanks. I'm surprised you remember."

"My mind is a steel trap." Liam grinned and tapped his temple. He was holding his own cup close to his face, and the steam from the coffee was fogging his thick-framed glasses. They sipped in companionable silence for a moment.

Rosemary found herself studying Liam out of the corner of her eye. She was immeasurably grateful for his predictability and openness. He was who he claimed to be; more than that, he was better than he thought he was. Kind, compassionate, and excitable, Liam was consistently himself, no fuss, no drama. Rosemary noticed he'd let his sandy hair grow out a bit. It was tousled high on his head. Combined with the scruff on his face, he looked a bit like a rumpled mess, but an endearing rumpled mess. His thick frames made his gray eyes seem larger, and his round face and dimples, combined with a propensity to laugh, gave him a perpetually youthful look.

"Hey, so I was thinking." Liam turned to her, a fleck of foam on his upper lip. "What do you think of visiting my classroom next month as a guest author? You can talk to the kids and read your book to them."

"That sounds wonderful. I'd love to."

"Awesome. We're not that far away from you, you know." Liam lived and taught in an Indianapolis suburb, less than an hour's drive from Rosemary's mother's house. "Now that you're home, we'll be able to see more of each other."

"True. I'm glad to be close to at least one friend. That was the hardest part about graduating, knowing we're all going separate ways and not knowing when we'll see each other again."

"Well, I'll make sure we stay in touch. You'll be sick of me by the end of the semester." Liam grinned at her and rested an arm on the back of her chair. "And I'm holding you to your promise. My kids will love you."

Rosemary smiled and tapped her lip, indicating Liam had something on his. She watched in amusement as he licked his lips dramatically. Shaking her head at him, she turned to the front as the session started and leaned back in her chair, the back of her shoulders brushing Liam's arm. She was thankful that the caffeine was beginning to kick in. Her mind felt freed from conflicting thoughts of BJ and Ben. There wasn't anything that a good friend and a

Caramel Macchiato couldn't fix. Rosemary welcomed them both as a blessing.

◇◆◇◆

"Where's my hair spray? Clare, do you have my hair spray? I promise, if you do . . ." Becca stood in their shared bathroom, half-dressed for bed, her bright polka-dot pajama pants clashing dramatically with her navy business casual blouse. A bag of toiletries dangled from one hand and a lathered toothbrush pointed accusingly at Clare from the other. Although her frame was petite, her presence filled the room with the heat of her frustration.

"I don't have your hair spray, Becca," Clare groaned from the bed. She'd finished packing before the closing banquet and was now enjoying a rerun of *Gilmore Girls*, her long bare legs stretched out lazily in front of her with pink polish flashing brightly from her toes.

"Ugh." Becca stomped out of the bathroom and began shoving clothes into her suitcase, jamming the toothbrush into the corner of her mouth and speaking around it. "I despise packing and unpacking, traveling in general, really."

"Yeah, but it was a great few days, you have to admit," Rosemary commented from her squatted position in front of the dresser. "This trip was just what I needed. Oh, and I forgot to tell you all, Liam invited me to visit his classroom next month to read my book and talk to his students. Not sure yet what I'll say exactly, but it should be fun. Kind of surprised he asked."

"Really, Rosemary?" Becca stopped packing and plucked the toothbrush from her mouth, placing a hand on her hip.

"Becca!" Clare jerked her attention away from the television to glare warningly at her friend.

"What?" Becca challenged. "I'm tired of all the ingratiating nonsense Liam throws around."

"What are you talking about?" Rosemary frowned.

"Never mind. Don't listen to Becca."

"No, if there's something wrong, tell me."

"There's nothing wrong, Rosemary." Clare sighed and sat up, letting her long blond hair spill around her face. "It's just that, well, Liam likes you."

Becca snorted. "Understatement of the year."

Rosemary's heart was pounding, and she felt the heat rush up to her face. "You mean he *like* likes me?"

"Oh really, Rosemary!" Becca snapped. "Wake up, girl. He's only been in love with you since our freshman year of college."

"What?" Rosemary rocked back on her heels and stared openmouthed between her friends.

"Oh come on. It's obvious. He hovers around you and can't stop singing your praises." Becca, ever blunt and honest, began packing again.

Rosemary shifted her gaze to Clare, who shrugged and nodded. "Yeah, it's true. It's kind of a well-known fact."

"But he's kind to everyone!" Rosemary protested. "That's just the way he is." Instance after instance of Liam singling her out, showing her extra care and courtesy, came to Rosemary's mind. She gulped. "Right?"

"Sorry, girl. But he has it bad for you. You might want to be careful about leading him on."

"Unless you like him back, that is," Clare offered with a smile. "You two would make a cute couple."

Rosemary started pulling her clothes out of the dresser drawers, her body on autopilot while her mind swam. "I-I don't know. I guess I've never thought of him in that way. He's always been just a great friend."

"Well, we're just giving you a heads-up before you go waltzing off to his classroom. It's going to mean way more to him than it does to you."

"Unless you like him, that is," Clare added again, gentle, helpful, doing her best to soften the blow of the revelation.

"I don't know . . . ," Rosemary repeated. "Did he tell you he liked me?"

"Honey." Becca stilled her busy hands, her tone uncharacteristically gentle. "He doesn't need to tell us. The way he is with you . . . we just know."

Rosemary grew quiet, and for a while she and Becca finished packing in silence, the only noise that of Lorelai Gilmore holding a heated debate with Luke in the background. Finally Rosemary spoke. "Thanks for telling me. I guess I'd want to hear this from Liam if it's true."

"You know Liam," Clare said. "Brave in all things but love."

"Yeah, you get to talking about feelings and he kind of shuts down," Becca added. "But I just thought you should know what you could be getting yourself into."

Later that night, Rosemary lay in bed, staring at the ceiling, her mind awash with yet another complication. She was thinking of how great Liam made her feel—valuable, interesting, special—and she wondered if her feelings counted in the way he needed it to count, in the way *she* needed it to count. The BJ-and-Ben split personality had been replaced by Liam's bright, cheerful face. "Lord," she prayed, "I don't know how I feel about all of this and I'm too exhausted to think about it anymore. Please just give me guidance. You see the heart, after all, so if You could clue a girl in, it'd be much appreciated."

The next morning was a blur of checking out, loading up the car, and ensuring everyone had enough caffeinated beverages to tide them over for a while. Rosemary ended up in the front passenger seat, Liam was driving, and Becca and Clare took up residence in the back seat among a mountain of pillows and snacks.

Clare stretched out her long legs and propped her feet up on the console between the front seats. "Try to get us there in one piece, please," she shot out to Liam. "No crazy speeding or weaving in and out of traffic."

"Hey, I don't see any of you offering to switch places with me," Liam shot back.

"And navigate all these toll roads? No thank you." Becca shifted in her seat and tried to position a pillow between her head and the window.

"So I'm doing a unit on creative writing this semester." Liam turned to Rosemary, his eyes bright. "This will be the perfect time for you to stop by with your book. I'm sure whatever you decide to talk about will be great."

Becca, slumped over her pillow with her eyelids at half-mast, laughed. "Yes, it will be spectacular. The spectacular Rosemary."

It had clearly been a joking comment, which anyone who knew Becca would instantly pick up on, but Liam straightened and glanced at her in the rearview mirror with a scowl on his face. "Hey, watch it, Becca." This was about as stern as Liam had ever gotten around his friends, and because of that it was as good as a slap in the face. Becca, thick-skinned and unfazed, just shrugged and looked away.

"Sorry," Liam mumbled. "Shouldn't have snapped at you."

"No big deal."

Rosemary glanced into the back seat with a furrowed brow. Clare and Becca were both giving her pointed looks. Clare raised her eyebrows and nodded her head in Liam's direction. Becca splayed her hands upward, beseechingly, silently mouthing, "See?" Rosemary's heart stuck in her throat, her own eyes widening as she saw the truth in their eyes.

**The girl cannot stop drawing.** *After leaving her sketch for the boy, she fills notebook after notebook with images, cramming into the margins, wrapping around the outer edges, eating their way across the page. She wonders if the boy found her sketch yet and dreams of Christmas, when she'll be back for a visit and able to run to the Room and check.*

# Chapter Fourteen

## SHE'D BEEN STANDING THERE ALL ALONG

Ben had spent the last two weeks cleaning every nook and cranny of Palermo's. He'd channeled his anxiety over his decision to sell and the quickly approaching appraisal into making sure that every square foot of the property looked spotless and well kept. He'd oiled the doors so the hinges wouldn't squeak, and he'd made other minor repairs throughout the building. He'd even gone so far as to organize storage shelves and closets, which is what eventually drew him to the Room.

When he'd first taken over Palermo's, this was one of the first places he'd gone. He hadn't known what to expect. Was the Room still mostly empty? Would he find traces of Rosie? He'd been disenchanted during that first trip back to the Room. It wasn't quite the secret hideaway that he'd remembered. The hidden door within the closet wasn't hard to spot. His adult eyes detected that the wood of the door was completely different from the surrounding wall, so even though it was seamless and lacked a doorknob, it wasn't difficult to see where the wall ended and the door began. It'd been more than fifteen years since he'd set foot in the Room. At some point in those years, the Room had been appropriated by the needs of the store, its corners cluttered with cleaning supplies and old furniture. Clearly it hadn't stayed secluded and forgotten. He'd looked for traces of Rosie but had found none. He'd expected to feel the comfortable twinges of nostalgia, but instead he'd felt panicky. The walls, vibrantly full in his youth with the voices of the Story People, had gone silent and instead slowly drew in upon him, reminding him of all he'd lost. He'd only been back a handful of times since, until today when no part of the store was safe from his organizational touch.

It was the evening of August 28, close to nine o'clock, which meant the rows of shelves stood quiet watch as Ben climbed the stairs to the third floor, where the Room waited for him. He took a sharp left and approached the closet door, opening it and flicking on the light. It winked a few times and then died out. Sighing, he went back out and turned on the main lights, letting their beams illuminate the small closet. The back wall was blocked by cardboard boxes, slumped with age and repeated handling, their edges fastened with numerous layers of packing tape, gleaming in the light like shiny gray bandages. A set of partially empty metal shelves sat to the right, and Ben began moving the cardboard boxes onto the shelves, clearing a path to the door. He planned to start in the Room and work his way out. Clearing the back wall took just a few minutes and then Ben was pushing against the wooden panel, urging the door inward. The narrow hallway to the Room had seemed much longer as a child, like an enchanted entryway to another kingdom, the rabbit hole leading to Alice's Wonderland. Now he saw it for what it was, a simple threshold—two steps and he was in the Room.

The light from outside the closet was sufficient for Ben to look around but not enough for the cleaning he had in mind. Ben dug into his pocket and pulled out his phone to use as a flashlight in order to get a better idea of what was in the Room. At some point, Uncle Louie had updated the front desk, and apparently the Room had been the resting place of the old furniture. A worn office chair sat facing a corner, and two old cabinets stood against the wall, their doors warped and yawning open. A collection of old tools lay scattered beneath a bench, and an assortment of rolled-up rugs leaned in one corner like slumped, oversized slugs. With all the large items in the Room, there was barely space in the middle to move about. Ben began to second-guess his cleaning and organizational initiative. Would the appraiser even look at this room? And if he did, surely all he'd be interested in would be the dimensions of the Room and not the chaotic collection before him. It was getting late, and Ben didn't think he had the emotional energy to tackle the Room after all. He decided to make a quick pass before heading back out. Slowly he began by walking the cramped perimeter of the Room, testing the floorboards, looking for any that might be loose or squeaky.

He didn't recognize any of the Room's current occupants. As a boy, he'd smuggled in a couple of metal chairs with cracked vinyl seats. There'd been the bedsheet he'd used for his fort and, in later years, a beanbag chair that his uncle had given him but that he'd smuggled up two flights of stairs to the Room rather than taken home. None of these items remained. In their place was an assortment of tossed junk, neglected over the years.

Rosie had been on his mind even before he entered the Room. Although it'd been transformed from an open, imaginative space to a cluttered mess, the Room still held her presence. She'd been a little kid when he'd seen her last, maybe nine or ten. He'd been close to fourteen, and even though their carefully cultivated game of the Story People had lost some of the enchantment it had held for him in his younger years, he'd still clung to it tightly, nostalgically, and he had enjoyed seeing the hold it had over Rosie. Ben reached the corner with the rugs and shoved his foot into their midst, testing the floorboards beneath. He was about ready to move on when the beam from his phone caught a flash of white. He bent closer, nudging a flap of rug out of the way. Yes, there was a piece of paper stuck beneath one of the rugs, but what really caught Ben's attention was the slash of purple on the paper. It looked like a drawing of some sort. Ben's heart picked up pace as he gently pried the piece of paper out.

A girl, depicted in bright purple colored pencil, greeted him. She was curled under a tree, reading a book. The image, although clearly captured by a child, was well drawn and beautiful in its simplicity. But more than that, Ben recognized it. With a catch in his throat, he brought the page closer to the light and slowly shook his head. *Rosie.* This was her sketch, but not one he had seen before. This must have come after. She had remembered him after all, and she had left a message. The lump in his throat grew as he turned the page and read the short note.

> *BJ, I know you haven't received my other two notes yet, but I guess I'll keep trying. Who knows? Maybe someday you'll be back and then we'll have a lot to catch up on. I think you owe me a really long letter because you're making me wait a really long time.*

Ben sat on the floor, hard, and buried his face in the crook of his elbow. At fourteen, confused and grieving, he'd focused only on the fact that he'd never be able to come back here with his parents. And then the years slid by, and his thoughts of his uncle and this Room and Rosie had continued to be centered on how it affected him. He was missing out. He would never be back. Even if he came back, it wouldn't be the same. He had never stopped to think about how his absence was affecting those he'd left behind. Clearly it had affected his uncle, and now he realized it had affected Rosie too. He had not seen it from her side, wrapped as he was in his grief. She would have left a note and then seen it still there during her next visit. She would have been confused at his sudden silence. She would have had no way to know what had happened to him or how to reach him. "Lord, why do You keep sending me reminders of what I lost?" Ben groaned into his arm.

Through the pain, a line called out to him: "You haven't received my other two notes yet." The other notes!

Ben leaped to his feet, the page clutched in his hand like a rumpled tissue, the beam from his phone jerking into random corners. He saw now what must have happened. Rosie had left him notes, probably in the same location, nothing obvious, just folded pieces of paper on a chair or on a blanket, as was usual, someplace safe and obvious for the intended reader. But the intended reader had never found them.

Ben could just envision his uncle entering the Room, dragging a cabinet behind him, shoving it against the wall, the rough wooden edges catching the edge of the blanket that held the notes, or knocking against the chair that held them, spilling the papers onto the floor. He could see his uncle returning a few months later with a stack of chairs, placing them over the fallen pieces of paper, scattering the notes even further. A year goes by, maybe two, and he imagines his uncle returning with some old rugs, lugging them into a corner, their edges snapping at the papers, which by now have migrated into hidden spaces far from their original location. Who knew how many scraps of paper were hidden in this place? Ben felt his chest constrict at the thought of the unread messages. They called to him, and once again the walls seemed to come alive, this time with whispers from Rosie.

There was nothing left to do but get to work. Ben rushed to gather all the things he thought he'd need: a portable work light and plenty of empty cardboard boxes to gather up odds and ends. After letting JC out one last time for the evening and locking the connecting door to the shop, Ben hurried back up to the Room. The sense of dread he'd connected to the Room earlier that evening evaporated under his new mission. Gone, too, was the sadness, at least momentarily, for there were more messages to be found. Ben turned on some music, filling the small space with more sound than it had experienced in years. He began by dragging everything out of the Room, cluttering the rest of the third floor with piles of junk, inspecting the items as he went. He checked to see if there were any pieces of paper stuck to anything or crumpled beneath long-forgotten debris. The smaller items he boxed in the Room before carrying them out, unfolding and inspecting each piece of paper he came across. He hadn't been this meticulous even in preparing the store's financials for his real estate agent.

Ten minutes in and he had found another note. He resisted the urge to read it right then and there, instead carefully folding it and putting it in his pocket next to the other one. He wanted to read them all together. The speed with which he'd found the first two gave him a misleading sense of hope, so after an hour more with no further messages, Ben began to get discouraged as his energy flagged with the lengthening evening. It wasn't until he reached the final few items in the Room that he found the last three. They were huddled together beneath a tool belt, all three, one right on top of the other. Ben's heart sang as he added them to the other two in his pocket and finished clearing the Room.

Five notes total. Ben sat in the middle of the now-empty Room. He aimed the work light so that its beam didn't blind him and spread the notes out before him. Silently, he bowed his head and breathed in deeply, calming his nerves. "God, I'm sorry. Thank You for these reminders of Rosie. Help me see them as blessings—as gifts—and not things sent to torment me." Slowly he unfolded all five notes and pieced together a chronology. The first note was cheerful and full of the usual banter.

*BJ, I've never read* The Phantom Tollbooth, *but it sounds like fun. I'm going to read it next, unless the Story People have eaten it. I don't see how you think you can hear the Story People at night. They're not nocturnal. Unless you think they should be? That would change things, wouldn't it? Maybe they only come out at night, but then where are they during the day if they're not in the Room?*

She'd drawn a row of Story People's heads with various expressions, all with pajama caps on, several books open and partially eaten by their side.

The second note was surprised but not upset. The fact that he'd missed a note wasn't yet alarming.

*BJ, you didn't get my letter! Well, I'm just going to leave you another one anyway, OK? I loved* The Phantom Tollbooth. *I wanted to be Milo the whole time I read it. I just finished reading* The Silver Chair *again. It's the fourth book in* The Chronicles of Narnia *and my favorite. The girl and the boy in the story remind me of you and me. They go on lots of adventures and meet a lot of creatures much stranger than the Story People. I wish I had thought up Narnia. I wish it was real and we could go there. Wouldn't it be cool if we could pick a book to walk into? Which one would you pick?*

She'd drawn a strange amphibian creature with spindly legs and a pointed hat. This creature was greeting one of the Story People, who seemed to be aghast at making its acquaintance.

The third note was the one he'd originally found. Ben skimmed it again and moved on to the fourth. The confusion was becoming apparent now.

> *BJ, I don't know what's going on. I think I'm going to have to stop leaving you letters if you aren't getting them. If the old ones were gone, then maybe I would think you'd read them and decided to just not write back. That'd make me sad, of course, but it would be an explanation. But all my letters are still here, so that means you haven't gotten them, and I don't know why. Are you in trouble? I think when we see each other again or you finally write back, you should send me your actual address and we could write that way. You know, like pen pals? That way I know I can find you.*

There was no illustration with this fourth one and no mention of the Story People. Ben moved on to the final and fifth note, his heart in his throat.

> *BJ, I honestly don't know why I'm writing this, but here I am again. You probably will never read this, but that's OK. I like the idea of leaving it here, to maybe or maybe not find you. If you could only see our Room now . . . it's filled with storage and all my old letters are gone. I'm trying to decide if that means you found them? I hope so, but then again, that'd mean you'd found them and not replied. And then again, maybe they just got lost in the shuffle. There's an awful lot of junk in here. Our Story People must be feeling irked, don't you think? There's no place for them to repose after sating themselves on their books! Anyway, I just wanted to leave this note as a good-bye.*

*I hope life has given you only good things and that wherever you are, you are happy. God bless you. Good-bye, friend.*

Ben sat staring at this last note. It'd clearly been written many years later. The handwriting, the language, everything pointed to a mature Rosie, making her way back to the Room one final time. Ben set the note down and covered his face with his hands. Tears pricked at his eyes, and the lump in his throat was hard to swallow past. He sat and did something he hadn't done in a while—he let the past catch up to him. The work light hummed in the corner. The Room was silent and still as Ben sat, a quiet nucleus to the five messages scattered around him. After years of dodging, Ben turned and greeted the past. She'd been standing there all along.

**It's two and a half years before the girl and the boy see each other again.** *But in that time they continue to leave messages. The girl visits the Room three times each year, during summer and at Thanksgiving and Christmas, leaving a note each visit. For a while, their system works, but the girl begins to forget what the boy looks like and twice she discovers her note in the same state as she left it. She is not expecting the Room to be occupied this Christmas when she visits. But when she opens the hidden door and sees a light, she is surprised and delighted.*

# CHAPTER FIFTEEN

## COMEDY OF ERRORS

"The key is subtlety." Mrs. Gardner stood before her distrustful and hesitant group of volunteers, her hands agitatedly darting to and fro as she tried to garner enthusiasm and elicit confidence. "You've all been given instructions and know what to do. Just quietly and naturally go to your stations, and avoid detection at all costs."

"I already told you, Matilda, I'm not doing it." Mrs. Frank was whispering through her teeth even though there was no one around. The group had gathered in a corner by the poetry section on the second floor of Palermo's. "I absolutely refuse."

Mrs. Gardner sighed and pinched the bridge of her nose. "Emma, I'm tired of arguing. Can we compromise? Please just go to your station, and when the time comes, I pray you will let your conscience guide you."

"That's exactly what I'm doing, letting my conscience guide me," Mrs. Frank snorted. "Deceiving Ben is wrong." Mrs. Gardner rolled her eyes but said nothing, and Mrs. Frank knew that her argument for honesty had been rejected. "Fine. I'll stand there like a fool if that will satisfy you, but in no way am I making any noise."

"Fine, fine. Anita, I've already planted the specimen. You'll simply need to make sure that attention is drawn to that area. It had to be an out-of-the-way area so as not to be obvious before we needed it to be, if that makes sense."

"Got it." Mrs. Baumgartner nodded vigorously.

"Now, I have the trickiest part. I'm going to have to stay hidden until the very end before I put the icing on the cake, so to speak. It should all work. It should. It should." This last bit was spoken more to herself than to the others. Mrs. Gardner worried her lip, clasping and unclasping her hands as the adrenaline coursed through her body. Her plan just had to work.

◇◆◇◆

Ben began the big day raw with emotion. Rosie was everywhere he looked. Finding the last of her notes had reminded him of exactly why Palermo's was special to him in the first place. It was a family business, sure, but even more than that, it held a strong place in his identity. How could he possibly give it up? He'd debated and wavered, but in the end he hadn't canceled the appointment. Didn't he owe it to himself to at least weigh his options? Still, his heart wasn't focused or ready, and he found himself anxiously checking the clock throughout the day.

At one forty-five, he was preparing to do a final sweep of the building before closing early for the two o'clock appointment when he saw a gray Honda Civic pull up in front of the shop and a man, who looked exactly like Professor Jenson, pull himself out of the driver's seat. Same shock of white hair, same leathery skin and big-boned features, same gait—it could have been the Professor's slightly sprier twin rather than his cousin. Ben met him at the door.

"Ben? Arnold Jenson. Good to meet you."

As Ben ushered him in, a yellow pickup pulled up and a tall, thin man in khakis and a bright checkered shirt stepped out.

"That's Scott Rogers. Early as usual," Arnold explained.

Scott was up the front steps in no time, clipboard in

hand and a stubbed pencil behind his ear. A hefty camera dangled from his neck. "Arnold, good to see you! And you must be Ben. Beautiful place you have here."

"Yes, thank you." Ben ushered the two gentlemen inside, feeling like a shepherd leading wolves to his flock. "I can give you a quick tour of the place and then let you loose to do your thing, if you'd like."

"That'd be great, thanks." Scott made a note on the official-looking form attached to the clipboard, flipped it up, and looked at the page beneath as if for reference. "I've already gone over the documentation you sent, tax statement, survey. I'll just be asking you a few questions as we go. I see this place was built in 1832."

"Yes, this is quite a historic building." The tension in Ben's shoulders eased a bit as he began talking about the building and guiding his visitors around the first floor. He'd given countless tours over the years and always enjoyed talking about the place. If he could just pretend for a moment that this was only another tour and his companions were simply interested, book-loving passersby, then maybe, just maybe, the panic and guilt would subside a bit.

They were approaching the second floor, and Scott had already made numerous notations on his form and had snapped photos of every room, which made Ben nervous. He felt like he was being graded, and the old pre-test anxiety reared its ugly head in response. There was a lull in the conversation as they paused near the nature section. Arnold was checking his phone, and Scott was writing something down. It was completely silent, and therefore the soft intake of breath sounded loudly throughout the second floor. Ben whipped his head around as he heard a fluttery, hesitant, and *familiar* voice.

"Oh-oh my, ha-ha, oh dear. How horrible and . . . disgusting and . . . *unhygienic*. Is that—? Yes, I think that's *m-mold*!"

◇◆◇◆

Mrs. Baumgartner danced from foot to foot. Then she paced a few steps and then paced back. She leaned against the wall and sighed. The longer she waited, the more she questioned this plan. Mrs. Gardner's fearless certainty that they were doing the right thing had buoyed her spirits and carried her this far, but without her friend present, Mrs. Baumgartner was left to confront the moral choice she'd just made. "First I invade Ben's privacy and snoop in the worst sense of the word, and now I'm outright breaking the Eighth Commandment through horrifying levels of deceit!" she whispered to herself. Who had she become? "Lord, help me."

Mrs. Baumgartner bent and took another peek at the "specimen." What had Professor Jenson called it? *Fuligo septica,* that was it. He'd given them a good amount, which Mrs. Gardner had planted along the baseboards. Mrs. Baumgartner squinted at the dull yellow fungus. Its surface was fuzzy and textured, and it looked alarmingly like vomit.

Mrs. Baumgartner put a hand to her mouth and straightened. She heard footsteps and froze. Could this be the moment? She wasn't ready! She hadn't decided exactly what she would say! But no, it was a handful of customers leaving. She sighed and slumped against the wall.

What *should* she say when the time came? Mrs. Gardner had admonished her: "Just speak off the cuff, Anita. Don't be too practiced or it will come off as fake." But how did one deliver a practiced startled discovery without sounding scripted? She wasn't an actress, for crying out loud!

"There's a sign on the door that the store is closing at two, which means Ben is closing the store for the meeting. We have to be there before he closes. And we must make sure we are quiet and out of sight," Mrs. Gardner had informed the group. Easy enough for Emma to pull off; she was sequestered in a closet. Not so easy for Mrs. Baumgartner, who was just standing here, idly loitering against the back wall of the nature section. Inspired, she grabbed a random book off a shelf and opened it, hoping to blend in with her surroundings. Mrs. Baumgartner leafed through *A History of Swallows in the United States*, her mind racing through various compilations of things to say during the crucial moment.

The store had grown quiet, but now a chorus of masculine voices suddenly sounded from below. Mrs. Baumgartner froze and listened. She could make out Ben's voice and two others. Surely this was it? She quickly shoved the book back on the shelf, knocking another off in her haste. It landed with a thump. "Oh oh oh!" Mrs. Baumgartner scooped up the fallen book with a panicked gasp and shelved it upside down, quickly corrected it, and then scuttled as quietly as possible back to her station. Should she pretend like she was directly upon the "mold"? stand more off to the side? She finally settled on an off-to-the-side position so as to better showcase the specimen.

The stairs creaked, footsteps grew louder, and the chorus of voices drew closer. Mrs. Baumgartner could barely breathe. From her position, she could just make out the top of the stairs. She watched as Ben's curly head appeared first. He was talking about the age of the roof. She strained to see past him to the two gentlemen following him. They were taking notes and listening intently. Yes, this was it. Should she wait until they were closer? For a split second she entertained the idea of ditching the whole thing and letting them pass her by. The relief at this thought was intense. But no, she had fumbled her way to this point and must see it through. The three men were standing at the top of the stairs. All was quiet. It was now or never. *Speak, Anita, speak!*

"Oh-oh my, ha-ha, oh dear!" She paused. *Well,* that *was awkward.* Why did she have to laugh when she was nervous? Should she stop there? No, specificity was required; plant the image firmly in their minds. "How horrible and . . . disgusting and . . . *unhygienic.*" Yes, that was good, very good. It implied potential health problems. Now to seal the deal. "Is that—? Yes, I think that's *m-mold!*"

◇◈◇◈

Ben stood and stared in astonishment at a blushing Mrs. Baumgartner, who was standing with her body half-turned toward them, posed and with her arm outstretched like a game show hostess about to uncover the prizes. The subject of her gesturing arm was a disgusting yellow mass running along the baseboards. His heart sank.

"Mold!" Mrs. Baumgartner repeated, shaking her arm for emphasis. "Oh dear me!"

"Have you historically had problems with mold?" Scott squatted and began snapping pictures of the yellow growth with a bit too much interest and enthusiasm for Ben's liking. Ben resisted the urge to throw himself between the lens and the offensive subject.

"No, we haven't!" Ben turned to Mrs. Baumgartner, who was slowly backing away with a guilty expression on her face. "Mrs. Baumgartner, what are you doing here? The store is closed. Oh, I forgot to lock the door!" He made a start for the stairs but stopped, loathe to leave his visitors alone with the incriminating evidence.

Scott continued to snap pictures like crazed paparazzi outside a Hollywood nightclub. Arnold stood silently by, a graveside expression on his face.

"Is the store closed? Really? Ha-ha. That's so odd. I must have lost track of the time. I didn't realize . . ." She had backed halfway down the aisle at this point. "Well, since the store is closed, I probably better get going."

"This isn't mold."

Mrs. Baumgartner froze and Ben turned back around. "What?"

"It's not mold," Scott repeated, his picture taking temporarily halted as he peered closer. "It's some sort of fungus, all right, but it's not mold."

"How on earth did it get here?" Arnold interjected.

"This is an outer wall and near a window. The windows *are* old." Scott had resumed taking pictures, this time of the surrounding elements. "I can't imagine that there was enough dampness for this volume of growth, but . . ." He trailed off, and all three men stood and stared at the yellow mass.

Ben finished the thought in his head: *but there's a mound of fungus on the floor.* The floor creaked behind them, and Ben turned to find Mrs. Baumgartner gone. A moment later, a distant ding told him she'd exited the building.

"Excuse me, gentlemen." Ben dashed back downstairs and to the front door, opening it and looking both ways down the sidewalk, but Mrs. Baumgartner was out of sight, deceivingly quick. Gritting his teeth in frustration, Ben closed the door, making sure to lock it this time. As he approached the steps, a scurrying noise came from the back of the store. *What now?* Ben did a quick sweep of the first floor, finding nothing, before joining his visitors on the second floor.

"His uncle didn't leave any record of having dealt with, uh, fungus growth, did he?" Scott was questioning Arnold.

"No, nothing," Ben answered, slightly out of breath from running up the stairs. No sooner were the words out of his mouth than he began to doubt himself. His uncle hadn't been the best record keeper. It'd taken Ben a full year just to sort through and make sense of everything and impose his own order on the accounts. "We haven't had this type of issue at all since I've been here, and I really don't think this was here even yesterday. I would have noticed."

The three men stood silently staring at the growth, the unspoken objection hanging between them: *Uh-huh, sure, but there's a mound of fungus on the floor.*

"Well," Arnold briskly broke the silence, "I suggest we wrap up this tour until this problem can be addressed. Then we can revisit all of this afterward."

What had started out as a nerve-racking experience had quickly descended into a horrific one. As Ben led the group around the rest of the second floor and Scott continued to ask questions and take pictures, Ben's mind was only half-focused. The other half was worrying about what this would do to his property value and whether he actually did have dampness issues and whether there was damage to his inventory and what this would cost him in the long haul. Arnold was trying to be helpful by pointing out the beautiful crown molding and wooden paneling, but Ben could tell that it was just damage control at this point.

They had moved to the third floor, and Arnold was commenting on the historic charm and importance of the building, the aura it created, et cetera, when a low murmur reached them. At first it wasn't loud enough to interrupt them. Arnold kept talking and Scott listened while Ben frowned and looked over his shoulder. It sounded like a conversation, but they were too far up for anything to reach them from outside. As abruptly as it started, the hushed conversation stopped. Ben had turned his focus back to Arnold when a low humming noise replaced the earlier voice. Was someone mowing outside? The humming noise morphed into a pronounced moan. *"Mmmmm ooooo!"* Arnold stopped talking and Scott stopped his polite nodding and all three men stood stock-still and listened.

◇◆◇◆

Mrs. Frank had never in her life been in a more compromising situation. She stood rigidly by the closet door, which was open just a crack, every muscle in her body tense and coiled. It was no surprise that sweet Anita had fully embraced Matilda's dark side, impressionable as she was, but that she, Emma Frank, would also be dragged over that line? Unthinkable! She'd tried to argue her way out of it. "Why does it have to be *me* in the closet?"

"Honestly because you have the best vocal register to pull it off, and I imagine it won't take much to summon up enough angst to make it convincing."

"What is *that* supposed to mean?"

"See? Exactly."

She'd tried another tactic. "Surely these men aren't superstitious. These are practical, business-minded men."

"I know, I know, but some people really believe that stuff! The world is full of practical people who believe impractical things. All we need to do is plant the suggestion, the seed of doubt, the 'could it be' thought."

"I don't even know what one is supposed to sound like, Matilda."

"Just put what you're feeling now into nonverbal form."

Mrs. Gardner had an ironclad rebuttal for every concern Mrs. Frank had brought forward, and so here she was, standing in a dark closet, having been instructed to humiliate herself by *impersonating a ghost*. The only thing keeping Mrs. Frank rooted to the spot was a genuine desire to save Palermo's, no matter the cost to her personal dignity.

"Now, it's important that you hide afterward," Mrs. Gardner had explained. "It would defeat the whole purpose, wouldn't it, for them to find you."

Mrs. Frank had begrudgingly located a suitable spot. The closet she was in looked like it'd been recently organized, but fortunately, there was still a stack of boxes on the far left that she could duck behind.

She kept telling herself that she wasn't going through with it, that the fact that she was standing here didn't actually commit her to anything. She could just stand here silently, ducking into her hiding spot should they come to the closet of their own free will. Or, to add deception upon deception, she could simply tell Matilda that she had done it but not actually do it.

"Now, Emma, what do you think you're doing?"

Mrs. Frank jumped and looked over her shoulder. Pastor Andrews's voice was so vivid in her mind that she found herself answering audibly. "Pastor, I know what you're thinking and I agree, I really do, it's just . . ."

"I would expect this of the other two, but *you*, Emma?" Pastor's voice sounded so saddened that Mrs. Frank almost wept.

"Oh Pastor, I'm so sorry!"

"And a ghost?" She could almost here the tsking of Pastor's tongue. "Emma, you know what we believe about ghosts."

"I know, Pastor, I know!" Mrs. Frank sobbed, thoroughly chagrined.

"God's grace can reach you, Emma, even—what was *that*?"

Mrs. Frank froze and listened to the creaking stairs. From her location, she could make out the bare bones of what the approaching men were saying—something about the historic nature of the building and its first owners. She smiled grimly. Quite the segue into her little performance—

"If you were going through with it, that is," Pastor reminded her.

"Of course, and I'm not, I won't!" Mrs. Frank replied hastily. She watched through the barely cracked door as all three men entered the third floor. Ben looked horribly shaken. His face was strained and sad and confused all at once. Mrs. Frank was reminded again of how young he actually was. *God bless that poor boy.* He was only doing what he thought was best, which, of course, was utterly the wrong thing to do. Mrs. Frank felt a twinge of conviction to aid him by completely derailing the sale of Palermo's. It was for his own good really, the dear boy. No one would ever have to know it was her.

"*God knows*," Pastor was quick to remind her.

"He does indeed," Mrs. Frank assented. But she could keep her integrity intact in the community by never ever speaking of this moment to another living soul.

"Ah, you who hide deep from the LORD your counsel . . ."

"Pastor, please!"

". . . whose deeds are in the dark . . ."

"I know I'm literally in the dark, but I'm not a person of the darkness, I promise!"

". . . and who say, 'Who sees us? Who knows us?'"

"Yes, yes, I understand."

"You turn things upside down!"

"Isaiah 29:15–16! See, I know my Scripture, Pastor!"

Oh dear, Ben was looking directly at the door. With a start, Mrs. Frank realized she'd been hissing an entire conversation out loud through clenched teeth. She watched in panic as Ben frowned in her direction and began moving toward her. Hardly realizing what she was doing, Mrs. Frank let out a low hum, almost a Gregorian chant, anything to throw off Ben's suspicions and redirect them to something otherworldly. Surely that was ghostlike enough, but the rest of the group didn't seem to notice. Ben was shaking his head and looking away as she hummed a little louder, putting more oomph into it this time.

"It doesn't appear to be working," Pastor offered unhelpfully.

Mrs. Frank thought back to her sole reference for ghostly behavior, a classic black-and-white adaptation of *A Christmas Carol*. There had been quite a bit of moaning, if she remembered correctly. Mrs. Frank switched from humming to moaning.

"Yes, that got their attention!" Pastor let out an unchecked hurrah.

Mrs. Frank watched as the group stopped talking and began looking around for the source of the noise. A strange, deep satisfaction welled up in Mrs. Frank. She was pretty good at this! She moaned a little louder. What had Matilda said? Put angst into it? She tried to imagine that she was the original owner of the store, horrified at the potential sale of the building. How outrageous! She inserted a little wail. Next she imagined her own disgust at being put into this horrible position. She fairly howled at the indignity of it all. It was working! It was working! She saw three confused faces pivot in her direction. Ben began walking toward her, causing Mrs. Frank to abruptly choke on her last moan, which fizzled out as a whimper. *Oh good gracious, it's working . . .*

"Emma, I would move along right about now if I were you."

Pastor didn't have to tell her twice.

◇◆◇◆

Ben walked toward the closet as if in a dream. What could be causing that horrible noise? It sounded like a cat being skinned alive. In the back of his mind a silly thought popped up and took hold: the Story People disapproved of what he was doing. They knew and they were not happy. A shiver ran down his spine. *Pull it together, Ben*, he counseled himself as he threw open the closet door. He'd replaced the burnt-out bulb the other night, so he flicked on the light and peered inside. Scott and Arnold were right behind him, both peeking over his shoulder. The noise had abruptly stopped, but there could be no doubt that it'd come from this direction. The silent closet stared back at him, neat and organized and devoid of any screaming cats.

"I didn't imagine that noise, did I?" Ben turned to the other two.

"No, that was kind of hard to miss." Arnold was staring straight ahead, a look of concentration on his face, most likely trying to figure out a way to positively spin this latest development.

"Old buildings often make odd noises," Scott added, graciously leaving out the obvious: *but usually not hysterical, hair-raising moaning noises.*

There was one other place to look, and Ben couldn't resist the pull to check it. He pushed the secret door and for the first time since Rosie, allowed others to see the Room.

"This is an unusual space," Scott commented, standing on the threshold.

Ben stood in the middle of the Room and looked around. He didn't know what he had expected to find, but the place was silent, nothing out of the ordinary, still clean and tidy from the other day. "Yeah, I'm not sure how this room came to be sectioned off," he said.

"No window, so nothing to give it away from the outside," Arnold added as he entered the Room.

"It's not uncommon for old buildings to have rooms partitioned off or passages, corridors, and so forth that don't make much sense by today's standards." Scott began snapping a few photos, and Ben clenched his jaw so hard it ached. To have his Room, his Rosie's Room, catalogued this way didn't feel right. He felt like herding them back out and putting up an Off Limits sign, but instead he stood to the side and let Scott finish.

"I just don't know what could have made that noise," Ben said as they finally exited the Room.

"Maybe it was ghosts," Scott suggested, raising his eyebrows and cocking his head in an exaggerated, suggestive manner. "You never know."

"Ah yes, Palermo's is haunted," Arnold laughed as they entered the main floor again.

Ben was beginning to feel queasy. First the fungus and now this? What else could possibly go wrong? It was at this point that a loud thumping noise and a series of shrill shrieks filled the air.

◇◆◇◆

Evading detection was actually quite thrilling; it was like playing hide-and-seek, and who didn't love that shivering sweet sensation in the pit of your stomach as you heard the seeker, peeked at him from your hiding spot, content in the comfortable knowledge that he couldn't see you . . . yet? Mrs. Gardner had felt like a child again as she ducked and weaved behind the first-floor bookcases, always just out of sight of the three gentlemen. Still, it had been a relief when they'd finally finished with the first floor and moved to the second. She could be a little less cautious. When Anita had come barreling downstairs, face bright as a cherry, Mrs. Gardner had resisted the urge to go to her. She couldn't risk exposure. She was glad she hadn't, for not a second later, Ben had come barreling down after Mrs. Baumgartner. She had watched in frozen fascination as Ben ducked outside then back in, locking the door behind him. He was on his way to the stairs when Mrs. Gardner had realized she was in his line of sight. Quickly she'd ducked behind a bookcase, but not quietly enough, for Ben had turned and looked in her direction searchingly. The ensuing few moments were laced with no innocent hide-and-seek frivolity; instead Mrs. Gardner had felt like someone in a horror film being chased through dark corridors. She'd half expected Ben to start chanting "Fee-fi-fo-fum." It was a miracle, really, that she'd evaded detection. Ben had left the first floor and she'd been left in a quietly gasping heap in the back, having never moved that quickly in her life. Eventually the group had moved to the third floor, and confident of not being disturbed, Mrs. Gardner snuck out and took up her position on the first-floor stairs.

Carefully, Mrs. Gardner ascended and descended the stairs, testing each step, plotting the various ways to feign a fall. The key was to be dramatic. It needed to be clear that she'd tripped on these horrible, unsafe stairs and nearly broken her neck. She finally decided upon a suitable location for her dramatic pose. Near the bottom of the staircase made the most sense, but not at the very bottom; it'd be much more attractive to lie in pained repose on the stairs than sprawled out on the floor.

Mrs. Gardner sat on a step and practiced being a tragic figure. Slowly she stretched out, legs tucked together, neatly crossed at the ankles (modesty was important here). She leaned against the wall with one shoulder and the other she flung back dramatically, resting a hand on her forehead. *Hmmm, yes, this is suitably dramatic but perhaps not quite believable.* Mrs. Gardner sat back up and smoothed out the creases in her skirt. Why on earth had she worn a skirt today? Slacks would have been much easier to work with. "Nice thinking, Matilda," she muttered. Not much time remained. Quickly she leaned back and placed one leg on the step above her, the other on the step below, and eased to a prostrate position. No, this one was just plain ridiculous. It looked like she'd cast herself headfirst down the stairs. Not to mention that she'd be giving them a front-row seat to looking straight up her skirt. Sitting up again, she decided that she was approaching this the wrong way. With a bit of difficulty, she turned and faced the stairs, carefully sinking to a sitting position and tucking her legs to the side. Gingerly she eased forward until she was sprawled in an almost worshipful position. But no, this one didn't make sense either. It looked like she'd fallen *up* the stairs.

Mrs. Gardner grunted as she righted herself. She needed to just pick something and go with it before she ran out of time. So it was with a touch of panic that she scrambled to her feet. As she rushed to straighten, her right foot landed on the edge of the step, causing her leg to fly out from underneath her. Desperately, she flung an arm to catch the banister. She caught it but managed only to wrench her arm painfully as her body lurched. With a yelp she let go and landed with a thump on her bottom, half-on and half-off a step, causing her to bounce from one step to another in an awkward sideways position until the momentum finally cast her forward onto the floor, as if the stairs were spitting her out. She landed with a crunch and rolled a good few feet, finally ending up in the middle of an aisle, her skirt hiked up, her legs splayed, arms pinned lifelessly beneath her. The pain shooting up Mrs. Gardner's right arm completely masked the irony of the situation. She didn't realize she'd been shrieking nearly nonstop until the last fall knocked the air out of her. She lay in a silent, graceless heap and awaited discovery.

He didn't really care about any of this business about the bookstore, and he certainly didn't care for Mrs. Gardner. It was just that he hadn't seen his cousin in a while, so he might as well swing by Palermo's to see if Arnold was available for an early dinner. Professor Jenson wavered on the front walk outside Palermo's like an arthritic bird on a branch—two steps forward, three steps back, two steps to the left, four to the right. Finally, he ascended the steps and peered through the glass door. The store was lit but empty. He tried the door. It was locked. He took this as a sign that he should leave and descended the stairs, but something pulled him back up the steps. He could always call Arnold on his cell phone to come let him in. If he knew Arnold's cell phone number, which he didn't. Had he even brought his own cell phone? No, he hadn't. He could knock, then.

He'd just raised a fist when he had an arresting thought: knocking would draw attention to the front door and perhaps upset the devious plans already in motion. He'd bowed out of any direct involvement, but he certainly didn't want to get in the way of Mrs. Gardner's plans. If her scheme meant they could keep Palermo's, then so be it.

Professor Jenson lowered his fist and turned back around. He supposed he could loiter until they came out— pretend like he'd just been in the area. He was still hesitating by the door when he caught sight of Mrs. Baumgartner eyeing him from inside the shop next door, her round face and unblinking eyes completely unnerving him. "Anita!" He raised a hand to get her attention. Perhaps she knew what was going on inside and could enlighten him. He watched her duck out of sight just as a loud banging along with a series of shocked feminine screams reached his ears. Professor Jenson turned and hurriedly hobbled back to the door, clutching at the doorknob and peering inside. His heart was racing and not just from the exertion. He scanned as much of the interior as he could from his position. His eyes finally settled on a pair of bare legs sticking out from an aisle deep in the store. He could only see from the knee down but he was convinced those were Mrs. Gardner's calves.

"Matilda!" Professor Jenson pulled on the doorknob, as if urgency alone could open it. "Matilda!" Could she hear him? She wasn't moving. Professor Jenson switched from rattling the doorknob to banging on the glass pane. "Someone help! Matilda!" His heart was pounding, slow and hard, then it caught and abruptly picked up pace. He stared at Mrs. Gardner's helpless bare legs and let the fear course through him.

◇◈◇◈

As Ben raced to the first floor, he racked his brain for who else could be in the shop. Had Mrs. Baumgartner somehow stayed inside and gotten hurt? Arnold and Scott followed quickly behind him, down to the second floor and then the first. As they reached the top of the first-floor stairs, a sorry sight greeted them. Mrs. Gardner was sprawled out on her stomach in the middle of the floor. Her skirt was twisted around her knees, and her legs were at awkward angles. She wasn't moving or speaking, and Ben had a moment of dread like he'd never known. But then she moaned and the relief came crashing in. She was alive. Thank You, God!

"Mrs. Gardner! How did you . . . ? Are you . . . ? What happened?" Ben jogged down the steps and raced to her side. Arnold and Scott pounded down the steps behind him.

A loud banging on the front door drew Ben's attention. A hysterical-looking Professor Jenson was plastered to the front door, both fists raised as if he'd been trying to break the door down. He heard a muffled "Ben! Thank God! Matilda is hurt!"

"Yes, I can see that!" Ben shouted back and turned to the prostrate Mrs. Gardner.

"Ben! Let me in!"

"Do you know this woman, Ben?" Scott was squatting by Mrs. Gardner, who was still moaning.

"That's Matilda Gardner, one of my customers." Ben squatted down and placed a hand on her shoulder.

"Ben! Let me in!" More hysterical banging.

"I'm trying to see . . . would you just . . ." Ben started toward the door and then turned, torn and confused. What was happening? He needed to turn Mrs. Gardner over and make sure she was okay, see if they needed to call an ambulance.

"I got it, Ben." Arnold dashed to the front door to let his cousin in. Gratefully, Ben turned back to Mrs. Gardner and, with Scott's help, slowly turned her over so that she was facing up. Ben gently loosened the twisted fabric around her knees and arranged it over her legs.

"Mrs. Gardner, can you hear me? Can you understand me? Can you tell me where you're hurt?"

"Matilda! Oh, dear Lord, no." Professor Jenson was walking as quickly as he could to the small group forming around the fallen Mrs. Gardner, Arnold close behind him. "I heard the shrieks. She must have fallen down the stairs."

"Matilda?" Mrs. Baumgartner suddenly materialized in the front doorway. "Is everything okay?"

"Aha, there you are!" Professor Jenson pointed an accusing finger at the new arrival.

"Just everyone be quiet for a moment," Ben snapped and leaned closer to Mrs. Gardner. "Please let me know where you're hurt. Can you move your legs? your ankles?"

Mrs. Gardner moaned but moved both legs and swiveled both feet to prove that her ankles were intact. There was a collective sigh of relief.

"I-I think she's okay." Mrs. Baumgartner was kneeling next to Ben now. "You're okay, right Matilda? You just took a little spill on these unsafe stairs, right?"

Mrs. Gardner clutched her friend's hand and pulled hard, raising herself slightly from the floor. "Yes," she gasped. "I fell, I really *did* fall."

"I know, dear. Poor thing." Mrs. Baumgartner patted her friend's hand. "You'll be just fine though. Something really should be done about these unsafe stairs."

"No no, I fell, Anita. I *fell*."

"Yes, dear," Mrs. Baumgartner placated. "But you'll be okay."

"What's going on here?"

Six heads simultaneously turned to see Mrs. Frank standing in the middle of the first-floor stairs, her brow furrowed as she observed the cluster of people below.

"Mrs. Frank? Where did you come from? Were you upstairs?" Ben's head was beginning to pound.

"Matilda fell down the stairs." Professor Jenson had shoved Scott aside and was attempting to squat next to Mrs. Gardner without falling himself.

"Yes, of course she did." Mrs. Frank didn't appear to see the reason for all the fuss.

"No, she really fell. I saw it happen, almost," Professor Jenson insisted.

"What do you mean, *really* fell?" Ben looked from person to person, but he was being largely ignored.

"I think you've quite made your point, Matilda." Mrs. Frank reached the bottom of the steps and hovered by Mrs. Gardner's feet.

"Point?" Ben questioned.

"Do we need to call an ambulance?" Arnold piped up.

"I don't know. I'm trying to see if she's okay, but . . ." Ben gestured helplessly at the constricting crowd of people.

"Can you move your arms? your hands?" This from Professor Jenson, who had finally managed to squat.

"No, really, I think she's okay," Mrs. Baumgartner chimed in.

Mrs. Gardner slowly stretched her left arm out, but when she tried to move the right, she winced and let out a whimper. "I think it might be broken," she gasped.

"Anita, I think she might actually be hurt." Mrs. Frank's expression had shifted and she shoved Scott out of the way so she could lower herself to her creaky knees next to Professor Jenson.

"That's what I've been trying to tell you!" Professor Jenson shouted in a voice that indicated he'd about reached his limit.

"Matilda, blink once if you're hurt and twice if you're not."

"What? That doesn't make any sense, Anita. She can speak."

"No, I mean, I'm just saying . . . so we can know for sure."

"That still doesn't make any sense."

"What do you mean, *actually* hurt?" Ben interjected. "What's going on?"

"Just blink for me, Matilda. Yes or no?" Mrs. Baumgartner was speaking slowly and loudly.

"For crying out loud, she's not deaf or dumb, Anita."

Mrs. Gardner wasn't doing any blinking. She had her eyes squeezed shut and was now clutching Professor Jenson's hand. "I—fell—down—the—steps," she managed through gritted teeth.

"Don't just stand there, all of you!" Professor Jenson was patting Mrs. Gardner's head with his free hand. "She's hurt and needs medical attention!"

"I have a car right outside," Arnold spoke up. "I can drive her to the nearest hospital."

"Do you need that, Matilda? Do you need to go to the hospital?" Mrs. Baumgartner pronounced slowly and loudly.

Scott was helping Professor Jenson to his feet and Arnold and Ben were helping Mrs. Gardner to hers. "Yes. Hospital. Thank you," Mrs. Gardner said, wincing.

"Emma, you're right, she's hurt. Oh Matilda, I'm so sorry!" Mrs. Baumgartner's calm shattered, and she began to cry. Mrs. Frank put an arm around her friend.

"It's okay." Mrs. Gardner's teeth were gritted and she was hunched over. Clearly most of her body was in pain and not just the arm. She'd latched on to Professor Jenson's hand again. Ben supported her on the other side, careful to avoid the damaged arm, and together they all hobbled to the front door. Scott propped the door open for the slow-moving cluster; Arnold raced to his car, started it, and moved it parallel to the door. Mrs. Frank held Mrs. Baumgartner, and Mrs. Baumgartner wailed.

The front steps were the trickiest part. Mrs. Gardner refused to let go of Professor Jenson's hand, which made matters a bit more difficult, seeing as Professor Jenson couldn't sufficiently support her. As Ben moved to Mrs.

Gardner's left side, Professor Jenson stood in front of her, holding her left hand and staring up into her pain-filled face. Scott helped steady the group from behind as Ben, who was holding most of the weight, urged the group forward. Somehow they all made it to the bottom, Professor Jenson treading the steps backward in order to keep ahold of Mrs. Gardner's hand. Arnold opened the rear car door and helped usher Mrs. Gardner inside. Professor Jenson followed, still attached by the hand.

Scott stood panting next to Ben, his camera hanging down his back, most likely to keep it unscathed and out of the way. "Ben, I'm thinking we'll just reschedule, in light of everything."

"Hmm? Oh yes, yes, I'm so sorry, Scott. Thank you for your time, and thank you so much for all your help. I don't know what happened back there. Nothing like this has ever happened before."

"Don't worry about it. I'm just glad everyone's okay, or at least will be." Scott clapped Ben on the back and headed to his truck, readjusting his camera as he went. Mrs. Frank and Mrs. Baumgartner had joined Ben on the front walk and were tearfully waving at Mrs. Gardner, even though the car hadn't moved and was only a few feet away.

Arnold popped his head above the car before getting back inside. "Another time, Ben?"

"Yes, sorry, we'll be in touch."

Arnold nodded and ducked back inside, easing the car onto the ragged brick road. The car banged along, Mrs. Gardner moaned, Professor Jenson fretted, and the remaining spectators stood in various stages of tearful, openmouthed disarray on the sidewalk in front of Palermo's as the curtain closed on the day's comedy of errors.

**The girl walks toward the light and experiences a sharp sense of déjà vu.** *The fort is back up, the blanket draped across the backs of three chairs this time, formed into a triangle. A soft light is emanating through the blanket, turning the fabric blood red. A pair of sneakered feet stick out and there is the sound of crunching. The girl experiences none of the fear she'd felt two and a half years before. Instead there is a blinding joy as she rushes to the fort and playfully pulls on the feet. "BJ!"*

# CHAPTER SIXTEEN

## ONE STEP AT A TIME

Ben entered St. John's with a lump in his throat and an uncomfortable tightness in his chest. He'd done something he hadn't done before—he'd made an appointment with his pastor to talk pastor to congregant, friend to friend. The fiasco from earlier that week had left him shaken and questioning. It was high time to talk it through with Dale.

Ben walked down the hall toward the pastor's office, the bitter smell of coffee wafting toward him. "Hey, it *is* you." Dale poked his head around the corner, a smile spreading across his face, making his ears pop out even more. "I thought I heard something. Come on in, Ben." He extended a hand and clasped Ben's in a strong grip. Walking into Dale's office, Ben was instantly enveloped in a sense of studious warmth. Dark cherry paneling, built-in bookshelves, and overstuffed chairs all formed a tasteful, comfortable atmosphere. "I made some coffee for us." Dale gestured toward the French press on his desk. "I realize at ten in the morning you've most likely had your first cup, but I'm a strong believer in second and third cups of coffee."

Ben laughed and accepted the proffered mug, moving to the desk to fill it. "I'll second that opinion."

As Ben poured, Dale grabbed his full mug and sat in a chair by the window, avoiding, Ben noted, the chair behind his desk. "There's been a lot of chatter about you lately, Ben. I have to admit that I've heard some confusing accounts of things happening in your store this week. I was glad to receive your call."

"Yes," Ben sighed, sitting in the chair next to Dale. The sun streaming through the windows created streaks across the side table between them. "And that's partially what I wanted to talk to you about. I just . . . I don't really know where to begin."

Dale put his mug on a coaster and leaned back. "I sense there's something larger at stake here."

Ben didn't find it easy to confide in people. Since his parents died, he'd lost two major confidants, and he had never really found others to fill that void. Now, his heart in his throat, he allowed himself to return to a place of vulnerability. "Dale, I'll be honest with you. I've been entertaining thoughts of selling Palermo's for a while now. I just don't know what I'm doing here. I fell into this life, as you know. I love this town, this church, the people, but I feel restless ninety-five percent of the time—almost like I'm not doing enough or not doing the right things with my life. The problem is, I don't know what the alternative is."

"Have you felt like this since coming here?"

"Honestly, I never expected to be here this long. I'd intended to assess the business for a year at the most with the intention of selling, but then I just got into a routine, and I also couldn't avoid the fact that the place holds so many memories. I hadn't been back since I was fourteen. Not since my parents died."

"That must have been incredibly hard on you, especially at such a crucial age. I don't think I've ever asked you about it in detail."

Ben felt a twinge of discomfort. He didn't really want

to bring his parents into this. He'd much rather focus on what to do with the bookstore. "Yeah, it was rough. I didn't have the typical angst-filled relationship with my parents that you might expect from a teenager. They were always my best friends."

"And you went to live with your grandmother after that, correct?"

Ben appreciated that Dale wasn't rushing the conversation and instead, with gentle questions and a listening ear, was letting him talk as much as he needed to. "Yes. My grandma was older and had trouble getting around, which meant we didn't do any traveling. She passed away when I was in college."

"So coming here after so much time, it must have been difficult." They both sat in silence. After a moment, Dale said thoughtfully, "It's hard, when tragedy hits close to home, to have to be reminded of it every day."

Ben looked down at his hands. The conversation was moving in a direction he hadn't anticipated.

Dale spoke softly. "Ben, I'm not trying to presume upon your emotions. Listening to your story made me realize how hard it must be to be confronted with your past day in and day out, to be reminded of it constantly."

"Yes, that's been the hardest part of living here, of running Palermo's."

"It might be easier to make a clean break with painful histories, to purge ourselves, so to speak, of the reminders. But that's not always possible and, I might add, not always helpful in the long run."

"I've kind of made a life habit of moving forward."

"Yes, driven people are sometimes driven by fear rather than passion."

"I hadn't thought of it that way." Ben grew quiet.

"You know this, Ben, but I'll say it anyway. We are not a people without hope. First Thessalonians 4:13 states, 'But we do not want you to be uninformed, brothers, about those who are asleep, that you may not grieve as others do who have no hope.' It is with that hope that we can move forward. Without it, and without relying on the Holy Spirit for daily comfort, there is no moving forward; there is only reliving the past and, with it, the pain. Jesus assures us in John 14 that He 'will not leave you as orphans; I will come to you.' And He gives the Holy Spirit as our Comforter, precisely so that in times of unspeakable tragedy, we will know that we are not alone in this world and have the hope of the world to come."

Ben hunched over and let the words wash over him, his face in his hands.

"In regard to your store, Ben, I can't tell you what to do or not to do with it. But I do know that the decision you make shouldn't be based on a desire to run from the past."

"Is running the store what God wants me to do then?" Ben lifted his head, his face stricken. "How do I change how I feel? I want to be passionate about what I do and not feel trapped. How do you know you are where you're supposed to be?"

"Vocation is a tricky thing. Our culture has it backward, you know. We infuse our children with platitudes: 'Follow your heart,' 'Find your bliss,' et cetera. And then the Christian response seems to be a belated 'God, bless what I've already decided to do.' Instead, we need to flip this around and seek God first. Also, if you think about it, the world and even Christians view what they do in primarily self-centered terms. How does this serve me? How does this fulfill me? When really, vocation was never about finding personal fulfillment—that can only be found in our identity in Christ. Instead, vocation is about serving God and others through our various callings. Luther had it right when he called vocation a 'mask of God.' God is at work through human means."

"I understand what you're saying, and I do realize that I've perhaps been looking at this backward, but I guess I'm still just wondering how to get a sense of direction. I mean, if God wants me to move on, I should do that, right? But making that determination seems so difficult. I wish I had a sense of peace about where I'm at right now."

Dale took a sip of cold coffee. "I understand where you're coming from, but I would challenge you to look at this differently too. It's not about finding the perfect set of circumstances—there is no such thing in this fallen world. It's about being faithful in the circumstances you're in. God simply calls us to be faithful, but even in faithfulness, peace can elude us if we're not fully trusting God. If we spend our time worrying over a perceived lack of peace and direction, we are missing the point and skipping over the whole trust part. The point is to be faithful and to set our minds on Christ, and trust in Him alone. It may sound simplistic, but oftentimes we complicate and muddy things through human reasoning. As Paul says in First Corinthians, God chooses the simple things to confound the wise. Just look at the cross—there can be nothing more simple and powerful than that, and yet how we humans love to tamper and play with the clarity God has given!"

Dale stared down at his empty mug. "I'm going to admit something to you, Ben." He leaned back, set his mug down, and rested his clasped hands on a knee. "I've struggled with this very thing myself in recent years. When I received this call, Sarah and I were hoping for a call out east. That's where most of her family is, and with twins on the way, we wanted to be near family. But God had other plans; we received a call to St. John's Lutheran Church in New Holden, Indiana. Neither of us have family in this area. Neither of us are even familiar with the Midwest. Honestly, it felt like exile. Sarah should have had the harder time adjusting. She was the one, after all, carrying our twins and setting up our home thousands of miles from her mother, but she was such a rock for me during that time. Every time I questioned God's call, she replied, 'Dale, who are we to decide how and where God wants to use us? If we're here, then that means we have something to accomplish here. God isn't in the business of deserting His children.'" Dale smiled at the thought of his wife. "She is an incredibly strong woman, and so very right. God's desires for us are so much bigger than our earthly plans, and all He asks is that we are faithful and trust Him and His love and care for us. Isaiah 26:3 tells us that peace comes from a mind trusting in and 'stayed on' Christ. Peace is never to be found in circumstances and always to be found in Christ."

Ben had been listening silently the entire time, his mug of coffee forgotten, his hands clasped and trembling in his lap. He felt embarrassed at the emotion coursing through him and unsure how to contain it. At Dale's confession of his own struggle, Ben finally broke down. He didn't realize he was crying until Dale finished speaking and turned to him with a concerned look on his face. He didn't say a word. Instead he stood and grabbed a tissue box from his desk, proffering it to Ben in silent support. "Thanks. I don't remember the last time I cried, let alone in front of someone."

"Hey, that's okay. No judgment here. The Lord knows I've shed my share of tears."

Ben laughed, and the tension eased. "Thank you for sharing with me and for everything you said. It was exactly what I needed to hear."

"God be praised, Ben. I'm happy to talk anytime." Dale paused and then looked at Ben out of the corner of his eye. "So . . . is it true that a group of women tried to sabotage the appraisal of your store?"

"Sabotage is the perfect word for it." Ben laughed and shook his head. After Mrs. Gardner had been ferried off to the hospital, he'd cornered Mrs. Frank and Mrs. Baumgartner and extracted a full confession. It hadn't been difficult, given the state of their nerves at the time. "What have you heard?"

"Well, I'm almost embarrassed to say . . . something about a ghost, of all things, and 'treacherous' stairs."

"Well, let me set the record straight." Ben recounted the misadventures from the other day while his friend listened with great amusement. When he'd finished, he stated, "I was furious at first, but then I began to see another side to it. It's kind of humbling, really, to know that you and your store are so loved that people would be willing to risk so much to see you stay."

Dale laughed. "That's what I was thinking. You may feel restless, Ben, but you are clearly very much loved here."

"I know, that's what keeps running through my mind— that, and the way I felt taking the first step toward selling. I didn't feel an ounce of peace the entire time. I just felt so unsettled about the whole idea, and not just because it's a big endeavor or because I don't have another job to go to. I think I need to take time to really process all of this and pray."

"That's always a good idea," Dale said with a nod. "And perhaps take the appropriate precautions against Mrs. Gardner and her gang." There was a gleam in his eye.

"Poor Mrs. Gardner. Turns out, she actually did break her arm."

"I heard about that," Dale said. "Professor Jenson called the office to add her to the prayer list."

The two men stood and clasped hands. "Thanks again, Dale. I can't begin to tell you how helpful you've been."

"The mask of God, Ben. We are all given the privilege of being the mask of God in the roles He's called us to fill."

Ben left the church lighter than he'd entered it. He still wasn't entirely sure what to do about the store, but he had gained a sense of peace and clarity for the moment. It wasn't his place to know the next one hundred steps. God was simply calling him to faithfully take the next one. Wasn't that how life was lived, after all? He would trust God to direct one step at a time.

**The boy feels a tug on his foot and hears the sharp exclamation, "BJ!"** His heart stops and then quickly starts again. For a moment, he imagines that the Story People are there, ready to drag him from their home. But no, it is the girl, her face open and lit up with joy and enthusiasm.

"Rosie!" The two friends stand and regard each other. The boy notices that she's grown much taller since he's seen her last. Her hair isn't any less poufy and still forms a halo around her head; her eyes are just as bright as before, just as mischievous and ready for adventure. Finally, he grabs her in a hug and then pulls her into his fort by the hand.

"I can't believe you're actually here," the girl says breathlessly. "I got all your notes. Did you get all of mine?"

"Yup! I got all of your messages. I really liked your drawings." It's just like before, the two of them in the hideout. The boy passes her the open box of crackers he'd been snacking on. There is a cozy sense of safety beneath this blanket, like they are the only two people in the world but safe as long as they are here, sheltered by this blanket, hidden away in this moment.

# Chapter Seventeen

## ASKING HER TO REMEMBER HIM

W asn't there a survey or something that proved that people were more frightened of public speaking than of dying? Rosemary stood outside Liam's classroom at Glen Park Lutheran School, waiting to be introduced, her hands shaky. Surely she hadn't made that crazy statistic up. Standing here, feeling like she was ready to pass out, she could almost believe that this fear was worse than the fear of death, however improbable that sounded. As Rosemary often did when she was nervous, she had overprepared for the event. But preparation, however helpful at the time, did little to assuage the nervousness now coursing through her. Who knew third graders could be so intimidating? "Lord, calm my nerves. Help me to just speak from the heart and honor You."

Also worrying at the back of Rosemary's mind was the fear of failing in front of Liam. Only a month had passed since their Chicago trip, but the knowledge of Liam's interest had created an awkward strain. She was certain Liam remained oblivious, but she felt like she was on tiptoe around him, not knowing whether to feel flattered or annoyed; in either case, she definitely did not want to let him down today. His admiration was oddly compelling and frustrating and attractive and confusing all at once, which created a desire to live up to his impression of her.

"I've invited a friend to come here today." Liam's voice was muffled through the glass-paned door. Rosemary watched him move in her direction. She gripped her book tighter and hoisted her tote bag onto her shoulder, taking a deep breath as Liam opened the door. "My friend Rosemary is here to talk to us about being an illustrator and an author. Let's all welcome Rosemary." Twenty-five pairs of little hands clapped their hardest as she entered the room.

"Thank you very much for having me here today. I'm so glad I can visit and talk with you all." Rosemary deposited her bag on Liam's desk and turned to face the children with her book. "How many of you like stories?" All the hands shot up in the air. "Me too! In fact, when I was little, I liked to imagine that I could walk into my favorite storybooks. Wouldn't that be awesome?" There were lots of affirmative nods and noises.

"Unless your favorite book was *Jurassic Park*, and then it wouldn't be so good," a little boy in the front piped up. The class laughed and Liam made a shushing motion.

"That's true," Rosemary laughed. "Well, when I was a little girl, I kept track of all my story ideas in my head. I eventually began writing them down and drawing pictures to go along with them, and that's how I came to write and illustrate my book, *Spectrum*. It's a story about a little girl who goes into a storybook." Rosemary showed them her book. "Would you like me to read it to you?"

A chorus of yeses filled the air. Rosemary positioned the book so the children could see the pictures and began. "Once there was a little girl named Ivy, who lived in a world of black and white." As Rosemary continued to read, she relaxed into the familiar narrative, the nerves and tension from before all easing away in the comfortable environment of her story. The children all sat in rapt attention, leaning forward with elbows on their desks. She was aware of Liam standing nearby, hip against the wall, observing her with a smile. When Rosemary reached the end of the book, Liam was the first to lead the applause.

Rosemary set the book aside and turned back to the class. "I hope you enjoyed my story. Now I want to talk to you about *your* stories. There is a story inside each and every one of you. God made you unique. Your thoughts, your ideas, they are all good gifts from Him; so don't be afraid to share those ideas with others. That's how we learn from one another. I know you all have been studying creative writing, and I want to encourage you all to continue writing. I've brought each of you what I call an 'idea journal.'" Rosemary handed out notebooks and brightly colored pencils. "Personalize your journal, make it your own, and then keep it somewhere handy. Then, anytime you get an idea, whatever that idea is, write it or draw it in your idea journal. Look, I brought my very first idea journal to share with you." Rosemary pulled out a tattered purple notebook with Hello Kitty and Lisa Frank stickers plastered all over it. *ROSIE* was scrawled with gel pens in large bubble letters across the top.

A little hand shot up. "Can you read us some of your ideas?"

Rosemary flipped open the notebook. "Here's a poem called 'I See.' Look, I even drew blue glasses and crazy eyebrows to go along with it." She turned the notebook around and showed it to the kids. There were some appreciative murmurs. "Okay, here goes: I see a tree and he sees me! / Me and the tree traveled out to sea, / so we could see all the things there could be to see! / I see another tree climb on board with me and my friend, tree. / I see a bee! / But that is another story!"

Snickers rippled throughout the class, and a little boy in the back row shouted, "That's silly."

Rosemary smiled. "I agree, it is kind of silly, isn't it? But you see, that's the whole point. These journals are places for you to be as silly and creative as you want to be. Who knows? Maybe a silly little something will inspire you to write or illustrate your own book someday. In the meantime, don't let the fear of being too silly or of getting it wrong hold you back."

Rosemary sucked in her breath and stopped. A sense of God's presence surrounded her. It was as if God was using her own words to target and speak to her. She closed her eyes briefly and smiled, then opened them again to look at the eager faces turned to her. Some of the kids were already flipping through their notebooks or drawing on the covers. "Yes," she repeated, "don't let fear hold you back. Use the voice and thoughts and ideas God gave you, because they are valuable, just as each and every one of you is valuable to Him."

Liam led another round of applause, his eyes shining as he walked toward her. "Thank you, Rosemary, for taking the time to talk with us today about sharing ideas and stories, and thank you for the gifts."

"It was my pleasure." Rosemary smiled and gathered up her things. As she turned to leave, she caught Liam's eye. He silently mouthed, "I'll see you later." Rosemary smiled and nodded, her cheeks burning. She'd agreed to have dinner with him while she was in the area. She'd done so out of a desire to get back to the old times when conversation had been easy between them. He was, after all, her good friend. But seeing the expectant look in his eye and feeling the small leap in her chest in response, Rosemary wondered if agreeing to dinner had been a wise move.

◇◆◇◆

"They loved you! They couldn't stop talking about you!" Liam leaned back in their booth at the Sushi Bar and beamed at Rosemary.

"I'm so glad. Honestly, it was such a blessing to me as well. You should have seen me pacing outside the classroom door though. You would have thought I was about to face a crazed mob."

"Well, that's not an entirely inaccurate description of my kids some days." Liam smirked as he took a drink of water.

"Oh come on, they were wonderful!"

"They were on their best behavior. But you're right, I have a great class, and I know it."

Rosemary settled into her seat with a twinge of hope. Things felt familiar and free between them again. Maybe she didn't have to distance herself from her friend after all. Maybe, in fact, Clare and Becca had been wrong.

Their rolls and miso soup arrived and Liam asked the blessing. For a while, they ate in companionable silence. This was something they both ardently agreed upon: truly good sushi is an experience. There'd been a sorry shortage of decent sushi restaurants near their alma mater, much to their chagrin. Locating a Sushi Bar so close to Liam's school had been an exciting discovery. Near the end of the meal, Rosemary set her plate aside and leaned forward conspiratorially. "Want to know what I've been up to this afternoon?" She reached into her bag and pulled out a sketch pad. The inspiration she'd received in Liam's class and the conviction she'd felt at hearing her own advice to the kids had sparked an idea in Rosemary that wouldn't shake loose.

"Please tell me you're working on another book."

"You stole my thunder!" Rosemary laughed. "I just realized something when I was talking to your kids. The only thing that's been holding me back this whole time is really just a disgusting mixture of fear and pride."

Liam cocked his head. "How do you mean?"

"Well, fear of failure, sure, and fear of not being able to find a subject I'm passionate about. But it's more than that. I realized that I'm such a perfectionist and am so caught up in how people see me and my work that I'm afraid another book won't be as good as *Spectrum*."

"Ah, like you hit a home run and now it's time to just turn in your bat and end on a high note."

"I guess. Silly, right?"

"Um, yes, certifiably insane, actually."

"I realized that if I'm going to stand here telling these kids that all of their ideas are valuable and a gift from God and to not let fear hold them back from sharing their ideas and stories, then I had better start taking my own advice."

"Yes, otherwise you're just . . . what's the word?" Liam stroked his chin as if in thought. "A *hypocrite*, that's right."

Rosemary smacked his arm from across the table. "Hey now. So I've been spending the last few hours trying to take my advice to heart." She gazed at the sketchbook in her hands, suddenly nervous. Her return to Palermo's, the discovery of BJ, it had all brought back the Story People to her—old, familiar friends, who were waiting to be told and to be shared. "So, when I was a kid, I had these imaginary friends, sort of. They were more like imaginary creatures who lived in this bookstore back in the town where my Oma lives." She found she was leaving out BJ and she wasn't sure why. She just knew that she wanted to keep him and Liam separate. "They were called the Story People, and they snuck around eating the stories in the bookstore." Rosemary opened the sketchbook and handed it to Liam, who began slowly paging through it. "So I've sketched some preliminary concepts based, actually, on drawings I did as a child. It was such a powerful, imaginative story for me growing up, and I'm hoping I can translate that into pictures and a compelling story for others." There was a heavy silence as she watched Liam take in the sketches and the bits of description written in the margins. Rosemary cleared her throat nervously. "What do you think? Would it make sense to other kids? Or is it just some jumbled childhood make-believe story?"

Finally Liam placed the sketchbook down and reached across the table to grab her hand. "Rosemary, you are so incredibly talented. Seriously, these are fun and creative and will definitely resonate with kids."

Rosemary wanted to be happy at the positive feedback, but Liam was still holding her hand, which wasn't typical. He began to rub the top of her hand with his thumb. She gulped and pulled her hand back to tuck a strand of hair behind her ear in order to release her hand without offending him. "Thank you."

"These are based on an actual bookstore?" Liam was looking at a sketch of the Palermo's Books storefront.

"Y-yes." Rosemary was still shaken. It had been a bad idea to agree to dinner. The last thing she wanted was to lead him on, but she also didn't want to lose her friend. With a pang, she regretted showing Liam the sketches—it put him alarmingly close to BJ, to the special connection she had with her childhood friend. It felt like a betrayal. *I want to show these to Ben*, she realized with a start. It was Ben's store, after all, and if she were being completely honest, it was Ben's idea in the first place. He'd been the one to introduce her to the Story People. He'd invited her into the world he'd created, and here she was, taking credit for it and showing it to someone else. She felt sick to her stomach.

"I think you should definitely develop this. I'd love to look at your drafts as you go along. I'm always available if you want to bounce ideas off of someone."

"Thanks, Liam. That's kind of you."

They were interrupted by the server showing up with their check. Liam quickly reached for his wallet. "It's on me."

"Oh no, you don't have to, Liam."

"I insist. As a thank-you for taking the time to come all the way out here and for inspiring my kids."

Rosemary watched him pay, a lump in her throat. Becca had been right. Hard-nosed, emotionally closed-off Becca had seen right to the truth of this situation: this trip meant something different to Liam than it did to her. The sick feeling in her stomach intensified.

"I'm serious about bouncing ideas off me." Liam was handing the sketchbook back to her. She took it and their hands brushed, causing her throat to tighten. Why couldn't things have stayed the way they'd been? How many times had they bummed around together? Studying, grabbing late-night food, joking, commiserating, encouraging? They were friends, and now, suddenly, she couldn't decide how she should or shouldn't act. Every small action seemed to have momentous implications.

"Thanks for the encouragement. I'll let you know how things progress." They gathered up their things, and Liam held the door for her as they left.

"This was fun. I'd say let's make an evening of it, but I know you have a long drive back, and I have school in the morning."

Rosemary felt a twinge of gratitude. "It was fun though. I'm glad I got to speak to your class." They were standing by Rosemary's car. She had her key in hand, and there was an awkward pause.

"Well, I'll let you get going, but we'll have to plan something soon. Next time I can come to you, and I'll expect further development on this book." He grinned.

"Yes, of course. Just let me know."

She was turning to leave, but Liam stopped her with an arm around her shoulder. Her breath caught as he drew her to his chest in a big hug. Her head bumped against his, awkwardly at first, and then settled so that her cheek was resting against his neck. She could feel his pulse throbbing in his neck and smell the sharp scent of his deodorant. "Thanks again, Clooney," he murmured into her hair.

Rosemary stood stock-still, unsure of what to do with her body. This, she decided, was definitely not a friend hug. Friend hugs were quick squeezes with minimal body contact, oftentimes even conducted side to side. This prolonged hug in which she was completely enveloped in his arms? Well, it was definitely not a friend hug. His face and a free hand were in her hair, his fingers brushing the back of her neck, giving her goose bumps. Rosemary quieted the panic long enough to focus on the feeling of his arms around her. She had to admit that this non–friend hug wasn't exactly unpleasant. She felt a rush of warmth. Liam really was such a good guy, so encouraging and supportive. He was genuine and a wonderful teacher who truly loved kids. She didn't want to miss out on something good because of her usual reticence. She needed to be open, to let herself be vulnerable, right? Was her hesitation because of the idea of a relationship, though, or because of Liam specifically? When should she pay attention to her reservations and when should she push through them? And when should she just stop thinking, stop overanalyzing everything, and be in the moment? She found herself awkwardly reaching an arm around him, patting his back. "It was my pleasure, Liam. We'll talk again soon, okay?" She leaned back to break the hug, sensing that if she didn't, he might not do it either, and then who knew where that would lead?

Rosemary got into her car, her chest tight with a mixture of emotion. She dumped her bag onto the passenger seat and pulled out of the parking lot, Liam waving to her in the rearview mirror. As she merged onto the highway, she glanced over to see that her sketchbook had spilled open. Her heart clutched even more. It was a sketch Liam would have seen but not understood. It was a sketch of a curly-haired boy with dark, intense eyes surrounded by shadows, asking her to remember him.

**The girl learns that the boy's favorite books are The Boxcar Children, and the boy learns that the girl's favorites are The Chronicles of Narnia books.** They each vow to read the other's chosen series.

"I'll let you know how I like the books," the girl promises. "Do you think the Story People have favorite books too?"

"They must," the boy says matter-of-factly. "I bet you the different stories taste different."

"That's true!" the girl exclaims. "I bet the Narnia books taste like the tea Mr. Tumnus feeds Lucy."

"I'm not sure who Tumnus is, but that sounds delicious," the boy laughs. "The Boxcar Children books probably taste like milk, cherries, and bread."

"Booooring," the girl chants, and the boy gives her a grimace.

Together they speculate on the taste of every book they can think of.

# CHAPTER EIGHTEEN

## THE BEGINNINGS OF A BEGRUDGING AFFECTION

The man was beginning to be a nuisance. Honestly, she'd held his hand during one of the most harrowing times of her life, and now he'd gone and developed a superiority complex in which he behaved as though he were the only one who could adequately take care of her. Every morning at seven thirty sharp, Professor Jenson knocked on her front door, ready to make her breakfast.

"What will you have this morning, Matilda? Eggs? Toast? Oatmeal?"

Honestly, one would think she was confined to her bed, so closely did Professor Jenson monitor her. She'd tried shooing him away.

"Mark, I'm fine, really. The Ladies' Aid has things under control." And indeed they did. Spearheaded by Mrs. Frank and Mrs. Baumgartner, the women of the church had been bringing meals with such regularity that she'd begun freezing them. Her deep freezer in the basement rivaled that of a doomsday prepper. Dora, too, had stopped by with soup, apple tart, and her famous bread. Mrs. Gardner was a tad chagrined, however, that as soon as Dora had seen how much help was coming from the church, she'd backed off. Help from family was always welcome, no matter where else it was coming from. Mrs. Gardner sighed and tried to shoo away Professor Jenson yet again. "I can handle things for myself from here on out."

"You broke an arm and bruised your tailbone. You are hardly okay." The severity in Professor Jenson's tone allowed for no argument.

And so Mrs. Gardner spent her days waited on hand and foot by her next-door neighbor. It was oddly comforting, though, to have a male presence around the house again. She'd adjusted after her husband's death, but she couldn't deny it was good to look over at the armchair and see Professor Jenson reclined with a book. It was pleasant to hear a male voice in the other room, to know he was just a call away should she need anything.

Others came and went. Women from the church continued to stop by with baked goodies or just to sit and visit, but in the background, like a steady hum, was Professor Jenson.

"Is he here all the time, Matilda?" Mrs. Frank asked at one point, her face teetering between surprise and hilarity.

"No, not all the time! Gracious!" It was at that point that Mrs. Gardner began insisting Professor Jenson go home or at least hide somewhere when she had visitors.

"Are you ashamed of me, Matilda?"

"No, I wouldn't say that!" Mrs. Gardner fumbled. "But we womenfolk . . . we like our privacy, you see."

"Aha, so you can gossip about us menfolk?"

"Well, no, not exactly. It's just unnerving to some of the women to see you sitting around, like you're snooping on us or something."

"Huh," Professor Jenson snorted. "Fine."

"I see Professor Jenson has finally left you alone," Mrs. Baumgartner noticed not long after.

"Oh, um, yes, ha-ha, indeed." Mrs. Gardner cleared her

throat and shot a glance toward the hall, not wanting to admit that Professor Jenson was currently stuffed into her craft room, last door on the left, with strict instructions to remain there until the all clear.

What continued to surprise Mrs. Gardner the most was Professor Jenson's willingness to even come to her aid in the first place. She'd tried broaching the subject during lunch one day.

"Mark," she said past a bite of ham sandwich, "why are you doing all of this? Let's not pretend that you don't find me . . . annoying."

Professor Jenson ducked his head, staring with the utmost attention at the salad on his plate. "I feel partially responsible."

"Responsible? How on earth could you be responsible? Were you there forcing me to ridiculously parade around on the stairs? Were you the one who came up with the scheme in the first place?"

"No . . ."

"Then none of this nonsense about being responsible." Mrs. Gardner sighed and slumped in her chair, for once sincerely repentant and docile. "People have told me for ages that my interfering would get me in trouble someday, and here we are. No, if anyone is to blame, it's my own foolish self."

◇◆◇◆

Professor Jenson couldn't stand seeing her this way. He hadn't realized what a comfortable staple Mrs. Gardner's incessant cheerfulness and meddling had become in his life until he was forced to confront her sad and humbled demeanor head-on. Apparently he enjoyed the familiarity of her meddling ways more than he disliked her prying and chattering. Yes, her scheme had been ridiculous, but at least she had acted when no one else would. She was a woman who stood up for what she cared for, and he could understand and appreciate that attribute. This confounding, irritating woman was oddly inspiring and endearing. Quite beautiful too, come to think of it.

Professor Jenson looked at her downcast face and thought back to that thrilling moment in the store when she'd grabbed his hand. He, Mark Samuel Jenson, had been singled out, even above her closest friends, to be the provider of comfort and solace during her hour of need. Professor Jenson had often returned to this memory during the last few days, and it never failed to fill him with a startling, sharp joy: her desperate hand, fluttering, reaching toward him; her refusal to let go, even at the front steps; the way she'd only squeezed tighter, causing all blood flow to cease; how she'd fairly dragged him into the car with her. There'd been no sidewalk debate on who should accompany her. Mrs. Frank? Mrs. Baumgartner? No, only he, Mark Samuel Jenson, would do. His chest swelled at the memory. He'd brought Mrs. Gardner's desperate hand-holding up to her, slyly, importantly, but she'd hemmed and hawed and overall hedged the issue.

"Purely an instinctual thing, Mark. You were closest to me, and I needed the support in the moment."

Professor Jenson had pointed out that Ben had, in actuality, been in closer proximity to Mrs. Gardner at the time.

"Well, I don't know about that. I mean, you were the only one who actually *believed* me in the moment."

So it hadn't been simply . . . what term had she used? Instinctual?

"Well, what else do you call relying on the only person who believes you and doesn't think you're crying wolf?" Mrs. Gardner persisted.

Professor Jenson could think of several things, and they all made the pit of his stomach go soft. It was good to be needed, very good indeed. If only he could communicate effectively with the sad woman before him, assure her that she wasn't a failure—but Professor Jenson had always been a man of action over a man of words, and so he continued to make her food and get her mail and keep her company and shuffle out of her way whenever a visitor called as the only way he knew of telling her that she was cared for. His hand was hers for the holding.

◇◆◇◆

"No no, the teaspoon is the small one. Whatever you do, don't put in a tablespoon of salt or you'll have us gagging on the food." Mrs. Gardner fluttered around Professor Jenson, waving her one good arm this way and that.

"I've got it, I've got it, just sit down," Professor Jenson grunted as he squinted at the small spoonlike contraption. He could just make out "tsp" on the handle. "T-s-p, that's teaspoon, right?"

Mrs. Gardner sank into her chair at the kitchen table with a moan. "Yes, you want the one marked t-s-p." A week of ham sandwiches, breakfast foods, and reheated casseroles from the Ladies' Aid had taken their toll. That morning Mrs. Gardner had made an offhanded remark, "Spaghetti sounds good." Instantly the guilt had set in as Professor Jenson set out to make Mrs. Gardner an authentic home-cooked meal, one that didn't have to be thawed and wasn't yet another casserole.

It was quickly discovered, however, that Professor Jenson's idea of spaghetti differed widely from Mrs. Gardner's definition. Professor Jenson had imagined cooking a package of noodles and heating up some canned sauce, but no, Mrs. Gardner had insisted on her mother's homemade sauce recipe.

"You can't have spaghetti with *canned sauce*." Mrs. Gardner looked at him in horror as if he'd suggested they fry up a cat. "No, if you're going to do this, you must do it right."

Professor Jenson had quickly doubted his ability to pull this off. If it went beyond boiling water or heating things up, there was a high probability he'd end up making inedible slop.

"I'll be right there to guide you through it." Mrs. Gardner had rooted in her recipe box until she'd finally located the tattered and stained recipe card.

A trip to the grocery store to gather ingredients had proven to be a harrowing experience. They'd made the mistake of splitting the grocery list in half, which meant Professor Jenson had ended up spending the entirety of the grocery trip hopelessly wandering in the produce section, searching for chives.

At one point, he'd managed to snag an employee who, in retrospect, must have thought he'd asked for "hives," because she'd asked, "As in honey?" To which Professor Jenson had fumbled an affirmative, thinking she was calling him an endearment. It wasn't until he'd ended up in front of a shelf full of honey, staring at the options of "organic," "clover," "raw," "acacia," and more, that he'd finally realized he'd been misdirected. By the time he'd found the produce section again, he'd begun to feel like the walls were closing in on him. He'd cast a wary eye at all passersby and doggedly avoided the less-than-helpful staff until Mrs. Gardner had finally found him standing frozen by the asparagus. She'd made short order of the rest of his list and they'd headed back home where "harrowing" didn't even begin to cover the next steps of the process.

"Preparing the tomato puree is the most important part and the easiest to mess up. You must submerge the tomatoes in boiling water and then plunge them in an ice bath. Then you'll be ready to peel and seed them for the blender."

Professor Jenson submerged and plunged, hardly daring to breathe, handling the tomatoes as if he'd been charged with the crown jewels.

"You're being too impatient." Mrs. Gardner peered around his arm. "Slow down with the peeling or you'll take most of the flesh along with the skin."

Professor Jenson steadied the knife and tried to be as precise as possible with the peels, feeling like an intern performing his first operation with the head of surgery bellowing orders at his elbow. Blessedly, the seeding, chopping, and pureeing were fairly straightforward, and Professor Jenson allowed himself to hope that they'd turned a corner. But no, there was an endless amount of chopping ahead: the chives, the bell pepper, the carrots, the onion, garlic, additional tomatoes. He chopped them too thin or he chopped them too fat. There was a close call once with a finger, and at one point a tomato gone rogue landed on the floor with a splat. In the end, Professor Jenson felt that he'd completed some form of rigorous initiation. He was sweating and his fingers were stained and sticky from the food, but Mrs. Gardner seemed to be pleased.

"Excellent! Now we sauté the veggies in butter until softened."

Professor Jenson shoved the food around in a liberal swathe of butter but apparently had set the burner too high and ended up scorching some of the bell pepper and carrot pieces.

"It's okay, it's okay." Mrs. Gardner pursed her lips, and Professor Jenson could tell she was checking her disapproval. "Just turn down the flame and we'll add the tomato puree."

Professor Jenson humbly did as he was told. Mrs. Gardner dumped in two bay leaves and whole celery stalks and sprinkled some Italian seasoning and basil over the mixture, her singular contribution—aside from the back-seat cooking advice. "And now for a splash of Burgundy." She handed Professor Jenson the bottle and gave him a knowing look. "This is the secret ingredient. Anita and Emma have been dying to get their hands on this recipe for ages. I'm entrusting you to keep this a secret. No leaking the recipe, do you hear?"

Professor Jenson seriously doubted this was a concern. He couldn't remember much of anything at this point. The last three hours were a blurred conglomerate of panic and relief as the recipe tentatively came together.

"Now for the noodles. You must add a little salt to the water before boiling them. I said a *little* salt. That's too much. You'll have to dump it out."

Professor Jenson finally succeeded at achieving the correct salt-to-water ratio, then turned to set the table, leaving Mrs. Gardner in charge of determining when the noodles had reached the appropriate "al dente" level. They were finally sitting down to eat when a knock sounded at the front door.

"What on earth?" Mrs. Gardner set her fork down and glanced at the clock. "Oh goodness, it's six thirty already! Ben said he was planning on stopping by tonight to visit. I never eat at this late hour."

"I didn't know going in that the sauce needed to simmer for two hours," Professor Jenson grumbled. "That altered the time projection a bit."

"Oh pooh. We'll just invite him to sit down with us."

Professor Jenson rose shakily to his feet as if to leave the room. "I have to use the restroom anyway, so that's where you can find me when it's all clear."

"Sit down, silly man. No need to hide this time. Honestly, I'm glad you'll be here for this meeting. The thought of facing him alone after what I did . . ." Mrs. Gardner shivered. "Go get the door while I grab another plate."

Professor Jenson dutifully left his well-earned supper and ambled to the front door. His feet were killing him, his poor hands felt riddled with carpal tunnel after all that chopping, and his nerves were shattered, but Mrs. Gardner seemed to be pleased with the culinary result, and that's all that mattered.

◇◆◇◆

Ben blinked in surprise to see Professor Jenson's hunched form in the front doorway. "Professor, I didn't realize you'd be here."

"We're just sitting down to a late dinner. You're welcome to join us."

"That's kind of you, but I don't want to intrude."

"Come in, Ben!" Mrs. Gardner's voice trilled from the back.

As Ben walked past Professor Jenson, he tried not to stare. There were red splatters across his shirt and even hints of red in his mustache. His large, cracked hands were stained red as well, and he reeked of garlic. "Something smells delicious."

"Oh, it better," Professor Jenson muttered.

Ben entered the dining room just as Mrs. Gardner was setting out another place setting. "Oh, you brought me flowers!" Mrs. Gardner rushed toward him with a shy smile.

"Yes, I just feel so bad about the accident." Ben handed her the bouquet.

Mrs. Gardner blushed. "*You* feel bad? I'm the one who should feel bad." She fidgeted by Ben's side, the flowers clasped in front of her like a wedding bouquet. Ben couldn't ever remember seeing her quite this repentant. "I . . . I'm glad you made plans to stop by. I just feel terrible about everything that happened. Ben, I hope you can forgive me. I suppose by now you've figured it all out . . . our scheme, that is." She moved to the table as she talked and indicated that Ben should sit.

"Yes, of course I forgive you," Ben chuckled as he pulled up a chair. "I appreciate the apology, I really do, but I'm not mad. I have to admit I'm kind of touched. It's good to know that I'd be missed, that Palermo's would be missed."

"Of course you would, my boy." Professor Jenson moved to a seat across from Ben. "You're an integral part of this town. Wouldn't be the same without you."

"It wouldn't be the same," Mrs. Gardner echoed, taking her rightful place at the head of the table and gesturing for Professor Jenson to help her serve Ben.

As Professor Jenson piled a healthy amount of noodles on Ben's plate and Mrs. Gardner ladled a steaming scoop of sauce over the top, Ben leaned back and observed the dynamic between the two. They seemed to be perfectly in sync, as if Ben had interrupted a happy marital moment. The transformation was fascinating to watch.

"May I ask the blessing?" Ben asked as his hosts settled into their places. "Come, Lord Jesus, be our guest, and let Thy gifts to us be blessed. Amen."

"Amen. Mark made the meal tonight, Ben," Mrs. Gardner said. "My mother's recipe. I'm sure you'll love it."

Ben watched as Professor Jenson ducked his head and blushed at Mrs. Gardner's praise. *Fascinating, simply fascinating.* "So, Professor Jenson, it's nice of you to be helping out like this," Ben shamelessly pried. "Mrs. Gardner is lucky to have you right next door."

"He's been making such a nuisance of himself!" Mrs. Gardner exclaimed, twirling a wad of noodles onto her fork despite her cast. Her tone hinted at irritated nonchalance, but her rosy cheeks and averted eyes told a different story. "I really am doing okay. They have me on pain medication, but really it's not bad." Mrs. Gardner leaned toward Ben. "The worst part is at night. I usually sleep on my right side. I didn't even realize this about myself until suddenly I couldn't lie in that position anymore. Showers, too, are rather difficult." She paused and then abruptly blushed a deep shade of red. "But Mark hasn't been helping me with *that!*"

"What?" Professor Jenson's gaze jerked up, a forkful of noodles suspended between plate and mouth.

"I ... I mean it has been a challenge, yes, but I'm managing on my own. I don't want you to get the wrong impression, Ben." Mrs. Gardner laughed and her good hand fluttered by her face as if fanning herself. Professor Jenson looked mortified.

"Don't worry," Ben laughed. "No wrong impressions here. This food is delicious, by the way. Excellent job, Professor."

"Couldn't have done it without Matilda." Professor Jenson cleared his throat modestly and glanced surreptitiously at Mrs. Gardner, who laughed and pooh-poohed but looked as pleased as could be.

*What is happening here?* Ben thought in bemusement. He watched transfixed throughout the rest of the meal as the two formerly hostile neighbors fussed over and deferred to each other. Even Mrs. Gardner's barbs seemed more like arrows straight from Cupid's bow.

"This man is so bullheaded, Ben. I told him I have three perfectly good aprons, but would he listen? No! And now he pays the price." Mrs. Gardner reached out and brushed at the stains on Professor Jenson's shirt. Her hand moved upward and she dabbed at the red stains in his mustache. Professor Jenson's nose twitched and he swatted at her hand like it was an irritating bug.

"You should have seen these aprons, Ben. All pink and frilly and ... short! I doubt they would have extended past my chest. I would have looked like a stuffed sausage!"

Mrs. Gardner released a series of loose giggles. "It would have been camera worthy, that's for sure."

"That's all I need—you with your hands on compromising photos. I shudder at the thought."

Ben quietly forked spaghetti into his mouth and smiled back and forth at the affectionate bickering. The bickering part he was used to, but now there was a softening around the edges of the harsh words, and he wondered if the two had noticed the shift.

As the meal drew to a close and Ben stood to help clear the table, the dreaded question arose. "So, Ben." Mrs. Gardner was leaning back in her chair as Professor Jenson took her plate. Clearly she'd perfected the art of delegation when it came to cleanup. "What *are* you going to do with Palermo's, if you don't mind my asking?"

Ben sighed. He still didn't have a satisfactory answer to this question. "Well, honestly, at this point I'm not sure. I haven't rescheduled with the appraiser, and I think I'm not going to quite yet. I'm going to put a pause on listing Palermo's until I've had a chance to think and pray about it some more."

Mrs. Gardner appeared to be trying to squelch her enthusiasm. The gleam in her eye and twitching at the corners of her mouth indicated that even though she might be genuinely repentant of her actions, she took full credit for their fruit. Mrs. Gardner adjusted her features into an appropriately somber arrangement. "Yes, that's quite wise, Ben, quite wise."

As the group moved out of the dining room, Ben offered to help wash the dishes, but Mrs. Gardner would have none of it. "Don't worry, Mark can take care of it," she stated dismissively. Professor Jenson grunted but gave no argument.

"Thanks for dinner. It was great, and I'm glad to see that you're doing so well. I'm sorry it's taken me so long to come by to visit, but it seems you are in capable hands." Ben nodded in Professor Jenson's direction and grinned.

"Yes, well . . ." Mrs. Gardner seemed flustered at the knowing smile slowly spreading across Ben's face. "It has just been convenient since Mark's right next door," she blustered. "And he *was* a part of the scheme, you realize."

"Oh yes, I was informed of his role."

Professor Jenson appeared to be trying to escape down a hallway. Mrs. Gardner placed a restraining hand on his arm. "Yes, so seeing as he's just as culpable as the rest of us, I suppose it's his Christian duty to tend the injured."

"Penance, then?"

"Well, I mean to say, tending to my needs couldn't really be called penance, could it?" Mrs. Gardner seemed to realize that she was only digging her hole deeper.

Ben laughed and came to her aid. "Certainly not." He gave her a hug. "Rest up, Mrs. Gardner, and continue to feel better." He extended a hand to the fidgeting Professor Jenson, who took it thankfully. "All is forgiven, the both of you."

"Bless you, Ben. You are a much more forgiving man than I." Professor Jenson shook his hand, and Ben turned to leave. The front door clicked shut behind him as Ben descended the front steps into the cool September evening. He could still hear Mrs. Gardner's muffled voice from inside.

"Trying to run away, were you?"

"Now now, Matilda. You were throwing me under the bus." Their voices receded into the back of the house, the characteristic sparring softened by the beginnings of a begrudging affection.

**The boy and the girl exhaust their repertoire of books.** *They have speculated on the flavor of everything they can possibly think of and now they both know that the visit is coming to an end, but neither wants to admit it.*

*"We'll keep writing, right?" the girl says sadly.*

*"Of course," the boy agrees. "And who knows when we'll see each other again. Maybe soon."*

*"Yes, maybe," the girl sighs. "I don't have many friends."*

*"You have me," the boy says firmly.*

*"Yes." The girl's face brightens. "I have you."*

# Chapter Nineteen

## WALK ON WATER

Ben approached Sundays with a renewed zeal. It was too easy to treat Sunday mornings like any other morning, to mark church off as just one more item on a never-ending to-do list. His talk with Dale had reminded Ben of the fervor and passion he used to hold and which he had taken for granted until suddenly he'd realized it wasn't there anymore. How did that happen? How did the extraordinary grace of God become ordinary in his life? "Keep it fresh, Lord," Ben prayed. "May I never stop being surprised and overwhelmed by You."

Dale's message that morning was on Matthew 14:22–33. Jesus walking on the water was a familiar story, but as is the case with Scripture, God brought something new to the hearers that morning. The message was titled "Stepping outside the Boat." Poor Peter, the poster child for passionate blunders. But before Peter got distracted by the waves, he first stepped outside the boat, and that, Dale had noted, was an important moment to reflect upon and mimic. Faith is never comfortable, and a life lived loudly for God requires us to first step outside the boat.

Ben's mind was humming with a sense of calm as he walked into the sunlight after the service. He stopped and greeted a few people and was just getting ready to head to the parking lot when a soft hand on his elbow stopped him.

"Ben, do you have a moment?" Oma stood quietly at his side.

"Mrs. Berg, so good to see you! How are you feeling?"

"Well, thank you. I'm finally able to move around more on my own, though I still have this cane for now. I'm so thankful, but I miss Rosemary's help."

Ben nodded in understanding, his heart twisting in his chest at the mention of Rosemary's name. His earlier anger at how she'd ignored him had mostly dissipated. In its place was an aching sensation of an opportunity missed.

"Actually, it's Rosemary I wanted to talk to you about. I wanted to share something with you. She's so sensitive and funny sometimes. She gets shy and overly modest, but I'm her Oma and I'm proud of her, so . . ." She extended a book toward Ben. "Rosemary is such a wonderful story-teller and artist. She's been drawing since she was a little girl, and in art school she finished this book as her final project. It's been out about a year and doing so well. Since you're a bookstore owner, I wanted to share this with you. Perhaps Palermo's could carry her book?"

Ben took the book and held it gently, his mouth gaping open in surprise. It was a beautiful hardcover book. The cover illustration was done in charcoal and pastels and depicted a small girl sitting beneath a tree, a large open book in her hands. A warm yellow light was shining from the book and illuminating her face, which was in color. The light from the book and the girl's face were the only spots of color in the illustration, a glowing center that drew the reader forward. A spidery script across the top of the book spelled *Spectrum*, and Rosemary's name stretched across the bottom. Ben was speechless.

"Beautiful, isn't it?" Oma peeked around his arm, staring at the book with a smile.

Ben finally found his tongue. "Y-yes, it's stunning. I had no idea . . ."

"How could you? That's why I thought I'd show you this copy. See what you think."

"Can I borrow this?" Ben had flipped the book over and was skimming the back cover copy.

"Oh, that's yours, dear. You can have it."

"Are you sure? Thank you so much. I wish Rosemary had told me about this while she was here. I guess we didn't really get a chance to spend much time together. I just . . . I just . . . I don't know . . . wish I had gotten to know her."

"Yes, she's an amazing young woman, isn't she?" Oma smiled gently at Ben, her eyes lighting up. "I hope you do get to spend more time with her. She's worth knowing."

"Do you have . . . could I have her contact information?" Ben asked before he quite realized what he was saying. "I would love to carry her book in the store," he explained quickly. "I would just like a way to contact her." He realized he was fumbling his words and felt his face heat up. "You know, to talk about the book."

Oma laughed. "Of course. Here." She reached into her purse and pulled out a small, weathered address book. "I have her information in here." She flipped to Rosemary's name. "Yes, here's her phone number and email."

Ben pulled out his phone, opening his contacts and keying in Rosemary's info. "I hope she doesn't mind me having her information."

"Why would she mind?"

Ben ducked his head. *Because she has a low opinion of me*, he thought. "Oh, I don't know. I don't want to invade her privacy."

"Don't worry about that. You can just blame it on me." Oma patted his arm.

"I can't begin to thank you for letting me know about this." Ben was still staring at the book in his hands. His heart was beating hard in his chest, and his breath felt a bit short. Once again, his mind and heart were full of Rosemary.

◇◆◇◆

Oma watched Ben walk away as if he were in a daze and smiled in self-satisfaction. *Success.* It was true, of course, that she wanted to see *Spectrum* stocked in Palermo's, but she didn't mind admitting an ulterior motive. She'd seen the way Rosemary had reacted to Ben. It'd been a while since she'd seen that look of mental preoccupation in her granddaughter, the look that said her creative, sensitive mind was full to the brim with something good— in this case, a dark, curly-haired young man. She wasn't sure why Rosemary had resisted any talk of Ben, but Oma didn't mind giving her a nudge in the right direction. Ben was such a wonderful young man. It'd be enormously satisfying to be his Oma.

◇◆◇◆

Ben sat in his truck and devoured the book. He couldn't wait until he reached home. In fact, it'd taken a great amount of self-restraint not to sit down right where he was in front of the church and read it there. Each page was more delightful than the next. The full-page illustrations were detailed and breathtaking. The story, too, was clever and well thought out. Ben followed Ivy as she walked through a world of black and white. He smiled as he watched her find a book and cheered as she opened it and was transported into the imaginary world of the story, brimming with new, vibrant colors. He shook his head in admiration as he picked up on the story arc. Each time Ivy came back home from her story adventure, a new color painted her black-and-white world. Ben watched as the exquisite drawings were slowly infused with color. The final spread showed Ivy stepping out of the story into a world that was just as bright and colorful as the one she'd left.

Ben leaned back in his seat, full of emotion from the visual world he'd just inhabited. This was a book that celebrated the power of story and imagination. It was an inspiring book for young readers with a message that Ben could fully get behind. His heart ached with a sudden desire to see Rosemary in person, to let her know how moving her book was, how beautiful and fulfilling the world she'd created in the book's pages truly was. He kicked himself all over again for the false impressions he knew he'd formed. Could he come back from that? How could he reconnect with this beautiful, creative woman?

The drive home was conducted on autopilot. Ben hardly remembered how he made it into his living room. JC came bounding in to greet him, and Ben scooped him up automatically. He sat in his recliner, mind ablaze. JC's insistent tongue finally brought him back to reality. "Sorry, boy." Ben stood and clipped the nearby leash to JC's collar, exiting through the rear and out into the alley behind the store. He took JC to the patch of grass between Palermo's and the next-door boutique, the small strip of earth that was their standard stomping ground when Ben didn't have time for a full walk.

JC paced back and forth, sniffing each section of the grass in an effort to find the perfect spot for conducting his business. After numerous false starts and some prolonged circling, JC finally squatted. Ben pulled out his phone and opened his contacts. He stared at Rosemary's information, an idea forming in his head. Ben let the idea percolate. Yes, it was a good idea, a solid plan. JC finished and puffed out his chest as he methodically stretched first one back leg and then the other, swiping the earth with his back claws and kicking up bits of dirt and grass. Ben picked up after JC, depositing the bundle in the trash bin in the alley before heading back inside.

The question remained: phone or email? Ben set his phone down on the counter and moved to the fridge to scrounge up some lunch as he assessed both options. Email allowed for a bit of a buffer. She'd be dealing with him in writing only, his name the only personal touch. She could keep him at a comfortable arm's length and respond to him at her leisure. It was certainly the safer route. Easy enough to dash off an email—then again, easy enough for her to ignore it. A phone call, on the other hand, was more personal and immediate. It demanded attention. At the thought of hearing her voice again, Ben felt a flutter in his chest. He was done with easy, with hedging and wondering and admiring from the sidelines. He wanted to hear her voice, and he wanted her to hear his. She needed to know that he was genuine, and tone of voice was a much better conductor than email.

Now that he'd decided on the tougher route of a phone call, the butterflies in Ben's stomach increased. He ate his leftover burrito in a hurried state of anticipation, immediately regretting it as the heartburn kicked in. Ben swigged some soda to calm his stomach and sat with phone in hand, practicing what he was going to say. Dale's sermon from that morning hit him again with fresh applications. Nothing was to be gained by staying in the boat. Faith involved a first step. Faith was climbing out of the boat. *Climb out of the boat, Ben*, he counseled himself. "Lord, help me out of this boat." He released a shaky breath and pressed the phone number, placing the phone to his ear and breathing slowly and steadily to calm himself.

The phone rang and rang, then switched to her voicemail. This was an outcome Ben hadn't expected. Could she still be at church? Perhaps she went to a later service than Ben did. For a moment he hesitated. He could just hang up at this point and no one would be the wiser. He could try again later after he'd had a chance to repeatedly second-guess himself. "Hello, you've reached Rosemary." Her voice was sweet and joyful. "Leave me a message at the beep." How he missed that voice and the bright face that went with it. "And I'll get back to you as soon as I can." It was now or never. He needed to hang up now or he would commit himself. Step out of the boat. Beep!

"Hi, Rosemary, this is Ben Palermo." He hadn't thought this through! Should he ask her to just call him back? Tell her the whole idea via voicemail? "You might be wondering how I got your phone number. I promise I'm not stalking you." He let out a nervous laugh. *Nope, wrong direction.* He reined it back in. "Your grandmother gave me your number today at church. She also gave me your book." Good, keep it focused on the book, less awkward and personal. "I have to say, I'm very impressed. This is a beautiful book and a compelling story, Rosemary." *Good—complimentary without sucking up.* "I'd enjoy talking to you more about it and about stocking your book at Palermo's." Now to get to the heart of the matter. "Also, I hope you will consider coming to Palermo's for a book signing." A book signing: good for business, and the perfect way to see Rosemary again. How he hoped she would agree! "You could be considered a local artist and author, seeing as you grew up visiting this town. I know the community here would embrace both you and your book with open arms. Please consider it and give me a call back when you have a moment to talk. You can reach me at this number. It's my cell."

There, he'd laid it all out on the table. He ended the call, his heart in his throat and his hope in the God who helped Peter walk on water.

**It is hard for the girl to leave the boy a second time.** The first time he was just a fun stranger and she had the letters to look forward to. Now she knows him and she will miss him so much. She gives him the letter she was going to leave him.

"Don't read it until I leave," the girl says, suddenly embarrassed. It's one thing to leave a note and imagine him reading it later, but it's another to watch him read it in front of her.

"Okay, as long as you do the same." The boy pulls out his own note and hands it to her. They laugh, the two notes in their eager hands.

# CHAPTER TWENTY

## THE GOOD, THE BAD, THE MESSY

Liam didn't waste much time in coming for a visit. Not long after their sushi dinner, he surprised Rosemary with a phone call. "Guess what I'm doing right now?"

"Um, besides talking on the phone with me?"

"I'm in the car, driving to your church."

"What?" Rosemary stopped short in her bedroom, hairbrush suspended in the air.

"Surprise! Figured after church I can treat you to your restaurant of choice and we can talk more about your next book."

"Oh, that's sweet, thank you." Rosemary's mind spun. She couldn't exactly tell him to turn around and head back, so she just said, "I'll see you when you get here, then."

Sure enough, by the time she reached church, Liam was already there, hip cocked against his car door, a big smile on his face. "Hey, Clooney, just you today? Where's your mom?"

"Hey yourself! Business trip." Rosemary initiated the hug, figuring it'd be easier to control the nature of the gesture if she took the lead. "This is a nice surprise."

They headed inside together. All throughout the service, Liam kept an arm rested on the back of the pew, alarmingly close to touching her. Rosemary tried to pay attention to the sermon, but it was hard with Liam so close to her. Her mind kept jumping around, assessing the situation, speculating on what was to follow. Why couldn't Liam just be open with her? What was he trying to accomplish with this visit? Rosemary was irritated and confused all at once. This perpetual limbo was exhausting.

"So do you have a place in mind?" They were walking to their cars, his arm brushing hers.

"There's a great barbecue place in town that has the best pulled pork sandwiches you've ever tasted. How about there?" She'd picked it less for the sandwich—which was, admittedly, amazing—and more for the fact that it was noisy and public and would be much less intimate than their last meal together.

"Sounds great! I can drive us there and we can come back for your car."

"That's okay, I'll just meet you there. It's on the way home, so we'd have to backtrack. How about you follow me?"

Rosemary breathed a bit easier as Liam got into his car and she into hers. She closed the door and reached into her purse for her phone to charge it, noticing a new voice-mail from an unknown number. As she pulled out of the parking lot, making sure that Liam was behind her, she hit the play button and put it on speaker. "Hi, Rosemary, this is Ben Palermo."

Rosemary jerked the wheel and hit the brakes with a gasp, nearly popping the curb. Liam pulled up behind her, no doubt confused. The message continued to play, but Rosemary had stopped listening. She needed to keep moving or Liam would wonder what was wrong and come over to check on her. Trembling, Rosemary hit pause on the message and slowly pulled back into her lane. A two-second clip of Ben's voice was all it had taken to transport her back to his store, back into his disarming presence. She breathed deeply and restarted the message. "Hi, Rosemary, this is Ben Palermo." She listened to the message in its entirety, letting the various emotions course through her. Confusion. *How did he get my number?* Frustration. *Oma, the little sneak!* Fear. *He's seen my book.* Joy. *He loves my book!* Anxiety. *He wants to talk to me.* Uncertainty. *He wants me to do a book signing at Palermo's.* Excitement. *He wants me to do a book signing at Palermo's!* And back to confusion. *Oh no—he wants me to do a book signing at Palermo's.*

Rosemary pulled up to the restaurant, threw the car into park, and turned off the ignition. She sat staring at her phone, unable to fully acknowledge to herself just how great it'd been to hear his voice again, especially now that she knew Ben was BJ. It was such a good voice, deep and warm. It matched his eyes and smile perfectly. She closed her own eyes and imagined his face. What had he been thinking and feeling as he'd left this message for her? He'd sounded collected and in control, excited by the possibility of featuring her book in his store. The idea of *Spectrum* in the front window of Palermo's was a fulfilling thought. She'd received inspiration, after all, from the bookstore, so bringing her book there was, in a way, coming full circle.

Rosemary was jerked from her musings by a loud tapping on her window. She turned to see Liam's concerned face peering in at her. "You okay?" Rosemary opened the door and slid out. She'd completely forgotten about Liam, let alone that they were about to share a meal together.

"Yes, I'm sorry. I just got an invitation I didn't expect. It's about my book." She stopped herself quickly, but it was too late. Liam's interest was piqued.

"An invitation to what?"

"Oh, nothing, it's not important."

"Come on. If it involves your book, you should tell me. As your unofficial manager, I deserve to know what's going on in your literary world."

Rosemary rolled her eyes. They walked into the restaurant and found a booth by a window. "It's a book signing opportunity. You know that bookstore I was telling you about?"

"Yeah, the one where you received inspiration for the Story People."

Rosemary felt a twinge of guilt for taking credit for BJ's idea. "Yes, well, the owner of the store wants me to do a book signing there."

"That's fantastic! You're going, right?"

"It'd be silly not to . . ." Rosemary fidgeted with the strap of her purse and worried her bottom lip. "I suppose I could go around Thanksgiving. I was going to visit Oma then anyway, and I could do this at the same time." The thought of seeing Ben again made her stomach turn over and not necessarily in an unpleasant way. Now that she knew he was BJ, she had a burning desire to see him again in light of this new knowledge. Plus, it was only right to run her next book idea by him, get his permission.

"See? It'll work out. Why look so worried? If you go over Thanksgiving break, I can even go with you, if that'll make you feel better."

It would most definitely not make her feel better. "That's nice of you, but I'll be okay, really. I usually spend Thanksgiving with just my mom and grandmother anyway." She backtracked, doing as much damage control as she could. The last thing she needed was Liam, good, kind, enthusiastic, loving Liam, breathing down her neck while she reconnected with her past.

"I'll wear you down. You'll see." Liam grinned at her. "Now, let's order."

Rosemary ate her meal on autopilot, which wasn't that

hard to do given how talkative Liam was. She listened and smiled and gave answers when appropriate, but all the while her mind and heart were with a dark-haired boy in a bookstore far away.

"I've talked too much. We didn't get a chance to talk about your new book." They were leaving the restaurant and headed to their cars.

"That's okay. I've done some more preliminary sketches but not much else at this point. What I really need to do is draw up a plot outline. That might help me shape my drawings into something coherent. It's weird because my approach with this book is, by necessity, different from before." Rosemary unlocked her car and turned to Liam. Talking with him as an old friend was so easy. "I'm having to be much more intentional this time around, I think. My first book came together so organically over the course of a lifetime. With this one I have to be structured, if that makes sense. But I'll get there."

"I have no doubt you will." Liam faced her eagerly and Rosemary sensed that he was getting ready to prolong their conversation. She felt horrible turning him away, especially since he had driven all this way, but she was not in an emotional place right now to plaster on a smile and make small talk all afternoon. Liam knew her well enough that he would recognize if she was distracted. She needed to think, to pray.

To call Ben back.

"Thanks so much for visiting, Liam. It was a great surprise, and thank you for lunch. You really shouldn't have. I'd love to visit longer, but I have things I need to do this afternoon." She squelched the feeling of guilt as she observed Liam's crestfallen face.

"That's okay. That's what I get for dropping in unexpectedly." He laughed. "Next time, I'll skip the surprise and we can plan for a larger chunk of time."

"Okay." Rosemary nodded but felt once again a twinge of irritation. Since when was Liam so needy? If he was that interested in her, why not say something? Why the sudden weird clinginess and subtle hinting around? Rosemary thought back again to several missed opportunities for dates in college. "You're unapproachable, Rosemary," one friend had said. "I think guys are just intimidated by you." She was so sick and tired of feeling like she was shouldering the burden of proof in relationships. Why should *she* have to make the first move? Couldn't a guy just act on his feelings and approach her already? Why should she be made to feel responsible for a guy's actions? And here was Liam, eager and in her face, but unwilling to verbalize the awkward dynamic and emotion that *he* had placed in their friendship. She tried to scale back the annoyance and be fair to him. He was her friend, after all. She wouldn't appreciate someone casting judgment on her if the tables were turned. "Have a safe drive back, friend." Rosemary initiated the hug again. It'd worked so beautifully before.

Liam accepted her side hug, but squeezed harder and held on longer than Rosemary did. "Thanks, and I'm serious about Thanksgiving."

"I know. Thank you. We'll see how it goes." A noncommittal reply seemed to be the best route. Rosemary watched Liam hop in his car and drive away with a wave of his hand, and then she turned her thoughts toward Ben. She'd need to call him back; there was no getting around it. She spent the drive home in a conversation with God. Rosemary found that she prayed more directly from the heart when she talked out loud, as if God were a friend sitting right next to her.

"So . . . that happened, Lord. BJ called, and now I have to call him back. It's so confusing. I guess I first need to figure out what answer I'm giving him." She paused and thought. "You haven't given me peace, Lord, about this next book project. That's probably because it's not really my idea. It's BJ's. I think the right thing to do here is to get his permission. I just won't feel right otherwise, especially since I know how to get ahold of him now."

She pulled into her mom's driveway but continued to sit in the car. "I should do it, right? Right. I can go during Thanksgiving, visit Oma, do the book signing, and talk to BJ, to *Ben*, about permission to use his idea for my next book." Her heart was racing with the anticipation of talking to Ben. "Okay, Lord, so I'm calling him." She sighed and got out of the car, drawn to the privacy of her room. There she'd be free to pace while on the phone. She entered the front hallway and saw her mom's suitcase in the front room.

"Mom, you home?" Rosemary called, surprised to see her mother back already from her business trip.

"Yeah, hi, honey," came the reply from the kitchen. "Just got in actually, earlier than expected. Gary gave me a ride."

Rosemary entered the kitchen and gave her mom a hug. "How was church?"

"Good. Liam came down and surprised me. We went to lunch."

"That's nice," her mom said with a bit too much enthusiasm. "He's such a nice guy. You should have invited him back here for dessert and coffee."

Rosemary shrugged, uncomfortable. "Maybe next time." Rosemary couldn't help but wonder what her mom would think of Ben.

"Okay, I'm going to unpack, then maybe you and me can have a cup?"

"Sure." Rosemary pecked her on the cheek and headed to her room. "Come get me when you're ready."

Rosemary sat at her desk and breathed deeply. She looked at the time of the voicemail. Two and a half hours had gone by since Ben had left the message. Rosemary wondered what he was doing now. Was he nervous for her call back? Why would he be nervous? He had no idea who she was. Or did he? Rosemary froze. No, there was no way he'd have figured it out. Right? Or maybe he had. Maybe he'd recognized her drawings in *Spectrum* and identified her as Rosie. But no, the childhood drawings BJ had seen were much different from the artwork in *Spectrum*. Two years of art school had seen to that. No, much more likely that he was still in the dark. So she'd probably have to be the one to break it to him, but not over the phone. She had until Thanksgiving to figure out how to approach the revelation. She pulled up the voicemail and pressed the button to call back. "Give me peace, Lord—and the right words would also be much appreciated." Ben picked up on the second ring.

"Rosemary, hello!" His voice was even and excited, displaying none of the jitters she felt.

"Hi, Ben. I got your voicemail. I see my Oma has been hawking my books." She laughed. *Start with humor to break the ice—always a good plan.*

Ben chuckled, and it sounded loud and deep in her ear. Rosemary's stomach flip-flopped. "Yup, pretty much. I'm glad she did too. I wish we'd had a chance to talk about it while you were here. I had no idea."

"Yeah, sorry. I'm still getting used to the whole thing. It feels narcissistic to ply my book on people." Rosemary thought back to the moment when she'd brought the books to the store. Would he have pieced it together then? Her in the bookstore with her drawings? Would it all have connected for both of them in that moment? He was being so kind to her now, and she felt guilty for how she'd handled their last interaction—closed door, silence. Apologizing now seemed awkward, and Ben seemed to have forgotten the incident, for he was casual and friendly on the phone, no hint of angst or bitterness.

"I get that. No worries. I figured I'd place an order with your publisher, get your book on the shelves here."

"I appreciate that, thank you. And I'm so glad you like the book."

"I love it, Rosemary."

She warmed at the sound of her name on his lips. She wanted to reach out to him, look into his eyes, reconnect with the BJ she remembered.

"Truly, it's a beautiful piece of art, and it carries a powerful message for kids. Have you given thought to my invitation?"

Rosemary fought against the lump in her throat. "Yes, and I'd be glad to do a book signing at Palermo's."

"Wonderful! When are you thinking?"

"I know it's just under two months away, but I was thinking of Thanksgiving weekend. I'll be in town visiting Oma. Would that work for you?"

"I'm happy to work with whatever time frame works for you. Actually Thanksgiving would be great. Things get busier around that time with visitors during the holidays, tourists, early Christmas shoppers, et cetera. How about the Saturday after Thanksgiving? That's New Holden's official Christmas kickoff. I'll set everything up for you the night before and you could come first thing in the morning."

"That sounds great, thank you!" There was an awkward pause. Rosemary had always been horrible with conversational pauses. Pauses, she felt, were meant to be filled. She would often jump in to fill the void even if she didn't have anything to say. "So, um, I guess in the meantime if there's anything you need me to do, you can let me know." What would he possibly need her to do? Other book signings had required next to nothing from her. She'd arrived, read, signed, smiled, and left. Rosemary began pacing around her bedroom. Somehow pacing went hand in hand with talking on the phone, especially during difficult calls; it was an outlet for all that nervous energy.

"Sure, absolutely. So now you have my number and I have yours, so if either of us needs anything, we know how to get in touch with each other."

"Yup, sounds good. Okay. Well. I guess I'll let you go for now." She paused again, breathless. Was she cutting him off too soon? But what else was there to say? Knowing who he was made this difficult. She felt like skipping all the niceties and blurting out, "BJ, it's me! It's Rosie!" But news of that type was better delivered in person. Instead, she fell into the standard pattern of preparing to hang up. "It was nice talking with you. Thank you for the invitation. I'll look forward to hearing from you closer to the date."

"Sure, absolutely," Ben said, repeating himself from earlier. "Thank you for agreeing to come. We'll talk later."

Rosemary hung up and sat down hard at her desk again. Part of her wished she'd settled on an earlier date, so badly did she want to see BJ, and part of her wished she'd settled on no date at all, so badly did she shrink from Ben. What on earth would she say to him? "Hello, it's me, old friend, a ghost from the past. Surprise!" She had just under two months to figure it out and to prepare her heart for whatever was to come—the good, the bad, the messy.

**The boy opens the note as soon as the girl leaves.** It's a drawing of the two of them, hand in hand. They are standing at the edge of a cliff overlooking a beautiful landscape full of hills with round doors in them. A caption runs across the top: The Shire.

The boy smiles. They'd just finished discussing The Hobbit and had agreed that this story was most likely one of the Story People's favorites since it probably tasted like cakes and tarts and all things delicious. No one likes food better than a hobbit, after all.

The boy reads the accompanying note. It's full of random thoughts.

The boy misses the girl already.

# Chapter Twenty-One

## HOW TO WIN A WOMAN'S HEART

The next few days, Ben walked around in a state of emotional suspension. Nick gave him funny looks and once or twice attempted to pry but got nothing more than one- or two-syllable answers and so eventually gave up. The phone conversation with Rosemary ran on repeat through Ben's mind. He'd analyzed and analyzed again every word exchanged for any nuance of meaning he could squeeze out of it. More telling than the words they'd exchanged, however, was her tone. Maybe it was just his imagination, but he'd picked up on the nervous edges to her voice right away. She'd been kind and gracious and humble. Her voice was as sweet as he'd remembered, with the kind of sound that could easily be the voiceover for one of those heartwarming commercials for dog food or baby shampoo or some other equally heartstring-tugging product. But her voice had cracked at the end of her sentences, and she'd been slightly breathless throughout most of the conversation.

Oddly, her nervousness had put him right at ease, and he'd fallen into the role of the calm, supportive acquaintance with amazing speed. He'd wanted to reach through the phone and put an arm around her, let her know there was no need to be nervous, and if he couldn't do that physically, then he could do it through his voice. He knew he had a deep voice, and it was instinct to lower it just a notch to convey sufficient soothing. Silly, really, how intensely he felt those few moments of phone time, how persistently he speculated on the cause for her nervousness.

Was she nervous at the thought of the book signing, at meeting and greeting the people of the town and talking to them about *Spectrum*? Surely not, for she'd been published for a year and most likely had done some publicity for the book within that time. Perhaps she was just a nervous phone talker. Ben himself preferred texts or emails to phone conversations, and he knew many people just weren't at their best when having to communicate via phone. Running a business had forced him out of this squeamishness since he was communicating with vendors and customers by phone constantly, but maybe Rosemary rarely had reason to talk on the phone and this was her natural phone talking voice. Or maybe—dare he think and hope it?—maybe she was nervous at the prospect of seeing him again, at hearing his voice. Okay, so for the sake of argument, say it was the latter. Ben thought there were two possible reasons she'd be nervous to hear his voice and see him again: (1) she still had a negative impression of him from the unfortunate compromising moments she'd witnessed, or (2) she liked him. Ben allowed himself to lean toward the second option, for if she were merely disgusted with him, then wouldn't her tone be laced with hostility rather than nervousness? Also, wasn't the fact that she had returned his phone call at all a promising sign, seeing as she'd met his last overture with stony silence? For an entire afternoon, Ben sank into the idea that she liked him; he luxuriated in the notion that this smart, beautiful, creative woman actually found him attractive. After several hours of indulging this heady scenario, however, Ben's practical side took over. She was most likely just a nervous phone talker.

Ben wasted no time in calling Rosemary's publisher, even though the book signing was still a ways away. They were helpful and professional. He'd arranged for several boxes of *Spectrum* to be delivered a couple of weeks before the signing. He'd also be receiving *Spectrum* bookmarks and pencils to pair with the books. Ben had no doubt the book would sell well. His children's section was one of the most popular areas of the store, and *Spectrum* was unique in that it had a cross appeal with adults and would work as a coffee-table book, so beautifully was it bound and so stunning was the artwork. Ben was looking forward to the shipment as enthusiastically as a child counting down the days to Christmas. His heart was full with preparations and with an exhilarating sense that he'd finally received peace and direction. He couldn't imagine pursuing the sale of Palermo's now. Perhaps this was what he needed—to take a breath and to focus on moving forward with the store rather than entertaining ideas of leaving it behind him. The peace he'd lacked while considering the sale of Palermo's was present in large quantities when he thought of Rosemary. His every thought of her was one of quiet assurance. He was at a time in life where he was done hesitating. He was ready to take that next step of faith, out into whatever waters awaited him.

Professor Jenson looked at the nervous woman in the passenger seat and shook his head. Mrs. Gardner was clutching the center console with a white-knuckled grip, and at every red light and stop sign, she extended her leg as if trying to help him brake in time. "I'm a perfectly good driver, Matilda," he offered without hope that she'd believe him.

"Oh, I know. You're doing quite well for your age."

"My age?" Professor Jenson looked at her askance. "Excuse me, but I'm not that much older than you."

Mrs. Gardner gave him an indulgent look. "Of course, Mark. Ten years isn't that much of a difference."

"Certainly not," Professor Jenson huffed, and he turned his attention back to the road, braking abruptly when he saw he'd nearly blown past a stop sign. Mrs. Gardner sucked in her breath and arched back into her seat as if attempting to avoid a head-on collision with a nonexistent semi. "Stop distracting me, Matilda."

"Okay, I'm sorry, I understand you need all your concentration."

"What is that supposed to mean? I can multitask. I don't have one foot in the grave."

"Of course not. I never suggested you did. Just forget about me and focus on the road. Focus on the road, Mark!" This last bit was delivered in a higher pitch as Mrs. Gardner pointed urgently at a scattering of deer fifty yards to their right.

"I doubt those deer pose an imminent threat."

"Deer are unpredictable. Sandra was telling me the other day about her godson who hit a deer on a back road. Well, it was more like the deer hit him. He was just driving along and the deer comes bounding out of nowhere and runs smack into his passenger window. Head went right through, and Brandon got cut by all the shards of glass going everywhere. Can you imagine if someone had been in the passenger seat?" Mrs. Gardner gestured toward her compromising placement in the passenger seat. "Death, Mark. Instant death."

"Matilda, I promise, if the deer move in our direction, I'll stop the car."

"No! Absolutely not! That would be the worst thing to do!" Mrs. Gardner's eyes went wide at the very thought. "I heard somewhere that deer have poor vision and rely on movement to see you and if you stop your car they're more likely to run into you."

"Well, which is it, Matilda?" Professor Jenson sighed. "Do I keep driving or stop? Because it seems like you're saying that either way, we're bound to get rammed by a deer."

"Ease forward slowly." Mrs. Gardner nodded decisively. "That way you keep in constant movement so they can see where you're at but you aren't in danger of hitting them."

"Are you being serious?" Professor Jenson had already slowed to a crawl during the deer debate. "So just continue like this?"

"Yes, this is perfect."

They continued to crawl past the deer at fifteen miles per hour. Several cars pulled up behind them, honked, and passed them. "Ignorant fools." Mrs. Gardner shook her head in derision at the blithely passing motorists.

Professor Jenson propped his elbow on the car door and rested the side of his now-aching head in his hand, slightly shielding his face from those passing them. When they finally made it past the life-threatening deer, he sped back up.

"Thank you, Mark. I really do appreciate you driving me into downtown like this. I think that's been the hardest— not being able to drive."

Professor Jenson's irritation melted as quickly as it'd formed. "My pleasure. What are your plans again?"

"Well, I'm meeting Anita and Emma at Palermo's. We're going to have lunch together, but we want to meet there first to apologize together to Ben. You sure you'll be okay for a few hours without me?"

Professor Jenson noted the "without me" and frowned. Was he making a nuisance of himself after all? He had prided himself on her needing him, but now worried that maybe she was just indulging him. "I can keep myself busy," he said more gruffly than he'd intended. "I have things to do too, you know."

"Oh, okay." Mrs. Gardner raised her eyebrows and looked out the window.

Professor Jenson didn't want to admit that his only errands were to the bank and pharmacy, after which he intended to kill time until she needed him again. No, she most certainly did not need to know that piece of information.

Mrs. Gardner bent down and waved through the window to Professor Jenson as he pulled away from Palermo's, straightening just in time to see Mrs. Frank and Mrs. Baumgartner observing her from across the street. Embarrassment coursed through her at the look on their faces, and she nervously fidgeted in front of the store as they crossed the street to her.

"Was that Professor Jenson?" Mrs. Frank looked accusingly at her.

"Um, yes, he gave me a ride since I still can't drive." Mrs. Gardner lifted her cast-covered arm pathetically.

"Oh, that makes sense." Mrs. Baumgartner looked relieved. "He's right next door to you too, so that's convenient."

Mrs. Gardner laughed nervously. "Yes, very convenient. Anyway, you ready to go inside?"

"Don't try to change the topic, Matilda." Mrs. Frank was still looking at her with a shrewd eye. "You know that either of us would have been happy to pick you up. You looked awfully happy stepping out of his car just now, and how about that overly enthusiastic wave, hmm?"

"I'm sure I don't know what you're talking about." Mrs. Gardner tried to arrange her features to look suitably offended.

"It's just that we know how much you dislike Professor Jenson," Mrs. Baumgartner chimed in helpfully. "That's all. It was just . . . surprising."

"I don't *dislike* him. I've never *disliked* him," Mrs. Gardner snapped before thinking better of it. "I mean, I never said I hated the man or anything," she quickly recovered. "Is he frustrating sometimes? Yes, but I've never said that I dislike him." An overwhelming feeling of protectiveness came over Mrs. Gardner, and she couldn't help the words that poured out of her next. "He's really been so helpful, you know, more than the two of you have been, I might add."

"Now, no need to attack us, Matilda," Mrs. Frank frowned. "We've both been over multiple times a week, and if you needed more help, you only had to ask."

"I was attacked first," Mrs. Gardner muttered.

"Oh, let's not argue," Mrs. Baumgartner pleaded. "It just seems that you've had a change of heart, is all."

"Mark, er, Professor Jenson will always be a frustrating man, but he has been a helpful frustrating man, so I'd rather not speak ill of him, if you don't mind."

"Nobody is speaking ill of anyone." Mrs. Baumgartner raised her hands in appeal and looked at Mrs. Frank with raised eyebrows.

"Certainly not. *I've* always appreciated Professor Jenson." Mrs. Frank refused to let it drop. "I just didn't realize how much *you* seem to appreciate him."

"Oh, just stop it already, Emma." Mrs. Gardner realized she was incriminating herself by the blush spreading across her cheeks. "We're next-door neighbors and he's retired and has the time and has been helping me and that is all. Can we go inside now?"

"All right then." Mrs. Frank was still looking at her with suspicion, but she moved toward the front door.

"Oh, I'm so nervous." Mrs. Baumgartner hung back, looking skittish. "Have any of you actually spoken to Ben since, you know, since the *incident*?"

"He had dinner with me and Mark the other night, and he was so gracious."

"You were having dinner with Professor Jenson?" Mrs. Frank's eyes popped.

"Oh good, that makes me feel better." Mrs. Baumgartner joined her friends at the front door, apparently breezing past the dinner revelation.

"You had *dinner* with him, Matilda?"

Mrs. Gardner was beginning to care less and less what her friends thought and to feel more and more irritated at the incredulity in their voices. She didn't care to admit that their incredulity was because of the unfair bias she'd held against Professor Jenson all these years. The more time she spent with Professor Jenson, the more ashamed she was of her former hostility toward him and the more eager she was to put it in the past, which was hard to do when your friends were in a state of constant astonishment. In answer to Mrs. Frank, she opened the door to the bookstore, knowing that this would squelch further debate. She was correct. All further talk was hushed as the three friends entered Palermo's slowly, sheepishly, repentantly.

Ben heard the loud ding of the front door and poked his head out from the aisle where he was reshelving out-of-order books just in time to see Mrs. Gardner, Mrs. Frank, and Mrs. Baumgartner enter his shop. They hadn't spotted him yet, and he took a moment to observe them. First they looked expectantly toward the front desk and, finding that he wasn't there, began casting their eyes around the first floor and consulting one another in not-so-quiet whispers.

"Where *is* he?"

"It's a big store, Anita. Calm down."

"Does he have a bell to ring?"

"This isn't a hotel, Matilda."

"Should we call his name?"

"Let's just browse until we see him."

"Surely he heard the front door ring."

"Shh, just stop worrying and try to look natural."

The three women began spreading out. Mrs. Frank grabbed a book from the nearest display, Mrs. Baumgartner meandered to the front window display of craft books and pretended interest in its contents, and Mrs. Gardner made a beeline for the romance section. Ben ducked back into his aisle and shook with laughter. A renewed sense of belonging filled his chest. To be so loved by three such ferociously loyal women was a privilege. He shelved the book he'd been holding and decided to put them out of their misery. "Hello, ladies. I thought I heard the door. How are you today?" He walked to Mrs. Frank, who was nearest him, and offered a hand. Mrs. Frank was not the hugging type.

"Well, thank you." Mrs. Frank took the proffered hand and looked for her friends with a frantic air. "Anita," she hissed.

"Hi, Ben." Mrs. Baumgartner came over slowly.

"Ben, dear." Mrs. Gardner approached him from behind, and he was officially surrounded.

First Mrs. Baumgartner gave him a hug and then Mrs. Gardner, who held on the longest and who eventually took the confessional lead. "I know we've talked, but all three of us wanted to come and officially apologize."

"Yes, we're so sorry, Ben." Mrs. Baumgartner looked like she was close to tears.

"It was Matilda's idea," Mrs. Frank started, but then stopped at the glare emanating from her two friends. "But we participated of our own free will and for that I, too, am sorry. In fact, I'm hoping you will forgive and forget it ever happened. I usually don't stoop to, to . . ."

"Sneaking around in other people's closets?" Ben offered with a grin. "Impersonating ghosts?" At the horrified blush spreading across Mrs. Frank's face, Ben quickly added, "Of course I forgive you. Please don't worry about it a second longer. It's forgiven and in the past."

A collective sigh spread through the small knot of women. "You're so kind, Ben." Mrs. Baumgartner wiped at the tear that fell. "I hope we didn't mess things up too horribly for you."

"Well, you'll probably be pleased to hear that I'm not planning on selling Palermo's."

All three women's faces brightened, and he thought he also detected a hint of self-satisfaction. "Really? I mean, I'm so sorry. I hope we weren't the cause," Mrs. Gardner said modestly.

"No, actually. I've just been giving it more thought and prayer, and I don't feel at peace with selling. That's not to say that down the road a sale couldn't happen, but for right now, I think New Holden is where I'm supposed to be."

"Oh, I'm so glad," Mrs. Baumgartner squealed.

"Why the change of heart?" Mrs. Frank looked skeptical, as if the news were too good to be true.

"I don't mind telling you that it is due in part to an exciting upcoming event. I'll be advertising it soon." Ben ducked behind the front desk and retrieved Rosemary's book. He'd read it repeatedly in the days since Oma had given it to him. "We have a local author, Rosemary Berg, and she's agreed to come to Palermo's around Thanksgiving for a book signing." Ben couldn't contain the excitement in his voice. This was the first time he'd talked about the event with others, and his cheeks hurt from smiling.

"Rosemary Berg, Carol's granddaughter, who was so recently in town?" Mrs. Frank asked as she took the book from Ben's hand and began paging through it.

"Yes, I remember Carol telling us about this book when it first came out!" Mrs. Gardner exclaimed as she looked over Mrs. Frank's shoulder.

"This is beautiful work," Mrs. Baumgartner said. "Even though she's from Indianapolis, Rosemary really is a part of this town. She used to visit Carol often over the years. Is she still in town? I haven't seen her lately."

"No, she left back in August. She stayed with Oma, uh, Carol, for a month while she was recovering from surgery." Ben couldn't help the admiration creeping into his voice. "Unfortunately, we didn't get the chance to talk about her book while she was here. I didn't realize she was an author and illustrator until after she'd left. I'm just glad she agreed to come back. There will be flyers soon and eventually a window display. What?" Ben stopped abruptly. All three women had looked up from the book to gaze at him knowingly. Three matching smiles greeted him, and he looked from one to another in confusion. "What?" he repeated.

"You like her," Mrs. Gardner stated.

"Matilda," Mrs. Frank hissed.

"Well, he does."

"Oh yes, he does," Mrs. Baumgartner confirmed.

Mrs. Frank sighed and looked at Ben. "Sorry, Ben, I have to agree with these two."

Ben felt a rush of embarrassment followed by acceptance. He chuckled as the heat filled his cheeks. "Well, I guess the cat is out of the bag. No sense in denying it. I mean, look at this beautiful, creative woman." He indicated her picture on the back cover. "What's not to like?"

All three women squealed exuberantly and crowded in for hugs, even Mrs. Frank.

"I'm so glad."

"You deserve to be happy, Ben."

"Finally. Thank You, Lord."

"Success!"

"Not our success, but still!"

"Thank God, we can put that plan on the shelf."

Ben laughed as he received all three hugs simultaneously. "Plan? What are you talking about?"

"Oh nothing, nothing! We're just overjoyed that you've finally found someone." Mrs. Gardner's head was resting almost beneath his underarm, but she seemed not to mind. All three finally let go and stepped back to look at him with shining eyes.

"Thank you, but I'd tone down the enthusiasm because I haven't even spoken to her yet and who knows how she feels about me."

"How can she not love you?" Mrs. Baumgartner extended her hands in his direction as if showcasing a premium specimen of manhood, just as she'd done the fungi.

"Well, thank you." Ben shook his head. "I have to admit that I'm rusty with all of this. I haven't had a serious relationship in a while. I'm hoping I don't mess it all up when she gets here."

"Don't you worry, dear." Mrs. Gardner began ushering him to a stuffed chair in the small reading alcove near the back of the store. "You are in good hands. We can give you all the advice you need."

Ben allowed himself to be shoved into the chair as the other three settled themselves in surrounding seats.

"The important thing is to make her feel beautiful," Mrs. Gardner began.

"Yes, but you must also make her feel appreciated and valued. You don't want her thinking you're only out for one thing, young man." Mrs. Frank looked at him with warning in her eyes.

"You must romance her," Mrs. Baumgartner contributed breathlessly, at the edge of her seat. "Flowers and chocolates, all women love those."

"But don't be too over the top. Women don't like desperate men," Mrs. Frank interjected.

"Flowers and chocolates hardly communicate desperation, Emma."

"I didn't say those things did specifically."

"Well then, what? We're not counseling him to follow her around with puppy-dog eyes."

"I'm just saying, don't be too clingy."

Mrs. Baumgartner huffed but made no further comment.

"Anita's right about the chocolates and flowers," Mrs. Gardner jumped in. "You really can't go wrong with that route."

"Maybe if I had flowers waiting for her in the store?" Ben offered. Even though the advice was being delivered in a confusing mishmash, Ben found that he was actually listening. It'd been a long time since he'd received maternal advice.

"Yes, that'd be good," Mrs. Gardner approved. "Surprise her, Ben. Women love to be surprised and flattered."

"But don't be too artificial with your flattery," Mrs. Frank counseled. "Women can see right through artifice. It must be natural and genuine."

"Well, of course," Mrs. Gardner sighed. "We're hardly advocating that he be disingenuous. You're being so cautionary, Emma. Do you have anything positive to contribute?"

"I *am* being positive," Mrs. Frank objected. "Someone needs to communicate the pitfalls to him."

Mrs. Gardner just shook her head and turned back to Ben. "Don't worry, dear. Just be yourself. Let her see who you are and how much you admire her and the rest will follow." Ben smiled as the other three nodded, apparently all agreeing on this point.

Having completed his trip to the bank in record time and picked up his prescription with very little wait, Professor Jenson now looked ahead to the several hours remaining and wondered what to do with himself. He was out of milk, but he didn't want to pick it up so early and risk it spoiling in the car. He supposed he could head back to Palermo's. It was close to where Mrs. Gardner was having lunch, and he could kill the time there until he was needed to escort her home.

As Professor Jenson parked in front of the bookstore and headed up the front steps, he let his imagination return to a time not that long ago when he'd traversed these steps in reverse with his hand squeezed ardently by a beautiful woman. A soft smile played across his lips as he entered the store. He'd expected Ben, but instead Nick looked up from the front desk.

"Hi, Professor. Anything I can help you with?"

"No, just browsing, thank you." Professor Jenson wondered how the ladies' talk with Ben had gone. He was moving toward the now-infamous stairs when he heard a ripple of soft laughter from the back of the store. He stopped and listened. Yes, that was Mrs. Gardner's voice, and that must be her friends too. What were they still doing here? Professor Jenson had become a much more curious man since getting to know Mrs. Gardner better; her inquisitiveness, he'd found, was catching. Quietly he made his way to the rear of the store, following the sound of female voices. He knew he shouldn't eavesdrop, but he couldn't help himself. As Professor Jenson shamelessly peeked around a bookshelf, he blamed his lack of self-control entirely on Mrs. Gardner.

Ben was sitting in the reading alcove, surrounded by Mrs. Gardner and her two friends. They were talking animatedly, and Ben appeared to be listening attentively.

"You must romance her," he heard Mrs. Baumgartner say. Professor Jenson frowned. Romance? What on earth were they talking about? He leaned closer to hear but remained where he was, hidden behind a bookcase so as not to be seen. "Flowers and chocolates, all women love those."

"But don't be too over the top. Women don't like desperate men."

They were apparently giving Ben advice on romance. Who, Professor Jenson wondered, was the lucky lady? The women continued talking, their advice turning to bickering until he heard Mrs. Gardner jump in.

"Anita's right about the chocolates and flowers. You really can't go wrong with that route."

Professor Jenson's eyes lit up. So, she liked chocolates and flowers? Professor Jenson realized with a sharp sense of giddiness the gold mine he'd just stumbled across. Here was a way to unearth the path to Mrs. Gardner's heart. Professor Jenson quieted his enthusiasm. She was talking again, and he must hear every word.

"Surprise her, Ben. Women love to be surprised and flattered."

Professor Jenson was not a man of surprise and flattery. He rocked back on his heels and considered this setback for a moment. Mrs. Frank was speaking. He strained forward again to catch the last of her statement.

"It must be natural and genuine."

"Well, of course. We're hardly advocating that he be disingenuous."

Mrs. Gardner continued in her reprimand, but Professor Jenson was caught up in his dilemma. How to convey flattery while being natural and avoiding, as Mrs. Gardner had so adamantly denounced, disingenuousness? This was going to be challenging. Professor Jenson decided to concentrate on the first piece of advice: chocolates and flowers. That was pretty straightforward—hard to mess that one up. He'd worry about surprises and flattery later. With a start, he realized he'd missed a chunk of what Mrs. Gardner was saying. He leaned in for the last bit.

"The rest will follow."

The rest of what? He felt anxiety clutch at his chest. He needed more information, more! But the conversation appeared to be coming to a close and the group was making signs of leaving. Professor Jenson quickly ambled to the stairs and scrambled up them, trying not to fall and mimic Mrs. Gardner's disaster. As he topped the steps and hurried into the nearest aisle, he could hear their voices retreating. He breathed a sigh of relief that he'd evaded detection. The nature section, his usual stomping grounds, was on the second floor, but he found himself roaming in a random direction, mind awhirl with the information he'd gleaned. The day lengthened, the store quieted, and Professor Jenson wandered among volumes of poetry and wondered how to win a woman's heart.

**The girl and the boy continue like this for years—the notes, the drawings, the messages, and occasionally the sharp, sweet surprise of a face-to-face encounter.** The girl changes. She gets taller and she also begins to notice the boy in a new way. He is changing too. He is taller, and his voice is new each time she sees him. The things that stay the same are his crazy hair and smile and his joy at seeing her.

All of the girl's friends are now "boy crazy." The girl sometimes wonders what this means but gets the closest to understanding each time she opens a new note, each time she sees the beam of a special person's flashlight.

# CHAPTER TWENTY-TWO

## REJECTION DIDN'T HURT

Time pressed forward in New Holden, Indiana. The air grew sharper, and residents began hauling out their cardigans and pullovers and finally boxing up summer's wardrobe. The trees, too, began sporting new attire. The green ash were first, their branches melting from green to buttery yellow; the red maple followed, all fire and exclamation points. Hot beverages were enthusiastically and religiously consumed. People trekked up and down the roads of the historic district, lattes in gloved hands, scarves flung casually over shoulders, a studied air of shabby chic trailing behind them.

Ben drew shoppers in with vintage-inspired window displays replete with twinkly lights, rustic chairs with stacks of books on their seats, baskets of bright red wax apples, and twine-wrapped glass bottles with floral sprays in them. He enlisted Charlotte's help during each new season. As the owner of the consignment boutique next door, her eye for style was flawless, and Ben welcomed her expertise with gratitude. Her displays were exquisite and he'd happily agreed to put up a sign attributing each display to her store as compensation for her work. This year, however, he'd be temporarily taking over Charlotte's thoughtful work for a few weeks as he advertised Rosemary's book signing. He'd agonized over how to display her books and had accumulated stacks of paper with preliminary sketches on them. Thanksgiving was less than a month away, and her books and promotional material were due to arrive within a week. With Nick's help, Ben had put together an eye-catching flyer, which he printed in color and planned on posting throughout the town.

Aside from the logistics of the display and flyers was Ben's romantic angle. Mrs. Gardner had proved to be a most unconventional but appreciated friend in this regard. They'd met on more than one occasion to talk about Rosemary, and she was always bursting with encouragement and advice. In embracing the fawning attention she was so eager to give, Ben found himself less irritated with her idiosyncrasies and more thankful that God had placed people who cared about him in his life. He liked to imagine that if his mother had lived, she'd have offered him similar advice, helping him traverse the rocky terrain of offering one's heart to another.

Mrs. Gardner was living the dream. She'd always known that she had a gift for making romantic connections, but Ben's trust and confidence in her was validation. How she loved seeing his eager eyes looking to her, soaking up her every word. How she thrilled at the thought that she would have a part in securing his happiness. In the weeks that had passed after his revelation to Mrs. Gardner and her friends, she had met with Ben two times; their talks on romance were the highlight of Mrs. Gardner's day. But then the flowers arrived and disrupted the pleasant flow of events.

It was a crisp November morning when Mrs. Gardner opened her front door to get the mail and found them, lying on her front doormat, a scattering of late-season wildflowers pulled up by the roots, clumps of earth still sticking in places and muddying her mat. "What on earth?" She bent and picked them up. They were still wet with dew; their stringy roots tickled her hands and left smears of dirt on her palms. It looked like something the cat dragged in. "Well, where did you come from?" she questioned the flowers, as if they could relay the secrets of their origins to her. Perhaps a dog had been digging in a garden and tracked them onto her front porch. She looked around in confusion. There were no gardens nearby with these type of flowers. Still, they were beautiful. A shame, really, to let them go to waste. Mrs. Gardner brought them inside, trimmed them, placed them in a vase, and set them in the middle of her dining room table.

"Those are pretty," Professor Jenson remarked later that day. He'd taken to coming over in the afternoons after she'd insisted he could stop making her breakfast.

"Aren't they lovely? I found them scattered outside this morning."

"So you like them?"

"They're flowers. What's not to like?"

"Well, I'm . . . I'm glad you like them."

Mrs. Gardner looked at him sharply. Was it just her imagination, or was he acting unusual? More unusual than usual, that is. "You okay?"

"Hmm? Oh yes, yes, just admiring the flowers."

Mrs. Gardner thought no more of the incident until it became a pattern. Two days later she opened her mailbox to find a small wrapped package inside. She brought it into the house along with the rest of the mail, thinking that this is how bomb scares happen and chuckling at the thought, then nervously stopping and regarding the package in a new light, circling and staring at it, head cocked, brow furrowed, until she finally broke down and opened it. "Baker's chocolate?" She looked at the slim package and turned it round and round in her hands. There was no note, no explanation, just a package of unsweetened baking chocolate squares.

"That looks delicious," Professor Jenson remarked as he caught sight of the packet on her counter that afternoon.

"Not really," Mrs. Gardner laughed. "It's very bitter."

"Oh." Professor Jenson picked it up and studied it closely. "Should it have been semisweet instead?"

Mrs. Gardner looked at him with surprise. Since when did he know the various kinds of available chocolate? "No, that wouldn't have made a difference. You see, this isn't candy chocolate."

"What do you mean? Isn't chocolate . . . chocolate?"

Mrs. Gardner found his confusion endearing. "No, I mean this isn't meant for eating directly, like you would candy. It's meant for baking, like brownies or cakes."

"Oh . . ." Professor Jenson's voice trailed off and he seemed disappointed. "I suppose that's why it says baking on it. It's such small print."

"It's the oddest thing. I found this in my mailbox this morning. Can you imagine?"

Professor Jenson grew quiet. "That's strange."

Mrs. Gardner went to bed that night with her mind on fire. She'd made light of the situation with Professor Jenson, but she was consumed with the desire to know who was leaving her these bizarre gifts. She tried to dismiss her speculations and turn her attention to the next day. She planned on finally getting her fall decorations up, much later than she'd have liked, and then there was the visit with Ben. She'd promised to meet him during his lunch break. At the thought of her visit with Ben, Mrs. Gardner went still. Flowers, chocolates—who had she been talking to recently about those? Ben. She laughed out loud. *No need to be silly*, she counseled herself. It's not like Ben Palermo was wooing her! She continued to laugh into her pillow at the very thought, but she spent a sleepless night tossing and turning. It was impossible. Wasn't it?

Professor Jenson drove her to Carley's Café the next morning. "You look like you didn't sleep a wink."

"Oh, I'm fine, everything's fine," Mrs. Gardner answered quickly. "Mark, would you want to join me for lunch?" She watched as his expression brightened. "I'm supposed to meet Ben, but I'm sure he wouldn't mind if you came too." His expression faltered a bit.

"Are you sure? I don't mind coming back to pick you up if you'd rather."

"No, you're welcome to join us." It was ridiculous. Ben wasn't leaving her gifts. There was no way, but just in case, it didn't hurt to have Professor Jenson along, right?

They were early and so found a booth and sat down to wait. Mrs. Gardner busied herself by staring at the chalkboard menu behind the counter even though she often frequented Carley's and practically knew the menu by heart. Professor Jenson cleared his throat across from her, and she looked over. He seemed nervous. She had just opened her mouth to ask him about it when Ben walked up.

"Mrs. Gardner, Professor Jenson, hi!" He slid into the seat next to her before she knew what was happening. He was carrying a small takeout box, which he set on the table. He leaned over and gave Mrs. Gardner a side hug.

"Oh, uh, oh, hi, Ben," Mrs. Gardner giggled nervously and scooted away a little. "I hope you don't mind Mark joining us. He's been so kind to play chauffeur while I have this thing on." She raised her arm to indicate the sling she was sporting. "It seems I injured my shoulder thanks to that cumbersome cast. This sling means I *still* can't drive." She sighed. "Honestly, I'm wondering if I'll even remember how to after this whole thing is over."

"Well, I'm glad you have a such a good man to help take care of you." Ben smiled and nodded to Professor Jenson across the table, then turned back to Mrs. Gardner. "When can you take the sling off?"

"Not for another three weeks," she moaned. "I suppose it's an improvement from the cast. Still, if it's not one thing, it's another. We old people just don't spring back like you young folks." She laughed and hoped he'd gotten the not-so-subtle message. She was old enough to be his grandmother! Or at least an older aunt; yes, an older, attractive aunt.

"I'm sorry to hear that. Hey, maybe this will cheer you up." Ben slid the takeout box in her direction. She opened it tentatively. Inside was an enormous red velvet cupcake from the bakery down the street. Number three on the checklist. Ben had just surprised her.

"Oh my, you didn't have to do this." Her heart was pounding uncomfortably. She was confused. Didn't Ben like Rosemary? Unless that had been a ploy, an excuse to spend time with her. She fidgeted and the hard plastic coating of the bench squeaked in response.

"It's my pleasure. I know you like their cupcakes, and your birthday was last weekend."

"It was?" Professor Jenson's gaze jerked up. He looked stricken.

"Oh yes, it was," Mrs. Gardner laughed. "How did you know, Ben?"

"You mentioned it last time I saw you. Have you all ordered yet?"

Ben turned and glanced at the menu. Mrs. Gardner took advantage of his distraction and looked pointedly at Professor Jenson. Was he seeing this? No, he was too busy wringing his hands and looking worriedly out the window.

"I'm going to go order." Ben turned back to them and slid from his seat. "Be right back, and hey, you look really nice today, Mrs. Gardner." He smiled at her, and her heart fluttered with despair. Number four: flattery, the final nail in the coffin.

"Th-thank you."

"You didn't tell me about your birthday." Professor Jenson leaned across the table as soon as Ben was out of earshot.

Mrs. Gardner was surprised at the vehemence in his voice. "I'm sorry. Is that information you wanted to know?"

"I just . . . I don't know. I would have done something nice for you."

"Mark, you do something nice for me every day." Mrs. Gardner patted his hand. "Now, would you order for me while you're up there? A bowl of cream of broccoli soup and a small Caesar salad, please."

Mrs. Gardner tried to enjoy the meal, but it was hard when Ben was carrying on so. He joked with her, touched her arm on more than one occasion, and complimented her on the cookies she'd brought him last week. Oh, he was laying it on thick, even with Professor Jenson sitting right there! Professor Jenson, for his part, was no help whatsoever. Mrs. Gardner tried to send him small signs for emergency help, but he seemed utterly devoted to his meal—and unusually miserable about missing her birthday. By the time they'd finished, Mrs. Gardner was beside herself. Ben needed a young vibrant wife, someone to start a family with! What on earth was he doing, throwing himself at her in this way? And here she was, beginning to think of him as a son.

"Sorry to dine and dash, but I need to get back to the bookstore." They left the booth, and Ben gave her a quick hug, causing her to gasp and laugh at the same time, which in turn made her hiccup.

"See you later, dear." *No, wait!* Mrs. Gardner wished she could reach out into the air and take the word "dear" back. She watched Ben leave, then headed to the car with

Professor Jenson, who was quietly brooding at her side. She desperately needed to talk to someone about this, and preferably a man. She needed to know, from a man's perspective, how to let Ben down gently and still remain friends. But how to bring it up? It was so embarrassing that she hated to even give it words. Maybe she could just hint around and get what she needed. He'd seen firsthand what was going on with Ben. Hopefully he'd help her.

They settled into the car, and Professor Jenson pulled out onto the main road. "Home?" he said.

"Yes, thanks." Mrs. Gardner fiddled with her seat belt. "So, I, um, I think I've figured out who sent me those gifts." She looked at Professor Jenson out of the corner of her eye, gauging his reaction. "The flowers and the chocolate, I mean."

"Oh! Oh r-really?" Professor Jenson stared fixedly ahead at the road.

"And I just don't know what to do about it," Mrs. Gardner sighed shakily.

"I see. Is it . . . unwelcome, then?"

"Yes, of course!"

"Oh, I see," Professor Jenson said again and then fell silent.

"I mean, don't you think it's ridiculous? The age difference alone!" Mrs. Gardner moaned.

"I don't think the age difference matters, do you?" Professor Jenson said slowly, his voice coming across as hesitant. He really was being moody today.

"Of course it matters, Mark. We're not at all right for each other."

"Is that what you think? I know it probably comes as a bit of a surprise. It surprised me too."

"Surprise? Try shock on for size!"

"I'm sorry if it made you uncomfortable. I-I didn't think it was that ridiculous."

"You approve, then?" Mrs. Gardner couldn't believe her ears.

"Well, yes, obviously."

"Mark! You astound me."

"Is that bad? Is that good? I'm confused right now."

"I just need advice on how to let a gentleman down easily, gently."

Professor Jenson was quiet for a long moment. Then, "It's okay, Matilda," he sighed. "You don't need to say any more. Let's just go home and forget about it."

Mrs. Gardner looked over at him. There was genuine pain in his voice, and his features as he stared firmly at the road were twisted in an expression that she didn't recognize. "Are you okay?"

"I will be. Let's not talk about it."

"Okay, I just don't know what to do."

"You've done enough. Don't worry about it."

Mrs. Gardner sensed that the conversation was over. She turned to the window in a huff. Well, he'd been extremely unhelpful! How could he sit there after observing what he'd observed and say it was a good idea? All her old convictions of Professor Jenson came flooding back. *Crazy old man!* And then on the heel of that thought came another. *Crazy, compassionate, kind, wonderful old man.* She looked at him again, her heart softening. She reached out a hand to touch his but he jerked it away. She frowned and contented herself with looking out the window, trying to pretend that his rejection didn't hurt.

**The boy is slightly embarrassed by his friendship with the younger girl.** She has come to mean more to him than his friends back home. He is at the age when girls hold an intoxicating mixture of frightening and pleasantly mysterious qualities. Still, she is just a little kid, and he will turn fourteen in just two weeks. The idea of ending their game, however, leaves him feeling sad and anxious. He needs the Story People as much as he needs the girl's notes, her smiles, her enthusiasm, her drawings.

The boy enters the silent Room with a small flame of hope that is quickly snuffed. It's rare to find her in the Room; they've met face-to-face only a handful of times over the years, but still he can't contain the thought: Maybe this time. To add to the disappointment, there is no note this time. The girl hasn't been back since the last time he was here, which means his last note is still sitting where he placed it, folded neatly on a chair. The boy tries to contain his disappointment, but it is acute and won't be silenced.

The boy spends the afternoon reading The Phantom Tollbooth and plotting another letter to the girl. He stops only for a bathroom and snack break, returning with a bag of Doritos in hand and licking his cheesy fingers clean when it comes time to write his note to the girl.

The note written, the bag of chips consumed, and the book at a logical stopping point, the boy stands up and brushes the fine dusting of cheese off his pants. He sets his newest note next to the old one, imagining the moment when the girl will come in and see this surprise: two notes! He smiles as he thinks of her excited face. The boy says good-bye to the Room. He clicks off his flashlight, gathers his things, and leaves.

The boy doesn't know that this is the last time he will be in the Room for many, many years.

# Chapter Twenty-Three

## "SURPRISE!"

Thanksgiving was a quiet, sophisticated affair in the Berg household—much different from the Thanksgivings Rosemary remembered growing up. Her father was part of a large clan, and Rosemary had many memories of hectic meals at the kids' table while the adults laughed, joked, or more commonly, argued boisterously in the next room. She'd loved seeing her cousins, but visits with Dad's side of the family always ended with her mom crying in the spare bedroom, packing their bags, leaving as soon as she was able. The anticipation of this anguish had tainted the gatherings until Rosemary had come to dread them. It would start out loud and fun and entertaining, but she knew it was only a matter of time before voices were raised, slurred speech hurled back and forth, and her mom would be back to where she always was, quietly sobbing.

When her parents had divorced, Thanksgivings had become quiet. Rosemary and her mother were no longer invited to the large, loud family gatherings on her father's side, and to eight-year-old Rosemary, that had come as a bit of a relief. She particularly remembered a time during the peak of summer, when she was nine years old and getting ready for the pool. Her mother had been slowly lathering sunscreen on her, building protection layer by layer.

"Sweetie, how would you like to have a new name?"

"What do you mean, Mom?"

"Well, you would take my old last name: Berg."

She'd thought through this slowly. "So I would still be Rosemary?"

"Oh yes, dear. You will always be my Rosie. I don't mean your first name. You will always keep that. Just your last name, sweetie."

"So I wouldn't be Rosemary Williams anymore?"

"No, honey. You'd be Rosemary Berg."

She'd mulled this over. "And you'd be Stephanie Berg?"

"Yes, just like I used to be."

"I guess that would be okay."

In the end it didn't really matter what Rosemary did or did not want. Her mother changed their last name and she was no longer a Williams, no longer invited to the large, confusing Williams gatherings. She saw her father increasingly less over the years, always wondering why she had been so easy to leave. Maybe she shouldn't have hidden herself so much, or maybe she hadn't hidden herself enough. One thing had been clear: she'd done something wrong if he could so easily forget her. Now she continued to be reminded every time she signed her name or heard it called that she was not a part of her father's family anymore—she had no part of him left.

Her father had a new family and three stepchildren and spent Thanksgivings with them, Christmases too. Rosemary had eventually adjusted to the quieter holidays. Instead of a table full of arguing people, it was just her mother, Oma, and her. As Rosemary grew older and more able to help in the kitchen, the three of them would turn on the music, open a bottle of wine (sparkling grape juice for Rosemary), and make an event of preparing the meal. With these two strong women, Rosemary felt like she belonged, like she was a wanted and valuable member of the Berg sisterhood.

Oma had insisted that they still come to her house for Thanksgiving this year, despite her recent surgery. "I can handle this," she'd replied to their protests. "And you can help by cooking the sides. I'll do the bird," Oma said during her weekly phone call early in November. Green bean casserole, stuffing, and pies were all made ahead of time, carefully packaged and transferred, filling the car with a tempting aroma. They'd taken two cars because Rosemary planned on staying after Thanksgiving for the book signing and to continue work on her new book.

"I'm beginning to think you prefer your Oma to me," her mother joked.

"It's for the book, Mom. It's much better to sketch from real life than memory."

"I understand. Your Oma will be so happy that you're writing about the bookstore."

The lonely car ride over had given Rosemary plenty of time to fret over the upcoming meeting with Ben. She turned up the radio, but even the loud tunes and pungent smells from the back seat couldn't drown out her worry and anticipation. Ben had mailed her a flyer weeks ago, and it was a beautiful and thoughtful tribute to her book. She was humbled by how genuinely excited Ben was over her book and how wholeheartedly he wanted to promote her and her work in New Holden. He'd invited her to the store Friday evening to help set up, and Rosemary was torn as to whether she should reveal their connection during that time. She'd finally decided she would just play it by ear.

Oma detected right away that something was amiss. "You're as jumpy as a cat on a hot tin roof," she said five minutes after their arrival. Rosemary was carrying food into the house, the door propped open and letting in wisps of cool air. "Are you nervous about the book signing?" Oma stood in the hallway with a twinkle in her eye as Rosemary and her mom trekked back and forth with armloads of food and suitcases.

"What do you have to be nervous about, dear?" her mom asked in passing. "You've done book signings before."

"Yes, but not ones put together by a handsome young man," Oma chuckled, causing Rosemary to blush as she plopped a bag onto a kitchen chair.

"What is this about?" Rosemary's mom drew up short and glanced over at her daughter. "You didn't tell me about a handsome young man."

"She hit it off with the store's owner, Ben Palermo, last time she was here," Oma continued helpfully.

"Oma! Really, that's not it at all. My mind is just full with ideas about my book."

"Her new book, that is," Rosemary's mom said proudly. "She's going to write about the bookstore."

"Oh, and will Ben feature in this book?" Oma continued with a grin on her face.

"Oma, seriously, you're horrible!"

"Rosemary, you didn't tell me about Ben." Rosemary's mom suddenly looked serious. "Is he a nice young man? Are you interested in him?"

Rosemary didn't feel like talking through all the complicated emotions Ben raised in her; nor did she feel like exposing her secret childhood friend just yet. BJ had been important to her for reasons that would make her mother feel guilty. "Hey, Mom, remember when Dad abandoned us and you switched our names and suddenly my family shrunk in size and my whole identity shifted? Yeah, well, Ben helped me through that time." No, she'd kept BJ a secret all this time, and she wasn't about to talk *about* him until she'd actually had a chance to talk *to* him.

"It's no big deal, Mom," Rosemary said lightly. "Oma is just playing matchmaker." She stuck her tongue out at Oma affectionately and went back outside to grab another bag.

The rest of Wednesday was spent stockpiling the ingredients to make the rest of the Thanksgiving meal. Rosemary approached the Thursday morning church service with her heart in her throat. She tried not to be too obvious in her search for Ben, not wanting to give the two women with her any more reason to poke fun, but she didn't spot him and wondered if he'd attended an earlier service. She suppressed her disappointment with a reminder that she'd see him tomorrow. Afterward, the Berg women hurried home to begin work on the mashed potatoes, cranberry sauce, and deviled eggs. Oma opened the oven every so often to baste the bird, and a bottle of pinot noir was steadily consumed as the women cranked up the music, whipped out the aprons, and talked and laughed. Thankfully, Oma steered clear of talking about Ben, and Rosemary was able to relax and enjoy the day.

"Thank You, God, for my two girls." The room had quieted. Candles softly glowed in the dimmed dining room as the three women held hands and bowed heads over the fine china and bountiful feast. "Thank You for giving us family and friends and good health. Thank You for delicious food and good conversation." Rosemary felt Oma squeeze her hand, indicating it was her turn.

"Thank You, Lord, for these two crazy ladies." Rosemary squeezed both their hands and continued. "Thank You for Your provision over the years and the many blessings You give us each day. Help us not to take them for granted." She squeezed her mother's hand, indicating it was her turn.

"Thank You, precious Savior, for my mother." Rosemary was surprised to hear a catch in her mother's voice. "Thank You for the strong example of a godly mother she's been over the years. And thank You, thank You for my Rosie."

Rosemary felt a lump form in her throat. Her mother usually wasn't this emotional. "Thank You for giving her the gift of creativity. Bless her efforts, and Lord, if it be Your will, bring a young man into her life . . . soon. I really want grandchildren someday. In Jesus' name . . ."

Rosemary opened her eyes wide as Oma squeezed her hand and gave a full-throated "Amen!"

"That wasn't very subtle, Mom." Rosemary felt her face flush as she laid the napkin across her lap.

"Well, ask and you shall receive, right?" Rosemary's mom lifted her wineglass as if in a toast. "I've been praying for your future spouse since you were little. The Lord is very familiar with this prayer."

Oma scooped a pile of stuffing onto her plate and looked at Rosemary with raised eyebrows as if telepathically transmitting Ben's name to her. No need, Ben's face was already dancing in her head.

Friday was a day of recuperation. Leftovers were divvied up and frozen, and the rest of the day was spent lounging around in pajamas and watching television. The Berg women religiously avoided Black Friday shopping. They much preferred stalking online sales and spent Friday looking ahead and planning for Cyber Monday. This year, Rosemary spent the day looking ahead to the evening and her meeting with Ben.

"You look really nice." Rosemary's mom looked up from her spot on the sofa where she sat with her feet propped up and the laptop open and balancing on the armrest.

"Very nice," Oma agreed from her spot on the recliner. She muted her television show and swiveled to get a better look at her granddaughter.

"I'm helping Ben set up the store for the book signing tomorrow."

"I thought you were just going over early on Saturday," Oma wondered.

"Well, he invited me over tonight, so that's where I'm headed." Rosemary tried to act casually, dismissively. She rummaged around in her purse for nothing in particular.

"He's being awfully attentive to you," Rosemary's mother observed. Her tone didn't sound excited.

"Is that a problem, Stephanie?" Oma questioned her daughter.

"No, not necessarily. I would like to meet him though." Rosemary's mom looked back down at her screen with a slight frown.

"He's Louie's nephew. Remember Louie?" Oma continued. "Ben goes to my church. Trust me, he's a wonderful young man."

"That's good to know." Rosemary's mom looked relieved.

"Okay, enough scouting of potential suitors! You'll meet him tomorrow. This whole thing, it's not a big deal. He's just being a smart small-business owner. This will make him a profit, after all." Rosemary hovered by the doorway. "Got to get going. I'll see you later tonight."

The evening was brisk and biting, but Rosemary decided to walk the few blocks to the store anyway. She buttoned her green peacoat as she walked down the front steps and pulled on her mittens. Her pink fuzzy scarf fit snugly around her neck, hiding half her face from the wind. She tucked her brown leather purse under her arm and leaned into the wind, her eyes watering. She'd chosen her outfit with care. Skinny jeans and camel ankle boots with a flowing ivory top. The top, she realized belatedly, wasn't warm enough for an evening fall walk, and she shivered against the cold, shoving her hands into her pockets.

She walked quickly and approached the store in record time, her eyes traveling to the lit storefront. Her book was featured prominently in a beautiful display. An artificial tree with twinkly lights sat center stage with a charming rustic chair next to it, and on the chair sat her book, propped open and greeting the world. There was a green cloth spread on the floor to mimic grass, and the first line of her book was written in beautiful script on a chalkboard sign: "Once there was a little girl named Ivy, who lived in a world of black and white." More twinkly lights were strung across the width of the window, mimicking stars. Even though the evening was growing colder, Rosemary stood outside and looked up at the lit bay window; her body and heart shivered in unison, albeit for different reasons. "Oh Lord, I want this to go well. Please let it go well." She breathed into the air. "Show me how to act and what to say to him." Finally she tore herself away from the front walk and went up the stairs, swallowing her nervousness as she opened the door.

Ben stood behind the desk and watched Rosemary's face slowly light up as she observed the front window display. From where he stood, he could see only her face peeking out from her scarf and looking up with delight at his store. His heart sang at her expression. Charlotte had helped him with the chalkboard sign because his handwriting was practically illegible, but the rest was his own doing. The day was here, finally here. Ben had invited her over a day early because he'd planned to ask her out, but as the day had progressed, he'd thought better of it. What if she said no? It would make the book signing awkward for her. By the time the hour of her arrival had come, Ben had completely changed his mind. Better to ask her out after the signing when a no would be less awkward for the both of them. There really wasn't anything he needed her help on—the invitation had been made purely out of ulterior motives—so Ben had scrambled for something to give her to do, finally settling on stuffing bookmarks into books and signing a few copies for later sales.

Now, as Ben watched her watch his store, his heart warmed in his chest and then plummeted to the pit of his stomach as she moved out of sight. The door opened with a loud ring and she entered with a cold blast of air on her heels. She was unwrapping the scarf from around her neck as her eyes scanned the floor for him. Ben took a deep breath and made the first move.

"Rosemary, so good to see you again!" He held out a hand to shake hers. She quickly pulled off her mittens and took it. Her hand was small and cold in his own. He lingered over the handshake, drinking in the sensation of the pressure of her thin fingers against his own. "Did you walk all the way here?"

"Yes, I think I underestimated how cold it was." She laughed, which caused her eyes to flash appealingly. She broke their handshake to reach up and tug her scarf off. Her nose and ears were bright pink with the cold, and she rubbed her hands together.

"I was going to offer to take your coat, but maybe you'd like to hold on to it and warm up a bit." Ben smiled. The cold enlivened her already lively features, and he took in the sight of her appreciatively.

"I may do that, thanks." Rosemary smiled up at him, her eyes catching his and staying there. He'd missed that intense look. "I just love your window display. It's gorgeous. You've really put a lot of thought into this."

"I'm glad you like it." JC chose that moment to come bounding from the back. With great joy he jumped at Rosemary's legs and yapped.

"Is this your dog?" Rosemary bent and placed a hand on JC's back. "I saw him the other times I was here but wasn't sure."

"Yes, this is JC, short for Julius Caesar."

Rosemary laughed out loud. "I love that! It's a very sophisticated name for such a small dog, isn't it?" Her voice descended into baby talk as she leaned toward JC. "Aren't you the cutest little guy?" She glanced up at Ben. "Is he okay with people picking him up?"

"Go for it." Ben smiled at her obvious love of dogs, his heart swelling as yet another mark in her favor was added to his already expansive list. Rosemary picked JC up and held him close to her face, laughing as she accepted his slobbery kisses. *So far, so good.* The nervousness he'd been experiencing all day was melting in her bright presence. Ben moved toward a table where he'd placed a pod coffee brewer. "Would you like a cup? I started setting this up a moment ago. Figured we could serve coffee and tea tomorrow during the event."

"I love that idea. You've thought of everything. And a cup of decaf would be perfect right now." Rosemary set JC down and finally took off her coat, exposing a tasteful ensemble beneath. Her style fit her personality—understated, classy. Ben hung her coat on a coatrack and tried not to stare at her. There was a brief silence while the coffeemaker emitted a gurgling noise and began streaming hot liquid into a mug. They were exchanging niceties with ease, but Ben could sense an undercurrent of tension from her. He hoped he could manage to put her at ease.

"I see you have my throne all arranged." Rosemary gestured toward a comfy chair and another table containing stacks of her book.

"Yup, and I figured tonight you could help me stuff the books with bookmarks, and maybe we could finish setting up the refreshment table."

"That sounds great!" Rosemary accepted the cup of coffee and took a grateful sip.

"And I . . . I got these for you." Ben lifted a vase of flowers from their perch on the refreshment table and handed them to Rosemary, who stared at them as if she'd never seen a bouquet before. For a moment they stood with the flowers suspended between them, he staring anxiously at her face and she with a steaming mug, staring at the flowers. Finally she set the mug down and reached for the gift.

"Oh, Ben, they're beautiful." She touched a petal and looked up at him. In that moment, he knew that he wanted her to look at him that way every day, always. He looked back and let her see his feelings in his face.

"*You're* beautiful," he fumbled and paused. He was getting ahead of himself; he was careening over a line that once crossed was never to be uncrossed. He tried to rein it back. "And you deserve beautiful things, so I-I just wanted to treat you with this, as the store's featured author."

"Thank you. I don't know what to say." She was blushing and refusing to look at him. He kicked himself for making her feel uncomfortable.

"Actually, those flowers that you saw me give away last time we met? They were meant for you. I'm sure it was confusing—seeing what you saw and then me leaving them on your doorstep like that."

Rosemary looked back up at him in disbelief. "You mean the flower incident next door to Oma's?"

"Yes, those were for you." Now was prime time to dispel all the false impressions he'd made, and Ben was determined to take full advantage of it.

"I feel so silly right now. You left them on the doorstep because I wouldn't open the door. And when I found them, I didn't know what to think." She hung her head. "I owe you an apology. I overreacted."

"Don't worry about it. No need to apologize." The last thing he wanted was to make her feel ashamed.

"Why were you bringing me flowers?" Her gaze, usually so direct, had turned shy. She avoided his eyes and looked instead at the flowers, gently touching their petals.

"To apologize for seeming to blow you off at the bookstore. It was never my intention. It was just that Mrs.

Baumgartner . . . I was asked to give a tour and I couldn't get away from . . . I just know how it probably looked, and it's not at all the way I wanted you to feel. Believe me, there's nothing I wanted more than to spend time with you. I still want that." He looked at her pointedly. "Anyway, I hated that you maybe got the wrong impression of me, and I felt so bad about it. I still do." Ben turned his gaze to stare fixedly at the flowers between them. The flowers seemed to bloom more fully beneath the force of their combined focus.

"You're sweet, so sweet. I'm so relieved. How could I miss that?" Rosemary's voice grew soft and trailed off as if she were speaking more to herself than to Ben. She looked up at him quickly as if suddenly realizing she'd spoken out loud. Her face flushed. Ben felt his throat tighten in response. She'd called him sweet! He could get used to this— his name on her lips, her eyes following him as they were now. To save her further embarrassment, Ben moved to the stack of books and bookmarks and cleared his throat.

"Should we get started?" Rosemary stood where he'd left her, the bouquet in her hands and her coffee mug forgotten. She looked lost and confused, and when she finally turned in his direction, she looked ready to say something important. Ben swallowed hard. Had he gone too far? Had he made her uncomfortable and ruined everything?

"Ben, I-I have something to tell you. To ask you."

"Yes, anything. What is it?"

"I am . . . you are . . . I . . ." She couldn't look any more cautious and uncertain if she were suspended on a tightrope. He watched as the tension eased out of her face by degrees, beginning with her furrowed brow and finally resulting in her setting down the flowers and picking up her mug. "Can I leave these beautiful flowers here? They'll be perfect on the table when I'm signing tomorrow."

"Of course." Ben sensed there was more on her mind, but he didn't want to pry.

◇◆◇◆

Rosemary's chest was constricted with emotion. Ben was obviously interested in her and the realization sent an almost painful shot of exhilaration through her. This would be so much easier if she weren't carrying around the knowledge of their shared past. She wanted to show him how much she was interested in him too, but to do so without first telling him who she was seemed dishonest. He was seeing her as a woman and making her feel desirable and beautiful, but would that change when he found out that she was Rosie? That brought a whole different dynamic to their unfolding relationship. Rosemary watched Ben unpack stacks of *Spectrum* bookmarks, which were dwarfed in his large hands, and she decided to hold off on her revelation. She wanted to enjoy this sensation a little longer—just two people getting to know each other.

"Tell me more about yourself," Ben said as they sat in the reading nook at the back of the store, a box of books on the floor between them.

Rosemary grabbed a book from the box, inserted a bookmark, and placed it on the growing stack on the coffee table. "Well, what would you like to know?"

"Where'd you grow up? How'd you start drawing? Anything you want to share, really." His eyes were eager and fixed on her.

"I grew up in Indianapolis, so not too far from here. Then when my parents divorced, my mom and I moved to a suburb south of the city and my dad moved in with the woman he'd been seeing from work. They're married now and living in South Carolina."

"I'm sorry. That must have been hard for you. Were you young at the time?"

"I was eight." Rosemary stopped abruptly, a lump in her throat.

"I'm sorry, that was thoughtless of me. You don't have to talk about this if you don't want to." Ben was looking at her with a worried expression, obviously thinking that her emotion was due to the memory of her father.

Rosemary couldn't look him in the eye. *No*, she wanted to tell him, *I'm not about to cry because of my dad, I'm about to cry because of you, you amazing, beautiful man! You got me through that dark, lonely period. You were the safe place for me. You!* It was surreal, talking about this period of her life with the grown-up BJ. She sniffed and cleared her throat, moving to a different topic. "It's okay. Actually, my art really helped me through that time." *And you—you helped me too.*

"I've heard that art can be therapeutic." Ben smiled at her. "Reading was that for me. Books always helped me manage my emotions. Something about reading the stories of other people's lives was soothing, helpful."

"Yes, I agree. I think reading lets us know that we're not alone, that our experiences have been others' experiences. Sometimes we think our situation is so unique, but reading puts us back into context. We don't have to feel isolated or alone after all. Stories connect us as humans." She paused, realizing that she'd gone on one of her "riffs" that had earned her the label of "intimidating" in college. Ben, however, didn't miss a beat.

"Absolutely. So, for example, I'd always loved The Boxcar Children, but after my parents passed away, the books took on a whole new meaning for me. I was fourteen years old, but I'd fall asleep with the books in my bed every night. I read the entire series over and over. My mom read them with me when I was younger, so they made me feel close to her, but more than that, I could now relate to the characters. Reading about other kids who'd lost their parents, fictional or not, was actually very helpful."

"Oh, Ben, I can't even imagine." Rosemary's hands stilled, and she sat silently watching her friend. "Oma told me what happened to your parents, and I could hardly believe it. I wish I'd known." She stopped. That last part had sounded weird, but Ben didn't seem to have noticed.

"Thanks. It's hard some days being here, being reminded of them and my uncle."

"But what a way to also keep their memories alive," Rosemary burst in, her heart aching for her friend. "Ben, you've done such an amazing job with this store. I have no doubt that it's hard and some days maybe doesn't even seem worth it, but trust me, it is worth it! Your uncle and parents would be so thankful and proud of you. *I'm* so proud of you." She realized that she was crying, but she didn't care. This compassionate, hurting man needed to know that he wasn't alone, that his work mattered— *he* mattered.

◇◆◇◆

Ben watched the woman in front of him passionately defend his work, the tears coursing down her cheeks, and before he knew what he was doing, he'd left his seat and drawn her from hers and was holding her. Her hair tangled and stuck in his lips as he mumbled, "Thank you, Rosemary, thank you. You're so kind. I can't begin to tell you how much I needed to hear those words." His breathing was ragged in her hair. She'd stopped crying and had stilled in his arms. She drew her head back and looked him in the face, both hands flat against his chest. He'd expected embarrassment, but she looked calm and happy, her eyes brimming with emotion.

"I just don't want you to feel alone. I've been in dark, lonely places myself, and it helps to have a friend to remind you that you're not alone. A flesh-and-blood friend, and not just a book friend!" She laughed, easing the heavy emotion between them.

He felt right at home with her in his arms, but Ben knew he had to let her go. They both sat down again, a fresh affinity between them. "I could never feel alone with someone like you—so passionate and caring. You make this whole store come to life! You make *me* feel alive."

Rosemary laughed. "You're giving me way too much credit here, Mr. Dramatic."

Ben just shook his head at her, his smile widening. "Nothing dramatic about it. I'm just stating the truth." He raised an eyebrow at her and cocked his head.

Rosemary blushed, grabbing a bookmark. "Well, I don't know about that, but you need to stop singing my praises and start stuffing books or we'll never get them all done."

Ben continued to grin at her even as he complied and picked up a book. He watched as she glanced up at him briefly and noticed him still looking at her. He grinned wider, causing her to roll her eyes at him and shake her head.

They continued to work, their eyes meeting on and off throughout the evening, a newfound awareness between them. Ben soaked in every detail of her. He sensed, too, that she was studying him. He'd caught her thoughtfully appraising him when she thought he wasn't looking. Several times, he intentionally let her think he hadn't noticed her gaze, just to keep her attention fixed on him a little longer. He needed to be noticed by her, he realized; he craved her attention with an intensity that unsettled him. He felt a connection between them, running like an electrical current just below the surface. She'd spoken like she knew him. Funny—he felt like he knew her too. Like she had been and would be forever a part of his life.

As the evening drew to a close, Ben found himself scrambling for ways to prolong it. They were sitting in the reading area, their empty coffee mugs between them, the store sprawling in front of them.

"This was wonderful," Rosemary sighed and shifted JC from her lap to the floor. "But I better get going. It's getting late."

Ben didn't want the moment to end. "Let me drive you home. I know it's not far, but it's pretty cold out now and it's dark."

"Okay," Rosemary smiled at him, and he was pleased with how quickly she'd agreed.

She sat with JC in her lap for the short drive. The dog had taken to her quickly, completely besotted by her attention. *You and me both, JC,* Ben thought. They'd talked nearly nonstop in the store but now remained silent. Ben looked over at her, still sensing that there was more on her mind that she wanted to tell him, not knowing if he hoped that was the case or not.

"Here we are." He pulled into Oma's driveway and threw the truck into park.

"Thank you, Ben." Rosemary lifted JC to her face and gave him a big kiss before transferring him to Ben's lap.

*Lucky dog,* Ben thought as he accepted JC's wiggling body.

Rosemary looked up at him quietly in the dark, their shared breaths foggy between them. "Until tomorrow, then."

He wanted to grab her impulsively, gather her in his arms, kiss her upturned face and feel the heat of her breath against his skin. Instead he contented himself with simply looking at her. "Until tomorrow." He watched her slide out of his truck and make her way to the front door. She opened the door, turned, and waved at him with a smile. He waved back and flashed his lights in a friendly farewell. He waited until she'd closed the door before backing out of the driveway. Quietly he stroked JC's fur all the way home. He carried JC inside and locked the door for the evening, finally sitting and processing all that had happened. "I've got it bad, JC," he finally admitted. "And as soon as this book signing is over, I'm asking Rosemary Berg out on a date." He didn't think he could wait another minute in suspense.

◇◆◇

Rosemary waved to Ben with a full heart. The gulf between Ben and BJ was slowly closing. The hours she'd just spent in his company had left her feeling off-balance. She had felt his attention like a physical presence in the room. "You're beautiful." She played those two words over and over in her mind, and with those words, the feeling of his strong arms around her, the instant connection they'd forged. She never wanted that feeling to end.

Rosemary closed the front door behind her and made her way to the kitchen. The light from the living room was on. Her mom and Oma were probably watching a movie together. Quietly she slipped down the hallway and into her room to change into her pajamas. She was back in the kitchen, pouring herself a glass of water, when her mom entered the room.

"Rosemary, you're back! We didn't hear you come in."

Rosemary glanced up and found her mom nervously glancing from the kitchen to the living room door.

"Yeah, I know, it's later than I thought."

"How'd it go?" Her mom didn't wait for a reply. "You might want to put something else on, or get a robe."

"What?" Rosemary looked at her mom, confused. She was braless and wearing an old extra-large T-shirt—immodest, yes, but hardly a concern given the present company. She moved to the living room door. "Why are you so jumpy?" She stood in the doorway, looking over her shoulder at her mom, a cup of water poised in her hand. A male intake of breath turned her attention to the living room.

Liam stood up from where he'd been sitting on the sofa, an embarrassed look on his face as he avoided looking at anything inappropriate. "Hey, Clooney! Surprise!"

**The girl is happy to receive the boy's two notes, but she is sad because she knows this means he was disappointed to not receive a note from her.**

The boy is reading The Phantom Tollbooth. *The girl decides this will be the book she buys during this visit. She tells the boy this in her letter and adds "unless the Story People have eaten it." She laughs and draws a picture of a partially devoured book, letters like crumbs spilling out of it. The girl finishes the note and leaves it on the chair. She looks around the Room, which seems empty without the boy. She leaves and imagines the boy laughing at her picture when he finds it.*

*The girl does not know that the boy will not find it for many, many years.*

# Chapter Twenty-Four

## COLDNESS SETTLING INSIDE

The day of the book signing dawned loudly—loud birds outside her window, loud breakfast preparations in the kitchen, loud turmoil in her mind. The day dawned loudly and only increased in volume from there.

Her mother, it seemed, had taken the liberty of inviting Liam to the book signing without telling her. Her mother, it seemed, liked Liam and hoped that Rosemary liked him too, and she wasn't above shamelessly throwing them together. Her mother had extended this invitation weeks ago, well before she had known about Ben. Her mother was sorry if this put Rosemary in an awkward position. Well, it did, and Rosemary was in no mood to be understanding.

After Rosemary had squealed and dashed for refuge to her room, where she'd changed into more modest clothes, she'd rejoined the group, where Liam continued to avoid eye contact.

The truth was, Rosemary didn't know how to react. It wasn't wrong for her close friend to want to support her in this way, and it wasn't wrong of her mother to take a liking to her friend, but it felt like a trap regardless, and Rosemary resented it. She'd acted poorly last night; she'd snapped at her mother and Liam and had been irritable and unfair. She'd tried to blame it on the surprise of finding herself half-clad in Liam's presence, but really she didn't need any other complicating factors in the complicated mess that was Ben/BJ.

This morning was an apologizing morning, a setting aside of her personal preferences and acknowledging that her friend and her mother had, in fact, done nothing wrong. Only Oma seemed to fully understand the distress she was under and quietly gave her looks of support. Rosemary had apologized repeatedly but still felt the tension radiating from Liam. She'd finally left for the bookstore—early, as she'd promised Ben. Oma, her mother, and now, apparently, Liam would meet her there later.

She showed up early, flustered and beautiful. Her green coat was hanging open, showing the brown and black striped tunic beneath. She wore knee-high brown boots and her hair was up in a messy bun.

"There are my beautiful flowers." She smiled at Ben and at the flowers brightening her table.

*And here is* my *beautiful flower*, Ben thought, eagerly looking ahead to the moment when he would finally make his interest known. Instead he moved to the business at hand. "We'll have you sign books here and then maybe around lunchtime you can give a reading in the children's section."

"That sounds great," Rosemary said as Ben took her coat and purse and placed them behind the counter. The conversation that had flowed so easily the night before now flagged. She was preoccupied and skittish. She asked for a glass of water and then didn't drink a sip. She needed him to repeat himself two or three times before processing what he said. Ben began to worry that he had truly bothered her with his attentions the night before.

The doors opened at nine, and Rosemary was perched in her seat, pen and smile in place. A line of people had formed. The first person inside was a young man with sandy hair and a huge smile. He was carrying a large bouquet of flowers and made a beeline for Rosemary. Ben watched as he offered Rosemary the flowers and leaned in close, whispering something to her. His heart sank in dismay.

Liam didn't know what he'd done wrong, but clearly he'd done something. He'd never seen Rosemary lose her cool that way, and it'd upset him to think he'd somehow been the cause. Flowers seemed to be the correct gesture, but his friend—his smart and gorgeous friend looking up at him with turmoil on her face—did not appear to like the flowers. "This is to say I'm sorry for taking you by surprise." He leaned in, noticing for the first time the bouquet already on the table. "I know you mentioned you'd rather me not come, but I thought you meant you didn't want me to bother. It's no bother, Rosemary. I'm happy to be here supporting you." He held out the flowers. She still hadn't taken them.

"Liam, thank you, but now's not the time. There's a line forming." She looked awkwardly past him, not at the line but at the young man standing near the front desk. Liam frowned and felt an instant uneasiness in his stomach. The young man was dark and suave and clearly in charge of the place. He was the type of unconventionally handsome man that made Liam feel inferior. He felt baby-faced next to him.

Liam turned back to Rosemary. "Okay, I'm sorry. I'll just leave these here with you." He set the flowers down, wishing he'd brought them in a vase. They lay sadly next to the perky bouquet already present.

Rosemary's face softened. "Thanks for the flowers, Liam. They're beautiful." She smiled at him and patted the flowers as if to make her point, but it didn't make Liam feel any better. He moved to the side and watched as the line moved forward.

Liam felt the other man's eyes on him. He turned and met them with a challenge. The other man moved toward him and extended a hand. "I'm Ben, owner of Palermo's. We're glad to have you stop by today."

The man had a smooth, deep voice. Liam wondered if Rosemary's resistance to his presence had anything to do with the man standing before him. "Good to meet you, Ben. I'm Liam." He paused. He was about to say, "I'm Rosemary's friend." But something kept him silent, as if he knew it'd be torture for Ben not to know his relation to Rosemary. The mystery didn't last long, however.

"I see you know Rosemary," Ben continued. "I assume you already have a copy of her book. You a friend?"

There was no uncertainty in this man's tone. Liam looked at him with a bit of respect. The man obviously knew what he wanted. The problem was, so did Liam. Before he could think it through, he blurted out, "Boyfriend, actually." He instantly regretted it, but the words were out there, and he couldn't help feeling a deep sense of satisfaction at the dismay spreading across Ben's face.

"Oh, I didn't realize . . . I mean, she never mentioned . . ."

"Yeah, Rosemary and I go way back. We went to school together. I teach third grade and she came and did a presentation and reading of her book for my students just a few months ago." Liam paused and looked at Rosemary, who was smiling at each customer, talking animatedly, and signing copy after copy. He watched her eyes stray in their direction, her expression slipping. "She really is something, isn't she? So talented and beautiful." He was met with silence. Liam glanced over.

Ben was also staring at Rosemary, his expression sad and thoughtful. "Yes, she really is. Truly one of a kind."

His voice was soft and resigned, and for a moment Liam felt guilty. He suppressed the feeling, however, because he wasn't exactly telling a lie. He wanted to be Rosemary's boyfriend. He intended to be her boyfriend, and as soon as this event was over, he meant to make his intentions known. So was it that bad if he jumped the gun a little bit? Ben glanced over at him. "You are a blessed man, Liam." The guilt returned full force. Liam tried to ignore it by mumbling good-bye and heading toward Oma and Rosemary's mom, distancing himself from the sad and reflective young man.

◇◆◇◆

"Is that Ben?" Rosemary's mom whispered. She and Oma had come up next in line after Liam.

"Yes," Oma answered for her. "As you can see, he inherited Louie's dark features. Handsome, isn't he?"

"Definitely," Rosemary's mother agreed.

"Okay, move it along, you two." Rosemary felt like crying and had no patience for the whispered exchange.

"I can see why you like him, Rosemary," her mother continued. "I'm sorry if I complicated things by inviting Liam. Still, Liam is such a nice boy, don't you think?"

"I didn't say anything about . . . Liam isn't . . . there's a line forming!"

Her mother and Oma took the hint. "We just wanted to say hi and be the first in line," Oma apologized.

"I know, I'm sorry. Thank you! I'll meet up with you after, okay?"

They moved off, and Rosemary watched them leave, completely beside herself at the way events were unfolding. Liam and Ben stood talking by the front desk, and what was worse was that she couldn't be there to referee. Seeing them side by side accentuated their differences. Ben was tall and dark, and Liam was much shorter and lighter in complexion. Even their bouquets seemed to be fighting it out, vying for attention. She tried to ignore the two men. She put on her happiest face, and she shook hands and smiled and thanked people and signed copies to whomever they wanted copies to be made out to. Most of those in line were families with children in tow. She was delighted to see the children's happy expressions as they handed her copies of her book. Their eager faces were almost enough to make her forget the two men standing nearby—almost. She was grateful to the crowd of people who were waiting in line to talk with her, and happy to see so many children present, but her thoughts ran wild. Eventually, Liam left Ben's side and went over to stand next to her mother and Oma. Rosemary breathed a sigh of relief and looked around for Ben, but he was nowhere to be found.

◇◆◇

Mrs. Gardner desperately needed a ride to the book signing, but Professor Jenson mysteriously could not take her. She'd relied on him for so long that his pleas of being too busy came as a shock. Come to think of it, he'd been awfully preoccupied the last few weeks, ever since their conversation about Ben. He'd found one excuse after another not to visit her, but this was serious—he'd never refused to drive her anywhere before. "But Mark, this is the big event, and we should go to support Ben," she said through the phone.

"You can go without me, Matilda. I don't have time right now."

Mrs. Gardner wanted to ask him what on earth he could possibly be doing when he'd been spending every available moment with her, but she bit her tongue. "Well, okay then. I'll have to ask Anita." She hung up the phone in confusion. She sensed that she was losing her friend, just when she'd come to really rely on and cherish him. *Why the sudden change of heart?* she wondered. She picked up the phone, determined to make it to Palermo's. Even though Ben was in love with her and it would be horribly awkward, she'd promised to support the store, and support it she would, even if she had to walk there on foot. A promise was a promise after all. "Anita," she barked into the phone, "come fetch me."

They arrived at Palermo's forty minutes after the event started. The place was packed and they were forced to park several blocks away. Mrs. Baumgartner offered to drop her off out front, but Mrs. Gardner didn't like the idea of entering and facing Ben alone, so they parked and walked the several blocks together.

"Isn't this the young woman Ben is interested in?" Mrs. Baumgartner stood breathlessly outside Palermo's, looking up at the display.

"Um, yes." Mrs. Gardner averted her eyes, not caring to correct her friend. *No, this is the young woman he used as a front to get close to me*, she thought and blushed miserably.

The store was alive with happy chatter as they entered. Mrs. Baumgartner grabbed a book from a display and stood in line, looking through it with interest. "Aren't you going to get a copy?" she asked, looking at Mrs. Gardner with a frown.

Mrs. Gardner had caught sight of Ben in the reading nook near the back of the store. He had apparently left Nick to manage the front desk alone, which seemed unusual, and he looked upset and agitated. Mrs. Gardner's heart filled with compassion. *Poor boy.* "I will, yes. But I need to go talk to Ben. I'll be right back." Mrs. Gardner wound her way to the back of the store.

Ben was alone. The noise and bustle from the front of the store trickled back and was amplified by the domed ceiling of the alcove, but despite the projection, a deep feeling of silence seemed to surround him. He was sitting in an overstuffed chair and was leaning forward, his face buried in his hands. Mrs. Gardner stood and observed him with concern, finally venturing a tentative "Ben, dear? Are you okay?"

Ben's head whipped up, and Mrs. Gardner's concern skyrocketed at the stricken look on his face. He hadn't exactly been crying, but the anguish was certainly present. Mrs. Gardner forgot that Ben was in love with her, forgot that she had schooled herself to be careful and not to lead him on. Her heart cried out to the young man in front of her as she hurried to his side. "Oh, Ben, what is the matter, dear? Why are you back here all by yourself?" She stood next to him and patted his shoulder and crooned to him as she might to her own hurting child.

"Mrs. Gardner, I'm sorry. I'm so embarrassed." Ben groaned and ran a hand through his hair. "This is very unprofessional. I can't believe I'm hiding back here like this."

Mrs. Gardner continued to emit soft, soothing tones. "Shush, shush, there, there. You can tell me what's the matter."

"It's just . . ." Ben's voice trailed off, and for a moment, Mrs. Gardner feared he'd keep it all in and not confide in her, but then he resumed talking, his words rushing out of him. "I've never felt so strongly about anyone, like it was just . . . right."

Mrs. Gardner froze and all the old fears came coursing back, but as Ben kept confiding in her, she relaxed as a slow realization came over her.

"I almost asked Rosemary out last night. I even bought her flowers, like you told me to." He glanced in her direction and laughed. "Thank goodness I didn't though, because who walked in this morning?" He laughed bitterly. "Literally the first person through that front door. Can you guess? Her *boyfriend*! She seemed like she wanted to tell me something last night, and now I realize that she probably sensed I was interested and was trying to find a polite way to tell me she had a boyfriend. I feel like such an idiot. Of course she has a boyfriend. I mean, look at her. How could she not?"

Ben's face was back in his hands. Mrs. Gardner should have been feeling continued concern, but the realization slowly spreading over her was so complete that she had little room for any emotion other than pure joy. Benjamin Palermo was not in love with her! He was, in fact, really and truly in love with Rosemary! Mrs. Gardner laughed right out loud, abruptly stopping as she saw the look on Ben's face. "I'm so sorry, Ben. I just, I thought . . . oh, it doesn't matter! I just mean to say that I'm so glad to hear that you love Rosemary."

"*Love* is a strong word, seeing as we don't really know each other." Ben paused and frowned. "No, you know what? You're right! I may not love her right now, but I got the feeling that she was someone I *could* love. You know what I mean? That she was a person I could continue to get to know forever and never get tired. That's what's making this so horrible. I could see the potential, the whole she-bang right here in front of me. Right *there* in front of me." Ben gesticulated wildly toward the front, where the sound of busy shoppers continued with a happy hum.

Unbidden, Professor Jenson's face came to Mrs. Gardner's mind, and she swallowed hard, tears suddenly prickling the back of her eyes as her throat tightened. "Yes, I think I do know what you mean." She sighed and sank into the chair opposite his. For a moment, both of them sat in agonized silence.

"So, that is that," Ben finally said, standing up briskly. "I caught sight of a good thing, but the Lord must have something else in mind for me. Thank you for all the time you took with me, Mrs. Gardner. I'm sorry that it was wasted." He laughed, that note of bitterness creeping back into his voice.

Mrs. Gardner looked up at him from where she was still seated, her heart aching. "I'm so sorry, Ben. Don't let it make you hopeless or bitter. I wish I had better advice for this or could somehow fix it, but I think that if God's been teaching me anything it's that sometimes we need to step back and just let Him work." She sighed and looked down at her hands. "That's a hard lesson for someone like me to learn, and sometimes doing nothing feels like giving up, but we're not giving anything up when we give it to Him, are we? There's no one better we could entrust things to."

Ben smiled down at her and reached out to squeeze her hand. "You're right, of course. Thank you for the reminder. I better get going, though, before Nick comes back here with a pitchfork."

Mrs. Gardner watched Ben leave and then sat in silence, her heart in turmoil over Professor Jenson and her mind in a whir of confusion and speculation, for if Ben hadn't given her the gifts, then who had?

The book signing was a success. It seemed that all of New Holden had turned out for it. At the close, Rosemary transitioned to the children's section for a reading. The children's section was limited to only a small area of the first floor, tucked behind and to the left of the stairs. Over a dozen kids and their families showed up for the reading, and Ben hovered near the back, distracting Rosemary from the kids. Each time she looked up from the page, her eyes were drawn toward Ben. He'd been mysteriously absent during the signing. She'd seen more of his assistant, Nick, than she had of him. Now, she tried not to let his presence unnerve her as she read aloud to the children. It was hard when he was staring at her so intently. She could feel his dark eyes on her even as she smiled and talked with the children.

As Rosemary closed the book and the kids began to disperse, she looked around for Ben, her heart sinking as she saw him in conversation with Liam. What were they talking about? Why was Liam back? Before she could reach them, however, Ben was dragged away by a customer. She looked after him as he disappeared in the direction of the front desk.

"Looks like it was a success!" Liam approached her with a big smile and bumped her shoulder with his own.

"Yes, I was surprised by how many people came." Rosemary felt antsy. She'd been hoping to have a private conversation with Ben, but now—with Liam at her side—didn't seem to be the right time. "What are you doing back?"

"I've been commissioned to come get you for lunch. Your mom and grandma are meeting us at a café down the road to celebrate."

"Oh." Rosemary tried to mask her disappointment. She'd imagined having lunch with Ben, which, she realized now, might have been wishful thinking since he had a business to run. "Okay, let me grab my stuff from behind the front counter and we can head out."

Ben was checking out a customer as Rosemary and Liam approached. Liam seemed jumpy. "Hey, I'll just wait for you out front, okay?" He gave her arm a squeeze.

"Okay." Rosemary watched him leave, confused by his moodiness. First he was all in her face, and now he was practically running away. The customer left and Rosemary came face-to-face with Ben. "Hey, you." Rosemary smiled and leaned on the counter, feeling flirtatious and not a little nervous now that the event was over and Liam was gone and her revelation to Ben was that much closer. Why had she been so hesitant before? Surely he'd be happy to know that she was Rosie. It wouldn't change what they already had between them now.

"Hi. Glad it all went well. You were a hit."

His words were nice, but the tone was markedly different from earlier. Rosemary looked sharply at him. He was avoiding her eyes, feigning business behind the counter.

"Everything okay?" she asked tentatively.

Ben finally looked up at her, but his eyes were a mask. There was none of the openness they had shared the night before. "Of course. I'm glad this day was such a success. Thank you for agreeing to it."

Formal, polite, businesslike. Where had their rapport gone? Rosemary felt a lump forming in her throat. Was he mad at her? Did Liam upset him somehow? "You're welcome. I see you met Liam," she ventured. "I didn't realize he'd be coming. Sort of surprised me. I hope he didn't bother you too much. He can be very talkative." She'd hoped to diffuse the situation, gloss over anything that might have offended Ben, but it seemed she'd said exactly the wrong thing, for Ben's features hardened even further.

"No, he seems very nice."

Rosemary fidgeted where she stood and continued to watch Ben pretend to be busy behind the counter. She finally gave up. "Well, I have to get going, but I'd love to come back for a visit before I head home."

"You're welcome back here anytime. I'm busy most of this week, so I can't guarantee that I'll be here when you do come back, but of course you're welcome to stop by anytime."

Rosemary fought tears. He used to go out of his way to see her. He'd been over the top in his welcome to her the night before, and now he was dismissing her as just another customer. Maybe she'd read the signs wrong. She still needed to have the talk with him. She couldn't move forward with her project until she'd spoken with him. "Maybe if I stop by Monday afternoon?"

"That'd be fine." Ben had moved to the refreshment table now and was beginning to clean up.

"Do you need any help with that?" Rosemary had picked up her purse and coat but set them down again and moved in his direction.

"No no. I'm fine. No need for you to pick up. This is just part of the job. Besides, I know you have a lunch date to keep." He was avoiding her eyes again.

Anger kindled in Rosemary. What had she possibly done to deserve this cold shoulder? "Okay, fine. I just thought I'd offer. Thanks again for all your hard work in setting this up. I'll stop by Monday."

Ben didn't say anything in reply, so Rosemary scooped up her coat and purse. She paused to also snatch up the vase of flowers, which seemed to mock her now with their bright faces upturned so hopefully. "And thank you. You know, for the flowers," she mumbled, not daring to look at Ben as she swiftly left the store. Her heart was thudding loudly in her ears, warm and heavy in her chest, vibrantly aware of being slighted. She needed to have the talk with Ben, but how would she move forward now that she was confronted with his coldness? How did you bare your heart to someone who wasn't receptive? Rosemary jogged down the front steps. Liam was pacing on the front sidewalk. She realized with a jolt that she'd forgotten Liam's bouquet back in the store, but she didn't care. She wasn't going back in there to face more of Ben's silence. She brushed past Liam, who gave her a funny look before sprinting to keep up with her. She'd also forgotten to put on her coat, she realized as the wind blew against her, eager to nip at any exposed flesh. She hardly noticed the cold against her skin for the coldness settling inside.

**The girl returns almost a full year later, much later than usual.** *Her heart sings as she makes her way to the Room, for she knows that she will find at least one letter. The boy comes to the Room much more frequently than she, so she wonders if perhaps there are two letters waiting for her. Her expectation is so high that at first she doesn't recognize the one letter in the Room as her own. The girl picks it up and unfolds it, just to be absolutely sure. But there is no mistake. This is her last letter to the boy, still sitting unread. The girl sits down hard on the floor and stares at the letter, the disappointment bringing tears to her eyes. Halfheartedly she decides to leave another note, but worry, sharp and persistent in the back of her mind, wiggles its way into her thoughts.*

*Why had the boy not come back?*

# CHAPTER TWENTY-FIVE

## "SAY YOU RECOGNIZE ME"

The day after the book signing was a Sunday, and Rosemary found herself dreading church. She, Liam, her mother, and Oma were all going together, and Rosemary wondered how she'd handle seeing Ben again after their awkward parting the day before, but she needn't have worried because Ben was nowhere in sight. Either he wasn't there, had gone to an earlier service, or had just successfully evaded them, but Sunday service came and went and there was no confrontation with Ben.

"Where to for lunch?" Rosemary's mom asked as they all reached the car.

"Actually, I was hoping to treat Rosemary." Liam's voice sounded hesitant. Rosemary looked at him searchingly. He was standing on one foot, rubbing the back of his calf with his other foot.

"Oh, I think that's a wonderful idea!" Rosemary's mom said eagerly. "Oma and I will leave you two alone then."

Liam had taken his own vehicle to church, as he was planning on leaving that afternoon. Now he opened the door for her. Rosemary found her irritation surging. She'd become convinced that Liam had said something to Ben that had set him off. She had no idea what it could be, but friendship or no, she was becoming irritated by his dropping by uninvited into her life. Perhaps a lunch to hash things out before he left was just what they needed. As Rosemary moved toward Liam's car, she caught sight of Oma's apologetic face. Rosemary sighed and mouthed, "It's okay," before getting in the car.

"Any place you'd recommend?" Liam asked as they left the parking lot.

"There's a Mexican restaurant nearby. How about there?"

Liam must have sensed that she wasn't in a chatty mood, for the quick ride to the restaurant was completed in near silence. As they were seated in a booth, Rosemary auditioned numerous ways to start the hard conversation ahead of them. "What did you say to Ben?" was high at the top, but "Kindly butt out" was a close second. They ordered quickly, distractedly, and then Liam surprised her with a straightforward revelation. Gone was his hinting around; instead, he jumped in with both feet.

"Rosemary, you've been one of my closest friends for a long time, but I need to be honest with you. I like you as more than a friend." She watched as he fidgeted with the wrapping from his straw, twisting and untwisting it from around his fingers. "I've liked you for a long time actually. You are creative, beautiful, smart, kind. I just like every-thing about you."

It was a good speech, even if it was delivered without eye contact. But Rosemary's heart sank in her chest and then stilled, suspended, silent. She thought she should feel something, anything. Liam was confirming what she'd suspected, what apparently Clare and Becca had known all along, and she should *feel* something. But all that was there was a numbness and heaviness slowly spreading through her chest. Liam was looking at her now. The ball was in her court, and the longer she waited to say some-thing, the more his expression hardened.

"Liam, I . . . I really appreciate your kind words. You're such a great friend to me. You've always supported me, encouraged me. I've always appreciated that about you." She paused and made herself look him in the eye. She needed to be honest. She needed him to see her and know her heart in this matter. "I appreciate a lot about you actually. You are so great with your kids. You have such a passion for what you do, and I really admire that."

She could see it in his expression. The anticipation of "but." She watched as he frowned and looked away from her. She faltered and tried to continue. "It's just that . . ." She trailed off at the look of anger on his face. His anger sparked her own. She had a right to what she was saying! She had a right to not return his feelings! She thought again of Ben and the abruptness of the change she'd seen in him, and she let the suspicion and anger course through her. She'd wanted this to go well, but Liam was making it impossible. Before she could rein it in, her anger opened its mouth and spoke. "Liam, would you please look at me when I'm talking?" His startled eyes jumped to hers. "I'm trying to tell you something important here, and I can see that you're mad. I'm sorry if you don't like what I have to say, but I have a right to tell you how I feel, how I honestly feel."

Once started, she couldn't stop. She hated herself even as she continued to speak. "I'm flattered that you like me in that way, but I just think of you as a friend. I wish you had been open and honest with me earlier because I feel like you've been following me around, hanging this over my head but not saying anything, and it's been kind of obnoxious and really put me in an awkward position. I mean, I care about you and don't want to lose you as a friend, but honestly, you've made it difficult."

"I'm glad you see me as such a pathetic figure," Liam snapped. Their food had arrived. The server stood by their table, quietly distributing plates without interrupting the blowup occurring before his eyes. "I'm surprised at you, Rosemary. I'm not in need of your reprimand here."

"Is there anything else I can help you with?"

"No!" Their answer was unanimously vehement. The server bowed his head and left quickly.

"It's just that you've been dropping by uninvited, expecting me to what? Fawn all over you? You've been clingy and needy, and honestly, it's exhausting. If you wanted to ask me out, you should have just done it."

"That's what I'm doing now!" Liam fairly shouted, drawing the attention of the next table.

"Keep your voice down," Rosemary hissed.

"I don't know why you're being like this." Liam had unfolded his napkin and was shoving food around his plate. "I don't deserve this. I'm just trying to be honest with you about how I feel. If anyone should be angry, it's me. I feel like you've been leading me on."

"See, this is what I'm talking about." Rosemary gestured toward him with both hands. "You've put me in an impossible position. I feel like you've been taking anything I say or do as encouragement. It's what I feared, but since you weren't saying anything, I felt like I couldn't say anything either. Don't you see how you put me in a bind here?"

"No, I don't see that." Liam had shoved his plate aside and was violently dunking a chip in their shared salsa. "It's natural, Rosemary, for a guy to hesitate. It's natural to feel nervous and not know what to say or do. You can be intimidating sometimes."

"I wish people would stop saying that." Rosemary threw down her napkin, dismayed at his words. "How am I intimidating?"

"You're just so . . . perfect and self-sufficient. You don't appear like you need anything or anyone, and it's hard to approach that."

Rosemary was close to tears. Was it true? Was she stand-offish? unapproachable? It must be true if more than one person said these things about her. She did need people. She needed others desperately, just like anyone else. Why couldn't people see that? When would someone finally see that? "I'm sorry you feel that way." She managed to push the words past the tightness in her throat. "I don't think I'm a closed-off person."

"I didn't say you were closed off—"

"If you were afraid to say something, then did you stop to consider that maybe that's a reflection of you and not of me?" She stopped, breathless.

Liam appeared to be grinding his teeth. "I'm just saying that I didn't know what to expect approaching you. You can cut a guy some slack, you know."

"And I'm just saying that I'm worth it. Am I expected to anticipate every guy's need? hand myself over on a silver platter? This is me, Liam. This is who I am." Rosemary rocked back in her seat, her breathing ragged. She realized she was laying into him more than he deserved, dumping years' worth of dating frustration on his poor, unsuspecting head, and the realization gave her pause.

"I know who you are, and I'm trying to tell you that I like who you are." Liam's face was still twisted in anger, but his words were softened by sadness.

There was a strained silence during which Rosemary found that she was tightly crossing her arms across her chest and her body was turned away from Liam. She was, in fact, perfectly embodying what he had described. On the heels of that discovery came embarrassment and re-gret. She'd come into this with fists raised, not at all how she'd wanted things to go. "Liam, I'm sorry." She relaxed her arms and bowed her head, trying to gather herself. "I think I just came into this whole thing already defensive."

"You think you can just say sorry and fix it like a magic

wand?" Liam had finished drenching his chip and had left it stranded in the salsa, his hands now in his lap, his face indicating that he'd checked out of their conversation.

"No, of course not. I'm trying to genuinely apologize here."

"For what? For calling me obnoxious? For accusing me of being clingy? For mocking my feelings?"

"Hey, that's unfair." Rosemary felt her anger flare up again. "I really am trying to apologize. I came into this defensive because I felt like you might have said something to Ben that offended him. Crazy, I know, but he did a complete one-eighty on me, and it was after he met you." Rosemary saw a flash of guilt on Liam's face. "*Did* you say something to him, Liam?"

"No. We talked, he introduced himself; that was it." His answer was too quick, too defensive, but he clearly wasn't going to offer a further explanation. "You like him, don't you?"

Rosemary sat back in her seat, stunned. "What?"

"You like him, I can tell, and maybe that's why you're treating me like this. It's not fair. You should have told me."

"Should have told you? We weren't—we *aren't* dating. Why should I have told you?"

Liam just clenched his jaw and looked away with a closed expression. By now their untouched food had grown cold, as had the air between them. Rosemary sighed and closed her eyes. She needed to diffuse things before their friendship was irreparably damaged. "Liam, I don't want to lose your friendship."

"Are you sure about that? Doesn't appear that way from this side of the table. And don't think I didn't notice that you didn't deny your feelings for Ben."

Rosemary's anger, at first so brief and hot, had now burned itself out. In its place was a sharp sense of regret and sadness. "Honestly, Liam, what I do or do not feel for

Ben is not your business. I'm sorry that I've hurt you. I'm sorry that you feel betrayed and led on. It was not my intention whatsoever. I care about you so much as a friend, which I know you don't want to hear, but it's the truth. And because I care about our friendship, this whole thing has been really hard to handle. I don't want to lose 'us,' so I think I just tried to ignore the signs for as long as I could. I'm sorry."

Liam was quietly staring at the table. "I'm sorry too. I'm sorry that this blew up, but just because I'm sorry doesn't mean I'm not mad. I am." He finally looked her square in the eyes. "You're right; it's not my business who you do or do not like. Consider this me butting out of your life."

"Liam, no, that's not what I meant."

"I know you want to remain friends, but I don't know how to do that. I'm sorry, Rosemary. I wish this had gone better."

"It doesn't have to end like this." Rosemary felt the tears gather in her eyes.

"We want two different things out of this relationship. I need time to come to grips with that."

He'd expected a completely different response from her, Rosemary realized, and she needed to give him the time and space he said he needed in order to process the letdown. She reached across the table to grab his hand, but he stood abruptly.

"I'm sorry, Rosemary, I can't. I just can't." He grabbed his jacket and backed away from the table.

"Where are you going?" Rosemary stared at him in confusion.

"I can't be here any longer, to just sit here stupidly and eat while you try to continue apologizing or whatever. I just need to leave. Nothing is going to make this conversation go any better."

"You drove me here!" Rosemary's cheeks burned in humiliation as he backed further from the table.

"I know. I'm sorry. I need to leave."

Rosemary watched in shock as he bumped into another table, apologized, shrugged on his jacket, and fled the restaurant. She swallowed hard, her eyes flitting to the tables around them. Several other people had noticed the exchange and quickly looked away from her. Rosemary's hands were trembling. Had he really just deserted her in the middle of lunch? left her stranded in the restaurant, humiliated in front of everyone? How selfish—how incredibly selfish.

"Excuse me, miss, did you need boxes?" Their server stood tentatively by the table.

"No, we're fine. I'm fine. I'll take the check, please." And Liam had saddled her with the bill—the icing on the cake. Rosemary paid and left the restaurant in a haze. She'd made it halfway back to St. John's, her mind on autopilot, before she considered calling her mom to come get her. But no, she didn't want to explain this to her mom. She'd been humiliated enough for one day. And so Rosemary walked home. Passing the church, she hoped no one would be left to see her, alone in the bitter cold. She purposefully skirted Palermo's. The bookstore, along with the other downtown businesses, was closed on Sunday, but still she didn't want to take the chance that Ben might see her. *That would just be the cherry on top, wouldn't it?*

Rosemary huddled into herself and picked up her pace, eyes wide and streaming from the cold, heart pounding. Liam. Warm, joyful Liam. He'd never call her Clooney again, never enthusiastically talk about her book again or their mutual love of children's literature and sushi. She'd been defensive and had completely messed things up, and he had been a complete jerk and had messed them up even more. How could they possibly come back from this?

"How'd everything go, dear?" Rosemary's mom asked as she entered the kitchen. Rosemary was shivering from her long, cold walk and just shook her head and fled to her room, shutting and locking the door. Her mom and Oma both knocked on and off the rest of the day before finally giving up.

Rosemary lay on her bed, still in her church clothes and coat, the coldness from the walk lingering, her feet pinched and blistering from having walked miles in high heels. She tried to sleep, tried to gain some respite from the pain eating her alive. In just two days she'd managed to alienate both Ben and Liam. Was there something fundamentally broken in her that shoved the people she cared about away? Where, exactly, was her fault in all of this? Should she be more open and vulnerable? Maybe. But she also didn't want or need to be with someone who insisted on feeling intimidated by her and who saw this as her fault. She felt like Liam loved her focus and passion but then turned around and used them against her, an excuse for his own reticence.

Irrationally she felt the urge to write a note to BJ, but she was beyond the comforts of childhood. Adulthood meant acknowledging that there were no easy fixes in life. Sometimes there were no fixes, period. There were no tears, just an open, dry-eyed pain.

"Lord, why do the men in my life run away?" Rosemary moaned into her pillow. "I need to snap out of this pity party, Lord, I know, but it just hurts right now. Please show me where I'm in the wrong and show me how to make it right. Please restore my friendship with Liam. Please show me what to do with Ben." She buried her face deeper in the pillow, her prayer continuing with endless "pleases" until eventually she quieted enough to let the solace trickle in. "See what kind of love the Father has given to us," Rosemary whispered, "that we should be called children of

God." She sighed shakily, soothed by the repetition of a familiar truth. "And so we are." What wonderful truth from 1 John, establishing the type of relationship she could expect with her Creator. God was not far off. He was her Father and she was His child. One father may have run; Ben and Liam may not be speaking to her; but Rosemary knew her heavenly Father wasn't going anywhere, and that was all the comfort she needed.

Rosemary ventured out in the evening for some food, making her movements quiet so as not to draw the attention of the two women in the living room. She'd changed from her wrinkled church clothes to a pair of sweats and a loose T-shirt, much more comfortable attire for the productive evening she had planned. Retreating back to her room with a sandwich, Rosemary said a prayer of thanksgiving for the sense of calm now surrounding her and spread out on the bed.

The hours passed and Rosemary poured herself into her new book. Furiously she sketched. Drawing always helped relieve anxiety. There was no tension when she drew, no room for self-doubt or dead-end questions, just quiet focus. She could get lost in her work, in the sleek black lines from the charcoal, the deep smudges that drew her in and revealed a story to her. Rosemary sketched the Story People and the Room. She brought the boy and the girl to life. She gave them names and she drew them together in the Room, finding solace with each other. Even if that childhood sense of security was largely myth, she would draw it, recreate that feeling on paper for others to latch on to. Late into the night she drew image after image, infusing them with the anger and anxiety and longing she'd experienced earlier in the day, as if in drawing images representative of happiness she could make it be so in her own world. As if peace could be created through the sheer wanting of it. "Peace I leave with you; My peace

I give to you." Words from Christ to anxious disciples who would soon be missing their ascended Lord. "Let not your hearts be troubled, neither let them be afraid." Such words of love and comfort to those who were being promised the ultimate Comforter—a promise fulfilled in their lives and hers. Rosemary paused to consider the two happy children before her. "Unless you turn and become like children, you will never enter the kingdom of heaven." So maybe it wasn't myth. Maybe children in their happiest, most peaceful moments had it right all along and showcased not something unattainable, but something intended for us all along. Rosemary smiled at her girl and boy and continued, sketch by sketch, to reacquaint herself with the hidden, lost, safe world of the Room and its occupants. Piece by piece she reintroduced herself to the Story People. "Hello, it's me. It's Rosie. You may not recognize me. It has been a while, and I'm a little older and I've lost some of my kindness. But it's me. Please say you recognize me."

**The girl's fear and worry are confirmed when she comes to the Room months later to see her notes untouched: two hopeful notes, sitting right where she left them.** Now she wonders what she should do, but she doesn't know who to ask about the boy. She does not have his phone number or address. She doesn't know who his parents are or where they are. Whom can she ask?

The girl feels a pang of guilt. She lived so fully in their make-believe world that she never made an effort to know his real world. He'd known about hers. She'd confided in him as she hadn't in anyone else. He'd been there for her when she felt like she had no one else, but now she finds herself at a loss as to how to repay the favor. She was selfish, so selfish. She needs to see him, just see him one more time to tell him how sorry she is for not getting to know his world, for being so wrapped up in herself and the Story People that she didn't bother to really get to know him.

The girl sits in the empty Room with the untouched notes and cries.

# CHAPTER TWENTY-SIX

## CONFIRMATION OF HOPE

Mrs. Gardner returned home from the book sign-ing with a renewed desire to get back in Professor Jenson's good graces. How she had somehow fallen out of them, she had no idea, but back into them she must get, for it was becoming increasingly clear to her that life without Professor Jenson in it was a life she no longer preferred. However, Professor Jenson was still brushing her off. She'd invited him over for dinner and even said that she'd do the cooking this time, but he'd again insisted that he was busy. Nevertheless, Mrs. Gardner was a re-sourceful woman. If she couldn't get his attention through common means, then uncommon means it was to be.

Midweek, Mrs. Gardner bummed a ride from Mrs. Baumgartner into town and headed to the local library, where she pored over the magazine section, finally finding what she was looking for. She held the issue aloft between two fingers, as if the name of the magazine indicated what it actually was: *Fungi Magazine*. She'd seen copies lying around in Professor Jenson's home. Maybe if she showed him she was branching out in her interests, it would snag his attention. She was not a closed-minded busybody. She would show him that she had wide and varied interests.

Mrs. Gardner hurriedly grabbed several other magazines and even a few books for good measure, just to mask the *Fungi Magazine* and to avoid questions from Mrs. Baumgartner.

Later that afternoon, Mrs. Gardner found herself stalking the front windows. Restlessly she paced, *Fungi Magazine* in hand, hoping for a glimpse of Professor Jenson. Thinking that perhaps he wasn't home, she went out back and peered over the fence at his detached garage. His old Buick LeSabre was just visible through the small windows lining the top of the garage door. So he *was* home. Mrs. Gardner finally decided to simply plant herself on her front porch in the hopes that he'd make an appearance. A half hour went by, during which time Mrs. Gardner sipped at a mug of hot tea, bundled deep into her afghan, and leafed through a copy of *Better Homes and Gardens*, the *Fungi Magazine* close at hand. Her persistence paid off, for just over half an hour later, she heard the loud creak of his front door. Hurriedly, she tossed *Better Homes and Gardens* aside and scooped up *Fungi Magazine*, opening its pages randomly and lifting it high so that the cover was clearly visible. She peeked over the top of the page and watched as Professor Jenson trundled outside, watering can in hand. He moved to the side of his porch farthest from her to water his potted mums, his back to her. Mrs. Gardner fidgeted uncomfortably, her nerves in a state of awful suspense. Slowly Professor Jenson turned to the other side of his porch, fully facing her. This was her moment. Mrs. Gardner rustled the pages importantly and flipped a few, as if deep in contemplation. She peeked over the top again. Professor Jenson wasn't looking in her direction. Instead, he had his head determinedly bowed, as if watering required all the attention he could muster.

Mrs. Gardner frowned, irritated beyond measure that he was ignoring her efforts. Perhaps he simply didn't see her. She rose, abandoning the puddle of warmth created by her blanket, and walked to the edge of her porch, leaning a hip against the railing and raising the magazine at an unnatural height. Carefully she extended her arms and turned the magazine so that the cover was glaringly obvious. She made dramatic clucking and humming noises as if overwhelmed by the interesting content she was digesting, as if she were fairly brimming with a desire to discuss the finer points of the article "Getting to the Root of *Oudemansiella*." Furtively she glanced in Professor Jenson's direction. There could be no doubt that he saw her. He was glancing away just as she looked at him, his expression doggedly intent at avoiding eye contact. His face was flushed and furrowed. Mrs. Gardner felt a lump constricting her throat. It was as if they had not just shared months of constant companionship. It was even worse than before, when he had avoided her and she had good-naturedly pestered him. At least then he had acknowledged her with a begrudging acceptance. This . . . this was so much different, and worse. It was as if he no longer even saw her presence.

With a start, Mrs. Gardner realized she was crying, and in embarrassment she hid her face within the pages of her useless magazine. She let him amble back inside, unscathed by her attempts at reconnection. What had she done to deserve this? And what on earth would she do without him? Her home, her life, it all looked empty now without his large, quiet presence. She hurried inside to the privacy of her home in order to have a proper cry, the pages of *Fungi Magazine* slowly wetting beneath her dismay.

◇◆◇◆

Mrs. Gardner's second encounter with Professor Jenson was a happy accident rather than a calculated assault. Her emotions were still too high for any more scheming, and she was beginning to think that if she actually did care for

Professor Jenson, then she should just leave him alone. He clearly didn't want anything more to do with her. But only a few days after the front porch fiasco, Mrs. Gardner bumped into her neighbor at the grocery store. She was wheeling past the bakery, having just finished in the produce section. Professor Jenson was turning the corner with a shopping basket hanging half-full from the crook of his arm. They stopped and regarded each other in a state of surprise.

"Mark! Um, I'm sorry I almost ran into you there." Mrs. Gardner felt the heat rising to her face. It wasn't often that she was left with nothing to say. It was extremely inconvenient and uncomfortable.

"It's okay." Two little words, but more than he'd uttered to her in quite a while.

Mrs. Gardner watched him shift to the side and start to pass her, her heart in an uproar as she observed him. What to say to keep him here just a moment longer? Mrs. Gardner glanced into her cart and saw the answer. She'd actually been reading the *Fungi Magazine*; its contents made her feel closer to the disgruntled man now hurriedly trying to pass her. Maybe she could put her newfound knowledge to use. "I see you're picking up some staples." She gestured toward the bread and lunch meat in his basket. "I myself am picking up some items for vegetable soup. You know, some celery, carrots, and some *Amanita*." She indicated the small container of brown mushrooms in her cart. Her heart soared as Professor Jenson stopped abruptly and glanced into her cart. Aha! She'd snagged him at last!

"*Amanita* is a poisonous species, so I would hope that you are not picking that up." Professor Jenson sighed and shook his head. "That's cremini."

Mrs. Gardner gnawed at her fingernails, embarrassed and humbled. She looked at the mushrooms and back up to Professor Jenson, who was now past her and walking away. Her chin trembled. He must think her a complete fool. She took a small victory, however, in the fact that he'd said more than two words to her this time. Perhaps that was progress of some sort.

◇◆◇◆

Saturday dawned cold and dry. It'd been a week since the book signing and over three weeks since Professor Jenson had suddenly decided to disavow her. Mrs. Gardner had had plenty of time to fret and pray. The past few months had been a time of self-examination, to say the least, and now she brought her worries over the Professor to the Lord in anguished prayer. She'd slowly become convicted to stop thinking about herself and her need for Professor Jenson's companionship and to start thinking of him and his needs instead. She became worried for her friend. Perhaps he'd received a diagnosis and didn't know how to tell her. Perhaps there was a death in the family that he was mourning. She shouldn't make snap judgments. Instead, she should let him know that she was here for him, should he decide he needed someone to talk to. For the first time, Mrs. Gardner began scheming not for her own desires, but for someone else's, and an idea came to her, a marvelous olive branch of an idea.

◇◆◇◆

Professor Jenson rose slowly from his seat at the dining room table, where he'd been sorting the mail. The knock came again from the front door, more insistent this time. Professor Jenson reached the front door and opened it, expecting a salesperson. Instead a very nervous-looking Mrs. Gardner stood before him.

"Hello, Mark." Her voice was soft and shot an arrow of pain through him.

He'd been avoiding her as best he could, for the mere sight of her brought back all the wretched feelings of rejection. She'd thought his overtures "ridiculous," and honestly he couldn't blame her. Who was he to think she'd desire someone like him—an old man set in his ways, a confirmed bachelor who was used to being alone and un-bothered? She was a bright, bursting flower to his dry, cracked weed. She'd been right to reject him, but he didn't think he could go back to the easygoing companionship they'd once shared. Now here she was, facing him, and he found that he didn't know what to say.

"Before you say anything or close the door on me, please just hear me out." She seemed breathless, as if she'd jogged to his front porch. "I know you have been avoiding me lately, and I'm not sure why. But I've come to realize that it doesn't matter why. What matters is that you are okay, so I came here today to tell you that if there's something going on in your life that you're upset about, I am here for you. If you need prayer or a listening ear, I am here for you. And if it's me that is the problem . . ." He watched her pause, a catch in her voice. "If I've somehow said or done something to offend you, please know that I am sorry, so very sorry, and I ask you to forgive me. I know I can be difficult sometimes. I am loud and opinionated and like things done my way. I am bossy and overbearing and of-ten speak before I think. You've been so gracious to me these last few months, so kind and compassionate, so I've brought a gift with me, a peace offering, you might say." She pulled an object into view. It was a six-shelf storage unit on wheels. The metal frame held six colorful plastic drawers with lids. Professor Jenson looked from the gift to the red-faced Mrs. Gardner.

"Did you bring that all the way over here yourself?"

"Yes, and it was quite the feat." Mrs. Gardner laughed, a slight wheeze in her voice. "I had to drag it from my base-ment too. The wheels made it manageable, but still, it was a workout."

"Matilda, you should have asked for my help!" Professor Jenson looked at her aghast. "You only just got your sling off. Do you want to pull or break something else and be right back where you started? Please promise me you won't try something like that again."

Mrs. Gardner's flushed face looked pleased beneath his reprimand. "I promise."

"What is this, anyway?"

"I hope you like it." Mrs. Gardner turned back to the contraption at hand, excitement lining her voice. "I remembered how you were saying you don't have enough room for storing and displaying your specimens, so I thought this could help solve your problem. It used to hold my scrapbooking supplies, but I no longer scrapbook." She paused and laughed. "Honestly, what do I have to document anymore? I'm certainly not going to record my antics with Emma and Anita. I used up or gave away my supplies long ago, so this was just sitting in my basement." She pulled out a drawer, like a salesperson on an infomercial. "The drawers slide right out and each one even has a lid, which, I'm sure, is good for preserving your specimens. And look, there's even a place for little labels on the front." She pointed to the empty plastic sleeve on the front of each drawer. "So you can label them however you like." She stopped and looked up at him eagerly.

Professor Jenson's heart was melting in his chest. The gift actually wasn't ideal for housing his specimens, but he wasn't about to tell her that. The fact that she'd single-handedly hauled this up her basement steps and over here filled him with joy and a deep longing. She'd been listening to him. All those months in her presence, serving and caring for her, and she'd been paying attention to him after all. Her generous speech and gift touched him deeply and in a place that had once been so vacant. But then the memory of her rejection returned and he felt his smile freeze on his face. Why was she toying with him like this? "It's nice, Matilda, really it is, and so generous of you. I appreciate the gesture, but you don't have to do this out of guilt. You don't owe me anything."

He watched her face cloud over, confused and hurt. "What are you talking about? I want you to have this. Please accept the gift." He watched her face crumple and felt a pang of guilt. He wanted to reach out and comfort her but didn't think his touch would be welcome. "Mark, I-I'm trying to be nice to you as you've been nice to me."

"And I appreciate that, Matilda, but you made yourself perfectly clear weeks ago that my gifts to you were unwelcome, so can you see how I would feel awkward accepting this gift from you?"

"What do you mean, your gifts?" There were tears in Mrs. Gardner's eyes, which she seemed to be valiantly holding at bay.

"Are you really going to make me say it?" All the embarrassment came flooding back, but she was refusing to cooperate with him. "The chocolates, Matilda, the chocolates and flowers. You made it abundantly clear that they were unwelcome, so whereas I appreciate this gesture, I really do, I don't feel right taking it from you."

"Those were from *you*?" There was a soft wonderment in her voice as she finally began to cry, though Professor Jenson couldn't tell whether she was upset or happy.

"Of course. Who did you think they were from?" This conversation had taken a confusing turn and became even more confusing as Mrs. Gardner burst into laughter, the tears still streaming down her face.

"Oh, it was so silly! I thought . . . I didn't know, I imagined that . . . oh, it doesn't matter anymore!" She was practically dancing on his front doorstep.

"Matilda, what are you saying?" His heart, resigned to her rejection, now began to beat again, hard in his chest, filling his ears with the sound of hope. "Are you saying those gifts weren't unwelcome? Are you saying—"

"I'm saying of course they aren't unwelcome! They make me happy, so happy!" She was still laughing and crying simultaneously, sending him mixed messages. "*You* make me so happy." Her voice softened, and he found that he was moving toward her, as if his feet had their own mind, and she was moving toward him, her laughter gone, replaced now with a breathy sigh that went straight to his heart.

"Matilda, I know this seems crazy. We've been neighbors so long, and I've been a pain, I know."

She silenced him with a hand on his arm. "Be quiet, you silly man."

He reached a gnarled hand to her face and watched her nestle her cheek into his palm. He stilled and settled into the look on her face. It was a look of joy, of promise, a confirmation of hope.

**The girl continues to leave notes, because leaving notes makes her feel hopeful.** *To not leave a note would be to give up, and the girl will never give up on the boy. The Room has become her place now, hers without the boy, and it is not the same. She talks directly to the Story People now and draws endless pictures of them as a way to make herself feel less alone.*

*But the Story People need the boy. They tell her that they miss the boy. She tries to talk to them about other things, but they only want to know about the boy. "When will he be back? Do you know? When will he come back to us?" The girl tries to tell them that she doesn't know.*

*"Please," she tells them. "Please stop asking. I do not know."*

# CHAPTER TWENTY-SEVEN

## "ROSIE"

Rosemary entered the day raw and bleary-eyed, having spent most of the night sketching. She had entertained high hopes for Monday. Despite Ben's inexplicable cold shoulder, this was the day she would lay it all on the table. This was not a day for backing out; too much was riding on her being open with Ben. But the encounter with Liam had left Rosemary feeling unequal to the task before her.

As she usually did when confronted with too many emotions, Rosemary threw herself headlong into preparations. "Lord," she prayed as she got ready, "I don't know how I'm going to get through this day, but I'm trusting You to love me in spite of myself and to guide me in all I do today. That taste of peace you gave me last night, Lord? Please bottle it up for me today. I need it badly!" She stuffed a portfolio with her sketches and first attempts at a story outline and then attempted to cover up all traces of her sleepless night with concealer and mascara. She left the safety of her room for the common living space, prepared to meet the onslaught of questions. Sure enough, both women rushed her as soon as she stepped foot in the kitchen. Rosemary kept the recap of the previous day to a minimum.

"And he just *left* you there?" Her mom stared at her, openmouthed.

"What a cad!" Oma spat out.

Rosemary smiled at the outdated word. "Really, I don't want to make it one-sided," she sighed. "We were both to blame in the argument."

"But to just leave you like that . . ." Rosemary could tell that her mom's estimation of Liam had slipped irreparably, and it brought a small sense of victory and satisfaction to her.

After assuring both concerned women that she was okay and emotionally stable, Rosemary finally bundled up and headed to the bookstore.

Nick was at the front counter when she entered. He looked up with a smile as she approached. "You here for Ben?"

"Yes, is he around?"

"Somewhere. How about you make yourself comfortable in the reading nook, and I'll fetch him for you."

Rosemary thanked him and headed to the back of the store, setting her portfolio down on the coffee table and scanning the small seating area. She thought back to the previous Friday when she and Ben had sat here, stuffing bookmarks and talking. Had it really only been three days ago? Rosemary took off her coat, draping it over the back of a chair, and settled into the cushion with a sigh, her travel mug of coffee in hand. The walk to Palermo's that morning had brought back in full force the memory of the cold walk from the day before. The numbness she'd felt then had wiggled its way into this morning. The nervousness and excitement over this moment was dulled by what had happened between her and Liam. She needed to mentally prepare for this as best as she could in the remaining moments she had—shake off the anger and humiliation.

Taking a bracing sip of coffee, Rosemary set down her mug and began pulling sheets out of the portfolio. She played with several arrangements, spreading them out on the table and debating which to show Ben first. The nervousness began to creep back in as she considered her work and tried to look at them through Ben's eyes. Perhaps spreading them out was too premature. Maybe she should keep them hidden until she had the chance to talk to him. One look at these pictures and he'd know exactly who she was. She wanted him to hear it from her first. Just as she'd finished gathering the pages together, she heard footsteps and glanced up.

Ben was standing a few yards away, observing her. Quickly she placed the folder on top of her sketches and rose to greet him. "Hi, Ben. I'm glad I caught you."

She watched as he entered the alcove. His approach was tentative, as if he were testing shark-infested waters. "Rosemary, good to see you. I wasn't sure if you'd come. I figured you probably needed to get back home. I thought maybe you'd end up leaving with Liam."

"Liam? No. I thought I told you I was staying for a little while. I really wanted to have this meeting with you today." Observing Ben's guarded features, she felt her heart freeze over. He was holding himself in check, keeping her at a distance. Just as Liam had the day before. Would he walk out on her too? She didn't think she could handle another confrontation or rejection.

Ben finally entered the alcove, but she noticed that he didn't sit down. His posture indicated that at any moment he was ready to flee, because that's what the men in her life all did—run as fast and as far away as they could. Quickly she checked herself and offered up a plea. "Lord, fix my thinking. I feel powerless to fix it myself."

"So what did you want to meet about?" Ben glanced down at her portfolio, refusing to meet her eyes.

Rosemary felt defeated before she'd even begun. She couldn't do this. Did she really even need his permission for this? Could she just leave and never tell him? Could she live with that? without him?

On the heels of her panic came a gentle voice. As much as she'd been trying to pray through this situation, in reality she'd been shutting God out. She realized that now. She'd put on her hurt like an old coat, pulled it to her for its familiar warmth. There was a certain satisfaction with feeling wronged or misunderstood. Such feelings obliterated obligation and responsibility. Such feelings put the onus on the other for fixing the problem, while blanketing one's own participation in a cover of hurt. She was used to finding comfort in this role, but she needed to find comfort from a different source instead. "Lord, help me," she silently prayed now. "I'm sorry, please help me. I'm an emotional mess. I know I've asked this before, but I'm listening now, and I need guidance."

Ben was looking at her with a frown. "Look, I don't want to keep you. I'm sure you're busy and eager to get back home. Did you need something? I'm pretty busy right now." He half turned from her, indicating a readiness to leave.

That did it. Rosemary felt the tears overwhelm her and closed her eyes, willing them to stay in. She didn't want Ben to see her like this. Swiftly she grabbed her coat and shoved her arms into the sleeves. Blindly she scooped up her pages, her vision blurred by the unshed tears. She realized as she gathered her things that she was muttering the same phrase over and over. "No, never mind, I'm sorry." She needed to leave quickly before he left her. She couldn't be rejected by Ben, she just couldn't. She'd rather he never know than know and reject her. She would hate herself for this moment, she knew it, but she couldn't stop. She needed to leave. Now. Before she completely melted down in front of him and gave him even more reasons to avoid her. She needed to run from here and go to a quiet place where she could pray and think. She wanted to still herself long enough to pray and listen but just couldn't with all the emotional tension in the room. Ben was saying something, but she wasn't hearing him, wasn't hearing anything over the roar in her ears. This had been a mistake, the whole thing, an awful mistake. She mumbled further apologies and fled the store.

◇◆◇◆

Ben had half hoped that Rosemary would just leave town. Liam had indicated as much. He had to be back to school on Monday and had made it clear that Rosemary would be accompanying him on the road trip home, so Ben had been confused when Rosemary had said she'd stop by Monday. When Nick had told him that Rosemary was waiting for him, his heart had leaped. She was here! And then it had sunk. She was here. He would have to see her again, knowing that she was beyond his reach. The sooner she left, the sooner he could try to forget her, as hard as that would be. And then he'd seen her. Walking toward the alcove, he watched as she shuffled papers on the coffee table. She was exquisitely beautiful. Ben saw her strength and vulnerability, an intoxicating combination that came together perfectly in her. "Please, let me find a woman of her caliber," he prayed as he approached her. Maybe meeting her was God's way of showing him what he needed so that he'd recognize it the next time he saw it.

The encounter was brief and confusing. She'd come to him for some purpose. She'd even brought material with her, but she seemed hesitant and unsure. He watched the emotion playing across her face. Fear, hurt, confusion, anger. Her face was a shield, shifting every second, not settling on one emotion, keeping him guessing. Why was she here? She was making this harder than he wanted it to be. And then she was leaving—quickly, dramatically, her arms reaching for her coat, her fingers clutching at the pages on the table, her words hurried and embarrassed. "No, never mind, I'm sorry." His guard crumbled beneath her distress.

"Are you okay? Here, let me help you. You seem so upset. What's the matter? I'm so sorry if I said something to upset you. Won't you stay? I'm sorry if I rushed you. Please stay." His hands were reaching for her, but it was as if she'd already left; her expression, once a shield, was now an impenetrable fortress. She resisted his help, resisted his words, and hurried away from him, her pages clutched tightly in her hands.

Ben watched her go, upset and angry with himself. He'd driven her away. Dully he sank onto a chair, and that's when his gaze was snagged by a piece of paper. In her haste, she'd left a page behind. Ben reached for it, eager, and then stopped short.

It was a charcoal drawing, infused with the same artistry as her first book. But it was the subject of the drawing that arrested him. Most of the page was an intense black, and at its heart a nucleus of light. Two children, a boy and a girl, beneath a blanket fort, the boy's flashlight piercing the dark, creating a halo in which the girl smiled, and hovering above them, a ghostlike image of long, thin people, stretching like shadows, towering with their long legs and large mouths and toothy grins.

The Story People.

Ben stared at the page, mouth agape, and it stared back with intensity. "Rosie." It was a breath, a quiet scream in his mind, a continuous roar, the backdrop to every emotion and thought now pounding through him. "Rosie!"

He was all action. With long strides, Ben ran toward the front of the store, the drawing in hand. He paused to look breathlessly around. She wasn't there. His heart in his throat, he blew past Nick and several customers, out the front door, which loudly jingled his exit, and down the front steps. His heart was thudding painfully in his chest. He'd never known such adrenaline. He felt like he could run for miles just to catch her. Anything to catch her. He would keep running toward her no matter what. He looked wildly around him and caught sight of her figure far down Main Street, hurrying away. Ben ran. The wind streamed past him, slicing past his cotton shirt and grabbing at his flesh. She was turning onto a side street far ahead of him. Several people stopped and stared as Ben tore past them. He held her drawing firmly in his hand, the wind eager to snatch it from him, tugging at it, tempting it to leave him. He held it tighter and ran harder, pumping his arms in his effort, ignoring the stares and the calls of several neighbors. He could run forever. He would run forever to catch her.

Ben turned the corner he'd seen her take and without pausing kept running. She was closer now; he was definitely gaining ground. He opened his mouth to call for her but no sound came out. The wind snatched his breath, stole his words, and tore through his hair with vengeance. He was nearing her now. Her scurrying figure was no match for his long strides. Ben slowed his pace, willed his breath to even out. She was there now, a few yards away. She heard him. She was turning. She was looking full in his face. She was crying and wiping at her tears. He reached her and grabbed her and held her tightly to his chest, catching her off-balance, throwing them both into a tailspin. She was crying harder and clutching at him tightly, her head buried in his shoulder as the sobs shook her. She was gasping his name between sobs, while he laughed hysterically, like a crazy person, but he didn't care. He didn't care. He had found her. God had brought her to him. She was here in his arms. He placed a hand behind her head and rocked them both in crazy, loopy circles, their breaths mixing in the cold air. His whole body hummed with the cold, his breath sawing painfully in and out of his lungs. He'd never felt more alive, here with this woman in his arms. He held her and said her name over and over into her hair, "Rosie, Rosie, Rosie."

**The girl tells the Story People good-bye.** "I am sorry," she tells them, "but it has to be this way." Three letters sit unopened on a chair. The girl finishes the fourth and places it gently on top of the stack. She doesn't want to leave, but the pain of the unopened notes is too big. Too much time has passed, and so the girl knows it's time to say good-bye.

"No," the Story People insist, "please stay and keep us company."

The girl has to tell them again what they already know: the boy is not coming back. She patiently explains this again. "The boy is not coming back, and we cannot survive without the boy."

The Story People are silent, for they know the truth of her words.

"Maybe I will see you again," the girl consoles the Story People. "Don't be sad. Maybe in a different time I will see you again."

# CHAPTER TWENTY-EIGHT

## IT WOULD HAVE TO BE ENOUGH

The moment was caught in a whirl of senses. First there was sound—the sound of the wind whipping around her, her feet on the pavement, her muffled sobs, and the bustle of Main Street life. The further she walked, the quieter it became, until the loudest noise was her own quick breaths. Then a new sound, that of hurrying feet pounding the pavement, the sound of urgency, accompanied by ragged breathing, and then her name borne on a gasp.

First there was sound and then there was sight—the sight of Main Street through tears, her own hurrying feet on the sidewalk, Oma's familiar street, and then Ben, with crazy hair and wild eyes, her sketch clutched in his fist.

First there was sound, then sight, then touch—the touch of the wind upon her skin; her leather portfolio, sticking in her clammy hands; Ben's warm breath on her neck; his lips touching her ear; his arms around her; his large hand cupping her head; her face against the soft cotton of his shirt.

First there was sound, then sight, then touch, and then there was smell—the smell of pastry drifting from Carley's Café; the smell of fall, crisp in the air; the intoxicating woodsy smell of Ben's aftershave, full in her face, filling her senses.

First there was sound, then sight, then touch, then smell, and finally taste—the taste of tears, first sad and then joyous. The taste of tears, Rosemary found, remained the same—salty and sharp. This is how she would remember the moment: as sharp and arresting as the taste of tears.

◇◆◇◆

"I found them just a few months ago. They were scattered all over this place. It's what made me back away from selling."

"I kept them all, Ben, all the notes, and I kept coming. For years I kept coming."

"Crazy, really, that we never talked more about who we were. I couldn't find you after, after my parents . . ."

"I'm so sorry that I wasn't there for you. I felt that something had happened to you and I couldn't help."

"Honestly, the whole thing faded into a story for me."

"Me too; I know what you mean. It just became something beautiful locked away."

"And then when I inherited this place, I avoided coming to the Room because I think it just reminded me of . . . everything."

"This place, it hasn't changed."

They were sitting on metal folding chairs in the middle of the Room, a floor lamp illuminating most of the space. Ben sat with his legs straddling the seat and arms resting on its back. Rosemary sat with crossed legs opposite him and watched him gaze about the Room. Her heart was full and pounding in her chest. To be here again and with him was more than she could have asked for. Even though they hadn't seen each other in so many years and didn't even really know each other as adults, they slipped back into an easy familiarity, aided by their memories filling the Room. Rosemary had been afraid that the knowledge that she was Rosie would ruin things, but it made it better, so much better, for they had the foundation of friendship to make their newfound relationship as adults even sweeter. The closeness she'd felt and the interest she'd sensed from Ben on Friday night had compounded tenfold. Now as he looked at her, she felt her chest constrict under his gaze. She shivered and laughed, "This is so weird. I just got a flashback to the first time we met and you stared straight at me like that. Honestly, I was kind of scared out of my mind. I thought, *Who is this? A crazy person?*"

Ben chuckled. "And I thought, *Who is this little kid coming in here and ruining my fort?*" He grinned at her, then asked softly, "Am I so scary now?"

Rosemary felt the blush creeping up her face and quickly turned her attention to the portfolio in her hand. "I want to show you these." She moved her chair, knelt on the floor, and pulled out sheet after sheet, splaying them across the floorboards. "I've been looking for inspiration for a second book. I've been nervous that I wouldn't find anything I was as passionate about as I was with *Spectrum*, and then coming here to Palermo's again and seeing you . . ." She carefully avoided his eyes, turning her attention to the sketches, where she was on familiar territory. "It all brought the Story People to life again for me, and I thought if we found so much joy in this make-believe game, maybe other kids would too. Maybe my next book has also been a lifetime in the making. Please take a look and let me know what you think. The Story People are more your creation than mine."

Ben rose from his seat and knelt next to her, his side brushing hers. "That's not true at all." He was looking at her, but she couldn't bring herself to meet his gaze. "They're both our creation. You brought them to life in ways I couldn't." He quieted as he looked at her sketches, touching them, bringing them to the light one by one.

Rosemary fidgeted, self-conscious as she always was with her work. To fill the silence, she began talking through plot points. "So these are just preliminary sketches. I'm thinking of beginning with just the bookstore as the Story People are out." She pointed to a sketch of a row of bookshelves with a grinning face peeking out from between the books. "Then the boy and girl are introduced later." She gestured toward the drawing Ben had first seen of the boy and girl with the flashlight. It was a crumpled mess from being in Ben's clenched fist. "But I don't want this to be too creepy or scary, so I'm trying to keep the Story People looking friendly and not too ghostlike." She picked up a sketch of a grinning baldheaded person with long arms and a toothy smile who was pouncing on an open book. "What do you think?"

She watched Ben nod as she talked, watched him look at her work with furrowed brow, his face lighting up at the sight of her portrait of him. Finally, he turned to her. His face in the dim light was a landscape of shadows, his eyes gleaming as they met hers. "This is beautiful work, Rosemary, just beautiful." He set down a sketch to reach for her hand. "Yes, absolutely, I love it! You have my full support in this. I think kids will really connect to it, just like we did."

Rosemary beamed and squeezed his hand. He wasn't letting go, she noticed, which she didn't really mind, but it was slowly becoming awkward as they knelt hand in hand, looking at the sketches. She casually removed her hand to pick up one of the pictures. Instantly she missed the pressure and warmth of his touch. "I'm thinking of staying with Oma for a little while so I can come here and sketch, if that's okay with you."

"I would love that. You're welcome here any time." Ben sounded distracted. Rosemary watched as he leaned back on his heels and stared at her drawings. "In fact . . ." He rose to his feet and looked around the Room, then ducked out into the connecting closet. Rosemary watched him in confusion as he came back in with a huge smile on his face. "I think I have an idea. Come here." He extended a hand and helped her to her feet, pulling her with him into the closet. "I've been trying to figure out ways to really make Palermo's my own. I don't want to be content with just running the business as it has always been." He was talking faster and faster, and Rosemary's heart picked up pace in response to his excitement. They were leaving the closet now. Rosemary hurried to keep up, her hand still clutched in his.

"Where on earth are we going?" She laughed out loud as Ben dragged her down two flights of stairs to the first floor.

"You'll see." His voice was breathless. She smiled at the back of his head, recognizing the creative enthusiasm she'd loved in BJ. Together they hurried to the far left of the first floor behind the staircase and came to a stop in a small area with a handful of beanbag chairs and low bookshelves.

"The children's section?" Rosemary asked.

Ben dropped her hand and stood in front of her, arms outstretched. "Yes, so this is the original children's section. It hasn't changed much in all these years. You remember how cramped it was when you did your reading here the other day. It's really not meant for those types of readings."

"Yes, I see what you mean." Rosemary smiled at the small shelves, nicked with age. "But why are we here?"

"This section isn't that big." Ben walked to one end. "It starts here and extends here." He walked to the other end. "There's a total of three bookcases, hardly enough, don't you think?"

"I guess you're right. It seemed much bigger when I was a child," Rosemary laughed. "It's especially not big enough if you intend to continue doing readings."

"Exactly." Ben raised a finger. "Okay, so now that you've refreshed yourself on this, follow me." Ben grabbed her hand again, and before she knew it, they were jogging back up the stairs.

Rosemary laughed out loud. "You do know that you're being a crazy person right now, right?" Ben just shot her a grin over his shoulder. Now they were back on the third floor and standing outside the closet leading to the Room. Rosemary was struggling to conceal how out of breath she was.

"Your book is giving me a vision for this space. What if we turn this area into a new and improved children's section?" Ben gestured toward the shelves outside the closet. "Currently, these house all the clearance books. What if I swapped these for the children's books on the first floor? This whole area could be a new children's section." Ben indicated the space near the closet. "And then this could be a new reading room for a children's story hour." Ben grabbed her hand again and they ducked into the closet together. "We could combine this closet with the Room and turn it into one reading room."

They were back where they had started, in the Room filled with her sketches. Rosemary couldn't stop smiling. "Ben, that's fabulous. Kids love story hour, and what a wonderful way to use this space."

"That's not all." He stooped and picked up a handful of her sketches. "What if we had the theme of this reading room be the Story People?"

She noticed that he used "we," and it warmed her heart almost more than his suggestion did. "Wait, so you're saying—"

"I'm asking you, Rosemary Berg, if you would be willing to transform this Room into scenes from your up-and-coming book."

Rosemary's breath caught. She looked from her sketches to the Room and slowly began walking its perimeter. "I could have this be the focal point." She trailed a hand along the back wall. "The reader would sit here, so I would need to draw attention to this spot. I could have Story People stretching across here." Her hand continued to travel along the walls. "I could paint them emerging from books, so I could have several large books open here." She moved down the wall, crouching as the ideas continued to unfold. "And then maybe some of the scenes from the books themselves could be pouring out so that this whole room is a mixture of scenes from books with the Story People pouring out, all merging to this spot." She moved back to the end of the Room and the imaginary storyteller. She stood silently, letting it sweep over her. Finally she turned, and now it was her turn to grab Ben's hand. "Yes! This is perfect! What a wonderful idea. I would love to be a part of it. This is great timing too. I have several smaller assignments from different publishers at the moment, so I can take this on. I'll be happy to work on this."

Ben laughed and drew her to him, folding her in his arms and resting his chin on her head. "I'm so glad. Consider yourself hired."

Rosemary smiled against his chest, then pulled back as more ideas came to her. "Oh, Ben, you could do so much with this area, so much! To help direct people to the third floor, you could put in footprints leading from the first floor to the third so that kids can follow the path. You could implement summer reading and birthday clubs, have ways for kids to earn a free book . . . it will be such a blessing to the kids and their families. What a wonderful way to reach out and really involve the community! And really, besides combining the closet with this room and adding the murals, there's not much else that needs to be done, is there?" Rosemary paused for breath, realizing that she'd been talking in one big outpouring. She was looking around the Room as she spoke, but now she looked to Ben, who was remaining quiet. At the look on his face, she stilled. He was smiling down at her with such tenderness in his expression that a lump caught in her throat and she realized with a start how very close his face was to her own. His arms were still around her, and she was afraid he would be able to feel how hard her heart was pounding.

Her eyes faltered and she looked away, embarrassed. As she usually did, Rosemary continued to talk to fill the quiet. "I imagine you'll want some additional pieces of furniture, a chair for the storyteller, chairs or cushions for the children, maybe some updated, colorful bookshelves, but I think you could find those at consignment shops or even make some of it yourself. I mean, if you're handy in that way. I imagine bookshelves aren't that hard to make."

She was babbling, but she couldn't stop. He was still staring at her as if he wanted nothing more than to kiss her, and she didn't know how to handle the emotions coursing through her. "I'm a bit of an expert in scouring garage sales, so I would be happy to keep an eye out for anything that could work for this area." He'd moved his hand to her neck and was brushing her hair behind her shoulder, his palm coming to rest against the side of her neck, his thumb extending to just below her jawline. His eyes were moving across her face, and she found that she couldn't breathe, could barely think, and so she continued to talk, pushing slightly against his chest with her open palms. "I imagine you'll want to go over the financials. I really do want to help any way I can. Maybe I'll talk with Oma and see if I can extend my stay even longer." She watched as he pulled back, blinked, and looked away. She felt instant regret. *Why, Rosemary, why can't you just relax?* She wanted to draw him closer, say, "Sorry, never mind, I was being silly, please continue and kiss me." But he was turning away and looking at the Room. His arms were no longer around her, and she felt colder without his touch.

"Yes, everything you're saying sounds great. I think the first step is looking into the possibility of combining these two spaces." He moved to the wall between the closet and the Room. "I don't think that this is a load-bearing wall, but we'll want to be sure." Rosemary scooped up her drawings and joined him by the door as he continued to speak. "Of course I'll compensate you for your work. Just let me know your estimate."

"Sure." Rosemary smiled at him, but he seemed to be avoiding her eyes. A wave of anxiety washed over her. Had she offended him? She caught his hand in her own and squeezed it, forcing him to look at her. "Hey, you excited? I'm excited. Let's do this thing." She felt the anxiety recede as he smiled at her. She wanted him to smile at her like that always.

He'd almost kissed her. Ben could hardly believe it. He'd been caught up in the moment, in her joy and enthusiasm, in the headiness of their shared vision, and he'd almost kissed her. He'd felt her resistance; it'd been slight, just a small pressure against his chest, the way she'd kept her hands between them rather than lean toward him as he was leaning toward her. It had been enough though, enough to bring him back to reality with a snap, and that reality was this: she was taken. He'd been so blindsided by their reunion that he'd completely forgotten about Liam. Of course she had resisted; she had a boyfriend, and the thought brought back the pain in full force. She was looking at him now; she had grabbed his hand and was looking up into his face with expectation. "Hey, you excited? I'm excited. Let's do this thing." And he smiled back. It would have to be enough, to have her back in his life and working with him to transform their Room into something special to share with others. He was grateful to have this vision, this breath of new life and purpose.

He couldn't wait to share with Dale how wonderfully God was working in his life, granting him that elusive sense of purpose. Rosemary was helping him see all of Palermo's in a new light. It would be enough, he tried to convince himself, to be near her and work with her. It would have to be enough.

**The girl isn't a girl anymore.** *She enters the Room a young woman to find her friends frozen and silent. "Hello," she calls out. "Hello!" But there is no reply.*

*The Room is cluttered now, with odds and ends stacked against the walls. The Room looks tired and forgotten. Gone is the empty space where the girl and the boy used to hide in their fort. Instead the girl can barely move now for fear of knocking something over. She sits on an overturned bucket and waits for the Room to speak to her.*

*It has been a while, and the Story People probably do not recognize her. She sees that her letters are long gone. Found, perhaps? More likely they are just lost. The girl sits and waits to be recognized, and as she sits she writes, she writes to the boy, knowing he will not see it and will not reply. And as she writes, the Story People emerge, slowly, cautiously, hardly daring to hope.*

*"Hello?" they breathe out the question.*

*"Hello," she answers. "It has been a long time."*

# CHAPTER TWENTY-NINE

## A NOVELTY HE COULD GET USED TO

Mrs. Gardner anxiously awaited the arrival of her friends and practiced her speech as she paced and fidgeted, but no matter how she phrased it, the news was astonishing even to herself. She paced right and gesticulated in her imagined speech. She paced left and wrung her hands in worry. She gave up and checked on the scones in the oven. It was just as she was removing them that a cheery "Hello" resounded from her front door.

"Come in, Anita! I'm in the kitchen!"

Mrs. Baumgartner came bustling in, her arms full of knitting supplies. "So how do you feel, Matilda, now that you have the sling off? Must be so freeing." She dumped her supplies on the table and sniffed the air appreciatively. "Are those orange pecan scones I smell? This is a treat!"

"Yes, I wanted to surprise you ladies today. In answer to your question, it has been very liberating, although my arm still looks a bit alarming, so pale and pasty, and I feel like a snake shedding its skin." She shoved up her sleeve and extended her arm.

Mrs. Baumgartner was leaning in and clucking appropriately at Mrs. Gardner's pale arm when Mrs. Frank arrived.

"Orange pecan scones! What's the occasion?" She deposited her knitting bag next to Mrs. Baumgartner's. "Also, what on earth are you doing? Put that away."

"What occasion? There's no occasion," Mrs. Gardner said a little too quickly as she rolled down her sleeve.

"She was just showing me her disgusting arm," Mrs. Baumgartner explained.

"Yes, thank you, Anita. I can see that it is disgusting."

"No need to overly critique my poor arm," Mrs. Gardner scolded as she scooped scones onto a platter. "Let's take the food and knitting into the living room."

As the ladies settled themselves in chairs and Mrs. Gardner handed out small plates and napkins, she wondered how to broach the subject. As it turned out, she didn't have to, as Mrs. Baumgartner broached it for her.

"I know you said that Professor Jenson wasn't over here all the time, but I'm finding that hard to believe." Her voice was muffled around a bite of scone. "The two of you have been seen cozying up to each other in public on more than one occasion. Anything you want to share, Matilda?"

"Yes, spill it. We've seen him driving you around like a queen. Even though you must be capable of driving yourself now." Mrs. Frank nodded at Mrs. Gardner's two good arms. "I feel like we've seen considerably less of you, and I'm suspecting it has something to do with the Professor."

"Has he been eating up all your time?" Mrs. Baumgartner jumped in helpfully. "Does there need to be an intervention? Is he making a pest of himself?"

Mrs. Gardner swallowed guiltily. "Funny that you mention all this because I was going to bring it up today."

Both of her friends froze and stared at her intently. "Aha!" Mrs. Frank trumpeted. "An intervention *is* needed!"

"No no, nothing like that," Mrs. Gardner was quick to correct. "You're right; Mark and I have been seeing a lot of each other lately, but I don't want you thinking he's imposing on me."

"Posing as you? Why on earth would he do that?" Mrs. Baumgartner looked confused and then gasped in alarm as if receiving a sudden revelation. "Oh, has he stolen your identity? I've heard about this! Apparently it happens all the time to people our age." She looked wildly about the room as if a shifty character lurked behind every piece of furniture.

"For crying out loud, Anita. She said he isn't *imposing on her*. She doesn't need us to make him back off." Mrs. Frank shook her head as Mrs. Baumgartner calmed down. "Are you sure, Matilda? You're not simply putting up with him because he's been so nice to you lately?"

"It's nothing like that," Mrs. Gardner assured, blushing deeply. "Most days he's the one who has to put up with me. We, well . . . we just enjoy each other's company. If you've been seeing us together a lot, it's because it's by choice."

"Oh, I think it's just so romantic!" Mrs. Baumgartner burst in. "And really, it's not all that surprising, is it?"

"But he's so much older."

"Come on, Emma, he's what? Ten years older? That hardly matters at our age."

"I just wonder at his ability to endure Matilda's . . . chattiness."

"Yes, you have a point. He does like his peace and quiet."

"And Matilda doesn't offer much of either."

"True, but they do say that opposites attract."

"Do you think it's a necessity that she be interested in his hobbies? She could hardly care less about fungi."

"From what I recall, it's healthy to have separate interests."

"I think you're right, Anita. The only thing that kept Richard and me away from each other's throats was his weekly golf games at the club."

"See? Separate interests."

Mrs. Gardner watched her friends discuss her love life, finally clearing her throat as if to announce her presence. "May I say something?"

Both friends looked her way, the one with her knitting in hand, the other with a half-eaten scone.

"I think perhaps Mark has been one of the best things to happen to me. It's not to say that I don't still miss Robert. I do, each and every day. I think that since he passed, I've become especially set in my ways. Mark has shown me so much compassion, and for the first time in a long time I feel like I'm growing as a person. I didn't expect to feel that way again. I suppose he challenges me in all the right ways. He makes me want to be better."

"Oh, that's so beautiful." Mrs. Baumgartner dabbed at her eyes and shoved the rest of the scone into her mouth.

Mrs. Gardner braced herself for what was to follow. "But there's more to this news."

"More?" Mrs. Frank questioned. "How could there possibly be more?"

"I have to admit that it completely took me by surprise. I always thought him the most unromantic man alive!" Mrs. Gardner exclaimed as if that were a terrific character flaw. "How can someone be romantic who devotes his life to *fungi*? But then I began to see it differently. He's so *unromantic* that it's romantic!"

Both friends looked at her with knit brows, trying to follow.

"I guess what I'm saying is that because he hasn't a clue how to romance, when he does try, it is that much sweeter. And usually it just doesn't work out the way he intends, which makes it even better."

Mrs. Baumgartner and Mrs. Frank looked at each other with incredulous expressions.

"He asked me to take a walk this past weekend, and we were walking through Fischer Park. You know that especially woodsy area in the northeast corner? Well, this was just after that big rain, and it was unseasonably warm for December. We were walking along the path when he just stopped all of a sudden and dashed into the woods. It was so strange. He began shouting for me. I didn't know what to expect. When I caught up to him, he was standing in the middle of a huge ring of mushrooms."

"Oh yes. I've heard that mushrooms can do that," Mrs. Frank interjected. She was quickly shushed by Mrs. Baumgartner, who was leaning forward in her seat and steadily consuming a second scone, her eyes wide and focused on Mrs. Gardner.

"He was standing in the middle of this nearly perfect ring of mushrooms, like he was the mushroom king." Mrs. Gardner laughed and blushed. "He said something about a perfect example of *Marasmius oreades*."

The two friends raised their eyebrows at the flawless name-drop.

"He told me to come join him, so there we were, standing in the center of this strange ring. He said it's often called a fairy ring and is surrounded by much folklore. He said they're supposed to be the work of supernatural beings and are portals to other worlds and that we were being dangerous and daring by standing at its center." Mrs. Gardner paused to laugh. "Of course, these are just silly tales, but I have to say there was something special about standing there so daring in the center of this ring. And then what do you suppose he did?"

"What, what!" Mrs. Frank exclaimed, taking both friends by surprise with her eagerness.

"He . . . well, he knelt right there in the wet grass . . . and . . . and he completely went out of character and took my hand and . . . and . . . kissed it!" Mrs. Gardner blushed bright ruby.

Mrs. Baumgartner chewed furiously as the story intensified, managing a mumbled "Oh, this is *so* romantic!" and spewing a handful of crumbs in the process.

Mrs. Gardner continued with her story: "There he was,

his pants getting completely soaked with the rain, and what do you think he said to me then? He said, 'While we're being dangerous, let me tell you how much I love you.'"

"Oh oh oh!" Mrs. Baumgartner cried, choking on the crumbs in her mouth and gagging until Mrs. Frank handed her a glass of water.

"Did he actually say that?" Mrs. Frank was absentmindedly whacking a coughing Mrs. Baumgartner on the back, staring hard at Mrs. Gardner all the while.

"He did! He completely surprised me. He was kneeling there with my hand pressed to his lips again and that great bushy white mustache tickling my hand and his large blue eyes holding the most emotion I've ever seen in them, and I just said . . . well, I said yes!"

"Yes? To what?"

"Wait, *what*?"

Both friends sat up straighter, and Mrs. Baumgartner forced herself out of her coughing fit to press further. "Are you telling us that—"

"Yes, I'm trying to say that he proposed and I said yes!"

"No! Really?"

"I can't believe it!"

There was an uproar of commotion. Mrs. Baumgartner jumped to her feet, spilling the water glass in her hand, Mrs. Frank slumped backward in her chair as if suffering a heart attack and stared at the ceiling, and Mrs. Gardner just laughed and assured them, "It's true. I know it's crazy, but it's true!"

As the news sunk in, Mrs. Baumgartner sat back down and it was Mrs. Frank's turn to jump to her feet to pace excitedly about the room. "Who knew that old Professor Jenson had it in him?"

"I know. It was such a romantic moment, though I really don't think he intended it to be. I had to help him back up afterward because of his arthritis." She laughed shakily, tears forming in her eyes. "And he didn't have a ring. I don't think he'd meant to propose that day. The fairy ring must have inspired him. He said the fairy ring would have to do for now and that he'd give me an actual ring later."

Mrs. Baumgartner shook her head in wonderment.

"I know it seems quick, but really, when you're our age, what is there to wait on?" Mrs. Gardner laughed.

"Indeed, no time to waste! What with the grave right around the corner." Mrs. Frank sat back down again with a nod of approval.

"Oh, Emma, now is not the time to be morbid."

"I'm not being any such thing. I'm just agreeing with her. Life is short. Act now or lose the chance forever. Good for Professor Jenson."

As if on cue, there came a sharp knock on the door and then a creak as it opened. "Matilda, dear?"

All three women squealed—Mrs. Gardner over the novelty of being called "dear" and the other two at the novelty of hearing it.

"Did you want to take a ride into town?" Professor Jenson turned the corner into the living room and was quickly surrounded by three emotional women.

"Congratulations! What a blessing!"

"Good for you. We had no idea you had it in you."

"I'm sorry, dear. I told Anita and Emma. I assumed you wouldn't mind."

"When is the ceremony? Tell me you're having a ceremony."

"Where will you live? Here or over there?"

"Have you told anyone else?"

"Can we tell everyone else?"

"Well now, isn't this nice. Calm yourselves, ladies. Speak one at a time please." Professor Jenson blinked rapidly as if under a bright light, his gaze flitting from one woman to the next, startled and not a little pleased to suddenly be the nucleus of three bubbling women, all loudly extolling his romantic virtues. It was a novelty he could get used to.

**The Room sits silent, settling into its loneliness.** A year goes by since the girl-turned-woman visited, and then another year and another. The Room sees people come and go, but they are like quickly passing guests; they arrive and leave, carting items back and forth. The Room fills with junk, yet it feels emptier than ever. There is no eager boy with a flashlight, no bright-eyed girl with loud giggles. No notes passed back and forth. No stories. No imagining.

The Story People burrow deep into the walls of the Room and wait; they wait for a girl and a boy to find them again.

# Chapter Thirty

## WELCOMING THEM HOME

The past was something Ben had pushed back for as long as he could remember. The present was a protective barrier, a way to look away from a painful past and toward something new. But now there was Rosie; she was the past come to life, and when Ben looked at her, he didn't see pain, didn't see a reminder of things lost, but saw a promise of things to come. Maybe there was a way to embrace the past instead of being consumed by it.

She'd asked him questions, tentative at first, about his parents, about his life between then and now, and he'd answered as honestly as he could. There was something about her that demanded openness, so he gave it to her and drew comfort from her. Rosemary was in the process of moving in with Oma again, so as to work both on her book and on the expanded reading room and children's section. Ben was thankful for her proximity; he couldn't imagine doing this project without her. But the proximity came with pain as well. There were moments when he sensed a connection with her so deep that he felt guilty, as if he were betraying Liam. He was careful not to slip again as he had in the Room. He tried to be as chaste with her as if Liam were present with them. There were times, however, when she showed such interest in him and her eyes held a light seemingly just for him that made it difficult. And he wondered.

"You have to be honest with her, Ben." Dale sat across from him in Carley's Café, a plate of cheesy bread between them. "How long has it been? A week?"

"Yeah." Ben stared at the bread, his appetite gone. "It's been a week since we reconnected. I'm surprised she hasn't mentioned Liam."

"Why haven't *you* mentioned him?"

"I'm not sure. I guess I don't really want to ruin what we have."

"Ah." Dale broke off a piece of bread and nodded. "You don't want to ask the question because you don't want to hear the answer."

"Something like that. Cowardly, I know."

Dale took a bite and spoke around the wad of bread. "No, it's understandable. And she's probably not mentioning it because, well, why should she if she's not aware of how you feel?"

Ben frowned. "I seriously doubt she's unaware. I've been not so subtle at times."

"Hmm, then you certainly need to bring it up. Before it goes further and there's something to regret."

Ben halfheartedly popped a piece of bread into his mouth. "I know you're right. I need to clear the air. I just know that once it's out there, our relationship will feel different, and I don't want to ruin it. We've just reconnected after all these years, and I don't want to strain things."

"I get it, but for both your sakes, you should be open with her. After all, you're going to be working closely together on this project, which, by the way, Sarah and I are excited about. Am I right when I say that it seems you are more, how should I put it . . . settled? content?"

"Absolutely. I think 'content' about captures it. You

might even throw in peaceful! Regardless of what happens with Rosemary, I'm excited for the future of the store and thankful to be a part of it. You know, when we get this new children's section done, I'm expecting to see a lot more of you, Sarah, and the little ones. How is the baby anyway?"

"Excellent. The girls love having a brother. Poor little guy doesn't realize that he has two extra little mommies. They are taking their roles as helpers very seriously," Dale laughed.

Ben smiled and listened attentively as Dale continued to regale him with the twins' reactions to their new little brother. He loved listening to these stories, but he could tell that Dale hesitated to talk about his children too much, probably because Ben had none of his own and Dale didn't want to tire him out with stories of other people's kids' antics. It was the juggling act of good friends in different stages of life. Ben could sense that Dale held back on the family stories out of respect for his feelings, and he appreciated the sensitivity even though it was unnecessary. He loved the stories even if they left him feeling slightly sad and envious. There was such joy in Dale's face when he talked of Sarah and the kids. Ben wanted that for himself. Listening to Dale speak now, Ben realized with a doomed sense of certainty that he wanted it with Rosemary.

"I'll be praying for you, Ben." Dale slid out of the booth and led the way out of the café. "I'll be praying for strength to speak to her and peace afterward."

"Thank you." Ben clasped his friend's hand. He wasn't sure what peace there could possibly be for him, but he trusted that the Lord would provide it. He also knew he had tarried long enough. Whether or not he wanted to hear the answer, he needed to ask Rosemary about Liam.

◇◆◇◆

Nick's brother in the neighboring town was a building contractor and had assured Ben that the connecting wall between the closet and the Room beyond was not a load-bearing wall and could come down easily. Construction could begin as early as next week.

"That's fantastic!" Rosemary's eyes lit up at the news. They were standing in the Room, which had been emptied in preparation for Rosemary's work. "Things are moving right along."

"They are." Ben took in her artistic appearance with approval. She'd shown up in a pair of tattered jeans and a loose sweatshirt that said "Coffee is always a good idea." Her hair was tied back in a messy bun, and she had a box full of charcoals and a large pad of paper under her arm. "So what is your plan this afternoon?"

"Well, I'll have to wait to actually prep the walls until after the construction work is all done. So today I'm planning on doing more sketches, and later this week, I hope to ask your pastor if I can borrow the church's projector. I noticed they were using one in Sunday School last week, and it'd be so helpful if I could use it because then I can insert my sketches into the projector and just trace them on the walls. A group of us did a mural in the art building on campus our sophomore year, and the projector really speeds things up. I'm kind of nervous, though, with this being only my second mural. You sure you want to entrust me with this?" She raised her eyebrows at Ben searchingly. "Speak now or forever hold your peace."

"I have every confidence in you." Ben smiled at her. "I don't want this to take away from the work on your book, though, or your other freelance work."

"Don't worry about that! I've juggled multiple projects many times. Plus these sketches will easily double for the book, so I'm killing two birds with one stone."

She reached out a hand to his arm in reassurance. Ben welcomed the touch, but then felt the familiar twinge of guilt and backed away. "Okay, well, I guess I'll leave you to it then. I'll be downstairs if you need anything." He left the room, glancing over his shoulder to see Rosemary settle herself in the middle of the floor. He smiled as he watched her take in the Room, but the joy he felt at watching her was quickly subsumed by the ache of wanting her and the guilt of knowing he shouldn't.

◇◆◇◇

Rosemary did what she always did when seeking inspiration. She lay down in the middle of the room and closed her eyes. She let her memories of the place sweep over her. What had she felt as a child? Wonder, excitement, mystery. What had she felt the first time she'd entered this Room? Anxiety, anticipation, fear. What had she felt upon meeting BJ? A profound interest. Rosemary lay still and let the different emotions take her away from herself and root her in the past. What had been so captivating about the Story People? How could she distill that into an image that would translate to other children? Rosemary opened her eyes, sat up, and grabbed a well-worn bit of charcoal and her sketch pad. She settled herself on the floor and let the Story People take over.

The hours passed quickly, and Rosemary was so focused that the soft sound of someone clearing his throat took her completely by surprise. She yelped and spun around. Ben stood in the doorway with a plate in hand and a guilty expression on his face.

"Sorry to surprise you. I just thought maybe you'd be hungry." He entered the Room and set down a plate of food: a banana, ham sandwich, chips, and water bottle. "And you sure you don't need a table? That can't be comfortable." He grinned and motioned to her sprawled-out position on the floor.

"This is sweet of you, thanks." Rosemary smiled up at him. "Nope, this is perfect. I'd rather just spread out like this."

"Can I see what you're working on?"

"Certainly." Rosemary patted the floor next to her. Ben sat and looked over her shoulder as she held up a sketch.

"I'm trying to imagine what is so appealing about the Story People. Part of what made *Spectrum* so relatable was the idea that you could just walk into your favorite book. With the Story People, I'm trying to communicate that the stories can jump out of the book, kind of the other way around. The Story People live on stories, right? So I'm trying to show that visually." She held up the latest sketch. "As they consume the books, the stories come alive, kind of how they do in us. As you read and take in a story, it comes to life for you." She handed Ben the sketch, which showed the Story People feasting on *The Hobbit*, the bookshelves slowly giving way to hills with tiny doors in them.

Ben took hold of one side of the page with Rosemary holding the other. "This is great. It will translate so well for the Room too. It's a neat concept. Kids walk into the reading room to hear stories, and they're surrounded by scenes from their favorite books, as if the Story People are making them come alive and inviting them to dig into the books, just as they are."

"Exactly!" Rosemary turned to him, her heart catching in her throat. He was closer than she'd expected. His chest was nearly cradling her shoulder. His hand was stretched out behind her and he was leaning in close to see the sketch. She knew she should turn away but she couldn't. She thought again of the moment that had passed between them a week ago. His hand on her neck, his eyes roaming her face—he'd been about to kiss her and she'd ruined it. His presence made her nervous and jittery, like an extra shot of espresso. One second she felt herself melting into his presence and the next she was jerking away, a high voltage coursing through her veins. She'd never cared about someone like this before and didn't know how to just relax and accept the attention. Upon realizing that she'd missed out on a kiss with Ben, it'd been all she could think about, which made interactions with him hard to bear. She'd tried to send him signals that she was interested, that if he tried again, she wouldn't resist, but he'd withheld. Now she looked at his profile and willed him to look in her direction. Surely he could feel her eyes on him, but he remained turned toward her sketch, his eyes focused on her work. Finally, she sighed and refocused on the sketch. "I'm so glad you like it," she said softly, a wave of disappointment washing through her. Perhaps it was better this way. They would be working closely together, and why potentially compromise their renewed friendship and partnership with complicated romantic emotions?

"Well, I'll leave you to it." Only when Ben was standing did he look at her, the distance between them wider and safer.

"Thanks again for the food." Rosemary smiled at him and watched him leave. The Room felt smaller with him gone. She sat back and stared at the food, her appetite waning in light of the feelings Ben had left in his wake. Was it just her imagination, or did Ben seem subdued today? She remembered what Liam had said: "You don't appear like you need anything or anyone, and it's hard to approach that." Maybe he'd been right about her. Since she was a child, she'd learned to cope with things by retreating. If you didn't know how to react to something, better to just quietly retreat, build up walls, regroup, observe. This natural tendency had only increased once her father had left. But had her self-sufficiency made her unable to connect with others? She didn't think this was a hindrance with Ben. He seemed to be able to see her for who she was. He wasn't intimidated by her; he was inspired by her. She wanted to be with a man like that. Someone who built her up and who, in turn, she could build up. With Ben, she sensed an acceptance of who she currently was even as there was an invitation to grow. This was the type of mutual relationship she'd been waiting for. She needed to show him how very much she was willing and ready for it.

Rosemary reached for the sandwich and let her thoughts roam to Liam. She'd called him repeatedly after their blowup. She'd left two messages before he'd finally returned her call. Before he could say a word, she was speaking breathlessly, eagerly, repeating her earlier messages. "I was a jerk; I'm so sorry. I know you were only being honest with me, and I threw it back in your face. I built up this thing between you and Ben, and I let it make me so defensive. Please forgive me."

"It's okay, Clooney; it's okay. I was a jerk too, and I hope you can forgive me. I never should have walked out like that. I'm sorry. But I just don't know that we can go back to what we had before this, you know? I forgive you, but I think we both need time."

She'd assured him of her forgiveness, but it was clear that he didn't want to keep talking to her. He'd kept it brief, but she could still hear the pain in his voice, and something else, something that made him strained and tense. He'd almost sounded guilty, but she wasn't sure why. Still, she'd been grateful that he'd talked to her, and she took the return of his affectionate nickname as a promising sign. His words in the restaurant, however, remained with her: "You don't appear like you need anything or anyone, and it's hard to approach that." She didn't want anything holding her back with Ben. Rosemary prayed for the strength and courage to be open and vulnerable with the man she was falling in love with.

◇◆◇◆

Ben closed up the shop, a mounting sense of dread settling in his chest. It'd been hard coming into the Room that afternoon and seeing Rosemary's work, sitting next to her, listening to her passionate vision. He just kept thinking how fortunate Liam was and wishing he and Rosemary had connected sooner. Now it was just the two of them in the shop, and Ben knew he couldn't avoid it any longer. He made his way to the third floor and entered the Room to find Rosemary packing up.

"All finished for the night?" he asked and watched as she glanced up at him, her eyes flashing and face brightening, causing his chest to constrict.

"Yup. I'm going to call it an evening. I got a lot of work done. I can't wait to actually start work in here."

Ben walked to a wall and placed a hand on it, looking around the Room, delaying the inevitable. "Hard to believe we're here again. It seems like yesterday we were just kids making up stories."

"And now we're adults making up stories." Rosemary laughed and joined him, placing a hand next to his, facing him with a bright, expectant face that was so beautiful he had to look away.

"Ben, I-I wanted to talk to you and tell you how much it has meant to me to see you again and to get to know you all over again."

Her voice was tentative and nervous. He looked at her in surprise. He hadn't been expecting such a serious tone from her. "It's meant the world to me, Rosie," he said gently, slipping back into the familiar nickname. His breath caught as he saw the effect it had on her; the longing that welled up in her face was obvious.

"I'm glad to hear that." She reached out and took his hand, lacing her fingers through his.

Ben swallowed hard and looked past her into the far corner. Her openness was refreshing and intoxicating and . . . confusing. He knew he needed to say something before things went further. He knew he should pull his hand away out of respect for Liam, even if he didn't want to.

"I just wanted you to know how much you mean to me." Rosemary was speaking again, filling the silence. She'd brought his hand up and was clasping it tightly between her own. He could sense how honestly she was trying to communicate with him, to get closer to him.

Ben opened his mouth to speak. "Rosie, I—" His voice broke and he turned away, removing his hand from hers and clenching his jaw. "I feel like I need to stop you before you go further."

There was a strained pause. "Oh, I'm sorry. I shouldn't have . . . I thought maybe you felt the same." She sounded so hurt, and Ben couldn't stand it. He turned around and placed a hand on her shoulder. He watched her eyes dart away, embarrassed. "Forget I said anything, Ben. I shouldn't have."

"Rosemary!" Ben grabbed both her arms and pulled her close, looking down into her hurt face. "You're crazy. Stop apologizing. I like you so much. I'm actually falling in love with you, and I don't say that lightly. It's not a word I throw around. It means something to me." He watched her face transform from hurt to shock to joy. "But you're confusing me right now, you beautiful, wonderful woman. You have a boyfriend, and I don't feel right about any of this. It's been bothering me, and I feel so horrible. I came up here to clear the air with you and to be honest, because this is killing me, Rosemary, killing me." He realized belatedly that he was shouting into her face, his voice growing more and more strained. He watched in confusion as she laughed.

"What are you talking about, Ben? I don't have a boyfriend!"

"W-what?"

"No, I don't have a boyfriend. I'm completely available. If . . . if you're interested." She said this last bit with a sly smile on her face. She embraced him then, her hands on his back, bringing him even closer.

"But I-I thought that Liam . . ."

She was nestling into his chest and breaking his hold on her arms so that now they dangled uselessly by his side. "I don't know where you got that crazy idea, but Liam is just a close friend. We've never been anything more than that."

"So you're not seeing anyone." Ben realized he should be rejoicing right now, but it was such a surprise that he felt rooted to the spot, suspended as he took it all in.

"Nope." Rosemary's arms had traveled up his back and hooked onto his shoulders, pulling her flush against his chest, her elbows pressed against his sides. She rose up on tiptoe and placed a kiss on his jaw. "But I'd be happy for you to change that."

Ben let the revelation sink in. She was here in his arms and she felt so good and she was free and interested and he had never felt so incredibly blessed. "Praise the Lord!" His arms jumped into action. He grasped her tightly, bowing his head so that it rested against hers, shaking with adrenaline, and laughing into her hair. She was laughing too, her arms tightening their hold. Ben leaned back and ran his hand through her hair, finally resting it by her cheek and extending his fingers so that the outline of her face was perfectly cradled in his hand. He looked up, past the confines of the Room and straight to the One who'd been his comfort all along, who had seen his heart, and who had so graciously listened and answered his prayers. "Thank You, Jesus," he whispered. He closed his eyes, face turned upward, basking in the love he felt from above and the joy he held in his arms. Finally, he looked back into the pair of bright eyes before him and rejoiced in the love he saw reflected there. "So it's okay, then, if I do this?" He traced her jawline with his thumb. "And this?" He placed a soft kiss on her cheek and felt her shiver in response. "And this?" He bent and brushed her lips with his own, grinning at her soft intake of breath.

"Definitely," Rosemary murmured. She had a hand on his chest now, a fistful of his shirt in her hand, tugging him down. Ben complied, and she nuzzled the dimple on his cheek playfully, as if she'd been waiting a long time to do so.

Ben kissed her lightly once, twice, and then deeper as he settled into her embrace and gave praise to God, who was Father and friend, provider and comforter, all in all.

The Room quieted and settled in around the pair, who were completely captivated by each other. The air felt charged with both anticipation and fulfillment, as if the very walls were embracing them, welcoming them home.

**The Room shifts and shakes itself off. Its joints creak and moan from disuse.** There is a light and warmth kindling in the heart of the Room and it awakens to see what it is. Could it be? After so long? The Room blinks once, twice. It hardly dares to breathe; the joy is so intense. The girl and the boy have returned and they bring a spark with them, lighting dusty corners, illuminating dry walls with vision and purpose.

"Hurry," the Room whispers quietly and then louder. "Hurry!" it shouts to the Story People. "Wake up!"

The Story People yawn and stretch their long limbs. They are tired from too much sleep. They rub their eyes and shuffle closer to see what the commotion is about. "Quiet down," they tell the Room. "Stop your shouting." They are tired of false alarms, hopes that are dashed before they are begun.

The Room welcomes the Story People and turns their attention to the boy and the girl. "They are here! They returned!"

The Story People move about the walls, alive again, humming with excitement, brimming with realized hope.

In the middle of the Room the boy kisses the girl, and the girl kisses him back. The two of them stand in the center of a happy crowd. For the Room knows that once again, its time has come. After all, a room is just a room until it is made alive by imagination. And a book is just a book until it is opened and loved.

This is something the Story People know well.

# ACKNOWLEDGMENTS

Praise God that we don't have to do life alone! Instead, He graciously surrounds us with community, equipping and supporting us for what He calls us to do. Such was certainly the case with this book.

A big thanks to my editor, Peggy Kuethe, for being as excited about this project as I am and for being an encourager and cheerleader from day one. I appreciate, more than I can say, your insight and thoughtful treatment of this book. Thanks to Barbara Shippy, as well, for her spot-on observations and enthusiasm for this story and to all those at Concordia who worked on this book with such tender care.

Thank you to Lisa Clark, fellow author and friend, for all the encouragement and pep talks; to Scott Petty for his realtor expertise (consider this your 0.00000000000125 percent!); to Jordan Petty for being a first reader and a dear, sweet friend, whom I am blessed beyond words to do life with; to Alicia DeMoss, to whom God has given the gift of encouragement and whose priceless friendship and support mean so much to me; to Amanda Lansche (aka aglcreative.com), for being a first reader, art consultant, and dear friend and for making me look so good in my author photo; to Emily Hotard and Betsy Adams, for being first readers and sweet friends; to my book club gals Kendra, Kristin, Lauren, and Mandy for their excitement and support of this project; to Rich and Chris Schloss, huge encouragers and the best neighbors anyone could ask for; to my South County Bible Church family for their enthusiasm, love, and support, especially George and Jackie Howard for the steady doses of encouragement.

Thanks to my parents, Peter and Pamela Belmonte, for loving and supporting me in countless ways. Dad, my fellow author and bibliophile, and Mom, my confidant and cheerleader, this book is in large part thanks to you, and I want to honor you here for your godly example and endless support. And to my siblings: Michael, Laura, Efe, Anna, Isaiah, and Domenic—my thanks, with so much love! To my wonderful Kaufman family: Darris and Donna for your love and support; Aaron, Carrie, Lilli, Jenna, Adam, and Desiree—I love you all!

Tristan, who sparkles with so much personality, you are Mommy's biggest challenge and greatest privilege and joy. I love you beyond words, my beamish boy.

Thank you to Andrew—God knew what He was doing when He gave me you. You balance and ground me in so many ways. Your patience, kindness, and support form the cornerstone of this book. I love you, honey.

Above all, thank You to my heavenly Father, for persistently pursuing me with grace and for planting the love of story deep in my heart. I am humbled and grateful that You saw fit to use a broken vessel in this way. Soli Deo gloria!

*XO Heather*